MW01681305

WICKED APPRENTICE

(THE WICKED MAGIC SERIES, BOOK 1)

BY

MADELINE IVA

www.trollriverpub.com
Wicked Apprentice
The Wicked Magic Series (Book 1)
Copyright © 2016 Madeline Iva
ISBN: 978-1-939564-97-9

No part of this book may be reproduced or transmitted, with the exception of a reviewer who may quote passages in a review, without written prior permission from the publisher.

This is a work of fiction. All characters, names, events, incidents and places are of the author's imagination and not to be confused with fact. Any resemblance to living persons or events is merely coincidence.

WARNING: The author and publisher would solemnly advise you not to attempt any of the sexual or non-sexual actions of any of the characters in this book. Any damage physical, mental or emotional is the sole responsibility of the person/persons attempting such actions. Please be aware that this is a work of fiction and you are responsible for yourself and the consequences caused thereof.

Dedication

This book is dedicated to my sweetie of thirty years. If I'm a true romance believer, it's all because of you.

Special Thanks

Special thanks to my friends and romance family who held my hand during anxious times and without whom this book simply could not have been finished, including Joanna Bourne, Mollie Cox Bryan, Adriana Anders, Sophie Couch--who write with me and talk to me every week, Wendy La Capra who checks up on me, Elizabeth SaFleur--who hooked me up with Stephy at Troll River, Nara Malone--who set me on the path of writing this novel years ago, Kate Worth, Sue London, Joanna Jocelyn, S.A. Hunter along with my Lady Smut crew, including Elizabeth Shore, Alexa Day, Kiersten Hallie Krum, Rachel Kramer Bussel, Isabelle Drake, G.G. Andrews, K.A. Laity. Finally special thanks to my wonderful and amazing editor Stephanie McKibben.

Prologue

She left Ohio for the jungles of South America, doing unpaid grad work in the Amazon, hacking at vines with a machete until her arms wanted to fall off. The first damp log she sat upon was covered with a bright yellow-green fungus that promptly ate through the seat of her pants. After three months she was tired of her graduate director, tired of digging, tired of wondering when they'd ever find anything interesting. Then one day, when her graduate director was away, she discovered a mysterious green door and began to uncover it.

She should have waited for her grad professor to come back before clearing all the dirt away herself. She shouldn't have done it in such a hurry, but for once she forgot about the bugs that stung and bit at her, she forgot that she was watering the earth with a stream of constant sweat. She shouldn't have tried to spin the dial in the center of the door—it had to be ancient and could have broken. But her professor was swilling beer at a bar with air-conditioning more than one hundred miles away, and the dial wasn't decayed or rusted, it looked polished and new. Once the pebbles and dirt were removed it spun with ease.

Resting her palm on the door, she brushed at more dirt, revealing other fascinating knobs. She was leaning down into a pit almost three feet deep, so when the central dial spun, and the door suddenly opened wide into blackness, she fell through it, arms and legs comically flailing. The only thing more comical was the look on Hulgetta's face when she came tumbling out. The grumpy woman clutched at her heart, her body plastered to the wall, her face a big upside down frown of horror. Whatever the old sorceress was expecting to come through the door, it wasn't a sweaty, dirty, young archeology student flailing all her limbs before falling with a smack onto the castle floor.

CHAPTER ONE

Eleven months later…

Prin stole into the sorceress's lair.

"I got one. Oh! Sorry." She backed away and waited, slowly deflating as Hulgetta continued reading a spell book and ignored her. As an apprentice, she'd learned the hard way not to interrupt the sorceress while she was reading. Finally the grumpy woman turned the page and looked up.

"Found one," Prin said.

"And still you live?"

Prin bit her lower lip, her sense of triumph rapidly trickling down into doubt mixed with a small bit of outrage. *And still I live? Thanks for the word of warning, mistress.*

In fact, it had been a dangerous day's work and she would have appreciated a heads-up. She'd been handed a list and told to retrieve a subject from it. There were no names, only coordinates for the green door. By midafternoon she'd peeked into some quite nasty places, and was very afraid—not only of the subjects on the other side of the door but also because she hadn't brought someone back yet. She put up her chin a little. Never let the sorceress see you sweat.

"Well, do you want him or not? The door will be closing soon."

The mighty sorceress and dread cranky-pants Hulgetta sat hunched over a book all day, not caring if her apprentice was eaten by some wooly ice monster or clawed to death by a green smoke demon.

Finally, the sorceress stood in all her majestic frumpiness.

"Show me," she said.

Prin tossed her long braids behind her shoulders and turned into the short alcove. The lintel was low and covered in intricate carvings. The brass dials and knobs on the door were tarnished to a turquoise-green patina. The door was open, but the other side was mostly covered by some kind of tapestry.

Prin checked the central dial on the door one more time. It reminded her of a cross between a bank vault and a roulette wheel. If it began to spin while they were on the other side, the door would shut, and they'd be stuck there for good. Prin flipped the lever on the edge of the dial that Hulgetta had shown her. It kept the door locked in the open position—for a while at least. Then Prin slipped through the magic green door into another place entirely. Hulgetta followed her more slowly, her hulking mass hesitating while Prin slowly pulled back the tapestry that hung to knee height. She nodded towards the other side.

"Where?" Hulgetta mouthed.

Prin pointed. "Over there at the other end. Reading," she whispered softly. "Hasn't noticed us so far."

"Shhh." Hulgetta barely looked. She backed further away from the door. "Drop him."

"Yes, mistress. You mean, the sleep spell?"

"Of course."

"Right now?" Prin whispered.

The sorceress rolled her eyes.

"Okay, okay," Prin said softly, wiping her hands on her apprentice robes. *Here we go. First spell ever.* She ducked under the tapestry and pulled herself up to her full height, which was not very much, but it was the spirit of the thing that counted. She focused on the tall, lithe figure reading from an enormous fat book sitting on its own special stand near the windows. The light pooled over his shoulders and set his dark auburn hair ablaze. There was nothing more threatening about him than an aristocratic chill he threw into the room. Yet she stumbled over her words slightly as she started reciting the sleep spell, her voice reaching out towards him.

He looked up suddenly, aware of her presence. She sped up the words as a buzzing zap went out from him and struck her full on. She kept going, even as her jaw went numb and then tickled. The zap made her feel like a slot machine that had hit the jackpot. It left her head tingling as it traveled down her neck and into her chest. A strange sensation. The odd buzzing reached all the way down to her feet, and she shivered hard even as their eyes locked.

Keep going. Keep going. She recited the spell to the very end. She'd practiced the words for so long she could have said them in her sleep.

She finished and waited. After swaying for a moment, he dropped like a stone to the rug. She did a brief happy dance, shuffling her feet on the carpet. Ducking under the tapestry, she called to where Hulgetta was waiting all the way back at the end of the hall.

"Okay. Got him. What next?"

Hulgetta just stared at her. Such a long pause it almost made her doubt herself. *Did I do something wrong?* Hulgetta's mouth was slightly open and she blinked slowly. *Did she think I couldn't do it? Cause I just did.*

"Mistress?" Prin flicked her wrists a few times. Her arms were still buzzing and tingling from whatever it was he'd thrown out. The buzz left her wrists and sank right down into her lady bits. *Oh my. Yi-yi-yi.* She gave herself a little shake.

"Mistress!"

"He's down. You're sure?" Hulgetta mouthed.

"Yes," she hissed. Whoops! She ducked back behind the tapestry as a servant passed by the door. Did he see her? She peeked. No.

Hulgetta ducked past her and pulled the tapestry aside, peeking out.

She turned back to Prin. "Check his ears. If they're pointy, then drag him out of there and put him in the cell."

"The cell?"

Hulgetta cast her eyes at the ceiling. "Your old room."

"Oh. Right." She'd grown so used to the general decay permeating Hulgetta's castle that she'd forgotten her old room was one of the few with solid stone walls and a heavy bolt on the outside of the thick wooden door. Also it was clean and not too damp, and therefore one of the nicer rooms in the dump. The rest of the castle was crumbly, moldy, and falling to bits.

"Let me know when it's done," Hulgetta whispered.

"Yes, mistress," Prin said. She gave a tiny bow as Hulgetta turned and swept back down the hall. Prin crossed into the sunny room and bent over her unconscious victim. *Pointy ears? Check.*

She paused. He looked like Satan dipped in ice. A high, noble forehead fought for dominance over his features in contrast to his lush, sensuous lips. The lips won. Long beams of light fell about his pale skin and the black wings of his eyebrows. She checked the ears again. They were less pointy than Spock, yet pointier than your average geeky human. Good god, he was an elf! She was agog to see what Hulgetta wanted with him.

Dragging her eyes away, she looked up at all his books. From one end of the study to the other, the tall bookshelves followed the curve of the wall. Her eyes were caught by the sinuous moldings that snaked around the edges of yellow stone, outlining the walls with twining vines and then crawling back up to more and more bookshelves, all full.

The books gave off a silent persistent energy, a low pulse of magic that raised all the fairy dust inside her and sent it dancing about, covering her in goose bumps. She had lust in her heart.

So many magic books, so little time.

Yet orders were orders. She picked up his feet and began dragging him across the room. He slid easily enough across the silk-knotted carpet. His arms swept up over his head as she pulled him along to the green door. She tried not to look at the open books out on the tables. *Thou shalt not covet another's magical books. Okay, well, just one.* She hung over it for a second trying to read the letters. *Nope, don't know the language.* They sang to her nerves like a soprano choir hitting the high notes in an opera. Like being near a celebrity or the President of your country. Like that.

She'd been learning the low form of Anslod for potions and spells, as well as Berbainwick, the common language all the maids used. She prided herself on becoming fluent in two languages in a little under a year, but there were still so many other languages to learn.

One day I'll have a room in a tower like this and read books of magic all day.

Yet how full of briars was her workaday world. He had looked so slender standing up, yet his bones were large, and he was much taller than he had seemed clear across the room. She was breathless just pulling him along the patterned silken rug. She wanted to stop, but the green door was starting to slowly swing shut. Even with the lever, it would only hold the connection for so long. She dug her fingers harder into his pointy leather boots and gave a mighty pull. With one last heave, she made it under the tapestry and over the doorsill, bumping his head along the way. *Oops.* It took a final yank to drag his fingers clear while the door stood half-open.

With a hollow noise, the door behind her shut and clicked. The low corridor sank back into gloominess, and the familiar castle stench of wood smoke, boiled animal bones, and damp straw invaded her nose.

Leaving his body, she went around the corner. "He's bigger than I thought. Kinda heavy." She peered over at where Hulgetta sat, scratching away with her quill on parchment. *Hey, lady, a little help?*

"Get one of the maids from the kitchen," Hulgetta finally said, not even looking up.

"Yes, mistress." Like a heat-seeking missile, she headed towards the warmth and glow of the kitchen, trotting along the mezzanines and up and down the stairs to keep warm.

Wart was hanging a dead rabbit from a hook over the butchering table.

"Gotcha!" she said, grabbing the maid's shoulders.

Wart jumped.

"It's just me." She peered over Wart's shoulder. The eternal rabbit being cleaned for rabbit stew. *Gah.* Prin gave a shudder.

"Hey, Wart. How's your chin?"

Wart turned around and tilted her head up so she could see. There was no getting around the fact that Prin was short, but Wart was so tiny Prin towered over her. Prin looked at the perfectly charming chin that had just two months before carried a wart the size of a gumdrop. All gone now.

"Looking good," Prin said, "Is there any willow bark extract left?"

"I gave the rest to Kath for her chilblains."

"Aren't you sweet. Let's see the fingers." She caught the maid's hands and held up the tiny child-sized digits to the gloomy light.

"Excellent. These look good too."

The maid turned back to her rabbit with her small curved knife she used especially for skinning the tiny creatures. Prin smelled the fresh blood and her stomach turned.

"So what are we going to call you now that there's no wart?"

Wart gave the rabbit a pensive, sad look.

"Wart is fine."

The maid's taciturn nature stood out more than before. Dowdy kitchen maids could be a bullying bunch. She reckoned that the giant chin wart had been a sort of camouflage, along with hiding out by the rabbit hutch and in general trying to seem invisible.

Sad for her, but welcome in my lonely little life. Wart was someone she would call her friend. But would Wart call her friend back? Perhaps. If no one else heard her.

"Oh, I need your help."

A few minutes later, she had her arms under Hottie McElf while Wart took his feet.

"Who is he?" Wart asked.

"Dunno. He's an elf, though, which is so cool." They hoisted the man up, and once they were out of Hulgetta's lair and down at the great hall, Prin resumed. "She hands me a list this morning with coordinates on it for the green door. Says pick any one of these and bring back a subject."

Carry, carry, carry. She wished they had something to drag him on. Oi, he was heavy.

"Anyone on the list," Wart said. "Then why him?"

"Wart, you have no idea. For a minute I didn't think I could pull it off." She told Wart about the smoke demon, the monster in the ice cave. "Not that I saw it, but I saw its poo, and I left as fast as possible. Ugh!" She shuddered, remembering the slick ramp heading almost straight down and the eerie silence, broken only by the noise of cracking bluish ice. There had been a giant pile of human bones next to the spore of whatever it was that lived in that cave. "I mean, I had no weapons, just a sleep spell. I wasn't going to risk it, you know?"

"But you found him."

"Yes. At last. And! Bonus points—he has pointy ears. Huzzah!"

Whatever she did, her apprentice vows that she must never disappoint her mistress in any command. Wart knew that. Wart, when enticed to speak candidly about previous apprentices, said that they disappeared after they had invariably disappointed their mistress. Prin assumed they probably went back through the green door from whence they came. Wart didn't seem so sure, but wasn't about to speculate, either.

It had become a rather sinister question mark hanging over Prin's head ever since. She tried not to think about what would have happened if she hadn't succeeded today. Now she was almost high with relief.

"What's she going to do with him?" Wart asked.

"Ah, Hulgetta. Secrets shrouded in mystery, blah, blah, blah."

Wart gave her a peculiar look with her big dark eyes. She often kept her thoughts to herself, but Prin knew that behind that modest demeanor was a needle-sharp brain.

"What? Cough it up."

"You must have some idea."

"Nope. Not a clue. Can't read the book she's been studying up on. What about those spring rites we did last year? That was fun. Maybe we're going to do that again."

Wart made a frowny face.

Prin prodded her memory. "You remember. I hadn't been here long, but Hulgetta had finally let me out of the cell. And then the maids covered me in honey and rolled the herbs all over me." It made her smell like turkey stuffing, which was not bad, all in all. After that she had had to caper about on the greensward while they clapped, sang songs, and drank. No doubt she looked like a freak, but it was fun.

Prin prodded her friend's memory some more. "Spring ritual? Really cold. We drank spiced wine punch."

"Do you mean—the moss maid rites?"

"Holy bat turds—we were doing a moss maid ritual. And I was the moss maid. Duh. Okay, I get it now."

"The moss maid ritual only uses women."

"Really?"

"It's not spring yet."

"Close enough."

They continued dragging the gorgeous elf along until they reached a spot where the stones were a bit less clammy and Prin suggested they take a break.

"So if I was the moss maid, who was that tiny woman who showed up all in green?" Prin asked.

"What?"

"Really short woman, like way shorter than me or you. Covered in green." The woman's eyes had seemed extra white around the iris and blazed at her. "She showed up towards the end." Prin remembered the dance off they had. Crumping moves meets chicken dance.

"Sure it wasn't a kitchen maid?"

"Definitely not. No. She was, like, four feet tall."

"Not Kath?" Kath was the bread maker, and if the shortest, she was also easily the widest of all the kitchen maids.

"This woman was half the size of mighty Kath. Easily."

Wart just shook her head, puzzled.

"No? Okay." Prin was ready to go again, but Wart held up a hand, panting, so Prin waited some more. While biding her time she be-spelled herself by staring down into the elf's face.

"Are all elves this gorgeous?" she asked.

"I've never seen an elf before. I'm not sure." Yet the way Wart was staring at him didn't seem admiring. She looked like she was listening to a sad song.

"Okay, Wart, cough it up. You think Hulgetta means to harm him?"

Wart looked at her with a certain quirk to her mouth which meant yes. This was bad, very bad. She had to get someone else from the list. It had been terrifying enough to go through the green door into whatever place it opened onto by day. Except for him, all the critters on the other side reeked of danger. The idea of starting to go through that list and open the door at night? She shuddered hard.

"Is this a, you know, gut feeling, or have you seen Hulgetta do something bad to other people before?"

Wart looked at her and wouldn't speak. Just gave her those giant haunted brown eyes.

Prin compressed her lips. Hulgetta said jump, she asked how high. Hulgetta said put him in the cell, so he was going in the cell.

Still she hesitated.

"I can't put him back."

Wart was silent.

"What would I tell Hulgetta?" Look what her mistress had done for her. Taught her magic. Fed and clothed her well—better than the maids, even. She'd recited a vow where she pledged her loyalty and obedience. *Shit.*

Prin gathered her arms under his chest and heaved. The crumbling staircase climbed up along the wall, twisting around without any railing until it ended abruptly in a small landing with an arched wooden door. Bracing herself and taking a big breath, Prin lifted his upper body as high as she could and started up the steps. Wart followed behind. Though the kitchen maid did her best, Prin had to do most of the heavy lifting. After almost a year of chopping firewood and hauling buckets she was pretty strong. Still.

"No one. Talks about. How much grunt work goes into magic," she said through gritted teeth.

"Poor you," Wart responded, panting and slipping on the narrow stairs.

Once they were in the cell, they went over to the wooden pallet that ran from wall to wall almost three feet off the ground. Prin's old mattress sat on the pallet, stuffed with itchy straw. They dumped him on it. A certain cruel sensuality about his mouth added a touch of sin to his celestial features. She put her palm up to his cheek. It was cool and clammy. He turned his face into the warmth of her skin and his lips touched her palm. The buzz of energy inside her picked up a few notches.

She forced herself to slide her hand away, when what she really wanted was to dig her hands into his rich auburn hair and climb right on top of him. *No,* her brain said. *Yes!* her body cried.

CHAPTER TWO

She began stripping off the little jacket he wore. It had sleeves that laced up at the elbows and shoulders. Then she began rolling up his shirt, inhaling the male scent of him, like some unknown mountain herb, sharp and clean.

"This is a bad idea," Wart commented.

"Maybe he's not so harmless. I mean, he did zap me," she said.

"Really. Before you kidnapped him. The nerve."

"Not sure what he did. Kind of felt like a spell forming. Only this was hard and sudden." Her wrists still hurt from it. Her body, meanwhile, rippled with energy. She wanted to jump out of her skin.

"Well, he's an elf," Wart said.

"So?"

"So they're magic and all."

"Right." She paused one more time to look down at him as he lay on the pallet. If she let him go, what would she say to Hulgetta? *Catch and release only, mistress. Sorry.* She quaked just thinking the words. She picked up the gold manacle but hesitated. There was no time to think. If they were going to do this, they had to get him out quickly. And then? And then? She couldn't think of any way she could switch him out without Hulgetta knowing.

She made up her mind. "I can't do it. I can't let him go." She clapped the gold manacle onto his wrist, then bundled up his boots, jacket, and shirt into her arms.

Wart gave a cry of alarm and backed into the corner as Hulgetta, already at the top of the stairs, stormed inside.

Holy marbles. Her innards began to liquefy a little. Looking over at Wart's expression she knew they both looked guilty as sin. She took a pull on herself and strived to appear a little more composed. Yet her heart was stuttering and she couldn't concentrate as Hulgetta looked around the room like she could sniff out disobedience. The tall sorceress turned quickly, the grey rotting wisps of her robes swirling out.

"Here, girl. Did you check him over? Do those leggings have pockets?" she said to Prin, who started quickly patting down his legs. "I don't want him armed. Keep everything out of his cell."

"Everything?"

"Nothing metal. Nothing he can use to escape."

"Yes, ma'am," Prin said. She could feel Hulgetta's eyes upon her as she went from his knees down to his feet. Pushing on a wide shoulder and gripping his deerskin leggings, she half turned, half pulled him onto his backside and began patting down his front. She threw the bundle of clothing at the end of the straw mattress. A fine white shirt of crisp linen with tiny stitches. Clean and well mended. Boots that were well made and well worn, the supple suede soft in her clutches.

"Anything?"

Prin showed her mistress the shirt and jacket. "No."

"The boots too," Hulgetta said. Prin checked the boots and shook her head.

Nothing. Hulgetta tested the manacle's chain, jerking the other manacle around an iron bar set into the wall. Staring at the wall, Prin realized it was probably the only part of the castle left without crumbling mortar. Instead of stones wobbling about like rotten teeth loose in their sockets the bar was immovable. The elf was not going anywhere.

The last ray of sun fingered its way through the narrow slit in the stone wall, lighting up the room and tagging a section of his hair. Prin watched the dark brownish strands take fire and the auburn locks turn to copper. What had she done? She swallowed at the elf's cruel beauty and tried to ignore the twist of her insides.

∞

Even as a small child in Ohio, magic had always been her obsession. Something about the idea of magic made all the molecules in her body sit up and twirl, before she even left her own world for an enchanted one.

Her family would often tell their favorite story about her—the time she first saw Peter Pan and went berserker. Not quite four, she had been riveted by the show and lost it when Tinker Bell almost died. At first she'd wailed, but then she had looked around at everyone clapping. She swiftly began to clap her heart out. When the curtain came down, she made a break for the stage. Her dad, caught off guard, hustled to catch her just as she made it to the top of the orchestra pit and was about to dive off the edge. She struggled in his arms, sobbing, "Tinkybell," as he hauled her away.

They said she had sat in her car seat, kicking her foot with fury against her dad's seat, furiously pouting the entire way home. Her mother would do an impression of what she looked like that day, arms folded, her face crumpled with angry devastation.

"What's the matter?" her dad said, looking in the rear view mirror. "Too much fairy dust?"

"Yes," she said, drawing out the word in a woeful voice. From that day her parents always looked at each other whenever she was in a bad mood, and said 'too much fairy dust,' before turning to her with mocking boo-boo faces. It was infuriating, and she was so over it, but they thought it was hysterical each and every time.

She grew older and played make-believe with the other girls on her block until one day Mary Beth, the next-door neighbor and her best friend, led off with, "Well, nobody likes Tinker Bell, cause she's selfish and mean and everybody likes Wendy."

It was like sticking a sword in Prin's belly. She staggered off home that day vowing never to play with other children again and become an irritable bookworm instead. There may have been too much fairy dust inside her, but as she grew, the fairy dust stayed inert. Perhaps it had been uninspired by the Ohio landscape.

Sometimes she grew so bored she'd thought she was going to die. She remained in a quasi-coma of twelve-year-old ennui until her aunt had given her an eight-volume historical collection called *Mysteries of the Ancient World*. The book suggested that while there didn't seem to be real magic left in the world now, perhaps there used to be.

"I'm going to become an archeologist," she had announced at dinner one night.

She then majored in archeology in college and got into a pretty decent grad school. Once there she got an internship and traded Ohio for South America, over the loud protests of her parents.

"Sorry, there's too much fairy dust in me to remain here in Ohio." She had been convinced she would uncover evidence that magic once existed in our world. She would find some evidence of magic below the dirt and vines in the jungle—and boy, did she ever.

∞

Prin got a torch and lit it up. A gloomy thundercloud surrounded Hulgetta almost constantly, but Prin had never taken it personally before. Maybe she had a mood disorder. At any rate, Hulgetta, without waiting for the light, stalked off in the shadows towards her lair. With one look, Prin and Wart took the long way around. Wart wrapped her arms up in her apron as she paced next to Prin.

"Do you think…Do you think she's going to kill him?" Wart asked.

"Kill him! What? Whoa. Whoa! No. Why would she do that?" Prin peered into the gloom. "I mean, I know she's not…" So many words presented themselves, Prin didn't know which to pick. Kind? Caring? Sensitive? Warm? Compassionate? "It's another thing entirely to think she murders people in cold blood." Until now the sorceress's irritability hadn't seemed vicious. So far, they'd gotten along just fine.

Wart gave her a rueful look. Then her face returned to that careful neutral expression she always tried to wear, but it was sad underneath.

"Well, I've never seen her kill anyone, have you?" Prin challenged.

There was one exception. The hop toads. Prin used them to practice her sleep spell. When she had gotten the spell memorized and practiced it successfully, she showed

Hulgetta the tiny toads belly up and arranged in a star—for superstar. Hulgetta had sniffed at them and reluctantly said well done. Prin beamed and turned around for just a second when *wham*! She looked back and saw a giant book flat on the table where the hop toads had been.

"You looked at others through the green door," Wart said. "Were they all elves?"

"Not at all. I mean, I guess Hulgetta was looking for an uncanny creature. She didn't say, she just gave me the list. I didn't even try for whatever it was in the ice cave, just shut the door and moved on to the next set of coordinates. That was a room full of green smoke, and I almost stepped into it when some demon with red eyes charged the door."

Even now she felt sweat breaking out across her shoulders and between her breasts as she remembered the desperate struggle, how she had tried to hold the door closed, how the door surged under her as the creature on the other side tried to push out. She was convinced it was going to bust through and rampage all over the castle, killing everyone.

She'd inhaled a lungful of the green smoke in the process, but managed to hold off the creature on the other side of the door, until the door at last swung shut. Afterwards, she just wanted to go curl up in a corner somewhere and hide, but she couldn't stop coughing, so she had to go take care of that. That's when she had noticed seven demon claw tips on the floor, writhing.

"Such a close call. I saved the tips in a box." Wart looked disgusted. "I mean, who knows? They might come in handy someday."

"Hulgetta is sending you to all these demons and monsters," Wart said. "But you never once thought about why?"

"To dance around the Maypole? Spring's coming you know."

"She's not looking to dance on the green with a smoke demon, I can tell you that much."

"I keep telling you, she didn't tell me why. Hottie McElf was next on the list, that's all. I don't know about you," Prin said candidly, "but I'd dance on his Maypole any time."

"Prin!" Wart fumed. "It's not funny. He could, in fact, be very dangerous."

"Which is it, Wart? Are you sorry for him, or should we lock him up and throw away the key? And I had to bring him," Prin said, turning into the last long hallway before Hulgetta's lair, "because she's my boss. I vowed to be loyal. When she says jump, I say how high." And that was that. Yet it didn't sit right with her.

"You've heard what the kitchen maids say," Wart said.

"Like Hulgetta cut off the cook's ears for burning the stew once. Right," she rolled her eyes.

Silence. Wart kept her face downward, relentlessly studying her dirty apron hem.

"Don't even tell me—oh *crap*."

Yes, the cook wore her head wrapped in a cloth. True enough. But all the kitchen maids wore their hair wrapped up in a cloth. It was safer that way around the open fires.

No, no, no, no, no.

"Aren't you afraid of her?" Wart asked.

"*Now* I am."

She strode along, fretting. "Okay. It still doesn't matter. I had to do it. You saw—Hulgetta was already on the stairs."

"Just open the manacle—"

"Wart, I don't know how! Hulgetta didn't tell me how to open it."

Crossing the heavy stone arch that marked Hulgetta's lair, she slotted the torch into a bracket. Before pushing her weight against the heavy door she straightened up and took a deep breath. Turning to Wart, she said, "Okay, I'm just going to ask her straight out what the deal is with the elf. Ready?"

Wart nodded, and Prin braced herself.

Hulgetta was already back on her stool, hunched over her stinky spell book that permeated the air with the stench of rotting eggs.

"Mistress," she said, bowing low. Prin stood there, waiting to be acknowledged, flicking her wrists and shaking them out at her side. They felt like they had fallen asleep. Pins and needles ran over her arms, along with what felt like the mother of all static electricity. Either His Elf-ness had given her a powerful buzz or it was something else—a defensive spell perhaps. The elf packed a wallop. *Here's hoping it's temporary, whatever it is.*

CHAPTER THREE

A steady draft ran over her feet. They were in the new part of the castle, which meant it dripped less. No windows kept the corridors dark and dank, but also kept out the worst drafts in winter. Almost. She poked up the fire, quickly backing away from the smoke that blossomed forth. The chimney really needed cleaning. It was a miserable rainy day as usual, but the wood burned merrily, and the room was full of books on incantations and spells. Before this afternoon, she wouldn't have traded being an apprentice for anything in the world. After all, she had just done real magic, used a real spell, and she'd done it all by herself. It made her feel bad-ass. Filled her with a sense of wonderment.

Hulgetta turned a page—which was enough of an invitation to start chatting.

"So what do we do with the man behind door number one?"

Hulgetta kept reading from her book. The frumpy woman was six feet tall, with the robust, rounded arms of a blacksmith. There was reason to doubt Hulgetta had a sense of humor lurking somewhere in her chest. Still, one had to try.

"Should we take him out on the green and do some spring rites? A little moss maid action? A fertility ritual, perhaps?" she joked.

Hulgetta looked up at Prin, annoyed, her mouth a long, colorless white line.

"Is he going to be around awhile?"

No answer.

"Should I at least get him something to eat?"

"I wouldn't bother," Hulgetta said.

"So, he'll only be here for a few hours?"

"Overnight. At most."

"Oh." That could be encouraging.

She looked over at the loathsome book Hulgetta was reading.

Or not. She couldn't read the title of the book or the language it was written in, but the book stank, and the cover always felt slimy, no matter how often Prin wiped it down with a dust cloth.

Yuck.

"Bring me the hand from the cupboard in the North Wing," Hulgetta said. Prin bowed and scuttled off, pausing before she turned the corner.

Just a hand? Ew!

"Which hand?" she asked.

"The petrified one with two rings on it," Hulgetta said. Prin hustled off, grabbing her torch from the bracket, Wart at her heels.

"I'm glad it wasn't a pickled hand, or a mummified hand, or something even more gross," she said. They went down the stairs, turned right, and headed through the cellars to the northern wing of the castle where the roof of the great hall had crumbled away years ago, leaving it exposed to the elements.

"Mistress doesn't seem very candid about the elf," Wart suggested.

"I know. Maybe we can work this out ourselves. Why would Hulgetta need a magic creature for a few hours?" Prin asked.

"The real question is why would Hulgetta need *you* to kidnap the elf for her?"

"No reason. Just being nice and letting me practice an easy spell," Prin said, and then laughed. No way Hulgetta was just being nice. That was not how she rolled.

"She needed me because I can do a sleep spell."

"Yes."

"I was the one that dressed up like the moss maid, too," she remembered.

"Hulgetta used to dress up herself," Wart said.

"Now that I would have liked to see."

Under the failing light and the drooling dark sky she found the chest. Lifting up the warped lid with some difficulty, she shifted all the objects to refresh her memory, careful to use her sleeve over her hand.

The trunk held objects made from stone. Nothing too exciting. There were memory marbles and some small warty stones which, slipped into a pack or sack, would make it too heavy to carry. She found what she was looking for at the bottom. A large object wrapped in a dark blue velvet cloth. She handed the torch to Wart and unwrapped the cloth to inspect it.

A hand, made out of peach-colored rock. Heavy. Not rock, she remembered, flesh turned to stone—petrified. A woman's hand, she realized, almost like Hulgetta's. Large. Very long fingered, with a thick wrist and rounded forearm. On the forefinger was a large black ring made out of some sort of rough crystal gripped with silver ornamentation almost like claws. The jewel sparkled to life in the gloom when she touched it, glowing white-orange hot, like the inside of a burning coal.

The smaller ring adorned the fourth finger of the hand. It was in the form of two slender silver hands, holding a delicate silver chalice between them. Inside this chalice sat a round blue stone with cracks across it. When she touched the stone, the dark cracks turned milky white and threw rippling shadows, the way light moved across the wall when reflected from a pool of water.

"Prin, I think magical things like you," Wart said.

"Better than they like Hulgetta, at any rate."

She considered Wart's theory as they trotted back to Hulgetta's lair, Wart holding the torch, Prin carrying the wrapped-up fossilized arm. She could see their breath in the air.

A theory started to form in her mind.

"There's more to what you said, Wart. Hulgetta needs magic to make magic. She needs a catalyst of some kind."

Wart looked bewildered.

"Um," Prin searched for examples in her head, "like you need sourdough starter to make a new batch of bread."

"Ah." Wart's face lit up with understanding.

"The starter has to be some kind of magical source. Maybe an elf, maybe a moss maid ritual." She thought about it some more, pondering. These days Hulgetta's spells never worked. Ever. Each day she tossed out the proof, in the form of the soupy dregs from Hulgetta's failed spells. Yet her own limbs felt full of itchy elf charge, and she wanted to release it.

Wart suddenly put out her arm.

"Wait, someone's up there," Wart said. Prin stopped in her tracks. Wart held her torch up higher to see down the long corridor. They headed towards the flickering shape.

"Halloo!" Prin called. It wasn't a person. It was the moss maid shrine.

"I forgot it was here," Wart said with a little uneasy laugh, clutching Prin's arm and tugging on it with relief. The small statuette was waist high, with overturned bird nests for a bosom. Small offerings to the maid sat on a block of wood. Five upturned black beetles, two stub candles, and a whole line of eggshells, plus a saucer of new milk.

They made their offerings. Prin took the list of coordinates from her pocket and folded it up into an origami crane. Wart had an acorn in her pocket and set it upright on the wood.

"What is the moss maid supposed to actually do?" she asked Wart.

"You pray to her for love, for protection," Wart's finger traced over the face. "But the moss maid also dispenses fortune to those females full of *stritagga.*"

"Sta-what?"

"It's when a woman is very bold. Flirty. Or jokes a lot. You're—you're stritagga."

"You mean mojo? Or confidence?" Wart shook her head.

"Stritagga means strong, but also unexpected. There's a story where a troll snatches children and holds them in a cooking pot. Things are really bad, but in this story the troll always says, 'who dares,' and this girl always pipes up, 'I do.' And she always has some clever plan. She's like you. And in the story, the moss maid helps her in various ways to escape the troll."

The moss maid looked up at them, her hair crazy dried grass, and her eyes blank white stones. Small bird bones were used for her hag's teeth, and she grinned crazy and grotesque.

"*Moss maid, moss maid, marry me well*. That's what the maids say." Wart's face fell as she said this.

"Like some man is going to show up at the castle door on this remote hillside to pluck a kitchen maid away. Right." Prin laughed.

Wart flinched. Prin peered at her, and noticed Wart looked like she'd been slapped.

"Sorry," Prin apologized. "That was insensitive. Anyway, I guess it never hurts to hope," she said, mentally shooting herself in the head.

"Yes," Wart agreed in her soft, sad voice. The truth was, Hulgetta's castle might as well have been a run-down nunnery, only with a lot more vulgar gestures flying back and forth in the kitchen.

"She's not arranged in a very stritagga way, is she? Here," Prin said, and arranged the moss maid's spoon hands so they were over her head and to one side like she was cheering at a rock concert.

"Better?" she asked Wart.

Wart smiled. "Yes." Now the moss maid's teeth were smiling, her eyes happy.

Prin looked down at the statue. "What if the moss maid acts as batteries?" she said. Wart looked at her questioningly.

Her mind revolved. Last spring after the ceremony, the stones had whispered and the firelight danced. A vivid chartreuse moss grew all across the dripping walls like a dew-bejeweled carpet. Everything had felt alive and full of magical potential. Yet in two months it was all gone, the stones silent, the moss on the walls dead and blackening.

"I like moss maid magic," Prin told Wart. "Because it's the nice kind." She patted the dry grass hair. "No smoke demons, no ice monsters lurking."

Picking up the wrapped forearm once again, Prin turned and looked at Wart.

"Shall we?"

Arriving back at Hulgetta's table, she hoisted the arm up onto the desk, unwrapped the dark blue velvet square from the peach arm and then backed off a pace.

"Ta-da!" she said.

As Hulgetta came near, Prin watched the rippling crackle die across the blue ring and the flames vanish from the black one. She blinked at Wart. Maybe what Wart said was true: magic really did not like Hulgetta's stinkin' looks.

"So what do they do?"

The sorceress did not reply as she began to examine the rings on the hand. By now she knew Hulgetta's rule was *say as little as possible, show even less*. In these situations, blunt prodding was often required to get results.

"Mistress?" Prin said.

"Leave me. Go empty the bucket," Hulgetta said.

She stifled an inward groan. The slops bucket was full of gooey potions that hadn't activated. She grabbed the bucket with the sludge in it, and, with a toss of her head to Wart to come along, she went down the side corridor. After flipping a lever and popping the dial open on the green door, she turned the latch. Instead of facing the inside of the elf's sunny study, or some other place, she stood before the empty moat behind the castle. A panoramic array of stony mountains and stunted, straggling pines half hidden in fog provided a magnificent, if rather grim, view.

She poured the liquid out carefully, reserving the clotted sludge at the bottom of the bucket.

"Okay, so this is going to seem a little gross," she told Wart, "but I want to do an experiment. I told you the elf zapped me, right?"

Wart's eyes grew large.

"He was standing there all harmless, then this ball of energy whacked into me as we faced off. It felt very much like a spell forming. Only hard, really hard."

"Maybe not so harmless, then," Wart said.

Humph. She eyed her friend, nodding. Wart was on to something. A reluctant ache between her legs bothered her. If looking at him gave her this kind of zap, what kind of energy would he release during other sorts of activities? Her insides tingled with speculation. What would happen if he touched her? Fucked her? Her insides ached just from thinking about it.

Hiding her lusty pangs, Prin took a golf-ball-sized glop from the bottom of the bucket and focused. She'd been learning an animation spell recently, and she whispered the words to the glop while stroking it with her thumb as if it was a baby bird or little fluffy woodland creature.

*Sisnaeda sis naeda, uhulur er oonag vohlerm…*she whispered. The charge from the elf flowed into the ball of goo as she focused hard, repeating the words a second time.

Sisnaeda…

The glop shuddered. Wart stood stiff and silent next to her as the glop began to change from dish-suds-grey through a rich rainbow of colors.

Nice. "It's never done that before," Prin muttered.

She bent over the little ball of glop, encouraging it. Then she realized she was being greedy and held it out to Wart so she could see.

"Don't! It's nasty!" Wart cried, backing away, putting her hands behind her back.

"It's harmless," Prin protested, but Wart shook her head. "Just a bunch of unicorn snot. Nothing to be afraid of. Whoa." The glop was on the move. It fell off the edge of her hand, landed down in the mud and began humping towards the woods.

"Hey! Oh my. Excellent!" Prin pursued the glop with delight, picked it up, wiped the mud off, and then slipped it into her pocket. "Let's do it again!"

She animated the unicorn snot a few more times, until finally Wart said, "I know this is terribly fascinating, but it's getting dark and starting to rain."

Prin looked around her. *Indeed.*

"I still have rabbit to chop," Wart added apologetically.

The feeling of elf energy was pouring out of her, delivering lumps of adrenaline to her system. She shivered, shook out her hands and turned to go back inside. She flicked the lever on the green door then gave it a strong push, and they went back into the castle. She whispered to Wart, "Here comes the best part."

In a corner of Hulgetta's lair was a long narrow shelf attached to the wall with stone supports. A long chain was attached to the wall above the shelf. An ivory-colored lizard squatted at the end of the chain. Its head ruff was also white and hung down like a sad, dirty Shakespearean lace collar around its face and over its eyes. As Prin approached, the lizard raised itself with a rattle of the loose metal cuff around its scrawny neck and shook the ruff out of its face.

Prin pulled Wart close and whispered to her in hushed tones so as not to bother Hulgetta on the other side of the room. "It's a basilisk. Don't look it in the eye. It's been locked here forever." She stroked the lizard under its chin and it sat there, hypnotized by Prin's fingers.

When she first saw the basilisk, it was paper-white and curled up in the corner, not moving. Yet it cracked its eye when she poked it and drank a little water. At first willing to eat beetles and bread, under the new regimen of semi-animated unicorn snot, the basilisk was quickly reviving.

And it was a smart little fellow. As soon as Prin put the bucket back down, the basilisk sat up, and when Prin came over to the shelf, Wart drifting behind her at a safe distance, the basilisk began to look at her pocket, then back at her face, then back down at her pocket again.

It made little snapping noises with its jaw, putting one claw-tipped forefoot out to rest on her waist.

"Look, he knows I've got food. Hungry, aren't you, Baz? Just a second." She took out a lump from her pocket.

"Sit for me first. Sit!" The lizard sat on its back haunches looking alert. Gradually it balanced on its back legs, the front legs coming off the ground a little bit. "See how smart he is? Bark. Bark, Bazzy." The lizard sneezed and sparks flew out. "Ah! Good boy!"

Wart stifled a giggle as Prin let the lump crawl slowly off the edge of her hand and drop into the lizard's mouth.

Prin took out another lively golf-ball-sized bit of goo. This time it sprang off her hand immediately, but the lizard was on it faster than the eye could follow. Baz swallowed the lump down, looking less docile suddenly, as his eyes narrowed. His head turned pale blue.

"Oh, look at that. Baz, you glorious creature, you." She petted the lizard's fringe, pulling the leathery skin through her fingers, something he tolerated with half-closed eyes, while she let Wart feed the lizard the third lump. By the time he swallowed, he was turning in excited circles and his skin had changed to dark blue. His belly was still pale butter yellow but his neck was now mustard colored.

"Okay, Baz. Last trick. Sit up, boy. Sit!" The lizard reared up off his front legs, his frill fanning out.

"Good boy! Wow, look at him. Okay—catch!" She threw a bit of the unicorn snot into the air. The lizard jumped up, swallowed it, and sat back down. It shut its eyes.

"Bark!" she commanded. The lizard put its snout up and snapped its jaws together. Flames shot up into the air three feet high. Both Prin and Wart leapt back from the lizard then looked quickly over their shoulders at Hulgetta. The sorceress looked up briefly from her book, sneered at them, and then went back to mumbling over her reading once more. Baz had two tiny wisps of smoke coming up from his nostrils.

"Gracious!" Prin said. The lizard gave a slight shake of its head, the frill flopping back and forth. Then he shut his jaws and put his chin out for a scratch. Prin hesitated, but reached her arm forward to stroke the underside of the lizard's chin.

"What a good boy you are. Want to pet him?" she said to Wart, who was now standing a good distance away. Wart shook her head.

"Wow," she mouthed to Wart. *Batteries indeed.* Clearly if Hulgetta wanted some power to operate her spells, then an elf was as good as a car battery, if not better.

An arrow darted out of nowhere, hit the side of the table and bounced off onto the floor.

"Another message from the king," Prin announced over her shoulder. She undid the scroll wrapped around the arrow. Hulgetta pointedly sighed but didn't look up from her book. Wart looked at the scroll and then at Prin, gestured with her chin that she was going back to the kitchen, and left.

"Same as the rest. King Linus the great and blah blah blah, commands that you, his loyal subject, dread sorceress, blah blah blah. You'll offer aid and succor to him against his enemy Rupert the Red." Prin looked up. "I thought King Linus called him Rupert the Revolting?"

Hulgetta raised an eyebrow. "Perhaps the name didn't take."

Prin looked down and scanned the rest of the letter. "Same as the rest. Arm yourself, stand with them, etc. Shall I put it with the others?"

Hulgetta folded her arms and sucked her gums in distain. Prin interpreted this as a yes, and took the arrow over to the basket by the fire to shove it in with the rest. Broken up, the arrows made excellent kindling. They also gave off pretty sparks.

Hulgetta flipped open her stinky book. "I need the prisoner's name. Go wake him and get it."

Prin drifted closer to her mistress instead, trying to look casual, yet also trying to see what Hulgetta was reading. Craning her neck and holding her breath, she crept a little closer. Same book, same smell of rotten eggs. *Gag.*

Hulgetta suddenly noticed her there. "What?" she said and snatched up the book, placing it on her other side, away from Prin.

The maids were not allowed to even dust the spell books. Hulgetta often copied out a spell for Prin rather than allow her apprentice to handle one.

"You want me to wake him up?" Prin said.

"Who else?"

Prin didn't respond to this but continued to linger.

"You're afraid?"

"No. I got the drop on him. He never saw me coming." *Dangerous? Him? Nah.*

"I've lost several apprentices to slaughter when they weren't paying attention."

"Very funny."

Hulgetta gave a double take, her gorgon's stare pinning the apprentice to her spot. Prin felt her stomach flutter. Pushing it, as always. Now that she saw Hulgetta in a new light, she was full of wonder that she hadn't been fried into a tiny pile of ashes long ago.

"I will endeavor not to be slaughtered, dread mistress," she said, dropping a small bow. "But if I wake him and he sees me—I mean, won't he resent the fact that I was his captor? It's unlikely he'll tell me what I want to know, don't you think?"

"He won't remember you dropping him."

"Oh." Prin turned away. Then she turned back. "Not at all? You're sure?"

"No."

Prin turned away and then turned back one more time, her hands in fists near her chin.

"And what, exactly, are we going to do with him once I have his name?"

"I will do with him whatever I want," the sorceress said, looking at Prin like her apprentice was a brainless slime slug.

"Of course," Prin said with a hasty bow. Hunching her shoulders, she gave another little bob and left.

Crap. Crap, crap, crap, crap, crap.

CHAPTER FOUR

Standing over the prisoner's bed a few moments later, she spoke the waking words from the spell.

"*Ahlora voheh lessl nahama.*" Nothing.

"Hello?" She tried to speak more gently, and bending over, she stroked his cheek. She was feeling a little shaky, to tell the truth. Not full of the old *stritagga* now. The home team was not looking so good at the moment. Right about now she wanted to change sides. Hulgetta ruled with an iron fist and fear. Being crotchety and daunting was one thing. Being positively evil was another.

At the same time, best not be swayed by a pretty face. It was her responsibility to save him, but he clearly had magical power. Prudence dictated she wait and make sure the elf needed saving first.

"Hello?" she said.

He wasn't waking up. She said the words again. *Ahlora*… and shook his shoulder for good measure. Then she started to worry. What if she'd messed the spell up? What if she'd made him into a permanent sleeping beauty? She'd never forgive herself. She left off shaking his shoulder and gave his face a brisk little pat.

"Wake up! Wake up, beautiful man," she crooned. His eyes remained closed, but his hand grasped her wrist and she gave a startled little anxious scream.

His eyes opened. Wide and alarmed, they were the color of forest shade, a mix of green and brown, and just now they were frowning into hers. Then they changed to black for a moment. *Freaky.* His eyes throbbed black with emotion, and she felt it inside her. Then his eyes went back to green. He stared at her as if accusing her of something. She kept looking back and forth at his eyes to see if they were going to do the thing again. Then he looked down at his chained wrist and blinked.

Suddenly he half sat up on the bed with a little groan. She forgot caution and felt the skin on his forehead, cheek and chest. Cool, not quite so clammy. The spell was wearing off. Good.

As she placed her hand on the side of his face, his free hand covered hers. More thrillingly, those eyes turned black again. Whatever did it mean?

She did not want to take her hand away. So they stayed that way for a long time, as she measured his temperature. Indeed he was warming up. He was hot. Meanwhile, he just looked into her eyes until she gave a little shiver.

"Where am I?" he said, as he noticed the manacle. "Am I a prisoner?"

Duh. She pulled her hand away. "Careful, you've been bespelled."

She pushed him back down gently with her fingertips, all too aware of the heat from his chest.

"By you?" he said.

"Stay down," she warned. "You'll feel a little woozy for a bit." She tried to stand up.

"Don't leave," he said.

"Do you by any chance remember how you got here?" she said.

He shook his head. "I was reading in my study, in my tower." He frowned. So the big H was right. He didn't know she'd dropped him. Her heart leapt with a strange twisty ache. God, he was pretty. It was just sick how perfect his body was. And she'd never been one to fall for a pretty boy before. Or any boy, for that matter. She'd had things to do. Magic to find. Now she just wanted to dive into his eyes, fall onto his lips. Her hands, still full of elf zappies, itched to creep towards him again.

"Let me bring you some water and come right back," she promised, using her fingertips to push him gently the rest of the way back down. "Are you hungry? Rabbit stew?"

Happy and guilty all at once, she tore her eyes away from his naked chest. His dark, deep-set eyes were full of sensitivity and suffering. Involuntary smile muscles ached in her face, until she could hold it in no longer. She beamed at him.

He gazed avidly back at her, not smiling, but looking at her with—well, yeah, with yearning. Eventually she was able to pull herself away from the sappy staring contest and blink at the wall. Then, like a zombie, she got up and left, only to return a few breathless minutes later, leading a string of kitchen maids who carried in a basket tray with his food on a wooden plate, a clay pitcher of water, a tumbler of wood, a clay basin to wash in, a towel, and last but not least, a rounded porcelain pot pushed discreetly under the bed shelf for *necessaries*. Nothing metal, per her instructions.

He eyed the kitchen maids, stirred his food but did not eat it, and did not speak while they were there. The kitchen maids would not look at him directly. They put down the tray, the pitcher, and the basin then scrambled away from his cell as if it was full of snakes.

Once outside the cell they trooped down the stairs, their overloud voices carrying right back into the cell.

"No doubt he's small as me little finger," Lanky Sue said.

"S'not the size of a man, tis what he knows how to do with it," Kath replied. "This one looks like he wouldn't know his arse from his elbow."

Prin stood rooted in the middle of the cell with unutterable embarrassment, her cheeks burning hot with resentment, until they went out of earshot.

She tried to keep a dignified silence, turning to her captive, watching how the lamplight caught the copper in his hair.

"They all called you Prin," he said at last.

"Yes." He wasn't going to mention how they behaved. *Thank you.* She took a bigger breath.

"That's an odd name." His Berbainwick was strangely accented, his words all stretched out instead of clipped off. He kind of gargled them sometimes at the back of the throat. To her ears the language had never sounded half so charming before.

"It's a nickname," she explained, and then stopped, not willing to explain more. Touchy ground here.

"What does it stand for?" he asked. His voice was lilting and gentle, another tone entirely from before. "Princess?"

"Bet you say that to all the girls," Prin replied. In fact, it was an abbreviation for apprentice and a way of making fun of Hulgetta's speech. She wasn't going to tell him that, of course. Everything about him was gentle and refined. She kinda wanted to muss him up a little bit.

"I said nothing to them at all." He looked puzzled.

She wrinkled her nose. "Never mind."

"You are a princess then?" he said. He asked her a question in a language she didn't understand. She looked down at her calloused fingertips and didn't reply. Let him think what he liked. The silence stretched on. She looked up and his attractiveness hit her again like a physical blow.

His eyes had gone dark again, and he was a vision of sensitive torment. She felt herself involuntarily reaching towards him. Then, alas, the eyes changed back, and she regained a modicum of self-control. She stood up and paced around the cell, her heart still thudding about inside her chest.

"Who has imprisoned me?" he asked. "A murderous wizard? An evil enchantress?"

I did. "Technically speaking, she's a sorceress," Prin replied. "You don't remember?"

He sniffed at the water in the tumbler.

"It's not poisoned or tainted," she said. "I freshened it with herbs myself. See?" She drank from the cup and then held it out to him to show him the sage leaves and borage blossoms. "Perfectly safe." He took a tentative sip on his own, letting her hold the cup for him. The feel of his fingers sliding over hers. Her eyes widened, but he moved abruptly, pulling the cup away. As if he didn't want to touch her.

"Thank you," he said, not looking at her. Then he must have changed his mind about something. He looked up at her again, his eyes flickering black. "I thank you," he said, this time with a tone of grave respect.

"You're welcome," she said, using the same formal tone. *And did you know you're smoking hot?*

Lying there pliant, helpless, and half naked, he was so scrumptious her body itched to crawl on top of him. Moreover, all her fairy dust was up and screaming for him, and that just never happened to her with a guy. Ever.

She put the tumbler back on the wooden tray with the pitcher and stood there twisting her fingers up in her skirt. Nervous. Her mind strained for something to say. Her body looked for another excuse to bend over near him and reveal her cleavage. *Get a grip, woman.*

"And what are you called?" she asked, forbidding her fingers to play with her braids. The traitorous fingers took to the lacings on her corset instead, and she bit her lips a little to make them red. Where was her apprentice side? The scholarly side that wanted to learn? Pathetic.

"Princess, help me," he whispered.

How was she ever going to refuse him anything when his eyes were all big and noble, yet softly luminous? She had felt loyal to Hulgetta. *Had* being the operative word. Her loyalty was wobbling, big time. This was so wrong.

"Are you okay?" she said, filled with dread and concern. She leaned over the bed and put her hand on his brow again. Yes. It was warm now. She felt his cheek. It was hot. Spell all gone. Reluctantly, she took her hand away.

"Can you move your legs?"

He took her hand again and placed it back on his cheek, his lips parting a little. She went a little gooey and just stared at him, unable to think or move. He took that hand and kissed it.

"Help me escape."

She stood up straight, breathless. *Whoa.* There it was. Bright needle-thin fear suddenly pierced the bubble.

"It would mean my life," she said, simply.

"Then you're her captive as well?"

"What's your name?" she asked, nervous. She had to get his name and go. She was in over her head.

"But you haven't even told me yours, Princess," he said in his quiet voice. She gave a little curtsey in response.

"I know not. Hulgetta has taken it from me." Her name and her tears were the fee Hulgetta demanded in exchange for learning magic—and a bargain at twice the price.

"Hulgetta? Her magic is cruel, then."

He looked at her, as if dazzled. The way he said the word *cruel* and the look he gave her, it was as if he was really saying that she, Prin, was the cruel one, not Hulgetta.

She smoothed the front of her dress, feeling all feminine and cruel. She wished she'd laced her bodice tighter. He lay there enticing, helpless, and yet a corner of her mind still pricked with the need for caution.

"Um, I'll be back in a moment," she said, stalling for time. She leaned forward one more time to feel his forehead. If she was honest with herself it was because she wanted him to see her cleavage. Nor did she mind when he captured one of her braids, pinching it between two fingers, and tugged on it gently, playfully. She froze, stunned, her face inches away from his. *Oh, you are dangerous.*

The way he shifted on the cot was very promising for future slutty fantasies. She found herself giving him the tiniest soft kiss on the lips.

Just for you. Just because.

She hadn't meant to. The fairy dust was in control. She stared at him tentatively, waiting for those zappies to happen again. They didn't. Instead he just looked at her helplessly with big yearning eyes, which was much worse.

"I needed that kiss," he said.

She heard him swallow.

"I—I think I need another."

"I have to go." She fled down the stairs.

She sought Wart, who was, as ever, deboning a skinned rabbit.

"Okay. Okay. I've got to pull it together, Wart." She paced across the stone floor, sticky with dried blood, and paced back again.

"Hulgetta wants his name."

"Did you get it?"

"No. No. But I kissed him."

"What? Why did you do that?" At least five cloth-covered heads turned and looked in their direction. They clustered closer, like magnets drawn to iron.

"I don't know. He looked at me. He seemed to like it." She paced some more. "Hulgetta is going to kill me."

"Did you tell him you're her apprentice?"

"Somehow it didn't come up. He doesn't remember me performing the sleep spell, anyway. I'm such an idiot."

"And he wouldn't tell you even his family name or anything?" Wart said. Prin stared at the rabbit table, which was covered in a thin, watery pool of blood. She crossed her arms, trying not to lean against the blood-splattered wall, and worried on her lower lip.

"No." She thought back. Who knew what they'd said to each other—she mostly remembered feeling all gooey while staring at him. Names? Who cared about names? "No. I asked him, but he didn't tell me."

Two of the maids came to the edge of the entryway. Wart's voice started to change.

"Well, I wouldn't go near him for nothing. He's a wizard, he is."

Prin gave a start, suddenly realizing what Wart was saying.

"A wizard! You think?"

"Or another sorcerer. A fine-looking lord, if that's what he was, would be yelping up and down by now. They go on and on, saying their family are all high, important muckety-mucks and we'll suffer their vengeance. Threats or bribes, tis all their kind knows. He didn't try to bribe you, did he?"

"No." Unless a kiss was a bribe.

"He'll be showing her his bits next," Kath joked, cupping herself between the legs. "And asking to see hers." Prin turned away, not liking that thought at all.

Kath and Elfrieda started moaning in low and high voices. "Oh, Prin," murmured Kath.

"Oh, Elf! Oh, oh, oh," Elfrieda cried.

"What if he doesn't have any family?" Prin said.

"Everyone's got relatives if you're one of them," Wart said with admirable disdain for the aristocratic class. Prin narrowed her eyes at her friend, suspecting Wart *was* one of these aristocratic folk—she was copying the way the maids talked at the moment, and rather overdoing it. Prin let it go without commenting.

"Even if it's some fifth cousin by marriage three times removed, they all back each other."

"Oh. I see," Prin said, scratching her nose. She didn't see, actually.

"What I'm saying is," Wart went on, lowering her voice to a whisper, "is wizards, they renounce their families when they start, mostly." The two maids, Kath and Elfrieda, nodded.

"Don't you mean conjurers?"

"What would herself want with a conjurer?" Elfrieda said.

Kath spat on the floor in agreement. "They're rubbish. Only good for making a little rain in the garden. Or performing at fairs and such."

A wizard. He didn't smell right for a sorcerer. Hulgetta smelled of burned sage, ether, and witch hazel. Prin herself smelled like wood smoke, green beech, and moss. Earth, fire, and air. Not all of them unpleasant in their various guises. What did wizards smell like?

She closed her eyes and inhaled, trying to remember. Her prisoner smelled good. Cold and clean. Like silver keys or fresh snow. He smelled like ozone. She opened her eyes and wrinkled her nose, puzzled.

"They don't want you knowing their name, see?" Kath said, tapping her nose.

"Who doesn't?"

"How many times do we have to tell you—wizards!" Elfrieda exclaimed.

"What about a sorceress?"

"None of them do."

"Why not?"

"I don't know. But you don't see Hulgetta spreading her name across the land, do you?" Wart said. Dread trickled through her. She'd told the elf Hulgetta's name.

She was so dead.

CHAPTER FIVE

"Why can't you know their names?" she asked Wart slowly, carefully.

"You could use it in a spell, I suppose. All I know for sure is when we go down to the village we call her Our Mistress and the shopkeepers call her The Sorceress, and nothing else."

Crap.

"But why wouldn't he tell me his name?" Prin challenged the maids. "I'm just plain old Prin from the kitchen as far as he knows. I'm not going to perform some spell."

"Because you'd tell Hulgetta," Elfrieda said, "and claim your prize."

"What prize?"

"Your prize, a boon. You know." Sometimes the maids, or Wart, or especially Hulgetta, were so impatient with her for not knowing the most basic facts of this world. *So sue me, I'm still new here.* She shook her head, letting her braids swing. She started taking her hair out of the braids. Braids made sense in a comb-deprived world, but they made her look childish. All this time Hulgetta had seemed paranoid and overly suspicious. Prin hadn't realized her mistress had her reasons.

"If you gave up a wizard's name to someone like Hulgetta who works with magic, she would offer you coin or grant you a favor. Everyone knows that," Wart said, her accent suddenly gone.

Prin turned suddenly to her friend. "Would you go with me?"

"Don't do it, Wart."

"Don't."

"Thank you, and shut up," Prin said, shooting the other maids dirty glances. "Okay, okay. Fine. I'll give it another try."

"Careful," Wart said. "If he fancies you, that's dangerous."

There was nothing dangerous about him.

He fancies me. He fancies me. She drifted towards the corridor, thrilled and transfixed. What a word. *Fancy. Dangerous. He fancies me.*

Then her eyes caught the three scraps of leather nailed into the beam that marked the entry to the kitchen. Were *those* cook's ears? She'd seen them before but really hadn't thought about them. Looking again, she still wasn't sure. They could have been dried chili peppers and a bit of an old shoe. They must have been there for years.

She picked up her skirts and hurried back up the stairs.

∞

He woke to the scrape of the door opening. The light from the day was entirely gone, and one fat candle moved into the room. The princess hung over him, a worried pinch to her mouth. Seeing him awake, her expression transformed, her eyes going wide and the faintest hint of a dimple hovering about her mouth. Her bemused curiosity grew even more and he realized he was goggling at her again as the candle picked up the golden threads of her long hair locks.

Never had a human woman—any woman—looked at him with tender sympathy or joking regard. It was a heady experience. He was thirsty for more. Young love and all that other courtly nonsense seemed idiotic, at least to him. Now he cast his mind about for ways to express how the room sparkled to life when she was in it, how drawn he felt to her. Easy words dangled out of reach. To describe her and the effect she had upon him required a sort of poetry he lacked.

He sat up on one elbow and, hesitating, tentatively invited her to sit down near him, patting the mattress. She let the thick candle drip onto the other end of the wooden pallet that his mattress rested upon, out of his reach. Affixing the candle upright to the melty wax on the wood, and seeing it firmly set, she came over and sat next to him, setting the straw to rustling in the mattress, flipping her hair out of the way so she did not sit upon it.

She kept looking at his bare chest and then cutting her eyes away. So there was some modesty to her. Clearly she had been displeased with the vulgar kitchen maids earlier. Displeased, not shocked.

Either she had been here in the castle longer than he'd thought, or she hadn't grown up in that rarified environment that a protected princess would have experienced. The little blonde curls from her braids and slight dimples, along with her lack of height, had made him think her younger than she really was at first. Now he noted her wide open expression of curiosity and deep, upright bosom, those fully developed curvy hips, outlined by the bottom of her corset, and the tiny lines under her eyes. Not a girl, a woman.

She wore a silver chain of keys on her girdle. He held up the manacle, shaking it, and then looked pointedly at her keys.

"There's no keyhole for a lock," She pointed out. No luck there.

Her awareness of his half-clothed state made his inner elf struggle to get out. He wrestled the feeling, fighting for calm as he clenched his jaw and tightened his chest. With a big breath, he managed to pull away from the impulse.

"Who are you?" she asked.

"I am," he said, placing her reluctant hand on his bare chest, "a man. Can't you feel my heart beating for a woman?"

She wriggled her hand as if to pull it away. Obviously she did not like courtly flirting. He didn't really either, but he kept his hand on her wrist. To tell the truth, he'd never wooed anyone like this. His instinct said she'd immediately taken to him, but what did he know? Determined to get out of this cell, he needed alliances, and he needed to test them with her now.

"A man, yes, but also an elf?" she said. Leaning forward again, she looked at him as if she was listening to music far away. "And you're magical, aren't you?" She sounded impressed. Her fair face tilted. He was wary of the awe in her face. Captured elves had once ornamented a powerful king's court hundreds of years ago. Now such things were out of fashion. Still. Here he was.

"I'm half-elf," he explained, and felt a deep shame within. For centuries all human children had been told tales of elves. Stories that all started the same way. A fair and beautiful maid was snatched away by a cruel and handsome elf. The young prince who pitied a captured elf at the king's court was never seen again. The queen was seduced, suffered, and died. It always went badly for the human in the company of an elf. It had stopped elves from being held in chains in every court across the land, but had inspired a deep mistrust on the part of the commoners.

"It's high time you introduced yourself, sir," she said. He watched her closely. Her expression did not change—did not register fear or unease. He was bewildered, but stood swiftly and made a flourishing bow.

"I am your rescuer."

"My rescuer!" She laughed and grinned like a boy.

"I amuse the princess," he said, his mouth feeling stiff, his jaw tightening. He didn't care for being laughed at.

"No, it's just that I—never mind."

"I've decided to carry you from this place. We'll flee together." He slid forward, reaching for her, snagging her around her waist. She went still and small, and a thrill shot through him.

Was she afraid? No, no, her eyes looked back and forth up into his. Not with fear, though her breath started to come quicker. When he returned her look, she immediately cast her eyes down at his naked chest and then away again. She turned pink, but she didn't struggle.

"Your eyes change color," she said.

"Help me," he whispered softly.

"Who," she said, "is asking?"

"Who," he said, "wants to know?" She felt so sweet and yielding in his arms. He could feel the pulse beat in her wrist where her hand held him back.

He drew her down and onto his lap. He was going to have to go very slowly with her. He couldn't actually seduce her, yet time was of the essence.

Pulled in tight next to him, her head was even with his. "Are you of royal blood?" she asked.

"We wouldn't be speaking in the common tongue if I was," he pointed out, frowning.

"All right, I take your point, half-elf," she said. Raising her hand, she reached out and slowly stroked the edge of his ear from the tip down the lobe and then dragged her hand across his jaw line. He shut his eyes and almost groaned. She played with fire, but seemed not to know it. He slowly pulled her hand away, capturing it within its own.

"Where are you from?" he asked.

"Not from around here." That much he already knew. Her accent was not from the North and certainly not from the South. It was hard to place her.

"Where do elves live?" she countered.

"I live to the south of here," he said, eyeing the narrow window where cold seeped in and rain fell. It was already spring at the tower. "The majority of elves live in the North, in the woodlands."

"This is the North."

"Farther north. Their kingdom is a vast realm," he clarified. "Past the mountain ranges, beyond the Great Woods." The elf inside him wanted her exceedingly. His control was slipping. She shifted about on his lap as if she couldn't sit still. Desire rose up inside, blooming throughout his blood, singing like wine in his veins. His eyes throbbed in their sockets. He knew thcy'd turned black.

She was arrested by their change. What was she doing? She didn't look away. He had to avert his eyes and keep them averted, staring at her throat where a deep blush burned. His head began to fill with an infectious passion. Ancient poetic lines of battle and vengeance began chanting in his mind, beating in time to the pulse of his elvin blood.

Then great Torule, of silver lance and shield black with blood,
Struck far and wide to slay the knaves
Who sought to smite him down.

"If you told me your name, and where your people live, I could write them," she offered. He tried to focus on her words, but they were slipping out of his mind as the "Bane of Horslick" continued rolling through his thoughts.

Cursed elf wandering snowy lands
Hated by kindred and outcast.
Cold and all alone he fought as no elf
has to escape his doomed fate, written long ago.

Torule, like him, wandered friendless. Yet here he was on a bed with a maid on his lap. He grinned a little at the thought of railing against the cruelty he'd met. The world was full of wicked elves, violent men, and heartless women. This was just a bit of bad luck.

"I could let them know you were here. Perhaps they would pay Hulgetta a ransom to have you back," she said.

The heat of his naked chest radiated towards her. He could feel her lean towards him, warming herself. The telltale throbbing in his eyes began again. He watched it work upon her. She inspected his shoulder, mesmerized by his skin, her fingers skimming across the surface. Her hand slid up to his chest to touch him, then her other hand slid up higher to his throat. Her fingers slipped behind his head, her lips reaching up towards his, pulling him down to her.

He stared at her lips, and then her eyes tried to meet his.

No. No. No. That can't happen.

He let her go and pushed her off his lap, despite the way his blood sang to her. He closed his eyes, drew a deep breath. Family. She was offering to send for his kin, to ransom him, to rescue him.

"None of my family would claim me." Such a lowering, shameful thought. The pulse of his elf nature pounded.

She was almost in tears as she stood. "They might change their minds if they knew the danger you were in."

He shook his head. Only the dark family crypt would embrace him.

"I make no promises," she went on, "but I could find a way to get a message to—to friends who might help you," she said in a rush.

"There is no one," he said. Bitter memories rushed forth. His own father.

"Theo, it is decided. Nothing shall change my will. Leave and never return."

A tear tumbled from her eye, and her look of tender sympathy made her lips pooch out ever so slightly. She was completely unaware of how adorable and captivating she was. One who clearly had not faced the common cruelties of life.

"They are so awful to reject you. Is it because of your—your birth?" she asked.

"My human mother died when I was born. I was brought up by my father, and he did his duty by me. Then war broke out. He is our warlord, and saying I was too young for the fight and could not follow him, neither would he trust me to his relations while he was gone. He brought me South and left me with my mother's people."

"Why?" Her voice held a note of outrage.

"I now see he was right to do so. They hid their enmity well, but I would have been no match for their cunning wiles, and if he had left me there, I would have been dead or missing by the time he returned. Even as it was—I waited for him to come back, but he never did."

Her eyes were big and cornflower blue, with deep dark blue rims, just now brimming with sorrow. “Could I send to your mother’s people?”

“When I became a young man—you know about elves?”

“Know what?” He now believed she was indeed from another land, very distant.

“I lost my elfin side living with humans. Then as I grew older it came back. They would not have me near their women. I was cast out.”

“Because you—?”

“I had done nothing, harmed no one, yet it did not matter.”

He liked the way she listened, as if spellbound.

“I was glad in a way to leave. I fought my way through the mountain passes, infested with bandits, and sought out my father. War had ended in our land, yet when I returned, he never explained why he had neglected to claim me. We elves go fae as we mature. Passion overwhelms our reason. It’s a temporary stage, and swiftly mastered by most. Indeed, the companions of my youth had already passed this stage. However, being half-elf, I—” even in the telling his bitter remorse and self-loathing overwhelmed him.

“I could not master it.” His eyes throbbed. His neck and heart pounded with the pulse of his anger, his frustration threatening to overwhelm him once more at the memory.

“They knew it and purposely taunted me, watching to see how easily I was enraged. My father had taught me well, and I only stopped when a tormenter lay at my feet wounded. But my father said such childish rage was unforgivable. He was ashamed and once again, I was cast out.”

He stared ahead. Unspooling the memories dragged at his heart ache, plunging him into self-loathing. She stood up and took a turn about the room.

"Sit next to me," he begged. She paced, hands pressed over her chest. Finally, she settled down near him. He took her ice-cold hands into his own. She kept her eyes on their fingers.

"So now... you're a wizard," she said at last, very slowly. His heart strained to understand hers. She seemed horrified by his tale, but there was something more—something he could not understand.

He paused. There was a long moment of silence between them. He tried very hard to understand her expression, yet he could not.

"Yes," he said at last. "I traveled without knowing where I went and came upon the tower I now call home. I am a wizard."

CHAPTER SIX

She cringed, and tried to stand, pulling her hands away.

"Do not think I will harm you," he begged, tugging her towards him once again.

"I think you're not as helpless as you seem." She shook her fingers free and stood three paces off.

"I have told you all. Everything in my heart and of my past," he protested. Almost everything. "Princess, what else can I do to gain your trust?"

"Swear!" she said. "Swear you'll never harm me."

"I swear I will never harm you."

He held out his hand for her to come to him again, but she wouldn't.

"What good is that?" she said. "You swear an oath, but without your name as a seal it means nothing."

The elf in him flamed up and at once his eyes were throbbing. She accused him of faithlessness. His name was another source of shame. It was a name to make human kings feel the thrill of awe, but he was disgraced, and consequently spurned all things elvish.

The sullen bravado of his leaving his father and home still made him cringe. His eyes throbbed in agony at the memory. His wounded pride had never healed. He sought to ensnare her with a look, to subdue her to his will. For once her glance avoided his.

He could not use his real name. Neither would he stand for being insulted by the insinuation that he was a trickster. He was not. His word was gold, but the shame he felt in using his own name was too great.

"I, Eldred Fire Eater, swear I will never harm you, my princess." He used the name of his dead master. His second father. Yet memories of his late master held a bitter taste, more recent and unpalatable. Speaking the name again made his eyes and heart begin to throb with even more shame and misery.

"I swear I shall defeat the evil sorceress Hulgetta, free you from her curses, and protect you from her wrath." He meant every word.

She relaxed, and he snatched her into his arms, bringing her face up to his, breathing in her scent of linen and sage. Her poor, calloused fingers were wrapped within his larger hand. He promised himself silently that never again would she haul buckets or scrub floors. Never again would she wear such drab, simple clothes. His elfin side sprang forth at the faint taunting smile playing about her lips.

"I'm not sure what Hulgetta wants with you." she said, her voice deepening with emotion. "I've asked her, but she won't say." Her brow knotted with worry.

"Does she trust you?"

"She trusts no one." Her delicate nose and the sweetness of her expression had misled him. She was far quicker than he realized. She couldn't be a princess if she didn't know the aristo language, yet she came from someplace where she had been educated and lived a life that was soft and gentle. However, she had managed to survive here, like a flower thriving on rocky soil. She reminded him of a glorious purple thistle.

"Will you swear in turn to help me?" he asked.

She stared at him, uncertain and troubled. "I want to. I just don't know how."

Not enough. "Why has she captured me, Princess?" he asked. "Do you know?"

She shook her head. "She reads one book all the time."

"Has she ever said what the book is called?"

She shook her head. "It's slimy and stinks of sulfur."

His blood chilled.

"What?" she said, suddenly uneasy. "Are you familiar with it?"

"Could be a rejuvenation book. I'd have to see it to know for sure."

"If it's a rejuvenation spell, is that bad?" she asked.

"Yes. Most have been burned. They're deadly. Can you bring me this book?" he asked.

She shook her head. He looked up and thought. Then he looked at his manacle.

"I need you to find something else for me. Is there anything I can write upon?"

She hesitated. "I don't know how to open that manacle on your wrist."

"It doesn't use an incantation to open."

"How can you tell?"

"It doesn't have the feel of an incantation." She looked at the manacle as if it had just surprised her.

"Neither does it have a place for a key. It is some wizard's invention. Obviously very old," he said. "Someone made it, someone used it and, given that it's made of gold, it was probably made for someone at court. Were I back at the tower I could use my history books and reveal its workings in half a day or less.

There's a chance a court historian recorded the event and how the manacles worked." She listened to him, biting her lip. A wisp of memory tickled the back of his brain. But that delicious lower lip, so plump, and its upturned mate, distracted him.

∞

She emerged from the cell and felt as if she'd come back from some place far away. Was this really where she lived?

∞

While talking to him about the manacles she had felt herself transported to that warm court and the tower where the court historian scratched out a history of the golden chains. The castle was so cold when she wasn't near him.

She swiftly returned with a burned stick from the kitchen fireplace. He ripped away a long section from the deep hem of her shift. He scratched out the symbols that she would need to find with elegant fingers. He pointed with the stick.

"This symbol stands for history."

"What language is it?"

"Goinay. If she's got history books, they'll be in that language."

He turned to scratch out some other words, pressing down upon the shift linen stretched between his fingers. "These are other symbols you might see. Tales. Myths. Those words are often in a title of a history." He scratched out a final symbol with a flourish. To her eyes it looked like a two-headed fish sitting on a mirror. "This is the Goinay word for wizard. Look for books with any of these symbols. They will probably be history books."

He tossed the stick to the other side of the room and snatched her onto his lap.

She held the cloth crushed in one hand then folded it while he was kissing behind her ear, sending sharp ticklish shivers down through her chest to wiggle in her tummy. She put the scrap into her pocket reluctantly. He whispered. “Will you help me?”

“Yes,” she whispered back. There. She had said it. She had committed herself. The walls of her loyalty to Hulgetta had all toppled. All that was left in the rubble, aside from a healthy fear of her mistress, was her obsession for this elf-man and her even stronger desire to stay alive. But she still didn’t feel right in some measure. She owed Hulgetta. The woman had taught her magic, given her room and board. It was a debt.

What if to get him free of that manacle she had to cut off his hand? Her stomach turned over and she felt her gorge rising. Her fingers turned to ice and clumsy. She pressed them into his.

His eyes changed. He looked down into her face and down at her mouth. Those eyes were black. She could see her own face in them, and looked deeper, and then deeper still. Oh, what was this? A thick syrup of languorousness poured over her head. Her skin and lips and body wanted to whisper to him, while her mind was strangely hushed.

“The book. Bring it to me.” His voice held a compelling tone. Her mind fought with his, then went blank.

“I will.”

His eyes absorbed her with total concentration. They could suck in galaxies, those eyes, with their depths of sad understanding. A quivering under her sternum fell away. She felt steady on her feet once again. Under his gaze all worry leached away, like a pond that dried up in the sun. She felt a skeleton of strength again, propping her up from within. At the same time her loins were licked by the promise in his eyes, that mouth, the steady hammer of their regard as he bent towards her.

Like dark, slow treacle dumped upon her head, a sense of bonding with him enfolded her. Thick and full, it poured all the way down her throat, trickled across her breasts, and then down the center of her belly and between her legs. Her body felt covered with tingly pressure. She stood under his gaze, swallowed up by it, utterly absorbed.

He bent to kiss her, their mouths opening, eyes closing, his chain clanking as she yielded softly and fully to him. He pulled her up by her bodice, his hands high around her waist, one hand coming round to pull her hair aside, letting his lips rove across her neck. She felt an involuntary clenching deep down and pulled his hands lower, towards her hips.

One hand grabbed her buttock and pulled her up into the hard, prominent bar under his leggings. She rocked against it. The other hand cupped her breast, scooping inside her corset, lifting it free and caressing the nipple with his thumb.

His nose passed over her cheek, caressing her, and nuzzled the other side. Then those eyes were looking into hers, and she was falling into a thick featherbed of need.

His long fingers held her face upwards, and she basked in his touch, like warm rays of the sun. Yet there was a touch of despair in his desire. She drank it in, the optimism in her ready to defy despair. She inhaled his scent, her body aching. She'd die saving him if that's what it took.

∞

He stood, his head hanging above her own, the heat from his hot skin bathing her face, watching her clear eyes grow heavy. His eyes connected with hers, and again her irises shot wide, becoming vulnerable as her expression filled with a delicious resignation. He held her arms, one slender inch between his body and hers.

"Bring the book to me. You'll return it quickly. Hulgetta will never know," he said, the gold cuff rattling against the bar, holding it to the wall.

"She'll know if you escape." She spoke like a woman asleep, like someone resigned to her fate.

He let her go. In theory, her will was not entirely her own. He had never deliberately tried to enthrall anyone before. Was it working? He had no idea.

Among his mother's people he'd deserve death for even trying. The mindless instinct to survive had acted before he could completely stop it. Now it was done.

She was staring at his naked chest, and the elf in him wanted it that way. *Crave the feel of my naked skin against yours.* The elf side relished the challenge she presented. He wanted her with a kind of agonizing desire. She was under his thrall, and he wanted her to feel him, feel his powers, wrap them around her, protect her. He wanted her to struggle, try to resist, and discover all desire to resist was gone.

Stop. He forced himself to look away. He held onto her shoulders and, with a hard inner twist on himself, gave up the thrall. His eyes ceased to throb. He was back, the world hollow and dim, sliced down to a pale shadow of what he saw and felt in his elfin state.

"You will come back. You've fallen in love with me a little."

Her quick look betrayed the truth.

"If she discovers I've taken a book from her lair—"

"She won't. You're too clever." His eyes dragged across hers. He felt the slender skein of magical connection slip through her guarded mind.

A prickling sense of caution warred within him. He wanted to warn her and fought hard to suppress the urge. He was the one she should fear the most. He was cursed, unlucky—a betrayer with dark secrets she couldn't even guess.

Then she was gone. He let his vision darken with the fae-half pulsing inside. He stalked back and forth the short three paces his leash allowed. Every bit of the elf in him wanted to fight. If it could not fight Hulgetta, then his fae side wanted to take that pretty little maid apart inch by inch until she died from tormented pleasure.

∞

Wart was waiting for her at the bottom of the stairs.

"Well?"

"He thinks she might have a rejuvenation spell," Prin said. "He wants to see the book she's been reading and says I need to bring it to him."

"You can't! She'll kill you."

"Try telling him that. His eyes go all fiddly and then I can't think straight and I just want to—" Prin held out her hands and grabbed the air. "I have to do something, Wart."

"So she is going to annihilate him," Wart said.

"Probably. If this book is the one he thinks it is."

"But how will the book free him? Why does he want it?"

"No idea." She tried to calm the fretful tone in her voice. She opened the scrap of linen and once again studied the crude sketches he'd made of the Goinay symbols.

She folded up the scrap and put it back in her pocket. "Wart, he is so not innocent. Oh he looks it, but Hulgetta sent me fishing for some bad boy creature with magical powers, and he's what I dredged up. I have a bad feeling about all of this."

They turned into the sorceress's den and Wart gave her one look with big worried brown eyes. Prin gave her a quick shoulder squeeze and stepped up to the table. The feeling from the cell was passing, but she felt her strength remain.

"I need his name," Hulgetta said, dragging a clawing hand through her long lank gunmetal grey hair. "Now."

"Eldred. Eldred Fire Eater." Prin stood at the edge of the table. She hadn't wanted to hand over the name, and felt like a total shit about it, but let's face it, she liked her ears. She covered them with both hands, warming her icy fingertips on her hot face.

"He's a wizard, you know," she added. "A powerful one."

"Not so powerful, if he's lying prisoner in my cell."

Silence. *Well, that intimidation tactic didn't work.*

Another blue arrow came out of thin air. It hit the pillar with a zzzwift sound, landing with a clatter on the chamber floor. She didn't even ask, simply picked it up and put it in the basket. That made five or six in the last two days.

She thought of his face. Those elf eyes, such great big pools of feeling. How did he know how to reach deep down into her like that? Kissing him left her hollowed out. Trembling. When his eyes turned black—even now, just thinking about it hardened her nipples and left her clenching. Excitement mixed with a strange, intoxicating foreboding. She swallowed, her mouth dry. Now that she wasn't touching him, her confidence was shriveling. She'd just met him, and here she was contemplating magic book theft. Which was like contemplating suicide. She broke into a light sweat.

"Isn't it taboo, you know, um, to take a wizard?" she said. "I mean, you do magic, he does magic. Isn't there some sort of live and let live agreement? Like fellow magic workers unite, or something?"

"No," Hulgetta said and continued reading.

She drifted closer and waited, but apparently that was it.

"He seems to think you're going to kill him," Prin said.

Hulgetta looked her in the eye, and she didn't flinch away from those bloodshot, fishy grey orbs. Dread welled up from her stomach down to her guts, making them loose. *For the love of all that is holy, old woman, just answer my question. Are you going to kill him? Yes or no.*

"All magic has a price," Hulgetta said.

Sweat sprang up under her arms and she swallowed convulsively then looked at the sorceress again.

Yes, her mistress was old. Decaying right along with the castle, her face hollowing out, and at the same time crumpling in on herself while the books arrayed upon the shelves were growing dimmer, colder, and emptier of magic day by day. In Hulgetta's entire lair the enchantment was fading, dying. If you needed magic to make magic, then Hulgetta could revive her body, yes, but more than that, if rejuvenated, perhaps her body could hold a magic charge once again. Would the spell do that too?

Over the last month Hulgetta could barely raise a curl of smoke from the cauldron. So that was why her lowly apprentice was allowed to learn the sleep spell?—Hulgetta probably couldn't do it herself at this point. And how did she have enough magical zap to even perform the spell? Putting it together suddenly, she realized: from her encounter with the moss maid, that's how. *Ahhhhhhhh.* Yes, if magic worked like batteries worked, then her mistress's actions all made sense.

Prin edged closer to the sorceress again. She knew she was pushing it.

"I still don't understand how wizards are different from us."

"Why do you care? We have nothing to do with wizards," Hulgetta said and spit.

"Can you explain?" she said extra loudly. "How wizards and their magic are different from us?" She enunciated distinctly, as if Hulgetta was losing her hearing. Oh, how she hated that.

Hulgetta put down her book and gave her an exasperated look. "They don't work spells."

"What do they do, then?"

"Use instruments of wonder to amaze and stupefy."

"What kind of instruments?"

Hulgetta made a *whatever* flip of the hand. "Magical devices." Hulgetta's tone was dripping with derision.

"They invent them? That sounds pretty cool."

"Rarely. They steal. A wizard fears nothing more than another wizard in his domain. And then, after they've stolen whatever they can carry away, they don't even know how to use what they've stolen. They certainly don't create magic the way we do."

The way Hulgetta explained it, a wizard put together component parts of magical items created by—and stolen from—sorceresses and sorcerers in order to create a magical device. It sounded to Prin like the same way someone might add pesto sauce from a jar to some cooked pasta and claim to be a chef. It was more like assembling than magic. The magical parts all came from stones or glass or whatever item had been imbued with magic by a sorcerer or some magical creature.

"So did a wizard create the rings on the petrified hand?" she asked, trying to follow how it all worked. "Or was that a sorceress?"

"That's rather complicated. In fact—" Hulgetta abruptly snapped her mouth shut. "Never mind."

Prin knew when Hulgetta was hiding something from her. Hulgetta had some kind of agenda. Still Prin had to prod her mistress one more time.

"Are you sure we're safe keeping a powerful wizard locked up here in the castle? Shouldn't we let him go?"

CHAPTER SEVEN

Hulgetta gave her a look that plainly said, *Are you crazy?* "No. He would only retaliate against us."

"But we're safe from him, as long as he's locked up."

"And has no access to magical devices."

She nodded. So, a wizard without his toys was vulnerable. Thinking it through, she also realized a sorceress caught without her spells at her fingertips was a sitting duck. Speaking of which…

"Ah, it seems the elf-wizard knows who you are," Prin said. Hulgetta immediately whirled about.

"How? How did he learn my name?" Hulgetta was aghast.

Because I told him.

Hulgetta began muttering under her breath. She hauled out a giant map, unfolded it, and then, after searching for what she wanted, put a small pile of black sand over the spot.

"The name he gave?"

"Eldred Fire Eater."

Hulgetta invoked a High Anslod spell, her voice chanting out the short lines. Her mistress snatched a hand out and grabbed her own in a painful grip. Prin could feel the elf energy pouring from her into the spell, like water from a pitcher. She pulled her hands away from Hulgetta as fast as she could. Hulgetta, meanwhile, covered the pile of sand with a small curved glass—a cupping glass, it was called.

First the pile of black sand began to smoke. Hulgetta lifted up the glass and the spot of sand burned up, spreading wider, until the map was in flames. Hulgetta began slapping the map, trying to put out the fire with the flat of her hand. In the end it was like a game of whack-a-mole and the map was much the worse for it. By the time Hulgetta was done the map resembled tattered black lace, with spots and holes across the entire surface.

"That is not his name!" Hulgetta fumed. "He lied. Whoever Eldred Fire Eater was, he is now dead."

She was honestly shocked. *He lied? But—* "How d'you know?" she asked.

Hulgetta was clearly put out. "I tried using the location spell by invoking his name, and it didn't work." Hulgetta grimaced and glared down at the ruined map. *Obviously.*

Hulgetta grabbed the map, tearing it and balling it up. Then her large hand came out and with a crack smacked Prin full in the face.

"Idiot!"

Prin staggered back, shocked, holding the tingling side of her face with two hands, her eyes big with surprise. *Here it comes.*

"You should have known he was lying through his teeth, and instead, like a gullible mawworm, you come back here—ruining my map." She threw it onto the stones.

Like some bad LSD hallucination, Prin saw blue smoke start to pour out from the ceiling behind Hulgetta's head. She watched it, blinking.

"What are you staring at?" Hulgetta looked over her shoulder and gave a start of horror.

"Get my crossbow!" Hulgetta cried. Prin ran to the curtained alcove holding Hulgetta's bed and dropped down to the lower cupboard, snaking into the cobwebbed space. She came back out with the rickety bow, and an iron bolt, her cheek still tingling, her breath caught on half a sob.

The smoke was obliterating the ceiling, covering the vaulted arches completely like the rippling walls of a silken midnight blue tent being lowered down upon their heads.

Wordlessly she handed the dusty crossbow over to her mistress.

"Load it first, you idiot."

Prin braced the weapon against her diaphragm and began to struggle with pulling back the string. "It's the same shade of blue as the arrows," she said, coughing. The smoke was starting to make her head feel hazy.

"Are you loading it? I need it now!" Hulgetta snapped.

"It won't." Prin struggled and finally had to sit down on the floor, holding the cross-frame with her feet while pulling with both her hands on the string as hard as she could. Once she got her weight behind it, she loaded the string behind the spring clip. The entire weapon wobbled back and forth, then simply burst apart in her hands. The bolt shot across the floor, and she was left with a tangled, broken length of rotted wood in each hand.

Someone in blue robes and with long pale hair was emerging from the cloud.

"Shoot him, quickly. Shoot."

Prin dropped the fragments. "Oh, Criminy! You should have answered the king's letters!" She dove under the table.

"Come here at once," Hulgetta said, grabbing at Prin's hair. Her mistress continued twisting the long locks, trying to drag Prin's body up in front of her.

Prin didn't relish being a human shield. A deep baritone voice filled the room with chanted words. Hulgetta let go of her. The second Hulgetta let go, Prin sank to the floor, crawling backwards under the table.

"Here! Where are you going? Come back here!" Hulgetta cried, trying to snatch her apprentice back. But she kicked away Hulgetta's hand and crab walked backwards out of her mistress's reach, until she was safely behind a pillar.

"Prin!" Hulgetta hissed, looking around for her.

She crouched down low behind the pillar and shook her head. *No.*

So Hulgetta was left to stand tall and face the man emerging from the blue clouds.

Clearly a sorcerer, she thought, as he finished chanting and the blue clouds collapsed at his feet. His dark navy robes were certainly less ancient than Hulgetta's, but the runes embroidered along the hem in silver were almost identical. Her eye was drawn to his long pale blond hair, silky and straight. Though his features were even, he had a magnificent nose that jutted out from the cliff of his brow, while his lips were tight and pale with anger. He took his time to look around the room then faced Hulgetta, who was attempting to stand tall despite tucking her head into her shoulder, which was jerking.

A long snout of blue smoke humped across the floor like a snake. It made straight for Prin. The blue sorcerer followed its path and saw her. She started to shrink behind the pillar, but his expression relaxed. She thought she spotted a twinkle in the back of his eye. She started forward, but he gave one slight shake of his head, *no*, so she stayed where she was, avidly watching.

"Hulgetta." The blue sorcerer said the name with a weary distaste. "I come on behalf of King Linus. You are in violation of your oath. Tomorrow you must stand with us against Rupert the Red or face dire consequences. Spell workers are needed as the King faces the Valdean's mercenary forces hired by Rupert."

His voice carried through the low-vaulted chamber. She sank lower still, onto her haunches, while the blue smoke snaked about her and snuffled at her. Hulgetta looked like she was trying to tuck her face down into her breastbone. She could just see Hulgetta's lips moving.

"Rhine," Hulgetta said and held her hands out as if fending him off. She was afraid, backing away. Hulgetta turned her face and tucked her chin into her shoulder again. Suddenly Prin realized Hulgetta was muttering words. With an audible gasp, she realized that Hulgetta was speaking a spell against the other sorcerer, but trying to seem afraid and forestall him from realizing it. *A spell! Not fair!*

The sorcerer caught Prin's gasp and realized what Hulgetta was doing in an instant.

"*Lam alda extornimba, fra-lorsinqua bal dam*!"

Prin quickly pulled up her hands over her ears, but as she watched the sorcerers duel, there was a faint burst of light that speared out towards Hulgetta, who sank to the floor, writhing.

The sorcerer stood over her mistress. Hulgetta's eyes were open, her mouth gaping in silent agony. An elbow twitched upwards several times. Yet apparently the rest of her was frozen.

"Spell of stone. Your favorite, as I remember," Rhine said. He squatted down by the side of the sorceress. "I am a reasonable man." He leaned over the sorceress's body a little so she could see his face. "I know you hate people and want to be left alone. But you took this castle with the agreement to support your king in his time of need. Now your king commands you."

"I am no king's subject." Prin could barely make out the words Hulgetta muttered slowly through her stiffening jaw.

"You signed a pact." The sorcerer reached into his robe, withdrew a scroll. "I have it here."

"You cannot—make—me," Hulgetta muttered between stiff lips. "I'm no longer… a prentice."

"Brave words," Rhine said, "to speak while lying at my feet."

He stood up straight. Prin watched Hulgetta's eyes follow him. If looks could kill, Rhine would have twenty broadswords stuck through his body.

"The mercenaries Rupert hired are coming in from the sea, their battalion divided by storm," he said, his voice soft, "We must attack now, while half their force lies offshore. The king's men skirmish in small numbers, leading the Valdeans inland, where they will not have the sea at their backs. If we attack them on the morrow at half their strength, we will triumph. The other forces will return home without a fight when they see half their army decimated. This is why we must rally behind Linus's banner." His voice became more reasoning. "Less than a fortnight's service for an entire castle, Hulgetta. Tis a good bargain, and you know it."

Hulgetta could not speak. Nevertheless, she made a sucking noise that was familiar to Prin's ears and clearly insulting. The blue sorcerer smiled.

"Still your stubborn self, eh? Use your powers to help Linus, or I will not free you from this spell. It is your choice. You will stay here, as immobile as a stone, until it wears off."

How long would that be, Prin wondered? A week? A month? The sorcerer looked at her face, no, her cheek. Perhaps Hulgetta's fingerprint was still there.

"Frozen," he reminded Hulgetta. "At the tender mercy of your servants."

"Uh," Hulgetta said, but Prin thought her mistress meant *no*. Oh, he was clever.

"Yes, you will reap what you have sown," the blue sorcerer said, his voice hushed. "Have you been kind? Will they tend to you or torment you? Will they bury you alive outdoors? What if they simply walk away, leaving you here until the fire goes out, the candle gutters, and you are forgotten? How long before the rats creep out into the dark and find you?"

The spell would wear off. It only depended on the force of his magic to determine how long that would take. It wasn't much retribution at all. Yet Hulgetta's eyes were rolling, the giant frown of her mouth gaping as she struggled against the spell.

Suddenly Prin realized. All the wrongs Hulgetta had done over the years—how would those maids repay Hulgetta if she was locked into immobility? She looked terrified. This guy was a genius. His greatest power so far had been to use his enemy's imagination and bad karma against her.

"I've only been bitten by a rat once, but I will never forget the sting and ache of that bite on my forefinger. Look, I still bear the scar." He showed her his long forefinger. "How many times would they taste you? Remember, you won't die."

A gargled scream rose from Hulgetta's body.

"Change your mind?"

"Glah."

With a few words, Hulgetta was released. She slowly crawled away on all fours. Reaching the wall, she raised herself into a standing position. Prin hugged herself behind the pillar, watching her mistress.

"We meet in the eastern lands near Dorner," the blue sorcerer said. "In a forest ravine on the west side—Tully's ravine, it's called. Be there by morning. Look for the tents and fires." He held out a hand. Hulgetta looked at it with fear and loathing, and then back up at his face.

"You will not clasp my hand in promise? You, who were once my apprentice and owed me gratitude, loyalty? Very well." He closed his hand. "But never shame me with your cowardice again. We shall have a swift victory," he said, "if we remain strong, you shall once again be left in peace."

He darted one last look over at her, and Prin gave a little wave. Rhine gave her something that was almost a smile, almost a nod, and whirled around, chanting. White smoke came wafting up from the floor. When it touched the hem of his robe it turned blue, billowing everywhere, moving up toward the low ceiling in large plumy clouds. Soon it was all gone, along with the sorcerer. Only a tiny wisp of blue was left, snaking about wildly on the floor. Hulgetta stared at it, her mind clearly elsewhere.

"Come here," she said to Prin, but not looking at her. Prin crept towards her, but thinking of Rhine's words, she refused to cower.

Hulgetta gave her another sweeping smack on her other cheek. She should have been expecting it this time and wished it didn't hurt so much.

"Never show disloyalty to me again," her mistress said. "Disobey me in any way, and I'll have your ears off your head. Now tell the maids to fetch my armor." Prin swept towards the door immediately, eyes full of tears of surprise, and turning back from the hall she saw Hulgetta stamping in fury, repeatedly crushing the snaking curl of blue smoke that tried to dodge her foot, until it was mashed out of existence.

She returned swiftly with the maids in tow.

"Polish my armor," Hulgetta said. Turning to Prin, she added, "You. Find my padding." No sign of her recent weakness was in sight.

"And bring me my axe to sharpen. Wait. Bring me my mace first."

∞

It took most of the night to polish the armor. The maids used linseed oil and some kind of gritty grey paste until each fauld and tasset shined like nickel-plated pleats. Prin, who had found the purple quilted padding at last, nibbled by mice and covered in cobwebs, spent several hours polishing Hulgetta's helm.

It was carved like a demon's head with long metallic horns on each side. It was full of spikes and little sharp scales. Pushing the visor up made it seem like the demon was laughing.

A bad omen. And when was she going to have time to search for the books she needed to find? She would have to wait until Hulgetta was gone.

Hulgetta came back at one point, a bundle of moth-eaten wool under her arm. "Here, this should fit you."

"What?"

"Your tabard. You'll act as my standard bearer and cup bearer."

"But—"

"You're coming with me," Hulgetta said. "Now get that on, and find my standard while you're at it."

CHAPTER EIGHT

She unwrapped the bundle. A brown, matted, felt tabard-thingy and a matching skull cap, very moth eaten. *You're kidding me*. She put the tabard over her head. It was like putting on a dead rodent skin that covered her from her shoulders to just below her ass. She would look like the clueless servant she really was. Looking down she noted someone had stitched on the matted brown the head of a gorgon in purple and gold thread that had begun to rot and turn black. *Lovely*.

Wart came into the room and gave a double take.

"Don't laugh," she begged Wart. "Don't." She snuck up closer to the kitchen maid, speaking low so the others polishing armor wouldn't hear.

"I have to find the book now, before Hulgetta comes back."

"Too dangerous." Wart shook her head.

"You'll have to take the book to him then, while I'm gone."

"Absolutely not."

Wart tried to walk around her, but she backed up and blocked the maid then drew her over to the basilisk, where they stood with their backs turned to the room. Wart in her nervousness was stroking the lizard's neck.

"Look, it'll be safe, because she won't be here. You'll have it back before she returns. No one will ever know."

"No. I—no."

"What if I copy the page? You won't be taking him the whole book, just a page. No one would miss anything in that case."

"Take it to him now, yourself, if you're so determined. She won't notice, she's distracted. He can look at it while you're both gone."

The rejuvenation book was out on the table in plain sight. She walked over to the table, standing between the maids arrayed around the table. They sat on high stools or stood, busy polishing the armor with gritty paste, oily rags, and lots of elbow grease until it gleamed silver and moved freely.

She stood among them and then slowly drew off the tabard. She set it over the book. Ditto the skull cap. Then, gathering the cloth and book up into a bundle, she rolled it all together, watching the maids while her fingers made sure that the book was secure in the center of the roll, and turned towards the door.

"What you doing?"

Oh, she really didn't need this. She turned back. Five pairs of eyes stared, including Wart, who looked ready to bolt.

"Where you taking that?" Elfrieda demanded.

The bundle of cloth was faintly smoking. Prin waved the stray smoke away with a casual hand.

"What business is it of yours?" she said. Might as well go for intimidation.

"There's smoke coming out that bundle," Elfrieda said, pointing the awl she was using on the joints of the armored feet at the cloth. Baz had been watching this whole exchange at the end of his chain with lively interest. He shook his head, and lowering it, sneezed a small spurt of flame. Lowering his head dropped the cuff down over his head, where it stuck. The maids looked up, some suppressing a giggle at the ridiculous lizard looking out at them from the tube around his face. Prin got up and slid the cuff back down onto his neck again. He shook his head and his neck fringe flapped out, a glorious cobalt blue, which made the kitchen maids giggle again. The lizard looked around, taking an interest in them in a way Prin had never seen before. *Clown.*

"What you doing?" Elfrieda said again.

Kath turned with her arms akimbo to back up her friend. "She's had a funny look ever since being in that wizard's cell."

"You mean the elf-wizard?" Zephyr said. Shouldn't have. The kitchen maids all gave a gasp of horror.

"He's no elf. Where'd you get that idea, miss?" Kath said.

"His is. He's half-elf. Told me so himself." Another hiss from the peanut gallery.

"They enthrall women, you know," Lanky Sue said, her long arms wrapping about herself and hugging her shoulders with her large, bony hands.

"All I know is, she's got some book of the mistress's wrapped up in that bundle." Elfrieda was not to be distracted. "All my years here, I've never seen a book leave this room. And that's twenty years, almost, going on this spring."

"He's enthralled her, that's what it is," Kath stated to Lanky Sue and Elfrieda.

"What I do or don't do is none of your concern," Prin said, raising her voice. "I follow my mistress' orders."

"Not if you're taking one of them spell books up to that elf. The way I see it, that is very much our concern," Elfrieda said.

Prin put the bundle down on the table.

"Why are none of you polishing?" Hulgetta's voice boomed behind her. Everyone jumped a mile. The maids scurried and suddenly there was much rubbing and scrubbing going on, their heads bent over their work.

"There it is," Hulgetta said, and picking up a long handled mace, she turned to go. "I shall practice in the yard. Light!" Prin handed the torch over to Wart and whispered, "Go with her. I'm going to copy out a page. Then when we're gone, you'll slip it to him."

Wart silently shook her head, mouthing, "No, no, no, no."

"Go," she mouthed back, and Wart went off following Hulgetta with the torch. Once they were gone she pulled the book out from the tangle of tabard cloth, and with one glare at Elfrieda, flopped the book open to the beginning and sat openly at the table copying out the page. She waved away the sulfur smoke that rose from the tip of her pen as she copied the lines. Then she folded up the paper, put it in her pocket and with another look at Elfrieda dropped the book back onto the spot where it was and went back to polishing the tarnished helm.

Her fingertips were well pricked by the time Hulgetta returned and began putting on the padding. Prin helped her with everything else, strapping on the breastplate and gorget. She mounted a stool before gesturing for the helm. It was handed up to her and she staggered a little under the weight of the giant, heavy bull's horns. Putting it above the sorceress's head, she lowered the helm down onto Hulgetta's shoulders. Once Hulgetta was strapped in, they all stood back and stared. The sorceress was tall, her horns grotesque. Then Hulgetta started forward as if to menace them all.

The maids fled, terrified.

"Well?" the sorceress demanded, flipping up the visor.

"Most fearsome," Prin said with great sincerity, dismounting from the foot stool.

"Get that on and follow me," Hulgetta said, pointing at the skullcap. She crossed the lair with a ponderous stride as Prin dragged the skullcap over her head, letting her hair hang out on either side. Hulgetta went down the dingy narrow corridor that ended at the green door. Prin pulled on the tabard, and left the folded page, slightly smoking, next to the book on the table.

"What were you writing?"

Prin hesitated, her head suddenly pounding with fear. "I was taking notes. What about the prisoner while we're gone?"

Hulgetta stopped and looked back at her. "I forgot all about him." She swore. "I need his name and also his heart cleaned before the moon phase changes."

"That's in two days," Prin said. Hulgetta swore again.

"Will we be back before then?"

Hulgetta pondered then lifted her head. "You cannot go."

A shower of relief cascaded through Prin's body from shoulders to toes. She felt like she'd been pulled from an iron cage and could breathe again. She pulled the itchy wool tabard and the hood off her head, throwing them down onto the table.

"Not that you're to slack off while I'm gone," Hulgetta said.

"No, mistress."

"Find out what this elf-wizard's real name is."

"If I need to open the manacle—"

"Do not, under any circumstances, open the manacle!"

"But if—"

"Get his name even if you have to wrench out his tongue with a pair of pinchers," Hulgetta said without turning to look at her.

"Very funny."

Hulgetta gave a double take, her gorgon's stare pinning the apprentice to her spot. Prin's stomach fluttered. *Pushing it, as always.*

"I'll get it out of him." *Dangerous? Him? Nah.*

They continued to stare at each other. She would not cut her eyes away but stared her mistress down, fervently praying Hulgetta would not realize how scared she was.

"He's wily," Hulgetta said at last. "Do not fall for his lies. Do not underestimate him, and get out of your head whatever mischief you're brewing."

"Anything I should do while you're gone? I mean, with the elf-wizard."

"While I'm gone, I want him to starve. Then try asking his name. You're also to clean his heart of wicked deeds. The spell is in the primer. He'll struggle, so don't go all soft about it. Collect the pitch from the sponge into this bucket. I'll need it later."

"Right." Now was the time. Plucking up her courage, she said, "And when you get back? Then?" She made a throat slitting gesture.

"No," Hulgetta said, "it's more like this," and pointing with her armored gauntlet she used Prin's body to illustrate.

"Across the upper abdomen, then down. Around the belly button here," she said, dragging her finger across Prin's torso. "Then straight down again." The cut looked like a backwards five. Prin nodded, swallowing rapidly all the excess saliva that suddenly flooded her mouth.

"Lovely," she gulped. "So you kill him and then what?"

"Oh, we don't kill him. Not at first. No, we want him alive." Hulgetta's eyes lit up. It was as if suddenly the mentor Prin had always wanted was now happy to instruct her in these dark arts. Now that the magic had taken a sadistic turn Hulgetta was lit from within with glee.

"We want him alive as long as possible. In excruciating agony. It strengthens the spell."

"Does it—does it prime the spell? Like sourdough starter grows the bread?"

Another stare from her mistress. "An excellent way to put it. Yes, we torture the magic out of him, slowly, gathering it into the chanting bowl. Then, when the spell is strong enough, we activate it, all the while chanting Rhymaeic incantations to guide the spell as it starts to work. Timing is everything."

That's why Hulgetta needed to re-read the spell over and over. She was memorizing the incantation. That's why Hulgetta was telling her this. She would need an apprentice's help.

"And the pitch from his heart?"

"It feeds the spell, you see. We add it a little bit at a time to the bowl. The agony of a magical creature works just like bread starter. It's the strongest magical source there is."

"What if there's no pitch?" Brave words, they leapt out of her mouth before she could gather them back.

Hulgetta smiled. Or it was an attempt at a smile at any rate. She showed her teeth, creating a pile up of wrinkles on either side of her mouth.

"There'll be plenty. You'll see."

She handed her mistress her battle-axe and thought again about how many wizardly items Hulgetta had.

I bet she's killed others.

She viewed her mistress with fresh eyes.

How many?

Even so, she felt a pang at how two-faced she was being to her mistress. A traitor. A bald-faced liar. There was just no right way out of this whole situation, was there? She shuddered, wondering how far along this path she would have gone eventually. Would she have approved of Hulgetta torturing the green smoke demon? Absolutely not. She felt squicky enough having snipped off the demon's claws in the door—and she hadn't even been trying to harm him then, it was just an accident.

Hulgetta, her elbows sticking out awkwardly, her hands in her greaves, couldn't dial the coordinates for the battlefield. She said them aloud, and Prin spun the dial and slotted the levers to the right positions then worked the rotating knob. With a click the door unlocked. Leaning backwards, Prin began pulling the heavy door open.

Instead of opening onto the other side of the castle wall where the drained moat held the pig and a few bedraggled chickens, the door opened onto a sunny bright green hillside that sloped down to a gorge. A beech forest was off to the left, and the smell of leaf mold and fire smoke drifted towards them. A haze floated above the trees, proclaiming an army camped nearby.

Hulgetta stopped to give her apprentice one last sharp look.

"Remember. Starve him. Get his real name. Clean his heart." With the visor up, the helm looked like the demon was trying to swallow Hulgetta's face whole. The visor snapped down and Hulgetta began to slowly stride down the hill.

Prin watched Hulgetta framed against the beeches and drenched blue sky, then called out, "Wait! You forgot your mace!" She ran back to retrieve the weapon. She handed it off to Hulgetta and slipped back through the heavy door before it began to close.

With Hulgetta gone, she charged back into the study and skidded to a halt in front of the slender shelves of Hulgetta's books. *Where are you history books?* She looked around over her shoulder, quickly. The room was empty, the gritty paste and rags scattered all about the table and stools everywhere. Baz flicked his little tongue, head dark blue, expression alert and inquisitive.

She scanned the shelf. Nothing. She took out her spell book primer, put it back on the table and took a small break, tiny chicken scratch symbols from the spines of the books dancing before her eyes. She needed to relax. After a few minutes she tried scanning the shelves for history books again. Nothing. She took out the scrap of cloth he'd written on, and went through all five shelves again in a close and careful search trying to match the symbols he'd drawn. No! It just wasn't there. By the time she was done her eyes ached from the small, obscure print as the oil lamps ran low and the candles began to gutter.

She turned away in defeat, got out her small cauldron and slowly began to turn her primer to a page labeled "Recipe for Cleaning a Heart of Wicked Deeds." The letters looking like chopped-up worms, writhing in agony. She gathered the herbs and various ingredients, placing them on the table as well. Then she brought up the bucket and put it on the table next to the cauldron. The candles went out. She raised her head. It was late at night. Everyone in the castle was asleep. Even Baz was curled up on his shelf.

She left the room, began to run, and at last skipped up the crumbling steps to the elf's cell door, her body trembling and cold, trailing a little sulfurous smoke from the page of evil writing in her pocket.

They enthrall women you know. Oh, she was going to have words with him. She almost levitated at the thought and flew up the stairs even faster.

CHAPTER NINE

"I've never met an elf before," she said. Her fingers were trembling with excitement.

"Half-elf," he said. "I've never met anyone like you. Where is the land from whence you hail?"

"Far away. Further than the fastest ship can reach."

"Your accent is different."

She didn't bother explaining. She wasn't there to talk. She wanted to see his eyes change again and stood before him, the better to judge his expressions. She realized she was tired of mistrusting him. She wanted to believe him. Even more, her body wanted to crack open the magic inside him and taste it.

Without his shirt on, there was no way to ignore his body, the rounded meat of his shoulders, the flat plane of his pectorals, muscles that shifted and slid over his ribs. He had no hair on his chest, but a thin line of dark hair led from his navel down into the leather leggings. With his knees apart and legs relaxed, her mind couldn't help but slip down into the lacings and imagine what her fingers would find. She could feel the crisp hairs down there and sense the heat from his body. He was half naked but she was the one who felt exposed. She stared into his eyes. Just now they were mossy green-brown and quite nice. He'd look at home in the woods with a spotted hawk on his fist. She found her eyes skimming down his face over and over again. He lied, she reminded herself. He lied.

Play the airhead. Twiddle your hair around a finger.

"How do you know if someone is a wizard or not?"

"Why do you ask?"

"Hulgetta says all wizards are charlatans and liars. She said they don't do real magic. Is this true?"

"My master did real magic."

"Did?"

"What?"

"You said *did*—is your master dead?" She drifted a step closer to him and played with the ties of her corset.

"Yes."

She paused, then guessed. "Was your master Eldred Fire Eater?"

This time he paused, and she saw the muscles in his jaw bunching with tension.

"Yes—"

"Then you lied to me. You didn't give me your real name."

He gave her a pained, agonized look.

"It's alright," she said, relenting glumly. "I can see why, given the circumstances, you would lie. But Hulgetta knows Eldred's not your name." She watched him closely.

"Smart little princess," he said. "Come over here."

She came, reluctantly.

He hooked a finger into her bodice and pulled her down onto his lap. She let herself sit delicately as he buried his face into her collarbone. She began to melt. "I did not like lying to you," he said, his voice muffled by her neck.

"I can't trust you if you lie, and I'm not your little princess," she said, struggling to get up, struggling against his bewitching touch. "You know what I think? You're a scoundrel with a fair face, who wants to seduce and betray me."

With a sudden yank he pulled her back against him, and she felt the hard length of him under the padding of muscle.

"Seduce you, yes. Most decidedly. But I intend to keep every promise I speak," his voice was harsh and low in her ear. Then he kissed the tender space behind it. She swooned. His lips sent trails of ticklish pleasure racing across her collar bones until her head spun.

The magic inside him was closer now to the surface, expanding just under his features, making him, if possible, more beautiful, his lips full and relaxed. It excited her, blended with her attraction to him, until she had to strongly quell the impulse to squirm against him. The elf part was going to come out. She could feel it throbbing there, just under his skin.

"I like holding you here," he said in response to her helpless stirring. Gently taking her hand, he drew it over to his chest, resting it on the spot over his heart.

"Can you feel my heart?" Her palm felt his hot naked flesh and her own heart picked up its pace. He turned everything upside down.

"I feel the magic inside you," she said, leaning into him and closing her eyes. All her fairy dust was agitated like never before.

"It makes us very dangerous to women."

She pulled her hand from his chest.

He let her do so, but retained her fingers lightly in his grasp. She was feeling very Romeo and Juliet. Any second the maids could burst through the door and stop them, threatening to tell Hulgetta of her betrayal. Just the loose grip of his fingers holding hers made her breath tighten up. She stared at him. His masculine beauty far surpassed her own looks. She felt the magic in him, leashed and writhing. It was like trying to hold the basilisk's strong meaty neck when he was impatient for a treat and lashed his tail.

Yes, the elf was deceptive. He was so much stronger than he looked. His expression so hauntingly sad. She caught herself straining towards his lips.

"The land I come from has no elves," she said to distract herself.

"No elves?" He sat straight and looked puzzled, as if trying to imagine such a place.

"Nor wizards."

"None at all?"

"We have magicians who do illusions, but no wizards and no sorcery either."

He made a face. "For that you should be grateful. We are plagued with sorcery here. Gaybarth the Bold wrote, 'A sorceress, deadly as a snake, her soul an empty cupboard.'"

"Gaybarth." She had to sit up at that and look at him. "Seriously, Gaybarth?"

"Yes, the famous scholar and poet."

"Oh my God. Hey. So. Aren't there female wizards too?" she asked, edging towards her confession.

"No."

"No?"

"Magic turns women into vain, grasping creatures. Under its spell they seduce and deceive."

She was aghast. *Well this is a little awkward.*

I have to tell him, she thought.

"Not all sorceresses are evil."

"Hulgetta captured you, didn't she?" he said.

"Well, I'm not exactly sure." The face of Hulgetta when Prin landed through the open green door was impossible to forget. *Surprised? Ha! Definitely.*

"It's possible that my coming here was unintended, an accident. And she treats me no worse—perhaps a bit better even—than the others."

"Others?"

"The kitchen maids."

"But that is your due, as an educated gentlewoman of birth. Princess, do you know how Hulgetta found me?"

Awkward!

"Um, well. She gave her apprentice a long list of coordinates to use on a green door that opens in different places. And your location was picked. Then you were brought here."

"I have no memory of it. She used a knock-out spell of some kind, the wretched hag. Is that how you came to be here? Did you come through the green door?

"Yes—I was actually at a very old palace overrun by the jungle far south of Ohio."

"Ohio."

"That's where I'm from. You read about history, I dig it up at old sites where ruins are. I was digging with a team to find old artifacts so that we could preserve them. Do you follow me?"

He nodded, his expression intent, frowning a little. "You come from the land of O-hi-o."

"Anyway, that's how I found the green door. I dug it up. I really should have told my grad professor, but when I uncovered it, he was a hundred miles off at a bar, and I was kind of resentful that he was there with air conditioning and beer, while I was crouched over a hole, literally sweating into the dust. So I just kept uncovering more and more of this door, until it opened suddenly, and I fell through."

"I see. Did she clap you up in here?" He looked around the cell.

"At first. Then she let me roam the castle freely. So she really didn't capture me in the same way she did you."

What had she done? She stood up and paced.

A ray of early morning light fingered its way through a narrow slit in the stone wall, tagging his naked foot, illuminating his flawless skin. Prin put her little lamp up on the floor, her heart sore at the way the light illuminated his expression of heartbroken nobility.

"She left me with instructions while she's off fighting some battle against Rupert the Red."

"She's gone?" He sat up on his cot suddenly. "Then we must go now," he said. Their upper bodies were in shadow.

She froze. "What do you mean?"

"Now is the time to escape. Help me."

"I want to." She swallowed. "But how?" she said, her voice going up to a squeak.

She stood there looking at him. He had a five o'clock shadow, and damn, he looked good in it. At the thought of stroking it, a restless ache worked along her pelvis. *Stroke his face, kiss him again, deeply this time.* Another ache struck, this time so intense that she had to stop and look away from him.

His large hazel eyes gazed at her, she could feel them. She traded glances with him again. *Mistake.* His eyes were big and full of yearning. She wanted him. Wanted to be close enough to touch his skin and feel the slow, sizzling ache for him all over her body.

But who was he? She wanted those black eyes on her, so cold and indifferent they were hot and burned her. The weaker she became around him, the more her fear grew. *They can enthrall women.* It was happening to her. She was becoming enthralled. How many hours before Hulgetta was back?

The stinky scrap of paper was tucked into her skirt pocket, and a few strands of smoke escaped.

"You're not—I mean, you haven't put—a spell on me?" she said.

"Did I enthrall you? A little. I didn't really mean to." He looked rather unconcerned, she thought, for someone confessing. "When I'm with someone who… I… it got away from me," he confessed. Now he looked sheepish. "Is it bad? Has it worn off, I mean?"

"Yes." She stared at him. "Er, maybe. I don't know." She wanted him to enthrall her again, and this time she hoped it never wore off. He tried to reassure her but his manacle stopped him. He turned suddenly, yanking hard.

"The thing that's killing me is that I remember this," he said, pulling at the golden cuff. "I know I've read about it, but I can't remember the specifics. Did you bring the book?" he asked, turning to her once again.

"Yes," she said. "I mean, no, I couldn't. I was watched. I did manage this." She pulled the little twist of writing from her pocket, waving away the stench of rotten eggs. She bent down and picked up the little lamp, holding it closer. He took the scrap of paper from her.

"It's Rhymaeic," he said, looking at the writing. His tone was flat.

"That's not good, I guess," she said.

∞

The will to fight turned into a watery feeling of knowledge that he was going to die in the near future. His body felt riddled with weakness and sank back onto the stiff straw mattress, covered in his brown wool blanket. He was looking at the thin glimmer of light blue signaling dawn in a few hours' time as it leaked through the window. With any luck he'd die quickly when the time came, and not in too much pain.

He gripped his hair and flopped back on the crackling straw. There was something about her that was so fair and light that in his own panic he wanted to squeeze her half to death. He could only imagine the torture the evil sorceress would put her through. His rage at his own helplessness brought a bitter taste to the back of his throat and he swallowed it down, breathing deeply. *Not now. Not yet.*

She knelt at his side, examining the writing in the dim light coming through the slender column of window. In his pessimism, the dark burning part of him kindled to life. He had to touch her, and have her touch him. He wanted to ravage her with kisses and make love to her until neither of them could think straight. They would forget about the world for just a few hours. Yet knowing his fate, he also felt strangely immobile, as if his legs were too numb and heavy to move. She stared at the words then looked back up at him for an explanation.

"It takes so long to master magic. Those who succeed are often immortal," he explained, tracing out the words. "So they have time to enjoy the fruits of their learning. Becoming immortal is never easy. Some try a shortcut."

"What kind of shortcut?"

"The trick to creating a powerful Rhymaeic spell is to use a living sacrifice."

"Ah—!" she said. He nodded.

"The book is full of how to keep different creatures alive while torturing the magic out of them," he said. Keeping his voice calm and showing her the scrap, he pointed. "This page is an index." He pointed again. "This spell is for making dead thieves walk. Every spell requires a sacrifice. The bigger the spell, the bigger the sacrifice. This one," he pointed with a finger, "will revive an immortal, but see this symbol? It requires the sacrifice of an uncanny being."

"An elf."

"That would work."

"I don't know what to do," she whispered. She knelt by the pallet and gripped her hands together.

"Do you know the words to release me from this?" he asked, shaking the gold manacle.

She shook her head. "And I couldn't find any history books. I looked, I swear."

"Then I shall die," he said and lay back down on the cot. She lay down with him, her pale hair spilling over his bare skin, her head on his shoulder.

"I don't want you to die," she whispered. Her fingers began to stroke his jaw and cheeks. He listened to the scratch of his bristles against her nails.

"You're precious to me," she whispered, and her hands continued to stroke his face in a soothing pattern. "I thought elves didn't have beards," she added, and he roused himself from the feel of her fingers.

"I'm half-elf."

She grabbed his pointed ear and tongued it until he went boneless beneath her, only one part of him raging and hard, hot, like an iron bar. He felt his blood singing with tender, pitying love for his trapped princess.

The timid grey light continued to pour into the room through the narrow slit. He grabbed her and kissed her ardently, kissed the shadows beneath her eyes. She ground herself against the stabbing bulge between his leggings, tormenting him. The next second he'd flipped them so he covered her with his body, his tongue and teeth urgent upon her lips while all of her body strained and writhed against his.

He undid the lacings on her corset, and they both watched as he pulled the laces free. The linen unbunched under their eyes, slowly revealing her full firm breasts, pale and almost glowing through the thin shift. He traced a finger around the light square mark where the sun had freckled her skin. The mounds of her breasts were creamy, unmarked.

His fingers moved ever so lightly over her, marking a trail. Under her skin he could sense the unsettling ache in her; the way her body shifted told him all about it. For once he felt a sense of control, going along with his inner elf towards a kind of madness. Moving his hand lower still, he rested them on the bone just above her sex. She flexed her hips up into his hand. Pressing there, his fingers cupping inward, he kissed her hard on the mouth, her moans encouraging him to kiss her harder still. The melting pressure in his own hips grew unbearable, and just then he felt his control begin to slip away. If she continued squirming against him so deliciously, there was going to be hell to pay.

Unwrapped, she was all tender plump skin and slender bones. He didn't have a lot of experience with women, but her body called out to his and instinct led the way. He met her without hesitation.

Her naughty tongue on his lips surprised him, slackened his own inhibition even more, as his mouth opened again over hers. *Yes, yes.* Their tongues met and he gripped her hard, pulling her against him. She liked it, clearly. The hot, searing kisses progressed. His inner elf rattling to be free. *Can't stop. Can't.* He pulled back, not wanting to kick off the enthrallment.

Looking down, he saw her straining against him, those wicked fingers finding the lacings for his leggings and pulling them open. Her need was great. *Remain calm, distant. Let her have you.* He transferred his lips to her neck and she cried out as he bit into the tender skin there. She put a hand up, covering his, and moved it back to her breast. Then he moved lower, sucking on her breasts, while she arched up into his mouth. *That's it. Give to her, otherwise remain still.* He hoped that would be enough.

Her fingers were now pulling him free. He was hard, swollen, angry. He swallowed.

"Oh. Goodness." Her hand worked up and down his rigid cock as if by accident. *Oh, how did this get into my hand? Should I squeeze it, like this? Yes, please yes.*

He shook his head and closed his eyes in a pain that was the agony of pleasure. Did she know what she was doing? How it affected him?

The little devil was against him again, and eager, her skirt was up, breasts out, and his fingers found the sweet wetness of her, slippery and curved like the pink insides of a sea shell. Into that wetness he found himself sliding one finger, then two. She melted against him, riding his thigh. He jammed his fingers in more aggressively than before. In the growing light he watched her lips, swollen like they were stung and berry ripe. If she kept going, his dark elf would take her, would destroy her.

She will taste rapture, his inner elf assured him. She will ride across the sky.

No. No, if they kept going, she'd lose her maidenhead this very night. They had to stop. She stretched below him, wanton and sensual. She moaned and seemed to have such need for his bruising kisses.

"Stop," he said, tousled and undone, astonished he could still speak. "Stop. We must stop."

"We must?"

"I have to."

She gave him a wounded look—sweet, dim princess that she was. *Yes, play dumb.* He was no longer fooled.

"Your maidenhead," he said, reminding her, feeling his brow start to sweat with the effort of holding back.

"Oh. I forgot."

He frowned. Being a little careless, wasn't she?

He pulled her upright and paused. He thought them equal in this, but he took a big breath and interlaced her hand in his.

"Princess," he said, looking her right in the eye, "men and women are made to be quite different."

Her eyes widened and she looked horrified. "I know the functions of the body," she said flatly, her hand slashing away, as if begging him not to speak further.

"I wasn't sure." There was an awkward moment between them. He had no idea what to do next.

She looked off at the other corner of the room and said, "I would do anything with you."

She reached for him, closed her eyes, and—the devil!—started kissing him again, but this time he took it slowly, carefully. She didn't know what it really meant, he guessed, to lose her virginity. Yet even kissing seemed to drive her into a wild state of excitement. When he was touching her, his fingers slid up her thighs and she spread her legs a little. An invitation. He slid his hand up further, only to find his princess clamped her thighs shut around his hand. He looked up. The teasing smile she gave him made his blood pound.

"There are other things we can do," she suggested, hesitating. She stared, her eyes wide, their black centers huge.

He balanced over her, puzzled.

"What do you mean, specifically?"

"Um, things we could do—that would preserve my chastity?"

CHAPTER TEN

The pink blush of her expression contrasted with the hard stare she gave him.

"Is that wise?" He shifted around, uncertain just what she wanted. She pushed him onto his back and pulled down his leggings deliberately. Then, bending over him, she seemed to want nothing more than to torment his cock with her tongue. Her licking and sucking made him gasp.

He tried to withdraw from her mouth.

"Oh no! Please," she said, "let me." She went slowly, yet more deeply.

"I can't release," he told her. "I can't."

"Why not?"

"My fae side will come forth."

"And that's bad why?"

"It's dangerous. It will enthrall you."

"You'll have to be strong, then. Very strong. Because I like licking you," she said. "And I'm not going to stop."

"You like teasing me," he said. He felt her nod, her mouth around him.

The hellish effort of making her stop was draining away quickly, even as his fae side was building, rattling the inside of his skull, shaking inside his chest and hands.

No, no, no.

He could feel it coming.

"Princess," he swore. "Don't. Don't torment me." He didn't dare look at her. Instead, he was stretching his body wide, as if on a rack. She slid her hand up and down, stroking hard, squeezing. How did she know to do it hard, just like that? A prickling wash of pleasure and danger sparked down along the back of his neck and then cascaded down his spine like shivers.

"After I rescue you I'm going to take you to my tower." He couldn't talk for a minute as his face grimaced and his body bowed hard against her hand. She kept it up. He gasped, just stopping himself from letting the fae side take over, just barely, but he couldn't speak.

"Are you certain this isn't hurting you?" she asked, her tone all innocence and her grin completely wicked, as she bent down to her work again while his entire body went into a rictus of pleasure and pain.

"Little you care. Cruel. Cruel princess." His hand caressed her face then down to her breast, squeezing. His mind was losing this raging battle, his eyes beginning to throb hard.

"Am I?" She sounded like he'd just given her the greatest of compliments.

"You want me to die of pleasure."

"Yes. About the words for the spell? Can you read them?"

"The Rhymaeic? I know enough. It's a killing language. All the spells are based on the power of destruction. They got rid of all the Rhymaeic books a hundred years ago. I'm surprised this one is left."

She stopped. The remembrance of his chained wrist intruded between them, and she clung to him suddenly.

He stroked her hair, watching her. "I must escape. You have to help me," he said. "You have to find out how this manacle releases."

"She didn't tell me."

"Did you try everything you could? If there's a history book there, it would have something in it about this." He shook his wrist.

"I don't think she has any history books. I don't think she cares about history."

"It's dangerous for you. I understand."

She was trembling a little. He knew she felt for him. He knew she was brave or she wouldn't be there with him like this. "A true history book will have diagrams of the magical items in them. Measurements. Even if you don't know the language, they are easy to spot." How to outweigh her fear of Hulgetta? The surge of his inner elf pressed forward, overflowing his mind, as the hot-cold feeling of pure elfin soul invaded his senses. His eyes had changed, and a new energy assaulted him.

"You're afraid. But I need you to figure out how to open the manacle."

"I want to," she said.

"Not enough. Let me convince you," he said.

Before she could speak he'd thrown her onto her back, her skirts flying about her waist. She giggled then inhaled sharply as he began kissing her knees, the pale tender flesh of her inner thighs so tender and soft, his fingers dug into their plumpness.

"Oh no. You're not going to… oooh," she sighed. Soon his unshaven scruff was slowly rubbing across the tender inside of her sex until she was the tormented one. She groaned softly as he bent his head over her and let his tongue caress her, creeping closer and closer to the place she wanted. Then he blew upon that sweet bud and sucked it gently.

"More," she moaned. "Oh, the bristles from your beard. They feel so…" The short bristles of his beard apparently did something to her sensitive nerves down there. Something she quite liked. She arched her back hard. Her fingers threaded into his hair. *Yes.* She was holding onto his head and gripping it with two fists. *Yes.* He flicked just there and—.

She gave a sharp cry.

"Princess, what I'm doing won't harm your maidenhead," he said, his head still bent to his work.

"Thanks," she said, her voice hesitating and weak to his ears. He took her with his tongue. *Yes. Yes.* He'd discovered just what drove her mad. He bent himself to the pleasure of it, and used not just his beard and tongue, but his lips as well. Soon she was groaning piteously, her pelvis off the cot as she gave harsh little cries and her hips shuddered.

"Please," she whispered when she was done, a tangled mess under him. He looked at her judiciously and then went back to his work. No mercy. He reveled in the involuntary clutching of her hands in his hair, as she twisted her head from side to side.

"Oh no, I didn't mean it. I can't take any more, no, no," she cried out softly as he tongued her flesh, caressing her most sensitive quivering skin.

He sought out that special spot just… there. She gave an involuntary scream and her hips began thrusting again.

His raging soul was swept with the fizzy burn of pleasure. She was his. The hot feeling of possession made him strong, made the voice of his blood cry out. He longed to ride into battle. For her.

Kill for her. Slaughter men, capture their treasure and toss it at her feet. Bring her home to his people. He stopped suddenly. Home. He could never return home, never ride into battle at his father's side. Certainly never bring a human home.

The piercing thought brought pain and he renewed his efforts to ignore it. He wondered if she would like him rubbing his chin across that special place. He tried it and suddenly her body went into a rictus.

"No, no, oh, it's too much! Please—I'm coming. Coming. Oh!"

She fell back panting, caressing the back of his neck while he kissed her deliciously plump thighs.

Suddenly he felt his fae side snap, and he was only nuzzling her thigh, the elf side released. She panted heavily for breath above him. He could feel her core pulsing around his fingers, and the part of him that had enthralled her felt a similar pulsing joy racing through his loins and thighs as it was set free. Slowly her body relaxed and went limp.

Odd. His mind, now clear, began sorting out means and ways to get out of the castle once the manacle was off. His princess would find a way out of it. Their fate together was sealed by a powerful bond that would lick and torment her if she did not.

∞

She woke up with a start, her head on his shoulder. It was some time past dawn and she was starving.

Sunlight speared through the narrow window. The lamp was still lit, but dying, a small gold drop of light near the floor. His hand was on her backside, fingers tapping there. She looked up to see him watching her expression closely, his deep-set eyes lost in their forest shade and hard to read. She still hadn't told him her secrets. His eyes were pinned on her as if he suddenly read her mind, and she looked away, uncomfortable.

"What is it?" he said. Her cheeks burned. Her moist sex, both tender and sore, pressed right up against his bunched leather leggings. She pressed her lips to his chest and tasted the salt of his skin. Her hips rotated towards him and ground against his.

"Yes?" he said, as if she'd asked him a question. He began stroking her with one hand, and the slippery inside of her flesh responded to him, until she was holding back groans and biting her lips. She wanted to play it cool, but she was not cool, she was feverish and there was nowhere to hide from him. She felt like she had been flayed open, and he saw all her wanton desires. A dipper full of pleasure had been ladled over her head. Then her eye caught the scrap of dirty white linen and she remembered the Rhymaeic spells. How he was doomed if something was not done immediately. She sat bolt upright.

"What are you thinking?"

"I must go." She bent over to gather herself and her clothes together. This situation was entirely her fault and the knowledge ate into her like a canker.

How angry he'd be if he knew she was Hulgetta's apprentice. If she told him, what kind of fight would she lose then? To fight against his desire and win felt delicious. To fight against her own desires and lose felt divine. She shivered at the idea of his eyes turning upon her black in anger, and what he might demand in vengeance.

She wet her lips and felt a low throb within her. No, she would never be the same again. As soon as he was free, he'd be gone and she'd never see him again. She started to ache, to sob with dry eyes.

"Tell me. My eyes turned black, is that it?"

"Black is my favorite color. I have no problem with that."

"My fae side makes my soul twisted and deranged."

She pulled her shift up and let it drop. "I like your soul. At least, what I know of it," she said, trying to get her fingers to work. She thought about what she was doing and the clothes bunched up in her hands uselessly. "I have to get you out of here and I don't know how."

He looked thoughtful, tugging at his manacle. "The thing is, I almost remember this device. Something you said."

Just what would he do to her if he found out she'd captured him, dropped him, dragging him from his tower back to this place like a hunter dragging his prey?

She found her corset, turned it right side up and put it on, then realized it was inside out. She switched it around, grabbed the cord from the floor and began to lace it up. Her hands shook. He stood up and took over, his nimble fingers lacing her up quickly, his fingers tightening into strong fists as he mercilessly drew the edges of the corset together, despite her heaving ribs. He kept his eyes on hers, and breathless, she felt a buzzing in her chest and behind her pubic bone.

She dropped her eyes to his fingers tying off the lace, watching his knuckles. The middle one sported a deep silver scar. She stroked it with her fingertips.

He turned his head away. She raked through her half-undone hair with unsteady fingers, finding it hard to breathe in, breathe out. He stood close to her, their shoulders almost but not touching. He seemed tentative, uncertain. She would not truly rest again until Hulgetta unlocked that manacle. Another dry sob escaped from her lips.

"Are you crying?" he said, trying to take her chin in his fingers.

She turned away quickly.

"No, not at all." She wiped her hand with her fist, and there was no wetness. How much more it hurt to cry without tears.

∞

When she came back into the room, the maids were swiftly scrambling to pick up their mess from the night before.

The rejuvenation book was out there in plain sight, close enough to the bucket that she could feel the malevolence pouring out of it. She picked it up—

"Prin—" Wart said in a warning tone.

"What? I'm going to burn it. Then she can't kill him."

Wart grabbed the book and tried to take it from her. She hung on.

"Hey, Wart. Stop it!" Wart was grim while she hung on to the book as Prin tried to twist it from her hands.

Soon they were in a tug of war.

She looked up to realize the maids had gathered all around to watch them.

"A word," Elfrieda said. A cluster of maids backed her. They all had their hands on their hips. Everyone was there, everyone but cook. She let the book go and Wart put it back on the table.

"What do you think you're doing?" Elfrieda demanded.

"I don't answer to you," Prin said, standing on her dignity.

"She was in the elf-wizard's cell," Lanky Sue said. "I saw her," she told Elfrieda. "Going into his cell and being there all that time?"

"Those weren't mistress's orders," Elfrieda finished. Her large square face was mottled red with indignation.

Prin tried to stare her down. There were a lot of them. And they were strong. They'd been doing physical labor their whole lives. If it came to a fight, it was going to get ugly. On one hand, she was determined in her cause and in a way was more robust than they were—after all, she had enjoyed good nutrition her entire life. She thought she could take any one of them. On the other hand, they fought dirty. She knew she couldn't take them all at once. Yet she almost welcomed a free-for-all. Her nerves were stretched to the breaking point. She had more to fight for than they did. She realized, suddenly, that she wasn't afraid.

"Hulgetta left me her orders. Which are none of your business."

"Bosh," Elfrieda said.

"Tell her," Lanky Sue said to Wart.

"He's an elf, Prin," Wart said.

Lanky Sue took over. "Everyone knows elves ruin women."

Ruin?

Baz, on his shelf in the corner, was nodding his head up and down, letting the manacle slide forward over his head and then looking out at her through the tube of the manacle where it stuck.

"It's true," Lanky Sue said. The lizard looked at Lanky Sue, then back at the rest of them. He looked ridiculous. Lanky Sue took another step forward until she towered over the other maids all around her. "They put their black eyes on a woman and—"

"Back off," Prin said. Her hands came up and out, and she bent her knees slightly.

"—she bends to their elvish will. Happens every time," Lanky Sue finished. Kath at her side looked like she was burning to say something too.

"They do come back. Sometimes," Kath said.

"It's a cruel elf that sends them back," Lanky Sue said, turning to Kath. "The women starve, lovelorn and cursed. They don't care about nothin'. Not even their wee babes."

That sounded very much in line with what the elf had said.

"Others can't find satisfaction with the lads. One came back to our village and rutted with every lad who would have her, and then drowned herself," Lanky Sue said.

"I assure you, you don't have to worry about that with me," she started.

"It's not *you* we worry about," Lanky Sue said. "It's what he'll do to *us* when he gets you under his thumb."

Baz nodded sharply, and the manacle fell off the lizard's head and onto the floor. The lizard locked eyes with her then leapt off his shelf, falling clumsily onto the floor. He quickly scrambled up onto all fours and, tilting his head up, shot flames three feet long up into the air.

CHAPTER ELEVEN

The maids stampeded. They ran right past her and Wart, who was pushed against the big table as they scrambled towards the long corridor, shrieking a little louder than seemed strictly necessary to Prin. It happened so fast, she and Wart were left staring after the women.

Baz gave chase, gaining enough speed as he launched out of the room that when he hit the corridor he was running up on two feet, little claws dangling as he turned the corner. He paused there, for just a second, looking back at them. He seemed to be waiting for them to join him. Then he shot a snoutful of roaring flames down the corridor and was off.

They followed him to the door. The maids were shrieking again and Baz snapped his ruff out around his head and turned bright blue, and then he ran full tilt down the corridor after the fleeing maids.

"You think we're jealous, because we're plain and no elf would have us," Wart said.

"Not at all." She turned to Wart. "First of all, you're not plain, you're pretty and your soul is beautiful. Second of all, he loves me." Then she remembered she didn't even know his real name. Not that he knew hers. This was all going completely wrong.

"He'll wreck you. I've seen the signs before… I see it now," Wart said.

She didn't know what to say. She wanted to be wrecked by him. Wrecking sounded great, actually. At the same time she was acutely aware that their friendship was shattering into little bits. Then Baz was back. The lizard trotted around the corner, saw them, and froze, one claw off the ground.

They froze in turn. Then Baz charged them, his lizard mouth open and shooting forth flames. They turned as one, running around the giant table, while the lizard chased them through the room and down the long corridor.

"Wretched lizard!" Prin fumed, stopping half way and turning back. The lizard stood on his squat bow legs, observing them alertly. Prin made faces at the beast and shook her fist. The basilisk looked her up and down with independently moving eyes.

"I fed you, you little handbag!"

Suddenly Baz narrowed his lids and gave Prin the stink eye.

"Ow," she said, jumping back as her hand filled with pins and needles. "Ow, ow, ow!" She shook her hand and hopped about. The pain was like a rain of dull needles.

The basilisk gave a hissing roar, showing the inside of his big toothless mouth, and the blue frill, now tipped with yellow, opened around his neck again with a snap.

"Crap," she said. A stench like rotting sewage mixed with a hefty dose of mold assaulted her nostrils.

"Oh, oh you little beast!" she complained, stamping. She pinched her nose shut before she threw up. Wart, visibly gagging, hid her lower face in the crook of her arm. The lizard took a step forward. Then another. He wanted them to flee, like the maids. The hell with that. Flames roared from the basilisk's mouth, and then the stupid, mean little lizard charged again. Prin rapped out the sleep spell, practically singing it, and dropped the little punk right at her feet. Then, breathing heavily, she turned to Wart.

"You're smoldering," Wart said. The maid scooped up Zephyr's skirt and clapped the charred cloth hem of her dress together until the burning embers went out completely. She stood again and gave Prin a long-suffering look.

"I don't want to hear it," Prin said, clearly reading reproach in Wart's big sad puppy eyes. "It was just some unicorn snot," she said defensively. She opened and closed her hand quickly, trying to flick away the pins and needles. *Clearly none of my good deeds are going unpunished today.*

∞

When the fire in the main hall was blazing Wart arrived and once more tried to grab the book from her hands. She was more wary this time and was able to snatch the book up over her head before her friend could grab it. She might be short but Wart was practically a midget so there was no serious contest.

The logs were stacked three feet high in the fireplace, and the fireplace could hold five maids abreast with elbow room to spare. She lit it up and soon the logs were roaring merrily.

The slimy, slender rectangle threatened to slip right out of her hands. She could feel it pulling away from the fire.

"Don't!" Wart said, grunting with effort of reaching for the book. Prin easily held her off.

"She can't gut him for a spell if she doesn't have the book!"

"She can," Wart said, leaping up again.

"Well, she won't need to. There'd be no point."

"Fine." Wart gave up and sculked off to the opposite end of the hall near the entrance for the kitchen corridor, arms folded over her chest.

Prin tried to twist the book apart. The pages made her fingers prick and then go numb. The binding would not tear. It stretched instead, and then went back into shape. She gave up trying to tear it apart. She simply tossed it into the heart of the flames instead. Yes. She enjoyed the warmth, despite the smoke and watched the cascade of pink and white sparks from the fire as they leapt out onto the hearth stone. She felt strong. If this didn't work, she'd think of something else. And then something else. She'd go down fighting to the bitter end.

The flames raged and roared. Then purple-grey smoke poured forth out into the large hall, smelling of old rotten eggs. Prin backed off to where Wart was sitting on the step, chin on her fists.

Then the fire really took hold. The flames almost bursting out of the enormous maw of the fireplace, and Prin held out her hands to warm them only to realize the fire gave off no heat. That was when the prickling of unease took hold of her. The fire continued growing until it was licking tongues of pink flame out from the sides of the fireplace stretching a full seven feet or more into the hall. Sparks and smoke billowed forth. The fire belched and roared in fury.

She wasn't exactly worried about the blaze leaping from the fireplace and consuming the castle. The floor was stone. The walls were stone. What worried her, causing her to leap up and get as close as she dared, was that she could still see the book in the middle of the flames, and it was not burning.

"Not even the corners are turning black," she said, outraged.

"Watch out," Wart said and pulled her back. The flames had licked out, trying to grab her and draw her into the fire. She took the poker before the flames made it too hot and tried to poke the logs apart, but the flames were so mighty the heat drove her back before she could reach the logs with the poker. She went and got a bucket of sand, tossing it on the blaze. The fire turned orange for a bit and roared extra loud, but wasn't smothered by the sand in the least. Then she tried water, but the flames turned to black and the purple smoke poured forth even harder. The whole time it grew bigger, and she fell into a panic. The room was stone; the giant stones surrounding the hearth were turning black but there was nothing to burn. She paced back and forth and then picked up the bucket again and turned to go get more water.

"Stop," Wart threw out a hand. "You're only making it worse."

She looked at the fire and knew Wart was right. The flames were consuming everything up to twenty feet out from the fireplace. She looked up at the ceiling. If the fire burned those beams…

Worse still, the book sat open in the middle of all the logs, untouched. If the flames didn't die, what would Hulgetta do when she returned and stood before the obvious evidence that her apprentice had tried to destroy a precious spell book?

She was in such trouble.

The hall began to stink horribly.

"Now you've done it," Wart said, holding her nose. "What are you going to do?"

"I don't think she'll kill me outright, do you?"

Wart snorted.

"The spell is sixty pages long, and it's complicated, she's going to need my help." She only said this to pluck up her courage. The other half of her wanted to fall upon the stone steps and weep.

"When she opens the manacle to move him, I'll distract her, and while she deals with me, he'll escape."

"And you'll wind up dead—that's a terrible plan."

"But he winds up free. I owe him that. If you have a better idea, I'm all ears."

Wart looked at her.

"No pun intended."

Wart followed her back to the lair.

"Let's just hope Hulgetta's powers are so low she can't do anything," Wart said. "Of course, using a knife didn't require magical powers."

Could she overcome Hulgetta in a tussle if it came to that? The woman was tall and strapping.

Wart picked up Baz off the floor and put him belly-up on his shelf, then cleaned up the mess, while Prin started mixing up the potion for the heart-cleansing spell. Hours later she was done and Wart had curled up under the big table and fallen asleep.

She took a quick break to check on the fire—which was still enormous and roaring. Then she slunk off to the cool, damp niche where the moss maid shrine sat. A beam of sunlight shined down upon the frizzle-haired maid through a dirty diamond-paned window.

She prostrated herself in front of the statue, stroking and petting the mossy little feet of the goddess. "Moss maid, moss maid, protect me well." She was tired, worn out from all the fear and stress. Even here on the stones she just wanted to sleep.

"You like him, don't you?" she said to the little statue. "Well then, protect him too, along with all his magical goodness. Cause right now, you're all we've got."

The moss maid grew huge before her until it was a towering giant made of moss and other plants. With crumbly giant paws it picked her up and cradled her, and for the first time since she had dragged the elf into the castle, she felt everything would be all right.

She raised her head with a snap. She must have dozed off for a bit; the sunlight from the little window had grown long, stretching far across the floor. *Have to get up, get the heart cleansing done on the elf.* She staggered up to her feet, blinking, and looked around. Okay, she felt a little stronger, a little braver as she headed towards the lair. An apprentice's work was never done.

∞

He was awake. She saw those black eyes on her and her guts churned and her sex throbbed as she entered the cell, her nose filling with the smell of clean straw and his desperate impatience.

"Did you find a history book?" He looked at her hands, which held a very small cauldron.

"No."

"I'm not in the mood for rabbit stew, Princess."

"Good. Because this isn't stew." She put the tiny cauldron on the floor. "And you need to strip."

He sat up on his mattress. "If we're going to escape, we should do it today. Now," he said.

"Tell me how to get that off and I will," she said, pointing at his cuff but keeping her eyes on the liquid, making sure it didn't spill. She'd never made a heart-cleansing spell before, but so far so good. The liquid was silvery and ran around in the ladle like mercury. She closed the door, but didn't lock it.

"What does it matter? Hulgetta is going to kill me," he said softly.

"You should be so lucky," Prin said. "She's going to rip out my tongue with hot pinchers when she gets back. Then snip off my ears. At least that's what she did to the last person who seriously pissed her off. She told me to clean your heart with this."

She placed the small cauldron on the floor and took a sponge out of the pocket of her apprentice robe, dropping it in the silver liquid. "I'm going through with it," she continued as she stirred, "in the hopes that she doesn't kill me outright, so I can be around to help you escape when the time comes. Now shut up and take off your breeches or leggings or whatever they are. I need to do this on your bare skin."

He looked her up and down, eyes black and blank, perfectly at home in his half-naked body.

Then everything began to go wrong.

"Why are you wearing Hulgetta's robe?" he asked.

"How did you know I borrowed her robe?" Prin asked, surprised.

"Right there," he pointed to the hem. "It says her name. Written out in High Anslod."

She stared hard at the border of leaves and twigs that ran down the center of the robe until, yes, there it was. In stylized letters in Anslod woven behind the branches—PROPERTY OF HULGET. The rest of the name was folded over into the hem she had sewn up so it wouldn't drag.

He gave her a dirty look and slowly stood. His eyes were pinned on her, his cruel captor, as he stripped. She could see the throb of his pulse in his clenching jaw, and her own matched it. It was as if a strong current flowed back and forth between them. He lay down and she quickly cleaned his heart. Sweat was standing out across his face and torso, and he jerked and twisted a few times, but did not say a word. She tried to keep a poker face, but inside she was aghast. The pitch, it didn't stop. Six times she sponged his chest with the silver liquid and then, as he sweated and gritted his teeth, she wiped with the sponge, until it felt heavy. When she squeezed it out into the bucket the pitch flowed on and on until he put a strong hand on her wrist.

"No more."

Suddenly he was off his cot, his shoulders and arms reaching out. She tried to dance away but he got her, grabbing her with one arm around her waist and ripping off the shoulder of her robe. Then he was loosening her corset and pulled down her shift until her breasts tumbled forward as she was drawn to him, onto her tip toes, her pelvis grinding into his, his arousal evident.

"Stop. No. What are you doing?" she protested.

Naked, he reached for the sponge.

He squeezed it, letting it fill with silver liquid, as he hauled her upright with him. She kept struggling but couldn't worm her trapped right arm out from where it was pinned by his arm around her waist. That same long arm gripped her above the elbow, and while she could writhe around like an angry cat in a sack, she couldn't free herself. She stopped, feeling her face hot with exertion, her breath huffing her hair out of the way as messy strands fell over her face. He leaned in.

"Your turn, Princess."

CHAPTER TWELVE

"If you haven't done any wicked deeds this won't hurt a bit." He gritted his teeth, holding the sponge over her. He seemed to delight in watching her squirm about. She held still and tried to regain some dignity, but frowned and wanted to wriggle again when he eyed her exposed nipples, tight in anticipation.

"It's cold," he warned her. Her hips squirmed involuntarily before she could catch herself, and his eyes spotted the subtle movement. The silver liquid rained down from the sponge onto her breast and trickled down her ribcage. Before it could stream off her body it soaked into her skin.

She felt her heart skip a beat at the shock of the icy liquid sinking into her flesh. Colder than rubbing alcohol or liniment, and heavy like silver, the droplets felt thick as he stroked the sponge over, around, and under her breast. Her heartbeat began to slow and she shivered all over. Her chest started to hurt in a dull wave, growing numb as the cold liquid sank slowly inside her bones, little metal bullets of pain.

She braced herself. He was turned on, his head snapping back exactly as the pain turned to an excruciating thrill. The thrill ran down between her legs and she was arching her back. It hurt—her heart ached unbearably, while her loins throbbed, as he held the sponge up against her flesh.

It was killing her, *make it stop!* He held her to him, observing her closely, his breath jerking. He looked into her eyes and would not let her turn her head away.

The reverse feeling began. Her flesh crawled as if insects were inside her. She thrashed, while he continued holding her easily with one arm, ignoring her jerking legs.

The invisible insects bit her with pinchers. Before she could scream out loud, he lifted up the sponge and she felt sweet relief. He removed the sponge from her breast and squeezed.

A cooling balm flooded her body and a feeling of lightness pervaded.

The sound of thin liquid spilled into the bucket and there was a smell, reminding her of dill that had gone bad in the fridge and had started to rot. A kind of green, sour smell. He looked down at the pitch trickling into the bucket.

"You've been bad, my princess." She was too weak to raise her head, and her hair fell across her face.

"But surprisingly stoic," he noticed. "You didn't scream once."

He didn't stop holding her and looked towards the clean sponge again.

He was going to do it again.

"Don't," she said. She didn't want her heart purified.

The sponge released the silvery liquid. "Please, no," she cried out. "It hurts, don't!"

Inwardly she felt that excruciating thrill of pleasure at the idea that he wasn't going to stop. A part of her exploded in shame, while she could feel how strong he was, effortlessly holding her with just one arm. He stroked the sponge over her breast and nipple with deliberate slowness then pushed it underneath, along the curve of her rib. Her legs were kicking at him in resistance, and her free hand was pulling and twisting his ear, but he acted as if he felt nothing at all. She felt hot with shame and moistness.

She wanted to cry. She wanted to swear, but, annoyingly, a princess didn't swear.

"This arouses you," he noticed, squeezing his fist as drops of pitch splattered from the sponge. He released her and cleaned his hands thoroughly on her torn robe.

"Shut up." She felt too weak to answer. She had to get her clothes together. Hulgetta was coming back through the green door any minute. Any second.

He pinched her chin. "Answer me."

She was dizzy looking into his eyes. They were black and indifferent. They pinned her soul and stung. She felt herself slowly giving in to the slow treacle feeling of breathless anticipation.

He let his manacled hand roam lightly over her breast. "It does, doesn't it?"

There was a commotion below, but her mind shut it out, not caring. All her will was focused on their bond.

Probably the fire from the book had finally set the castle ablaze. They were doomed anyway, she thought with grim enthusiasm. Goody. They could all burn together. She needed sleep. She heard bustling and concerned exclamations—and in the distance, someone yelling in a deep, hoarse voice. She'd recognize that roar anywhere.

"Prin!" Hulgetta was back.

He was instantly suspicious, and she braced herself. She pulled herself away from his arm and tried to pull her shift up. "I have to get dressed," she said, her trembling fingers trying and failing to pull her corset back into place. But her hands were cold and weak.

"What is it?"

She couldn't answer, but turned away, sucking in her breath. How was she going to explain the torn robe? He turned her towards him. He pulled up her shift and corset, loosened the laces of the corset, then did it up again faster than her eye could follow. He tied the corners of the ripped shoulder together.

"That's her, calling below. The sorceress?" he asked frowning, still looking at the mini-cauldron.

"Yes.

"Apprentice!" Hulgetta's voice was a low boom, but rising in pitch, getting closer.

"That's right, the sorceress was gone. So, who made the spell, Princess?" he asked, kicking over the mixture. She was trying to pull herself together, watching the silver spill across the floor.

"A. Prin. Tice!" Hulgetta screamed.

She couldn't ignore the calls any longer.

"She's coming!" she cried. "I must go."

"Why?" he tried to stand in front of the door but the cuff wouldn't reach. "She wants the apprentice." There was a hectic expression on his face. He was thinking. "Unless—that's you?"

For a second she thought the manacle was going to rip out of the wall as he lunged at her, but she was out of reach. Just. Already across the room, she was pulling the door closed before she even consciously thought about it.

"I didn't know she wanted to kill you when I took you from the tower," she called through the door.

"You will pay for this betrayal." His voice sounded deadly calm, crawling through the door. She felt her heart give one big squeeze and then began running down the stairs.

She flung herself down the corridor, where it smelled like firecrackers and light grey smoke snaked through the air. Grabbing Wart coming from the lair, she said, "Is it the fire?"

"No, no, she's injured."

Another maid came flying from the lair.

"Then what's all this smoke?"

Wart shook her head. They both looked towards the big hall. Prin moved towards the big hall then back.

"No, smoke smells fainter when I walk towards the hall. It's coming from over here somewhere."

She turned to the maids. "Find out where this smoke is coming from." The maids started to run in opposite directions.

Wart on her heels, she turned and burst through the billowing smoke to find Hulgetta leaning against the giant table, roaring like a wounded rhinoceros. Kath and two other maids cowered back away from her. Hulgetta jerked, thrashing, as little silver sparks came from the metal.

Prin reached out to her.

"Stop!" Wart warned her. "Her power was magicked. It's rebounded upon her."

Hulgetta bayed at them in pain and pounded a fist on her table, pulling off her helm.

Prin thought hard, her eyes skittering over the titles of Hulgetta's books.

"I know what to do," she said.

"You have to get her to lie down," Wart said.

Hulgetta's pounding fist made the helmet suddenly fall off onto the floor. The basilisk, frightened, ran between their feet and into a crack between two cupboards.

Prin skipped back as the sharp horns on the helmet bounced at her feet. She reached down and picked it up, hefting it onto another table.

"I can deal with this. You find the fire and get it under control," Prin told Wart. "Tell them about it in the kitchen. If it gets any worse than this, just get everyone out of the castle." Wart turned and then turned back.

"The elf-wizard," she said.

Prin felt her insides shrink and convulse. "See if you can find the fire, I'll check on him."

"No, I'll check, you stay with her."

"Very well—hurry!" Wart rushed out of the room into the smoke, ducking down below it.

"Come get me when you find the fire!" she called after Wart. Fires were very common at the castle, especially in the kitchen. There were buckets around every corner. If it was a chimney fire, they might have to pull open the walls of the kitchen.

Silver sparks still snaked out of Hulgetta, Prin turned and ran to the shelves, getting down her Anslod primer. She memorized the words, moving her lips over their sounds, and then, looking up, put the book to one side, threw her shoulders back and said the words to un-hex Hulgetta's armor. Some of the buzz deep inside that she carried from the elf enchantment drained from her and she knew the spell had worked.

The sparks stopped, but Hulgetta lost all color and sagged. Prin sprang forward and grabbed her. Kath caught her on the other side.

"Put her on the table—clear the books first!" she said, and the maids scrambled to grab the books while Kath helped her lay Hulgetta down on the table.

Hulgetta's shoulder was wet. Prin looked and saw it was covered in blood.

"Get cotton wool and brandy wine," she said to Kath, who took off down the hall. Prin managed to remove the greaves from Hulgetta and the quilted padding from her arms, legs and head. The whole time she knew that these were not the problem. The problem was the breastplate. There were scorch marks along the entire left side. If it was a direct hit from a hexed blast and she opened up the breastplate—who knew what she'd find under there?

Five more maids entered and stood there gawking.

"Go see to the smoke. Put out the fire. Go!" she yelled at them. A few fanned back, but then reluctantly they all came forward again.

"Prin, we looked. We can't find a fire anywhere," one said. "Except the fire in the great hall, but so far it hasn't spread."

Lanky Sue walked in.

"Did it go out?" she demanded.

"Did what go out?" Lanky Sue asked.

"The fire in the great fireplace?"

"Not at all. Still roaring away. That's not where all this smoke is coming from." There was now a slight haze of grey smoke about the ceiling.

"Well, feel the walls for heat, then. And when you find it, come tell me," she ordered.

They all ran off, Lanky Sue slouching along behind them.

One thing at a time. Hulgetta first. The sorceress opened her eyes and moved her lips—Prin waited. Hulgetta couldn't speak. Her eyes kept looking at Prin, but the words from her lips were mute. *Should I step away? Let her die?* Then she remembered—she couldn't die. Hulgetta could only suffer and keep on suffering.

I can't. I can't. She couldn't stand the thought of standing aside and doing nothing. She put her fingers on the buckles. They were hot, steaming at the clasps of Hulgetta's breastplate.

"I don't know if I should open it," Prin said to her mistress, indicating the breastplate. Hulgetta tightened her chin and gave a nod. The apprentice pried off the top of the metal and dropped it in a smoking heap next to the table. The purple pad was dark red with blood. *Not good.*

She took several deep breaths through her mouth, steadied her hands and pried the pad off. Hulgetta's skin came with it. *Fat. That yellow stuff is all fat. Oh my god.* Prin dropped the breastplate and covered her mouth with her hand. She was looking into the woman's insides. The sorceress's face lost so much color she looked dirty grey. She sank back, losing consciousness.

The apprentice put the pad back in place. She hoped never to see such a sight again.

Running to the corridor, she yelled for help. The smoke was much thicker now and panicked voices were coming from the kitchen wing. She couldn't do anything without boiling water to clean the wound. She needed a book. She had to find out if her mistress's immortality meant that she could close Hulgetta up and leave good enough alone. Wart came rushing up to meet her.

"What's going on? I need boiling water," Prin demanded.

"He's gone."

"The elf-wizard?" Prin swore several times in her head.

Wart nodded. "The cell door is open," she said.

The apprentice's blood turned to ice.

"I need water." She ducked and ran all the way down the corridor, coughing. The raging fire in the great hall was a continuous shower of black sparks and purple smoke. It had grown, and she had to run through the room quickly past the licking flames. She went around to the servant's corridor to get up the crumbling steps up to the cell. She panted up the steps, hurtling through the open wooden door. Inside the room the empty pallet with the mattress and brown wool blanket were in the gloom. Only the open gold manacle gleamed from the finger of light coming through the window. She backed up.

Shit shit shit. Crap, crap, crap.

She ran below and ordered the kitchen maids to hurry with the water and supplies to Hulgetta's chamber.

"Bring any sage and basilicum powder as well. It'll have to do for now." If she could plaster a bandage on over it—infection was the main worry. Hulgetta was immortal, but her body was not repairing itself. Would she live on in agony, tortured by hideous wounds that would not kill her?

She tore back to Hulgetta's study, fear making her sprint. How could he have opened up that cuff? How?

She ran into the room and to the sorceress's side.

Hulgetta's face was livid grey, unnatural. The pad was no longer sufficient to soak up the blood. Now it was spreading onto the table. Pulling down a squat book of surgical procedures from a shelf, the apprentice flipped through it, fingers bloody, wondering how she was ever going to read it in the confusion of smoke and shouting of men's voices.

Men's voices? She put her head up. *No. Oh no.* With horror she realized the green door was still open, the battlefield outside it able to move right into the castle.

She hurtled around the corner to the alcove. The smoke was so thick she ran into it blindly, coughing and sputtering as she slowed down to feel her way, afraid of missing the door entirely and wandering outside. At last she found the edge of the door. Smoke blew aside in the breeze and brought the smell of gunpowder, while in the distance she heard the boom of cannon fire.

Fireballs of blazing pitch passed across the sky with a whistle. Arrows sang through the air, landing near the door. Battle smoke drifted near the door, the draft of the castle corridor sucking it in further. An arrow hissed through the green door and clattered onto the stone at her feet. Another hit the floor and bounced up high, right in front of her eyes.

She threw her body against the door, feeling it slowly pivot and finally secure, the clasp locking under the pressure of her weight. Suddenly the cries of men in battle, and the harsh scrape of their steel swords, stopped. For a moment she listened in the silence to her heart thudding. She felt someone bump into her from behind. Wart.

"It's not fire after—"

He was there. The elf-wizard clutched at her throat. Even as her own fingers went round his large wrists, his fingers dug into the tender skin of her neck with a firm grip, leaving her barely able to speak.

"*Alhor ramda—*" she said. Before she could squawk out the rest of the sleep spell, he clapped his hand across her mouth, shoving her back into the wall his forearm pinned across her throat his other hand grabbing the front of her corset and lifting her off the floor.

"You're no captive princess," his said, towering over her.

She shook her head in terror.

He was no tender lover, either. His eyes were cold, dark black, and indifferent, but his nostrils flared in fury, and his skin was livid white. Angry. Enraged. She couldn't breathe. Fear pounded in her brain. She kicked him with her feet, but that made everything turn brown and fuzzy, just like in a dream. For the first time in her life the world tipped sideways and she swooned.

CHAPTER THIRTEEN

"Come awake." Her cheek stung because he was slapping it. Not gently, either. She blinked, her eyes opened, and she flinched away from his hand. He stopped and took a step back.

She was bound in a chair with a high back. She looked down. All she was wearing was her thin shift. Overdress and corset? Gone. The long brown silk string that gathered the bunched linen together and tied in the front was gone as well. Without it, the linen collar of her shift was slowly opening and sagging around her shoulders. The feel of fabric sliding lower and slipping down to the tops of her arms made her aware of her big panting breaths. She glanced down again. Her skin was pink under the thin shift fabric, except for one thick black strap that pinned her arms to her torso under her breasts. It was the stuff of sexual fantasies gonc wrong.

She was facing a giant tapestry, the walls around it a pale yellow stone. *Wait. His tower.* She twisted her head around to the left and looked up. Yes, there were the diamond-paned windows. Looked right. Books everywhere. Wedding cake stone molding, all fancy and delicate, looping and tracing the arched doorways.

The tapestry belled out with a draft and then was pulled aside by a hand. A servant walked through, arms piled high with Hulgetta's books and other items from her chests and drawers. She cut her eyes away instantly. Still shirtless, the elf-wizard caught her attention. He'd put shoes on but was still unshaven. Yes, just like a sexual fantasy, until he looked at her, and then she could have peed herself right there. She began to gently hyperventilate. Which was embarrassing. Actually, she was sobbing.

Hot salty tears were rolling down her face. She'd given those tears and her name to Hulgetta. Now they were back. Something twisted hard inside her, mourning. She sobbed because she was no longer an apprentice.

"Stop staring at me," she said. He was looking at her like he was about to devour her.

"I am contemplating all the vengeance I can wreak upon you," he said. He was contemplating more than that. If the blazing stare from those black eyes was anything to judge by, some sexual fantasies were skittering across his mind right now as well. Those eyes dropped to skim over her shoulders and hard nipples, then down to her belly and thighs. All that pink skin visible through the thin fabric was rather more provocative than she would have liked, just at that moment, given the circumstances.

"This is all a really funny, big mistake."

He gave her a look. *Cunt.*

"Okay, look," she said, trying her best to suck up the sobs from her heaving chest. *Deep breath.* "Yes, yes. Obviously I neglected to tell you some, um, pertinent facts about myself. For that I'm very sorry!"

He turned away from her and leaned against a large, stiff-looking chair overflowing with books. It looked uncomfortable and matched the one she was in, which was uncomfortable. She knew those books—

they were from Hulgetta's study. One was still wet with blood. *Probably Hulgetta's. Probably.*

In the background she could see the tall, stooped servant coming out from behind the tapestry again, carrying Hulgetta's bottles and boxes of herbs and tinctures, piling them up against the wall. He went back behind the tapestry. *They're looting Hulgetta's chambers.*

"It feels wrong to kill you quickly," he said. "I should probably prolong the agony in some clever way. But at the same time, I don't feel in the mood to let you linger." His fingers came out and traced along the bottom of her jaw line.

Waves of numb buzzing sensations were rolling through her. Her hands and feet were icy with terror. He gave her cheek a few little slaps to prevent her from fainting again.

"Who are you?" he demanded. "Tell me."

She reached for her name—her real name. "Zephyr," she said and blinked. Yup, she knew her name and she could cry. No longer an apprentice, not any more.

"You swore you would not harm me." It was hard to talk with his fingers moving like that. He was instantly at her side, pressing her face into his ribs. His elf moves took some getting used to. Plus she just wanted to scream with fright, very badly.

"I did, didn't I?" He pulled her chin up to look at him. "And I promised to save you from that evil sorceress."

He looked over at his servant, who had come from behind the tapestry.

"Peter, bring the sack," the elf-wizard said to him. The servant paused then ducked back behind the curtain.

"You need to let me go," she said with a wince. "Hulgetta is vengeful, full of dread powers, and all that." Her tone was light, her shoulders shifting up and down trying to slide from under the binding belt, but it was just under her breasts and very tight. However, her wiggling was making the shift fall. Her nipples were barely holding it up. He watched her squirming and cocked an eyebrow, letting her know he enjoyed it. Which of course made her stop immediately and feel like a fool.

"Loyal to the end, eh?" the elf-wizard said, letting her go, and resting on the corner of a table, one boot swinging.

The servant emerged from behind the tapestry and handed over the burlap sack to the elf-wizard. It looked half empty, but something round and weighty bulged at the bottom. The elf-wizard turned back to her and emptied the sack over her knees. Hulgetta's head rolled out and sat in her lap.

She flinched and gasped. She tried to get it off her, but she was too shocked, and the head kept bumping around between the arms of the chair and her lap.

"Hulgetta, dread sorceress, isn't going to help you this time," he said.

She fainted. Again.

CHAPTER FOURTEEN

"Come awake." The command was impatient. Icy water splashed her full in the face and all down her front. Drenched and shivering, she sputtered. Water trickled crooked paths down her face, into the crease of her breasts. Looking down, she saw the horrible head was gone. Her nipples, cold and taut, were outlined under the sheer fabric of her shift.

A hand forced her chin up. She looked into his gaze. It was hot and hungry, black-eyed. No longer distant and sardonic. A fae spirit danced there in his eyes, wild to the point of madness.

"Deceiver. Did you enjoy your little games back there in that cell? Now you're my captive."

The compulsion to beg for her life was strong. Almost overpowering. But something about speaking smack to power was even stronger. "You deceived yourself. I just played along," she said.

He gave her a look.

"For which, as I said before, I'm truly sorry," she hastened to add, scrunching up her forehead. The slightly gleeful look in his eye was worrying. She bit her upper lip. "What, uh, what are you going to do with me? You swore you wouldn't harm me. Remember? That tender moment we had?" One of many he still cherished. She hoped.

"Yes," he frowned, his hands drifting over that part of his chest. "Yes. Despite the urge to throttle you, in general I loathe going back on my word." His hand fluttered over the area of his heart, and he looked uncertain for a moment.

Yet somehow she didn't think that meant he was going to let her go.

"Of course there are so many alternatives," he said, leaning back on the corner of a table now piled high with books. "I could order Peter to do it, for instance." Peter's head jerked up, startled. He was sorting books at the table.

"Or I could order the axe men to do it." *The axe men? What the wha—?*

She followed his gaze out the arched door to his study, and there in the dimmer grey hall were indeed two woodsmen, brown hoods and all. They stood with their long-handled axes resting between their feet.

Fuck me.

The axes looked ridiculously large and sharp. She swallowed. Hulgetta had been going to kill him with a knife, after all. Clearly her irate elf-lover embraced a strong "eye for an eye" ethic. With a little scorched earth policy thrown in, to judge from the sounds coming from behind the tapestry. Something was burning, and she could hear some female hysteria. She thought of the evil book she'd thrown in the fire.

"Ordering someone to kill me by proxy is cheating," she pointed out, looking at the axes, trying to sound persuasive. She tried to quell her rising alarm. *Calm. Calm.*

"It's not really in the spirit of the vow we made, is it?" he agreed, taking a turn around the room. "Then I think to myself, 'why should I care?'" he said, tapping into his fury again. She noticed he'd found a shirt. It was unlaced, but with it on he looked lean and lithe again. Elegant linen made him appear slender, nimble and, frankly, intimidating. She preferred the sensitive half-naked bookworm to this nimble-witted aristocrat before her whose eyes blazed with mad, wounded fury. Her hope for mercy and bygones sank a few notches lower.

Something about her shivering in her shift was giving him pause. He regarded her wet figure.

"Why should I keep a vow I made to you?" he said more deliberately. "You lied to me. Clearly. You distracted me with your favors while your mistress was away. You, who vowed to help me, kept me wrapped tightly around your pretty little finger the entire time." He grabbed said finger and held it, contemplating it while sitting on the arm of her chair. She braced herself as he bent it back a little more, but not to the point of pain. More like he was playing with her. He pouted at the finger.

"This same finger," he said, shaking it a little back and forth, "did nothing. Not one thing to save me." He let the finger go, and she swallowed air with relief. "So why should I honor such a vow?" A rhetorical question, clearly. She was learning at long last when to keep her mouth shut.

"Nevertheless, I could always get out one of Hulgetta's books and—here's one." He stooped low, scooping up a book, and opened it up between slender fingers. "Ah, a spell to turn you into a pig. Shall I? I could give you as a gift to the villagers."

He contemplated doing so.

"That wouldn't be killing you myself. I wouldn't order them to kill you, either. And they would treat you very well. They'd scratch your ears, feed you acorns and let you lie about pretty much wherever you liked in the woods. In fall they'd let you roam, hunting truffles and chestnuts. However, come winter…" he shook his head. Winter was when they slaughtered pigs, of course. His eyes crinkled with soft joy. The thought of winter seemed of great comfort to him.

He pulled her head back by her hair suddenly. Her hands gripped the arms of the chair. His black eyes pinned hers.

"That is, if I can rest easy with my conscience. About the villagers, I mean. Even transformed into a pig, I think you could still find a way to cause them trouble."

"I wouldn't. I'm not. I'm not even that brave," she chattered out.

He brought his face down very close to hers. "There is no underestimating the wickedness in you and the chaos you can cause," he said. "If I'm here alive, it's only because your mistress," he spit out the word, "underestimated you even more than I did."

He shook his head. She knew she was pushing him to the edge. Those black orbs were close enough, large enough and clear enough to reflect her own face back at her. *Nope, no bravery there,* she thought, looking at her own distorted pale face. Not brave, but, even so, mad as he was, he seemed somehow aware of her. His hands in her hair. Clenching and unclenching. Here it was, then.

She was aware of him, too, as much as she didn't want to be, as depraved as it seemed. She was miserable, but that hand with rubbing fingers, feeling the silkiness of her hair gave her a ridiculous amount of hope. She could feel desire radiating off him.

Not nasty rape-y desire, but something buried under the anger, a kind of silent music calling to her. *Oh, god.* It was the elfy thing.

She was staring into his black eyes and they were calling. She found herself leaning forward, though it pulled her scalp, and she was trembling, because on the very surface he was furious, enraged, wrathful. Underneath was something else, though, something hurt and wanting, caressing and full of enchantment.

It wasn't the feeling of thick treacle dumped on her head, it was more like a liquid shot of endorphin rush. Like hearing a favorite song when you have to leap up and dance to it. It gave her hope. Hope that a part of him remembered what they had done together, what they had felt.

Deeper down her mind was uneasy. *Whoa. It wasn't like this before.* The faint voice of sweet reason plucked at her. *Wrong choice! He's not merciful, and you're provoking him.* But she strained to get to within an inch of his face and just feel that thing, whatever it was.

"You're greedy too, aren't you?" she whispered. "What are you greedy for? Magic? Learning? Me?"

Her thin, clinging wet shift made her feel painfully vulnerable. Adrenaline coursed through her, making her shake. If she could have moved she would have dashed for it, she could not have controlled herself. He really frightened her. She heard more noises of timbers crashing, and a few distant screams from the direction of the green door. *He's ransacking Hulgetta's castle.* Her nerves thrilled and she felt herself vibrating like a tuning fork.

"I beg you," she tried, the words sounding artificial and clunky, even to her.

"Go ahead, beg. I am no longer taken in by your face. I know you better now."

"I beg you for my life," she insisted. If she could have gotten down on her knees it would help, but she was pinned in the chair.

"You were going to let me die." He said the words with relish, and a throb of desire began to compete with her fear.

"No. I tried to burn the book. I took great risks with my own life to try and save you. I think even in your elfie state, deep down inside, you know that."

Her mouth. Why couldn't she just shut up and look cute?

The tangled ticklish feeling of awareness between them began bothering her more the longer he stared at her. It was stronger, and she was sure he felt it too. The by now familiar tranquilizing effect had started. She stretched her neck, tilted her face to him, squeezed her thighs together. She tried twisting left and right. She was pushing it, but she seemed to have his attention.

"Hulgetta was going to maim me—literally—because of you. The maids told me what elves do to human women and I didn't listen. If she hadn't been wounded Hulgetta would have killed me and rained down poison frogs on my remaining lifeless bits."

He leaned forward and slowly, she had to back away until she was shrinking against the back of the chair, cringing, the carved wood pressing into her flesh. She had not thought her terror could increase. She was wrong. But that music…

"Is this what you wanted?" he asked her, his lips hovering just above hers. "Is your greed for more magic satisfied yet?"

"You're greedy too. You're ransacking her castle."

"The fire from that wretched book is spreading. That was you, was it? So stupid."

"I saw the pitch running out of your heart," she said slowly, aware of her mouth as she spoke, since he was looking at it like a cat eyes the bird outside the window. "I saw the visible foulness of all your wicked deeds."

"Wicked deed. One. About which you know nothing," he snarled. He was still staring at her mouth.

"It could have filled half a bucket."

"Silence!"

She dropped her gaze but noticed under her eyelashes that he was still looking at her body. He pulled back. When he did the thing with the eyes she could feel him inside her, somehow. Feel the attraction pulsing there, alive, overpowering. She caught him looking at her mouth once more. Did he remember those deep, hard kisses? The feeling of delicious richness started pouring over her head. *Uh-oh. Full-on bespellment, here we go.*

"If you're going to live, you'll have to be collared," he said slowly.

She looked at him. She couldn't help it, she could feel the defiance flash across her face.

"You're bluffing."

"Oh, you think I joke? Axe men," he snarled, and the men came into the room.

Fuck me!

"Die, then," he said.

"You repent?" he asked suddenly, watching her face.

"Ah! Too late." He gestured to the men, who started unstrapping the strap across her torso.

"Wait! Wait wait wait wait wait."

"I'll remember you," he said, his eyes lit with joy, his voice faux-sad.

"I didn't know how the manacle worked. If I knew, I would have opened it. I would have told you."

"You never told me anything of note. Not that you were Hulgetta's apprentice. Not that you were the one who knocked me out. Peter saw you dragging me from this very room. No, there is no honor in you," he said.

"Everyone feared Hulgetta—with good reason," she pointed out.

"Anyway, you promised not to hurt me. If you do, then you're the one without honor." He smoldered. Apparently it was not good form to argue with someone before they killed you.

"I won't have you killed. If," he said, wrapping his hands about her neck, "you vow not to use magic. You vow to do my bidding." He spoke Low Anslod. A contract spell. She knew it. It was the first spell in her Anslod primer. If she violated the contract, very bad things would happen.

Not do magic again? She bit her lip. A part of her would rather die—but dying was actually on the table. He did not care for her hesitation.

"When you're done," he told the men, "hang her head on a spike at the crossroads, next to her mistress's skull."

"Yes, magister," one of the men said.

"I am yours. My will is yours, my spirit yours." She started the spell in Low Anslod.

They released the strap, and she tumbled to the floor, her legs asleep. One man put aside his axe and began to haul her up from the floor.

"Here, use this to brace her neck," the elf said, kicking forward a small footstool.

She resisted the men, clinging to an arm of the chair while they tried to peel her fingers away. She bit and kicked out at them. With all the strength she had left, she shouted in Anslod the contract spell, breathless as she did so.

"I vow never to harm you. Never to use magic against you. I vow to forsake all spells and only be released at your command."

They pried her fingers away one by one. One began forcing her to kneel over the low stool, arms behind her back.

"No! Stop them! Tell them to stop it! *To do your bidding—*" One man had her hair, pulling her head over the stool. The other had picked up his axe. She knew the axe was raised high above her. Every nerve in her body was standing straight up, screaming. It was hard to drag in the air to force out the words.

"My will is yours!" she shouted. The spell was complete.

The men suddenly released her and she fell at the elf-wizard's feet, delirious, incoherent.

"Good enough. I accept the contract."

He whispered the sleep spell into her ear and she dropped like a stone.

∞

Wet. Again. She awoke on her side, on a stone floor. Blinking, she saw his feet in front of her. She realized she was still in the wet shift. Her hands felt heavy and cold. Pulling them up, she saw they were bound in the gold manacles. She sighed.

"Ironic, isn't it?" The elf-wizard was over her, his expression still lit with fury. Then, with a kind of upsy-daisy grunt, he picked her up and slung her over his shoulder in one action.

Despite the feeling that her eyelids and cheeks were swollen from the head rush, she looked at the tower upside down as he carried her up flight after flight of stairs. They hugged the wall, going up and around, an arcade of beautiful, carved arches lining their way. They passed narrow mullion windows, with oculus glass at the top, the arches meeting at junctions in fan vaults that led to a balcony on the second floor. They passed long, thin diamond-paned doors that opened to the warm breeze outside. She wanted to be there, be outside. They continued upward and passed some kind of grand hall then a narrow iron door. The steps themselves, stained over centuries of use, had dulled the marble to a speckled grey unlike the delicate fan vaults, which were still warm creamy-colored stone, that created the effect of elegant cake frosting as they dripped down to long points that ended in a carved ball. The steps continued upward, round and round, outlining the stair banisters, the fan vaults, and the gothic-peaked doorways. The irony of this reversal did not escape her, as they finally reached the top of the stairs, and he pulled her through a heavy door with iron straps into a large bedchamber. He set her down and she wanted to stand firmly, but her head was still in a tilt-a-whirl. He pulled her over to an empty fireplace and pulled her arms up above her head, taking the chain even higher and putting it over a hook, so high she couldn't reach but had to dangle there almost on tip-toe.

In the background over his shoulder was an enormous curtained bed covered in furs.

He'd shaved. The beauty of the dent in his chin struck her and warred with her fear at the frozen contempt on his face. She couldn't help but try to get out of the cuffs.

"Zephyr." He purred the name.

He stooped over her, his mouth closer still.

"My Zephyr." His eyes burned with cruel hunger. The treacle feeling began to build, her mind started to buzz, her lips involuntarily pursing for a kiss from him.

But he pulled away. Her hands were forced up to the level of her head. She felt like an idiot.

"These are the manacles of Jorgon the Undead," he told her. "He used these same manacles upon his mistress Beringia after her treacherous attempt to overthrow his kingdom. Appropriate, isn't it? Once I recalled the details of their history, I knew exactly how the cuffs worked. It's very simple."

He lit the fire. She welcomed the heat. She was cold and shivering wet. Her shift rapidly began drying in the heat. It was the only comfortable spot in the room for someone dressed in a wet shift. His actions were kind, even if the words coming out of his mouth were horrible.

"Teach me." She had breathed the words before she was aware.

He braced her against the wall, one hand flat in the center of her chest. "No, my little treacherous beauty, because that would go against your vow and you would choke to death before my eyes."

She became aware of the thin, uneven edges of slate that lined the fireplace and pressed sharply into her backside as he held her against the wall. Her nipples ached, feeling heavy and sensitive as they rubbed against the wet shift.

What kinky hell was this?

"So what then? What do you want from me?"

"Were you not a lying little snake, I would have enjoyed being alone with you here," he said, holding her chin. "I thought about you constantly in that cell."

"You thought about punishing me and hanging me here almost naked in my shift? That was your fantasy? What else? Spanking me?"

He frowned and shook her. "I thought of us—what's the use." He pulled her around and she felt the wet shift that was molded to her backside pulled away, and then she heard the sound of it ripping. A fresh draft of air made her break out in gooseflesh. A sharp slap of his hand stung her backside, and she jumped more from surprise than anything else.

"That's how you fancy my punishing you?" he said.

The elf magic was kicking into high drive in her system, but she was wiser now and hung her head.

"You want me to beat you?" he challenged. "I thought only human barbarians beat their women for pleasure. Yet I've never met someone who sorely tempted me the way you do."

"You might enjoy it." She didn't think she would. She didn't know. She really needed to shut up.

"I hear some do," he said, pausing. Unsettling desire snaked around in her belly. She turned back to him, the silent music kept calling her, beckoning her forward, until she didn't know what she was saying, she just knew that if she could capture his lips…

She was a fraction of an inch away from his mouth, and she gave a little groan of frustration. He let her get so close, but no further. His fingers, damn him, his fingers were there, right at the sweet spot between her thighs, pushing in just there, brushing her clit, cupping her, and she found herself grinding down into his cupped hand. *Ahhhh.* She pushed forward for more, and then, as if he'd planned it this way all along, he stepped away.

CHAPTER FIFTEEN

Curses!

He changed in front of a hulking wardrobe from his shirt and leggings into a black square-cut wizard's robe, then, still absentminded, pulled the long silk bell pull. She heard the sound of the bell echoing through the well of the tower down below and realized he'd sent for servants. They were going to see her, with her ripped shift. The mussed-up slut hanging from the wall. Her hair, all wet, had fallen forward into her face and she left it there. From beneath her tangled locks, she watched them come.

Her nipples were hard under the wet cloth, and she wanted him to rub them. A small sob of frustration worked its way up her throat, but she kept silent. Her head hung even lower.

Soon servants were entering the room, and he sat in the chair opposite the fire, near an open casement window. The fire, apparently, was just for her. Three large diamond-paned windows pushed apart above an inviting window seat underneath. Just perfect, she reflected, for Rapunzel to let down her hair. While her backside roasted from the fire and her shift started to spring away from her skin in the back, but still was damp and clammy in front, the servants came and went.

Peter was there. He's changed into sleeveless robes and now looked more, well, official. He was the only servant who sat in the window seat, a large book open before him, reading out *pipe rolls*, whatever those were. Something to do with crops. Threshed, winnowed. Barrels, bushels, heaps, quarters. She let the words wash over her, feeling pins and needles in her arms.

They went back and forth over parcels, demesnes, fields, woods. Every time pigs were mentioned, she felt herself give an involuntary jerk. He caught her doing it once and his eyes smiled. Now they were going round and round about barley. Barley seeded, barley harvested, and barley yields. Peter seemed to think something about the yields was problematic, while clearly the elf-wizard was bored and wanted to move on.

Soon she felt like she was getting roasted by the fire, and could not take it anymore. Her backside was now roasting hot, her front side still cold and wet. She found to her great humiliation that she had to twist the chains and turn around, revealing her torn shift and backside to the room. She rested her head on her shoulder, still peeping through her mussed hair to watch what was going on.

No one seemed to notice her, or if they did it was only in quick, darting glances, with expressionless faces. A short, plain woman with sandy hair, who in some way reminded her of Wart, offered to bring food to the elf-wizard. He nodded and listened to more tower business. It was mostly small stuff, but he listened carefully and seemed calm and sincere. What they thought of the human trophy across the room was anybody's guess.

Peter was muttering something from the bench, and suddenly the elf-wizard stood up and began pacing the room, his expression keen. Peter looked at her for just one moment, clearly worried, but then put his head back down and kept his face in his book. With the tray of food came enticing smells over to her side of the room. She didn't think she could eat, she really just wanted the ground to swallow her whole, but the fire was dying down, thankfully, and she was dry.

Knights came trooping in. They talked about the Valdeans. The wreckage of their ships. Gossip, basically. She didn't really pay attention, only coming to with a start when the wizard said, "Well, I do not approve. Go back to farming your pigs." She jerked from her daze. "You want to fight? You who have neither armor, horses, nor weapons, and lack all experience—this is foolhardy to say the least. Tell your fathers I in no way approve of your plan."

"It will end quickly, and we shall be the only knights not covered in glory," said a very red-headed man.

"It will end in your slaughter. Go."

∞

"That's enough, Peter."

Peter coughed. "It's quarter day, Sir."

Ah, an evil wizard's work was never done.

"I know. I'll pay them tomorrow." A sinuous sliding feeling under her skin announced his gaze. His eyes made her writhe against the wall a little.

Then he sighed. "Give me the accounts. You can pay everyone as soon as I review them."

She ached, she throbbed, alone with him in the room she arched her back, a wordless demand for attention. Down below she was now buzzing and numb all at the same time. So overstimulated. And it would not stop. Again and again she bit her cheek.

"Is that man your apprentice? Peter?"

"Silence," he said, making a mark on the paper before him.

Apparently not.

Her arms were burning non-stop from being up in the air.

There was a pause. The papers were swept away by Peter, and at last all the servants gone from the room.

"My arms hurt," she said in a small voice. He came over at once and released her, plucking the chain from its hook in the wall. She was allowed to lower her arms and she almost growled out in vexation while being held up by him. She righted herself, pushing against him, but the cost was a sharp, heavy pang between her legs.

"Do you know what's happened to you?" His voice came out of the darkness, calmer than before.

"Yes," she said, wanting him to take her by the chains, lead her over to the bed and bend her over it.

"Tell me," he said.

"I—you've enthralled me." What had Lanky Sue said? *He would put the black eye upon you.* Well, he had. She looked down at her wrists and hated the chains already. It was no use, however.

"Your desire will grow unless I release it."

"And if you don't?"

"That is what you're about to find out."

On the hard, ornately carved bench at the end of the bed she sat heavily, shoving her hands between her thighs then wincing as the sharp edge of the manacles caught on her flesh. She was so wet. He was changing again, into a nightshirt this time. The chain made noise, and she was torn between her pride and the need to press that throbbing place.

"I hope you're not touching yourself," he said, not even bothering to look. "It will only make it worse."

She quickly withdrew her hand. He was lying. Probably. She made a fist. She imagined herself bent over the bed with the elf-wizard behind her. She couldn't help but touch herself, the image was so vivid.

"There's only one way to be released," he said.

She slowly stood up. "So show me," she said.

He pushed her against the thick post at the corner of the bed. The wooden carvings twisted around. She could feel them on the back of her head and shoulders, the post as thick as her thigh.

He pulled on her shift and with both hands ripped the front down low, his fingers finding how wet she was. She felt her thighs parting at the sound of linen ripping, and her eyes closing, head tilting back. *Yes, please, oh god yes.*

Yet she had never felt so horny and miserable at the same time before. It was like intense break-up sex, but not the good kind. She could feel her orgasm building, but he just stared at her. She tried to pull him into her.

He wouldn't move, and her fingers dug into his flesh. She opened her eyes, and he was staring at her, his face hovering over hers. She met his eyes, not in defiance, not in anything, just letting her lips part, the flutter of her orgasm just out of reach.

Her hand reached up and the damn manacle chain hit his chest, but she caressed his neck, pulling him towards her.

"No, no!" He suddenly twisted and pulled her hand away from him. "I'm not going to. I told you, I don't—I'm not like that anymore."

Anymore?

His hand was on her waist, his other hand between her legs. He let her draw her leg up, pull it over his hip, and with one hand he held it there.

His fingers... so... unf—. An orgasm like a gold-flecked riptide pummeled through her, hard. He stayed close to her while it throbbed a drumbeat though her body from the tips of her breasts to the back of her throat.

She rolled her head. *Now that was something.* Like someone had turned her inside out, then sprayed her with whipped cream all over.

She put her head against his as the wash of release rippled, their foreheads touching, and then it all slowly faded.

"Thank you," she said.

He looked her up and down, his own thoughts hidden in those eyes, then turned away.

"You'll sleep on the bench," he said. He took the candle from where it rested on the wall sconce by the chair and brought it over to the bed. She went to the bench and sat. *Ouch.*

He climbed into the bed and snuffed the candle. All was dark and silent, except for a soft mild breeze that came through the casement windows.

"What makes you think I won't escape?" she said, her voice soft in the darkness. "I could walk right out in the middle of the night."

"And go where? Do you know where you are?"

"Good point," she admitted. For the first time he laughed.

"Glad to provide you with so much amusement, wizard."

There was no way she would be able to fall asleep on the hard bench when she could just get up and leave. Already the uncomfortable carvings were causing her flesh outrage in at least ten different places. While thinking of how uncomfortable she was, and how she would probably lie awake all night, she fell asleep.

∞

He thrust into her, and she lay under him in a half swoon of joy, kissing his chest over and over. "You do forgive me?"

"Of course, I can't help it. I love you."

He woke with a start, his body cold, thinking he was back in the cell, that tense ache of desperation waking him up, his body jackknifed from the dread. But instead, it was dawn and he was in his own bed, alone as usual. He forgave her.

He walked over to a wardrobe and used the basin inside it to wash. She lay there disheveled, a tumbled maid in rags, exhausted and out cold on the old bench. He shook her awake and she sat bolt upright, holding the manacles protectively over her head, unfortunately whacking her nose with them.

"Ow!"

"Go stand near the fireplace," he said, trying not to laugh. She shuffled off and stood there peering at him uncertainly. He hadn't thought about what to do with her. He hadn't thought about anything yesterday in his rage and exultation at being betrayed and getting free. He knew his eyes were changed back again. Calm reason was seated firmly in his head. She noticed as well.

"Your eyes are green again. I can tell even without looking because the treacle feeling is gone."

"The what?"

"I'm starving. What's for breakfast?"

He turned around and dressed, shaking his head. When Dorcas answered the double tug on the bell rope, he handed his captive maid off to her with instructions she was to be washed and clothed as befitted her station, then fed.

"But keep her quiet. And watch her closely the entire time."

"Yes, watch me, Dorcas. I'm wily," she said. Then she gave a hysterical cackle of laughter that left Dorcas looking at her bewildered. After they left, he ate quickly. Peter wanted him to look at the north fields, which were almost a league away, and he wanted to get it over with before the day was over.

∞

She had to escape. Not now, of course. Later. Now she was vigorously washing herself in a copper-lined tub in the dungeon of the tower. The first bath in almost a year. Not that this was a dungeon, really. Though it was in the basement of the tower it was more of a laundry room. There was lavender oil in the water, which was very hot. After the day before, she wanted to scrub herself inside and out.

Dorcas was working on her sewing right now, sitting in the corner of the dungeon laundry room, her needle flashing in the light that came from the half windows set up high in the wall. There were herbs hanging from the ceiling. Okay it wasn't a dungeon at all. *I give up*. She plied the sponge and soap and scrubbed between her poor, neglected toes.

A few of the other women servants drifted in and out, showing Dorcas their sewing, and smiling at Zephyr from time to time. They reeked of curiosity. A sparkling giant copper kettle simmered near the far corner. It held the heating water for the laundry, which was spread on drying racks all around the room.

Zephyr crossed one leg over her knee and scrubbed between her other toes. Steam came off them. Frankly, she stank. The elf-wizard hadn't seemed to notice last night. In the dark. Stop thinking about it. She shook her head hard, trying to free her mind from his helping fingers and the weird obligation of getting her off. She gave a little groan. Dorcas looked at her, concerned.

"I'm fine." She waved her sponge at Dorcas and went back to pensive meditation. He hated her. She squeezed the sponge with both hands and sank down into the water, perseverating on this. His touch was devastating. She had to escape, but the way she'd clung to his body last night and the way he had set off a firestorm in her senses made her whimper.

Stop being a ninny. What's your exit strategy here?

CHAPTER SIXTEEN

Go where? And what about these? She clanked her chains. Yes, she wore the manacles, even in the tub. Dorcas and the other woman had ripped the shift right off her because it was ripped to heaven anyway, so why not? They were madly sewing shifts and dresses that laced along the top of the sleeves and shoulders, so she could put them on and off. She didn't know whether to laugh or cry, really.

Okay, supposing somehow she got the manacles off. He'd done it, so could she.

Say she did. She imagined stumbling from the tower in the middle of the night and walking. Maybe even getting a horse or donkey to ride if she was lucky. Then what? Stopping at the next convenient castle? *Hello! Anybody need a sorceress in training?*

It didn't sound safe. Even if he was lying, it didn't sound safe.

Less safe than waiting around to be turned into a pig?

She didn't think he was going to do that—frankly, she didn't think he even knew how. He'd said that just to scare her. It had worked, but that was beside the point.

So far, the most powerful magician she'd ever seen had been Hulgetta's master, that blue sorcerer in his billowing robes. Appearing and disappearing out of the cloud of blue smoke—now that was something. But even that could be faked. Nothing about her elf-wizard indicated he could pull off anything of the magnitude of turning her into a pig.

No. Go with what you know. She needed to get back to the castle. Hulgetta was dead, so it would be a safe place to hide.

Why didn't she hate him? It was hard to focus her thoughts. They kept jumping about to uncomfortable topics.

Why didn't she?

No. Not going to think about that. She scrubbed her shins. Too uncomfortable. Perhaps when he stopped being so mad, he'd forgive her. At least a little.

Not the elf side. Her heart began beating a hard staccato rhythm thinking about his inner fae. Her emotions tumbled around with her sexual desires, like the spin cycle of a washing machine, making her so squirmy and uncomfortable and unhappy that finally she decided she didn't want to think. *Moving on.* She scrubbed her arms, the back of her neck, and then stood up abruptly from the bath and reached for a towel hanging on a rack, leaning out over the pea gravel to do so.

"I'm done," she announced to Dorcas.

"Just a moment." She speaks!

Zephyr dried herself on the linty towel. It was like drying oneself with a tablecloth, but at least these people washed. Did he bathe down here too? *Stop with the wistful thoughts already.* She had to control her feelings. Clamp those thoughts down and keep it together. She needed a plan. Any vulnerability she showed would provide him an excellent opportunity to hurt her all the more, glorying in his revenge.

And keep your eyes away from his at all times. The dark fae in him called to her, causing every inch of her body to call back.

Don't be grateful for last night. Remember the bench instead.

Eyes on the ground at all times.

Her arms were very stiff and sore—speaking of sore! Her lady bits were quite tender from their rough abuse at the hands of the elf-wizard.

Waiting for Dorcas to finish her dressmaking, Zephyr looked around the dun—ah, laundry room. It was bare, utilitarian, and neat as a pin. The curious maids reminded her of Hulgetta's castle a little, although there was one thing the castle had that this tower seemed to lack.

She reached up, wincing from the ache in her sore arms, and snapped off some springs of lavender, then some rosemary from the bunches on the rack. Idly she took a length of thread from the ground and twisted them together, still wrapped in her towel, her feet still standing in the warm bath.

"That's pretty."

"Yes."

"Is that a moss maid?" Dorcas's accent was difficult to understand. So different from the clipped-off dialect of Hulgetta's castle it was almost another language. But if she listened carefully, and Dorcas kept it simple, she could follow.

"It is." Zephyr showed her and smiled. The other maids drew closer and began to chatter. They insisted on placing the moss maid in the center of the mantle by the enormous copper kettle on display. Someone added a tiny pinecone, another added some smooth stones and soon enough a little shrine was in place. The moss maid stood upon her little clay hill, with a crown of lavender buds upon her hair of white towel threads.

Naked, like Venus rising from the sea, except for the white towel firmly tucked around her, Zephyr stood up to her shins in cooling water while they combed out her messy braids, wet her hair down, and re-braided it. She bent her head forward like a child while the oldest woman with the head cloth gave her a center part and then created a braid that went across her crown and wrapped it in ribbons, leaving a length of it to hang free down in the back. The maids were like girls playing with a new doll.

Like they were decorating a moss maid, Zephyr thought, and smiled. But she put up with it as they smoothed something nice into her shoulders and arms. It was cool and smelled minty. Perhaps it was meant to help her sore muscles.

It wasn't a damp room—unlike Hulgetta's castle, even with the bathwater, this tower was bone-dry and clean, the yellowish stone entirely free from damp. A yellow moth of the same color flew into to the room through the open shutters. It fluttered over to the moss maid figurine, landing on the breast of the crude representation. There it stayed, opening and shutting its wings, content in the warmth of the morning sunlight pooling on the mantle. Then she didn't feel so great. She felt a kind of wiggling from inside the figurine and at the same time it felt like someone was holding a pillow over her face. Oxygen just stopped. A flick of moth wings and the tiniest spark of enchantment—of magic—went into the fetish.

She was surprised, but even more surprised that she was growing faint. Like she'd gotten the wind knocked out of her. Her diaphragm could barely suck in the smallest thread of air.

"Help," she said to the women, her voice hoarse. She could barely speak.

"Dorcas," they cried.

"Get him. Now." she enunciated slowly, as a deep brown film covered her vision and she staggered out of the bath, her bare feet sticking to the pea gravel. Everything suddenly felt like a dream. She grabbed something. The towels, the drying rack. She couldn't speak, her hands pulling the towels, which slipped, and she fell, stretching out. The women were crying in alarm as Dorcas bolted up the stairs.

Clawing at her throat didn't help because there was nothing there. *Jesus, the contract spell.*

She realized she needed to stop struggling. Wait for him. Like she was holding her breath underwater. Be patient. He would come. What if he was far away? He was going to come. She could barely manage to suck in some air. Her throat was tightening.

It was just a moss maid. She couldn't see. Then cool hard fingers gripped hers.

A male voice said, "Not even a full day. You were warned, fair Zephyr, what the consequences would be."

∞

She woke coughing and sputtering, twisting her neck around.

"Lie still," a voice said, and so she did, cradled against something warm, the sound of blood cells in her head fizzing and popping loudly. She dragged in a deep breath. That restricting invisible choker gone, her skin still burned around her throat where she'd scratched at it helplessly.

She realized the elf was holding her. He'd saved her. Her leap of joy was stifled by the awareness of people all around. Then she realized he hadn't saved her. He was behind this all along, wasn't he? A stab of deep despair attacked her. She had snarled everything up between them. Her fault. Furious, she yanked herself up off his lap, clutching her towel around her, desperate to get away from him and keep her composure. He stood as well, reaching out a hand to steady her.

"Stay away," she snapped, and then coughed. He reached out again, but she danced away from his touch.

"That's the second time you've tried to kill me," she ground out coughing, her eyes watering. His expression shifted between amusement and caution.

"Think of what would have happened had I gone out to inspect the home farms this morning. They would never have found me in time, and you'd be lying here as blue as that dress."

"There's magic everywhere," she said furiously. "What happens if I eat a biscuit containing buttermilk and that same buttermilk was curdled because the cook said a spell over it? Or I step on a stair that someone waved a turtle stone over so no one would trip? Tiny little bits of magic. They're everywhere, and you just *knew* it would make me keel over at some point, didn't you? You *knew* I wouldn't last a week."

He looked at her, tilting his head, puzzled. "You really are from another land, aren't you?" His hands on his hips, he looked out the window. "If I'm honest, a part of me expected you would know how to dodge these folk ways. I forgot you didn't grow up amongst us."

Yet she sensed underneath his human form, the elf was gleeful. Exultant. His elf half was still angry, still burned with half-extinguished rage. The cloak of his logical side didn't hide it from her.

Dorcas stepped forward. "It's a subtle way that elf folk work. Like setting a pan on the edge of the stove. One knows it will fall, no matter who knocks it off because it is simply in the way. He may not, miss, have consciously planned this." Dorcas twisted her hands up in her apron. "But it's why one never makes enemies of an elf."

She watched his pale face. There was a twitching muscle in his cheek that jumped. With annoyance or humor? He just stood there, awkwardly, like he didn't know what to do with his arms. He really was a divided soul.

"The binding spell is broken," he said.

She held out her hand. "I won't say it again."

"No," he agreed.

She tightened her towel around her. "I was taking my bath. You're rather in the way."

"Try not to get yourself killed this time," he said, and then his long legs were taking him up the stairs.

An hour later, she was seated in a corner of his study, all done up like a prize cow for the state fair. Her frock was clean and simple, neat and plain. The shift light grey, the dress midnight blue, the ribbons light grey. The only significant difference between this dress and what she was used to wearing at the castle was that the shift had a low neck, and there was no fichu to cover up her breasts into perfect half-moons. The bodice cut severely across them and revealed far more than she was used to. She sat with a bowl of hot porridge on her lap, her hair slightly damp. She hadn't felt so pretty and clean in a long, long time.

The porridge was a little feast, with dried fruits and nuts in it, as well as cream, butter and some salt, but in truth half the contents of her shallow wooden bowl lay uneaten. Perhaps being corseted into the shape of a carrot was cutting off her appetite. Perhaps she was pining after the stupid wizard. She put the bowl down and drifted to the windows of the study. He and Peter were at the other end of the room. Instead of visiting the north fields, he'd decided to do an inventory of Hulgetta's possessions and store them away. There was a hidden door that was open, revealing an enticing store room that gave off the pungent, spicy smell of magic. She longed to peek into the room and examine its contents, but she was strictly warned to stay on her stool in the corner.

She stretched up on tiptoe to look out the window, aware of the delightful pair of curly-toed linen slippers on her feet. They had pretty little heels made of horn and were light grey embroidered with violets. Outside was the bare dirt yard and the corner of the outbuildings, a low stable, and the dark underwater green of the pines that led back into the woods.

Time to make a plan to escape. Where? How? Yes, she was well dressed and well fed. Never mind the manacles. Which no one did. Which was weird, so very weird. That spell could have instantly killed her in a dozen different ways without her half trying to do anything. Okay, the spell was gone and he didn't seem like he wanted to kill her anymore. She still felt shaken to the core, and adrenaline in the form of tremors shook her now and then. She needed a plan. A solid, well thought out plan. But she was scared. *This world will kill you if you don't watch out.*

She felt pulled back towards the hidden supply closet. That's where all the magic was. She could feel the power in there, like a sleeping dragon in its lair, alive and beating like drums, waiting to be used. It was drawing her like a child is drawn to all the exciting presents under the Christmas tree.

Meanwhile, Peter and the elf-wizard were completely ignoring the wonderment of the storage closet. Instead, they were absorbed in trying to figure out how all the dials on the green door worked.

"But you knew the combination to get back here," Peter said.

"If you set this dial to this spot here, it goes backwards. It went first to the battlefield, and then it came back here. Pure luck figuring that out," the elf-wizard said. Her back was to them. She caressed a geranium with tiny little white-and-peach-colored flowers and with her fingers pinched off the dead leaves.

The green door. She could go anywhere with the door. She wasn't stuck here. *Get the manacles off, and then what?*

Back to the castle. Find Wart. Her mind quickened at the idea. If the castle hadn't burned to the ground by that freaking awful evil book. Or perhaps the elf-wizard had torn down the stones and salted the earth. *No. No, he couldn't have. He didn't have time.* She wanted to skip about. To bring her back, hack off Hulgetta's head, loot the castle—no, it took too much time to do all that and tear down a huge decaying heap of massive stone.

So she had a plan. Yes. She was too excited to sit still. And it was a big castle. She could see if anything magical was still tucked away. They'd found the rings, but maybe hadn't dared venture into the room with the decaying roof. If the trunk was still there? There might be something inside it that she could use, and put herself out there as a sorceress maybe? Wart, Wart would know where they could go—a place where they would be safe and where no one would harm them. Though if that was true, what was Wart doing at the castle herself?

Zephyr didn't know a lot of details about Wart's past, but a few choice comments made her think Wart had once lived in a city. A big city. Maybe they could go back there. Zephyr could sell tinctures. Willow bark tonic, that kind of thing.

She wandered out of the study and stared up into the dim well of the inside of the tower. Drifting up the stairs, she stopped on the second floor before the open balcony. There was a view—not as grand as she'd had from up in his chamber at the top of the tower, but still. Across the rolling hills she saw a land of yellow and green fields dotted with many sprawling farms spreading out for what had to be at least forty miles.

No, what did he say? Fifty leagues? Below was the village with the crossroads where Hulgetta's skull was hung, apparently. From here she could only see a haze of wood smoke from the village houses against the turquoise sky and the crooked little pointy roof tops peeking out over the fields. The topography was surprisingly like the Midwest meets Eastern Europe, circa fifteen something. Ohio came to mind. Well, she didn't miss it. Okay, she missed her parents like the dickens. And maybe her annoying older brother. A little. But she wasn't going to think about that now.

The birdsong was making a racket. It was mostly coming from the forest that cupped around the tower like a hand, giving shade and darkness to the north. Which brought her back to the main goal for today: plans for escape.

What did they say? Fortune favors the bold. She stared at the manacles. Magic had a certain kind of energy, a certain density to it, sucking her attention towards it like gravity going down a black hole. No agitation of the fairy dust here. How had he gotten out of the manacles? She examined the heavy cuffs. *Time to give up your secrets.*

She tried to see outside in the bright sunlight if the cuffs actually melded together. After a long examination, they proved to have the tiniest of hairline gaps. So they were not magically sealed together, they only looked as if they were. *All right,* she thought. *That's something.*

The fit between each end was so precise it seemed impossible that it could be produced by hand. If a wizard made it by hand, she was impressed. Thinking about technology… maybe she could find the blue sorcerer who'd come to visit Hulgetta—the one in blue with long silver hair. Fighting the good fight with powerful King Linus.

He'd trained Hulgetta, she remembered. Perhaps he was in need of another apprentice? She could offer her services. He'd have to take Wart too. She drifted back down the stairs into her corner and sat on the stool.

She continued working on the cuffs, and at one point she looked up to find him staring at her.

"The midday meal is ready." Very slowly and carefully, she put her hands down. Maybe he hadn't noticed her playing with them. She wasn't looking at them, after all. They had weights in them. She could feel their shifting better if she looked at something else and focused on their feel as she moved her wrists about carefully.

"Plotting your escape?" he said.

CHAPTER SEVENTEEN

She couldn't control her involuntary jerk of surprise.

"If you're thinking of running off and approaching some lord in his castle, asking if anyone needs a sorceress, think again."

She didn't know what look she had on her face, but he grabbed her arm.

"Seriously. Don't."

"And if I told them I escaped from the evil elf-wizard and demanded their protection?"

"They would bring you right back here. Every knight, every baron, every lord within fifty leagues of the tower knows I am an elf-wizard. They also know I am no wicked seducer of maids. All of them desire my good will. They would truss you up and deliver you over to me."

"They suck up to you?" she said. "I'm shocked."

"Let us say I am their advisor and treated with profound respect. My actions so far they see as honorable. Without honor there is no trust. Without trust all is brutality and chaos."

Word.

"But does an honorable man hold a strange woman captive in his tower?"

"Instead of killing her for her evil betrayal? Yes."

"You say these men respect your honor, and they obviously must aspire to be honorable themselves, or they wouldn't really care. But what about women?"

"Women have no honor."

"So it's not just a sorceress that has earned your enmity. You hate all women."

"Only those who betray me. Unfortunately, these seem to be the only women I meet."

Feeling his eyes on her, she kept her own eyes pinned on her skirt and held her breath.

"Come clean. How did you get out of them?" she asked. "Show me."

He laughed. "I read about it. A certain come-hither female had seduced a king, and then secretly betrayed him to his enemy.

"The king could forgive her for the one time. He was very much in love with her, and the general of the enemy was her brother. But did she love him back? Or had she only seduced him in order to betray him? He could not tell. So he had the local wizard make the cuffs and placed them on her."

The elf-wizard traced his fingers along the edges where her skin touched the cuffs. She tried to jerk her hands away, but he held onto one wrist and kept making those little lines and circles there.

"He told her that if she loved him they would fall off. However, if she betrayed him to his enemy, and hated him, she would suffer terribly.

"He brought her back from the dungeons two weeks later and her hands were black," the elf-wizard said. "She was spewing venom for all the wrongs he had done to her family and swore her vengeance upon him."

"And?" she said.

"And the manacles cut off her hands. She bled to death before the entire court."

Zephyr made a groan and put her hands under her armpits, trying to hide them. Rocking back and forth and frowning for all she was worth, she said, "You're trying to scare me. They're not magic like that. I could tell if they were."

"But the story is true," he countered. "I can show you the chronicles if you like." He gestured to his shelves.

"No, thank you."

She spent much of lunch eating roast mutton, some kind of root vegetable and mushroom tart, and imagining various revenge scenarios involving the elf-wizard. These revenge scenarios, perhaps because of their dungeon setting, (a real dungeon!) happened to take a dark and edgy turn. He pled for his life on his knees. Mostly naked. They had a last goodbye in a proper dungeon cell where he was chained up. Mostly naked. If, while chained to the wall, he pleased her sufficiently while on his knees, then maybe she wouldn't have him beheaded, but he would have to work VERY HARD for her to show mercy—She shook her head and ate her slice of tart. *Okay, stop. You can stand life without a little wizard nookie. It won't be for long, anyway.*

The elf-wizard ate all alone, but she was in the kitchen. The kitchen occupied the other half of the basement next to the laundry room. She was learning the layout. Ground floor held the study, second floor had the balcony, and up on the third floor was a giant dining hall, where the wizard was all alone, seated at a massive table, staring at portraits of all the wizards who'd lived in the tower since the time of it being built. Their portraits crammed the dark oak paneling all the way up to the high ceiling. She, meanwhile, was crammed elbow to elbow with the servants at a crowded table under the window in the basement. Peter served his master, and then came to his dinner later than the others.

"Saved you some tart, Peter," Dorcas said.

"She saved the seat next to her as well," Zephyr told Peter. *Cause wasn't that interesting?* Peter looked down at Dorcas and gave a small, hasty bow, while Dorcas gave him a welcoming smile, surprised but happy. She went from plain to beautiful with one expression, her face lit from within. It was a useful bit of knowledge, wasn't it? That Dorcas liked Peter, and he was oblivious.

"Any luck with the green door?" Zephyr asked.

"We've finished that. We're on to the rings now and the petrified hand."

"Oh." She was impressed. He gave a cough, and was it her imagination or did a little bit of green smoke come out?

That was fast. Crazy fast. I mean, how'd he work it all out like that? Mathematical principles? Astronomy? Panic warred with envy. She envied Peter working with the wizard, that he was privy to the elf-wizard's methods, and got to see the wizard figure it all out. There were knobs on the green door she still didn't know the function of, but he had taken a bit of the morning and figured it all out. *Damn.*

She tinkered with her cuffs. The thought of going through the door and leaving him was not fun, but after all it wasn't like he loved her. Her chest burned. *You fell for all that Romeo and Juliet stuff didn't you? Idiot.*

She noticed that Peter kept coughing. And yes! Little puffs of green smoke came out as he did so.

"Smoke demon?" she said sympathetically.

"Yes," he coughed again.

"I can fix that cough for you," she offered. "I don't think it'll go away on its own."

He looked up at the ceiling.

"I'll be fine, miss."

"Oh, he's eating. If we're quick about it, he'll never know."

"I suppose if I were going into the study and you followed me, I wouldn't be able to stop you."

She followed him up the stairs and into the study.

"I'll need some camphor, and some colt's foot."

"Not sure we have those things, miss."

"Hulgetta has them. There should be an apothecary box, if you brought everything from her study."

"Nearly everything. Couldn't catch that dratted lizard."

"Ah!" And glory be! Peter went to the wall and pushed in a bit of molding that sprang the hidden door to the supply closet. The door creaked open.

Christmas had come early this year!

But he didn't let her in it. He shuffled around amongst the dark high shelves, all crammed together, and brought out the long apothecary box from Hulgetta's castle.

"Yes, look for the apothecary box," she said, peering in.

He gave her such a hangdog stare.

"Just looking! See? My feet aren't even inside the door." He had such a hang dog stare. Must be what got to Doras.

The feel of magic palpitated throughout the room and within her. Shelves and shelves of magical items crowded the walls. She tried not to gape, but it was like Aladdin's den. She recognized items in it, too. What a large collection Hulgetta had amassed. Yet it hadn't seemed large when spread throughout the castle. Here, all in one spot near the door, it was enormous. She recognized some things, like a curious carved elk horn. Peter coughed and she turned back to her patient.

"Lungs on fire?"

He nodded. He looked miserable.

"Malbrank. I need malbrank weed. Do you have any?"

"We have a—where is it?—a salve."

"I could use that." He drew out more apothecary boxes and together they began to open up the little boxes in the herbal.

"Not very fresh," she sniffed. The herbs in the wizard's box were mostly dust, but she poked around and found the odds and ends she needed. She knew the elf-wizard didn't study sorcery, but didn't he tend to his people and their health?

"Here," she said, picking up a shallow dish. "The malbrank. Bring it here. Also bring the tinderbox."

Peter returned in a second with a salve in a jar. However, inside the salve were whole leaves. She pried one out from the sticky goo. The stiff, curled-up leaf was tough. It looked a little bit like a green snail shell. She took a whiff and pulled back quickly. *Ugh!*

Malbrank, all right. Pungent. Hulgetta's maids washed the sheets with a tincture of it. The smell kept fleas out of the linens, but the herb had many other uses as well.

She crumbled enough into the small dish so that the bottom was completely covered and added the comfrey and then the colt's foot.

"Now light it," she said. He did, and the smoke hovered in the air. As they watched, the vapor formed into an oscillating bright yellow cloud.

"Okay, this is what you do. Open your mouth and leave it open. Don't breathe in, don't breathe out. Got it? When I nod, breathe out as much air as you can, alright?"

He nodded. The malbrank cloud hovered close to him. Even though he wasn't breathing, some of the green fog started to come out of his throat. It hovered in his mouth, almost poking out into the air.

"Breathe in. Now."

He did and the malbrank chased after the green fog, diving down his lungs.

"Now hold it. Hold it. Do not exhale."

She was good at this stuff. Stuff with air. And earth. She really wanted to get good with fire too, but so far hadn't had many opportunities. "Okay. Hold on."

Peter was turning a soft shade of rose. "Just let me get a bell jar. Now. In another second you're going to breathe out, slowly, all the air you can expel from your lungs. Every tiny bit."

She got a bell jar from a side shelf as Peter's eyes started turning red.

"Alright. Yes, let it out. As much as you can," she said. He exhaled and a yellow vapor engulfing the green vapor came forth from his lungs. She got it all trapped under the bell jar.

"This is the fun part." The seething mess of vapors began writhing and wrestling. The sight held her transfixed as the yellow cloud overtook and then ate the green vapor. Then the yellow vapor slowly dissipated.

"If your lungs ache, you can take a bit of nettle tea and that should help. How do you feel?" she said. Peter didn't answer. He was looking at the doorway. She looked up and turned to see the elf-wizard standing there.

∞

He had watched them from the doorway. He knew the green door was there, and a small part of his mind thought she might just use it.

"I swore I would not use magic to harm you, and I haven't," she said. "Peter had inhaled vapor from the smoke demon and was ill. I healed him, that's all."

"For helping my servant, I thank you." He gave her a mocking bow.

"You're welcome."

"Peter, there's firewood to be chopped for the kitchen." Peter said not a word and was gone.

"Yet you did not obey me. You will be punished."

"Right here? Right now? I see why you sent Peter away." She walked over to the table of books. "Where do you want me? Over this table?"

Her eyebrow lifted in flirtatious teasing, but he watched her lip twitch a little with excitement. Frustration coiled up inside him.

"Stop," he said at last. "I'm not going to beat you."

"No spanking? Too bad, it's one of my secret fantasies."

He hesitated, half shocked. The struggle to suppress the thrumming inside him took a considerable amount of time. He remained frozen in place as he wrestled those wicked desires.

"Right here." She patted the table. "Right on the books."

There was an empty space inside him, an ache for her.

He banished her up to his bed chamber. The guilty hot fantasies played out in his mind as he put away the herbs she'd used. His elf side, still rejected, still angry, simmered.

I can control it. I won't let it happen. You know how it all turned out last time.

He pottered around the table set trying to look up the stone forearm and rings resting on the velvet cloth. He was aware as the afternoon ticked onward of many maids stealing upstairs. They came down again, each one watching him and with some excuse for visiting Zephyr upstairs.

"Dorcas is wondering if miss wouldn't like to do some stitching by way of passing the time."

"Miss says she has a recipe for a tincture my mother's been wanting."

Clearly they were enchanted with her, and relished dressing her up fine, making her into a lady for them to pamper and serve. Dorcas came down eventually in search of a comb to use on Zephyr's fair hair. He thought of how some strands caught the light and glowed gold, while others were a darker color, but very soft overall. The shorter strands in front curled wildly, hinting at her tempestuous nature.

He wanted someone to love, a sweetheart to have a life with. That moment when she looked at him back at the castle—he thought it could happen, but the bittersweet hurt always followed. *Trust her. No, no, no!* Yet some stubborn element inside him, as hard as iron, would not relent. The stars had spelled out his doom. They were fated for each other and he only hurt himself in not bowing to the inevitable.

Peter came in, his shirt soaked front and back with sweat. "Master, the knights are back."

"What, all of them?"

He'd been so wrapped up in his reverie that he hadn't heard the noise of their approach. He climbed to the second floor, staying back just enough so he was out of sight. Horses, men with loud voices. "Tell them I am busy."

"They say there's news from Magor. The Valdeans are at the border and might invade. Less than five hundred leagues from us."

"No, that changes not one bit the problem of weapons, horses, and skill. I will not see them. Send them away."

"But sir, they say raiding parties—"

"No."

Peter left, defeated, and he continued watching from the shadows as the men mounted their horses and, grumbling loudly, left.

He turned to see her on the stairs behind him, watching. Her dull gold hair glinted like the manacles. "Well? What do you want? To torment me? Why didn't you use the green door when you had the chance?"

"Do you still hate me?"

"If you'd slipped away through the green door, then I would no longer have to see you. Or have you on my hands."

"How's it coming with those rings, huh?"

The exact wrong thing to say. He could feel his face clouding over the throb from the back of his eyes.

"Okay, I'm going, I'm going." And she turned, climbing the stairs, swaying her hips as she did so.

∞

She taunted him, and enjoyed taunting him. She was hoping that if she did it more he would get all elfy and slap her up against a wall, or over the table, and just let the spicy sexual sparks fly. Instead she was banished. Yes, banished. Up to his room. Like she was eleven years old. Grounded. She climbed the stairs in the late afternoon sunlight. *Okay, then. I'll just go to my room. But you'll be sorry, Mr. Elf-Wizard.*

She manipulated one wrist, a fraction at a time, taking up to two minutes to do so. After a tedious number of minute incremental shifts, she began to feel some tiny weights and counterweights moving back and forth inside the cuffs.

She was in the window, racing against the sun going down. She'd have the cuffs off by evening. Surprise him. Come down with the cuffs dangling from its chain on one finger, and look at the expression on his face! Buoyed up by this thought, she could have sworn one of the cuffs slipped. Just a little. A tiny bit.

She stared straight ahead then shifted it back and forth carefully. It went back to the way it was, but she realized that there were tiny weights inside each manacle, moving back and forth, making them looser so she could slide them off. Perhaps she'd even be able to open them all together.

Had she not been so relentless, she would have been having screaming fits of frustration by now. It was complicated to manipulate the cuffs. She had to keep trying new "feels" with the weights time and again.

This was exciting.

She felt the cuffs slip more. Just a little. A tiny bit. Somehow she had created a counterbalancing motion inside the cuff. She shifted it back and forth carefully. It went back to the way it was. *Okay, not that.*

She sat playing with the cuffs, her mind not on what her hands were doing. But by not thinking, she could feel the cuffs shift in a whole new way. She could feel a weight in them shifting down to a new level. She tried again.

A shift! And the cuffs grew tighter. Which pissed her off. "Curse you and your phallic tower too!" she shouted, shaking her fists at the floor suddenly. Suddenly the cuffs closed about her wrists like a trap, squeezing them hard.

CHAPTER EIGHTEEN

"Get them off! Get them off me! Wizard!" He heard her cries as he bounded up the last set of stairs to the bed chamber.

"Wiiiiiizard!" He swiftly sat next to her and grasped the cuffs as she cried out, her fists a soft color of pink.

"They suddenly got tighter," she told him as he examined them slowly, one at a time. "I don't know what happened!"

"You need to calm down."

"You calm down! Look at my hands!" she said, opening the pink appendages and flexing them. "Get them off me right now!" she shouted.

"Stop it!" he commanded.

She glared at him. Her eyes in that dress were deep blue, fierce, and irate. He tried using a soothing tone of voice. "Panic will do you no good. Calm yourself and I'll have them off in a moment."

She breathed heavily through her nose and continued to glare. Then her face crumpled and she held out both wrists to him again.

"Just get them off," she begged, tears spilling down her face.

"Breathe deeply," he said. He clasped her in his arms and as he heard her give hissing breaths in and out, he had her hold out her arms, wrist up. He grasped the cuffs and then manipulated them, shifting this way and that. At a critical point, he held her forearms and guided them firmly in a half curve swoop to the right and then a matching half curve swoop to the left.

"Hear that? That's it." He gave her forearms a hard shake downwards. The cuffs fell to the ground, open.

She snatched them up and threw them across the room.

"How could you put those on me!" she cried and threw herself into his arms. He held her, scooping her up, putting her head against his chest while she continued sobbing.

"I hate you," she added for good measure, clinging to him.

He held onto her. She snuggled in and his embrace grew more caressing and tender. This was what he had wanted. What he longed for.

"Can you feel your hands?" he asked, pulling her away from him.

She wouldn't look him in the eye. "Yes."

He blew on them. Looking at her bent head over her wrists, he felt a keen thrill go through him.

"What?" she said, looking up.

"Huh?"

"Did you say something? Anyway, thank you." She looked away, pulling a hand out of his to knuckle it into her eyes.

He bent his head and kept blowing on her other raw wrist. She let him. He felt breathless.

"You killed Hulgetta, but what about everyone else?" she said.

"Who?"

"At the castle. The maids. My friend, Wart. Did you kill her?"

"How could you think that?" he asked. "And why would I? I didn't kill Hulgetta, either," he confessed. "When I went back to look for her, she was already dead."

"She's immortal."

"Being immortal for a sorceress merely means you won't die of age or disease. She could still be killed by mortal injury."

"At least that wasn't my fault," she said. "Everything else was, though."

He blew on the red skin around her other wrist, and she seemed very absorbed in watching him do this.

"I could only get the weight to the middle of the cuff. The more frustrated I got, the tighter they got. I don't want to be your enemy," she said, fat tears dripping down her cheeks. Her head bent towards his, letting his nose dig into her hair. He breathed in the smell of her and gave a shrug.

"I can't seem to hate you for very long myself."

"You don't really hate me, do you?" she asked. In answer he let his nose slide down hers. His mouth gently kissed across her full lower lip, already swollen from crying. He nibbled on that lower lip.

"I wish everything was different," she said. "I wish…"

He kissed her very sweetly, feeling their fragile bond, and let his body go back to what was intuitive and uncomplicated. Soon they were crawling all over each other, her hands finding his skin as she made little impatient noises. And this time he kept his elf side so firmly in check there was nary a throb or feeling of losing control.

He stopped, and held her chin, which was pink and looked slightly raw from his beard. Nodding to the manacles, he said, "Do you know much about the items Hulgetta had?"

It was a test.

She bit her lip and said, "What do you want to know about?"

"The rings."

"I came through the green door, you know. That's how I got here from Ohio. Well not—"

He kissed her. "That explains the accent," he said. He wanted to know more, but he wanted other things first. Yet restraining himself he listened and she told him about her very odd life in a very odd-sounding place.

∞

"And what did you do in your old life?"

"I was a scholar," she said.

"Explains why a princess doesn't speak the aristo tongue," he said.

"Tell me more about the far left dial on the door. How did you figure out it was a 'go back' lever?"

He shrugged. "It's almost self-explanatory if you look closely at the little icons set around the dial. Hulgetta had a pretty thorough set of coordinates, though. Where did she get them?"

"No idea."

"How did she find your world?" he asked.

"I don't know." Her land was called Smalltown, Ohio.

"And you studied history," he said, fascinated. "Most, if not all, of what I've learned about magic, I found by studying historical chronicles as well."

"I did not study history. I went out into the world with questions, with mysteries about the past that I wanted to solve. I dug up old artifacts from the ground and tried to answer those riddles. It's completely different from just reading old books."

"Not at all. We find magical devices, and try to solve the riddles of how they work by using the ancient chronicles. My old master said that the history of wizards is mostly the history of charlatans. There are fantastical devices of sublime magic in history, but you have to dig."

"Really? So you agree most wizards were charlatans? Hulgetta seemed to think the same thing."

"Which isn't to say they didn't create magnificent illusions that fooled everyone. When I can find an account of real magic, if I read closely, I can often make sense of how to operate a device that hasn't been used in hundreds of years."

She nodded. "Those manacles."

"Quite clever."

"Quite evil."

"The weights you sensed were ball bearings attached together like beads on a necklace. They can roll around the curves of the manacle, but at the same time they can also be stacked vertically. You need the stack to have sufficient weight to spring the release."

"Clever," she admitted.

"Because they are gold, the mechanisms never rust. Do you know anything about the rings?" he asked, peeping at her after a little pause.

"Yes. Well. No, not really."

"Oh?" He didn't believe her.

"Why not just test them out?" she asked. "Fortune favors the bold."

"Curiosity skinned the cat."

"We have a similar saying in my world," she said, with a grin that made his heart kick.

"It's extremely dangerous if you don't know what you're doing."

"I'll admit I'm a bit of a magic addict. Always greedy to learn more. You keep asking about those rings. I think we're more alike than you want to admit."

"Who captured me? It was you, wasn't it?" he said. He couldn't stand this anymore. She looked at him steadily, back and forth in his eyes, as if to check he wasn't going to change on her suddenly.

"I did."

He wished he hadn't asked. His elf heat blazed through him, but he felt compelled to go on.

"Who placed the manacle on my wrist?"

"That was me too, but Hulgetta ordered me to."

"Ordered or asked?"

"I was her apprentice. I was loyal to her up until the end. Until I found out she was going to kill you."

"Did Hulgetta terrorize you into playing the part of a princess? Did she command you to sexually tease and torment me until my fae side burst forth?"

"No. That just happened." He studied her. She was trying not to laugh.

"You liked me, and I was scared by how much I liked you back," she confessed. "I've never been so stuck on anyone. It was like having a meteor crash into me. I can't help but shatter into a million little pieces around you."

∞

She was asleep in his arms. Since they'd begun talking frankly and calmly with each other, they had not moved any further apart than if they had been joined together. He drew her up into his arms as her head lolled on his shoulder, the rest of her body warm and utterly limp. It was a new feeling, to have someone trust him so utterly and completely. It made his heart hurt a little, and she was warm, so he pulled her in closer to him. He couldn't give her up.

Everything unpleasant was behind them. The road ahead was hazy, but if she was at his side, the way would become clear.

"I want you to be my chatelaine," he said, holding onto her, trying to convey through his tone and grip how important the next few moments were. "You would look after the servants, the entire household. Stand at my side. You would be called 'My Lady' and be first in all the land."

She was so still he wanted to poke her to see if she was still breathing. Absolute silence. His fae was slipping under his skin suddenly, his keen feelings turning towards irritation. He could feel it. She was going to say no. Going to hurt him.

Why? his spirit cried out. For a long moment agony paralyzed him even as he waited for her answer.

His fae turned the question inward. *Why did he expect anything else?*

She was a liar. A cold manipulator, so very much like Gabrina of yore. He pulled her face up to his. Her eyes were wide open in the dark, blind, but he could see. He could see the gleam of wetness in them.

"I don't know why I asked," he said, feeling the pulsing in his eyes, wanting only to lash into her with cruel words. "You have no heart. It's impossible for you to love another."

"To be with you," she said, her voice thick and deep with emotion. It did not fool him for one instant. "To be like this with you every night, our bodies wrapped together," she said. "I want this."

Was she starting to say yes? He didn't dare breathe.

"Being with you invited sunshine into my life," he said. The words were a plea, one last strangled hope she wouldn't cast him off into the cold void his life had been up until then. She was so silent, and yet he sensed her intensity.

"And you—would let me study magic with you? I could continue to study sorcery on my own?"

"No. Absolutely not."

Into the silence that was thick and heavy he said, "It's a fair offer."

Her thighs were trembling. He could feel her whole body shaking as she slowly slid away from him and off his chest.

His throat felt thick, the words coming out in a croak. "An honorable offer."

"I am honored," Zephyr said. In the high vibration between them, he wanted to retain control. His fae was there, ready to strike. Ready to get her into a full state of arousal, and then simply leave while she was tied to his bed. Ride off for lands unknown. Would she go mad slowly under the toppling desire that had no relief?

Did she want him to unleash his uncontrolled other half, to tumble onto her and do every lecherous thing his mind could conceive in order to drown out the way her body sang to him?

"You work with magic every day, right here in your home. To promise you I'd live with you and yet never use it, the whole time being near it day after day…"

She was saying no. The cold truth of her answer seeped into him slowly.

He became a block of ice next to her.

"So you won't have me? That's—that's what you're saying?" His mind couldn't quite grasp this fact. It kept slipping away from him. Like the wrong answer to a calculation, it simply could not be. His fae raged and he felt his control slipping away faster than he could yank it around him.

"Yes." She moved towards him. "But—"

"Stop talking," he said. The whip-snap of his tone had her struggling to move away. There was silence in the dark chamber.

He got up.

He was befuddled. He was numb. She loved him. So she said.

He took the tinderbox and lit a candle. He was aching for her and aching because of her. It felt like someone had died, like his own father had died. A raw hollow was all that was left inside him.

She didn't know what it was like to be stuck with magic whether you wanted it or not. Magic was like a tiresome crow outside your window that wouldn't stop cawing. To feel it crawl over your skin, down your mouth, in your throat, urging you onward, ever onward. He stood in the dark in agony. And what was he to do with her?

He changed his linen and put on a doublet over his leggings and tightened the laces. She started to rise from the bench.

"Stay here."

She was sitting up, her gown making a shushing noise around her lush little body.

"You want me to be with you," she said, "and I don't even know your name."

"I would have told you—had you said yes."

He left the chamber, crawling down the stairs to work while the dark cold hours slid at last towards dawn. He couldn't harm her. Not even now when she'd crushed him—again. But he had a plan.

∞

Her mouth felt swollen, her eyes felt swollen. It was blue outside, not quite dawn, but the day was beginning to brighten. She rose from the bed, feeling like a marshmallow, an insubstantial puff of squishy uselessness. She had to pull it together. She didn't want to wear a corset anymore and stripped off the dress she was wearing. She slipped on the nearest thing to hand, which was one of his dark square-necked robes. Pulling it on over her shift, she lifted the hem so she wouldn't trip on the stairs, slipped on the little violet slippers and crept down the long stairs. When she got down to the first floor she moved through the gloom towards the study. She heard him talking to Peter.

"And the man said."

"Said it was Flor-ee-da, not O-hee-o."

"But we're close."

"Same land, different county. That was all I could understand." She wanted to hurl. Surely, he was a brilliant man. Going backwards, he'd found his way back to South America. Now he was working his way north.

"Have you figured out the rings yet?" she asked, entering the study.

"I tried," he said, his voice cold. "I could not find any chronicles that mentioned them." He looked at her with hooded eyes, his mouth grim.

"What else?"

"I examined them with a magnifying glass."

"Yeah? So how's that working out for ya?"

This small mockery drove him ape-shit. A muscle in his forehead throbbed while another muscle in his jaw bulged in and out. All the bitterness of the night before and her answer washed over his expression.

She gripped him, and when he tried to turn away, she turned him back and pulled his head down to kiss him.

The kiss was searing. He pulled her up into him while making her mouth his own. She felt a small surge of triumph. He couldn't keep his hands off her. He couldn't control himself. There was only one solution. *Yes.*

Then he was dragging her towards the door.

"What are you doing?" she said.

"You're going home," he told her. It took her a moment to comprehend what he meant.

"No, no! You said you were going to turn me into a pig. You said you wanted to throttle me. You can't just let me go." It was so much worse than being let go. "I'll take my chances outside the tower, but I'm not—you can't make me go back to Ohio." He could though, he was.

"I could not harm you." He was pulling her towards the green door.

"Last night—"

"I've made no progress with the rings and I don't care. I don't care what you know about them. You are tearing my soul out of my heart."

She grabbed onto the chair with both hands and he had to yank her free.

"Who cares if it takes me a decade? I've worked on other projects longer." He was trying to get her to move forward, towards the tapestry, but the robe was big on her and she was writhing around in it, making it hard for him to get a grip upon her. She got her hands on the table leg again, but he was tearing her fingers away one by one. She wrapped her arms around the leg of the table.

"You're not trustworthy," he said, "and I can't be around you."

"You love me," she reminded him.

"That's right."

"You have feelings for me. I have feelings for you."

He pulled her free of the table. Digging in her bare feet, she grabbed onto the rug and tried to pull back with all her might. "Don't kill me!"

He stopped, and that was when she saw his eyes shift. What's worse, he let it happen. That was when she knew his resolve. She took the opportunity to grip the table leg again, wrapping her arm around it.

"If you send me back, it will be just like killing me. There's no magic back there." Her voice broke.

"I'm not going to kill you. I can't. You're too precious to me."

He cupped her face, but she didn't trust him and tightened her death grip on the table leg.

"Would you let me go back to the castle?" she asked, and she saw a flicker of wary hope dart through his eyes. They were even larger than normal, offset by curving wide cheeks. "I want to stay here. With you. I want to stay."

"No," he said. She fought him with every nail and kick and punch she had in her.

Soon he had her hands free. She did everything she could to squirm out of his arms, clawing at his chin and neck to get free, scratching him and leaving long pink scrapes, knocking her elbows about. Meanwhile he held her tightly, protectively, inhibiting her movement, like she was a precious package. Yet his determination was firm and he was easily the stronger of the two.

They were now at the tapestry and Peter was holding it aside, unlatching the final lock on the green door. The door was opening. She paused in his arms, watching it with a kind of horror.

It was a country meadow. A car sped past. His muscles were bunching as he prepared to cast her through the opening. Everything slowed down and she felt like she was in a nightmare, like she was struggling to move through thick syrup, half paralyzed.

"I am sending you back to O-hi-o," he told her, pronouncing the name with care. She looked through the door as another car passed by, and then up at him.

"I know exactly how the rings work," she panted. "I'll tell you."

CHAPTER NINETEEN

"So you lied earlier."

"Yup."

"Tell me," he commanded.

She knew nothing about the rings. She was stalling for time.

The key would be in making him believe that she knew something, and stalling some more, buying time somehow. Escape. That was all she could think of.

Through the green door, back to Hulgetta's castle. Once there she'd have minutes—if that—to destroy the door. It was her only option.

Meanwhile, she had to bluff.

"A sorceress made this," she said, tapping the blue ring on the fossilized hand. It lay between them on the table. She had her back to the windows, Peter hovered near the door, and her elf-wizard stood before her, his hair tousled, his doublet green like his eyes.

"How is that possible? A sorceress would not make a ring."

"Not ordinarily. But just because it isn't usual doesn't mean it can't be done."

"How can you tell?"

"The blue ring is an opposition to the black one. A sorceress would think of that, not a wizard. Sorcery always works in terms of oppositional forces."

She hoped it would sound obvious once she pointed it out. It seemed obvious to her.

"Look," she continued. "The blue ring has a chalice. The blue stone represents water in the chalice. What does a chalice stand for? It stands for wizardry, doesn't it? See, the two hands that made it are represented as well. But because of its shape, the chalice stands for a woman. And the blue stone stands for water, which quenches fire. The hands are a woman's hands. Which brings us to this ring," she said, tapping the black one and watching it flare momentarily with a reddish orange glow. She smiled down on it.

"It represents fire," he said.

"Yes. Fire is a base element for all sorcery. Fire represents knowledge. The strongest sorcerers control fire and earth."

"What do you control?"

"I—well, nothing. Yet." She thought of the moss maid, which was earth, but sadly, she hadn't gotten through much of the earth elements in her studies yet.

Water quenching fire. Desire quenching knowledge. The ring represented desire. She would have bet on it.

"The blue ring probably was made second, because it is more replete with symbology."

"So someone made the black ring, and someone else made the blue one in opposition to it."

"Could be. But they're linked. That's the important thing. A ring of knowledge and a ring of desire."

The black ring had a minimal setting of silver. Enough to encircle the finger—or thumb, and fierce claws. Very spare. Enough to hold onto the dark crystal and not much more. The blue ring was more ornate, elegant. An entirely different style. Actually, she bet that two different hands had made each ring.

"This is all speculation. How do they work?"

"You put on one ring and I put on the other."

"I tried that yesterday. Nothing happened."

"If you tried wearing both rings together, of course it didn't work. Like I said, they're oppositional. You need someone the opposite of you."

He looked at Peter, then back at her, skepticism plain on his face.

"And don't look at Peter, you need a woman. Were they glowing yesterday like they are now?" She stroked the rings and they both flamed up with color. Around him they glowed twice as brightly as before.

"A bit. No. Not as much," he admitted. For the first time she saw the elf-wizard hesitate, and she knew she had him hooked.

"You're methodical, logical. I'm impulsive and bold. You're a man, and I'm a woman. Sorceress and Wizard."

"Sane… and deranged."

"Har, har. Aren't you curious about the knowledge the ring might give you? You won't see what they can really do until we put them on."

He gave her a look, as if trying to judge just how far he should believe her.

"And then what happens?"

"Fire is knowledge, water is desire. The rings will manifest your knowledge and amplify my desirable qualities. Or my desire."

Moss maid, I'm telling you, I couldn't stand feeling any more desire than I already do. It would kill me. Talking over magic with him—was there any greater bliss in the world? If only it could be like this every day. She would ask for nothing else.

She watched the elf-wizard's face, and she could see he was riding the edge. The first person to fly, the first man to step into space, each one must have had to make the leap of faith. She was excited, curious, and so ready to leap.

He looked uncertain, trepidatious, as if he was leaping to his death. He was just like her though. They both wanted to taste the unknown. It was addictive.

Sometimes magic had a certain smell, like that of singed hair. It was in the air right now. She'd smelled it twice before, but never this strongly.

He didn't like it. She could tell, but he was looking at the rings silently pulse as she stroked them, and finally he could bear it no more. He took the black ring off the petrified hand.

"Don't do it," Peter said.

The elf-wizard shoved the black ring on his finger.

"No, master!" Peter shouted.

She grabbed the blue ring. Shoved it on her middle finger.

His eyes looked into hers.

He said, "Well?"

"Don't you feel it?" she asked. The throbbing was so quick and real between them. She could feel his pulse and taste his sweat from here. It was probably the elf side to him, but his eyes stayed green. And then she knew. She held him in her hand.

"Feel what?" he said.

"The desire."

His head went back and she knew he was experiencing the rush. She felt her power, raw power, while a yearning look came over his face. Was that what she looked like pining for him? Did he feel the thick want pounding at his senses? Yes. She watched as the sensation hit him like heroin. His eyes turned black.

Now it was time.

"No, master." Peter's voice was without hope.

"You feel it?" she said.

She felt the lust herself. Lust for power, lust for magic.

Your magic. Your tower. Your books.

She wanted to know him down to his naked soul.

Your ring.

"Give me your ring," she said. "I want it."

He gave it to her, his eyes turning her way, but it was too late to ensorcell her. Too late! She slid the black ring onto her left forefinger.

∞

Alarm flooded her system, tightening the back of her neck like an invisible hand choking her. The room tilted. Her hands flew forward, smacking into the hard edge of a wooden table, and her fingernails sank in. But the tilt-a-whirl was inside her. All her internal organs had gone on a sudden roller coaster ride.

Then it stopped. Her nose was filled with the smell of burning hair. Magic. Happening somewhere near.

Someone groaned. She knew exactly how they felt. She pulled her face up from the table, sweat springing out across her body. The headache releasing, like a tight hand lifting off of the back of her neck. She tentatively lifted her torso to find a delicate page of onion skin from a book clinging to her cheek. Saliva pooled in her mouth as she peeled the page off with care and stood straight. *Deep breath. Deep breath. Oh god.* It was like being carsick—only there was no car. *Make it stop, please.*

The burning hair smell began to fade. *Holy maggots. Look what I did.* She smoothed two badly creased pages on the book, a little panicked. She caressed it again, looking at the letters. The writing looked like long, excited worms making love across the page. Had to be high Anslod. She only knew the low form, which looked more like chopped up worms, writhing in pain. The low form was used for the recipe part of a spell or potion, the high form for incantations and other things. Hulgetta had usually translated the incantations for her into the low form if it was needed. Yet as Zephyr stared at the letters, the gnarled root clumps began making sense.

Yet. in. the end.

She smoothed the paper absentmindedly with her left hand. Suddenly the black rock of a ring on her finger lit up a blazing reddish orange. More worm words caught her eye.

King… Lurling… gave her the… Pearl… (something) elf (something)… Marcella… She blinked hard and stared, concentrating, swallowing down the sick feeling as best she could.

Yet in the end, even Marcella betrayed King Lurling. He gave her the Pearl of Thumrod, though she was of common blood, naming her Queen. This offended his men, who were all high-born, and they attempted to depose their king. As the men fought, creating unrest for over a decade, into this contentious land came elf warrior Halsong. The elf laid his black eye upon Marcella. Though she fought his will and attempted to drown herself, it was an enchantment most severe. In the end she followed the elf warrior from the kingdom. King Lurling in his rage threw their four children from the highest tower and spoke her name no more. To this day no one knows where the Pearl of Thumrod with great magical powers lies.

Bananas. She stared at the page, but yeah, she could totally read it. Thrilled and not a little confounded, she looked up and saw the green door. It was revealed underneath a tapestry that was on the wall opposite the table where she was standing. *Oh, this place.* She knew this room. She just couldn't place what she was supposed to be doing here at the moment. She looked down at the rings on her fingers. The black one had died down. The blue ring, however, threw up ripples of light like the water's dancing reflection.

My ring.

She looked around the room, which, frankly, was like her dream library. Books of magic? Check. Beautiful, quiet, serene? Check. Here she was somehow, a sorceress, in a beautiful tower, mistress of magic, and—

My books, my tower, my ring.

"I'm a freaking sorceress," she said out loud.

It sounded so unreal.

"The Sorceress Zephyr!" Better.

Yet something was wrong. Something felt wrong. She wasn't a sorceress. It seemed so obvious she was not a sorceress. Wait, wasn't she supposed to get something for Hulgetta? Bring something to her?

Yes! That initial splurge of great satisfaction and ownership immediately shrank down to nothing. She had the feeling time had passed, a lot of time. Was Hulgetta expecting her back? A hole of sucking dread opened inside her. *I didn't complete my task. I didn't get back to her with the whatsit. Agggggh.*

She had never failed her mistress before. Never. Perhaps it wasn't too late. What was it she was supposed to bring? She looked around the room on the tables. Nothing came to mind. Her eyes darted towards the tapestry. Then the door. She frowned. Still couldn't remember.

A man stood to one side of the door, pushed against the wall, his face frozen in horror, mouth agape. Her eyes darted from his balding long face and stooped shoulders to his plain brown clothes. A servant. No use asking him what she was supposed to bring her mistress.

Her heart was hammering.

She looked around at all the other books scattered across the table, taking up first one and then another while the dark rock of a ring on her finger blazed. *Okay. Get a grip. Stop scrambling.* She needed just a second to figure out what was going on.

Wait—this book. She held up the spine to the morning light streaming in the windows. *Enchantments of the Air*. She knew that book. Hulgetta had one just like it. And here was another. *How to Dry Spotted Creatures for use in Potions, Spells, and More*. She spotted another of Hulgetta's favorite books open on the large table. In fact, Hulgetta's books were stacked all over the entire table. *So I've got Hulgetta's books now.* She'd dusted the books so many times she knew all their covers by heart—even the covers of those she couldn't read yet. However, looking at them now, she suddenly realized that she *could* read them. *Swallow. Swallow. Don't be sick all over the nice books. Control yourself.*

"These are Hulgetta's books." She kept looking at them, but was talking to the servant. "How did they come to be here?"

"We brought them through the green door. Hulgetta is dead."

Now it was her turn to gape at the man in utter shock.

"Dead? You're absolutely sure?"

He nodded. Hulgetta dead? Hoooo boy.

The sensation of being utterly lost compounded. She remembered stepping into this wonderful library, but then: nothing. Just a blank and the stinking smell of bad magic wafting up her nose.

Well. She moved over to the windows and cranked them open. *Clear the air, clear my head, yes.*

Order out of chaos.

Someone moaned.

"Who's that?" She whirled, forgetting about Hulgetta, forgetting even about the books when she saw him.

He was in the shadow of the fifteen-foot bookshelf, plastered near the door, a midsummer's dream come to life. Dark reddish hair, darker eyebrows, pale skin that matched the dirty marble color of the column. He moaned again and an interesting flush stained his wide carved cheek bones. She drifted closer, taking in the tender pillow of his lower lip. Yes, he was fit to play the lover of a fairy queen. His face was as pale as if it had been washed in moonlight.

He gave another soft groan. *Poor man.* She reached up and touched his face. His brow was icy, and the feel of her hand on his face made him frown and shut his eyes more tightly. Yet when she tried taking her hand away, he took it and held it with his own to his face, like he was about to float away on a desolate shipwrecked sea without her touch.

She looked back over at the servant. He seemed familiar to her, but her brain hurt trying to place him.

"Forgive me, it's—"

"Peter."

"Yes, Peter. This man is ill. What can we do to help him?"

The servant looked at her, his eyes alarmed, and stayed right where he was. Not really so plain, but a long face, an intelligent face, and sensitive.

"Here, at least sit down," she told the midsummer prince.

“This way, come this way.” Her voice caressed him as she pulled him slowly by the arm down into a stiff spindly old chair of ornately carved wood and a tapestry back. Many such littered the room. It creaked and groaned as he sprawled in it. He was feeling sick too, wasn’t he? Perhaps with the same thing that had got to her.

A spell. Was it killing him?

CHAPTER TWENTY

He put one hand out, sharply clutching hers, like he trusted her. *A spell gone wrong in the study.*

"Get a stool," she said to Peter, who drew up a matching stool and helped her lift the gorgeous man's feet to the red crimson silk pillow.

He collapsed, more or less, his limbs sprawling, his head hanging off to the side. She stood next to the chair and he buried his head in her hip like it ached. A small, pathetic groan issued between his lips. Her hands crept out to hold either side of his head. *Poor thing. Poor thing!*

He seemed to like the feel of her hands on his head, and turned his cheek into her palm again, pressing it tight with his other hand. His lips touched her palm and a thread of buzzing excitement ran all the way down to the girdle of her hips.

"Dizzy? It'll stop soon. Take deep breaths." The servant was standing there, still gaping.

"Wine?"

The servant hesitated and she saw the wheels of his mind turning furiously behind his eyes. They were opened wide, showing the whites all around. She turned back to her moon prince, and that's when she noticed the ears.

An elf. She blinked rapidly. *Hulgetta's books. A beautiful tower.* Her mind could not put it all together. *Hulgetta's dead.* It was like a giant jigsaw puzzle, but she only had four pieces. Where were all the other pieces?

"What's going on," she whispered to the elf. He shook his head.

She glanced at the servant out of the corner of her eye. He was clearly of no use.

"Peter? Wine?" she said, reminding him. He startled and was gone from the room.

So she held the poor, incredibly attractive elf's head to her hip. He wrapped an arm around her and held on. Gradually, very gradually, he sat up a little. He put a hand over his eyes and rested. She could watch him all day. An elf. Like out of Tolkien—the hot kind, with a terrible beauty. Wait—weren't they usually cursed?

The servant came back with wine. A small slip of a woman with soft brown hair and big giant eyes followed behind him, carrying a plate of biscuits. "Thank you—?"

"Dorcas, mistress."

"Dorcas, thank you. I think he's feeling a bit better." Dorcas bobbed a curtsey, looked at her like she had two heads, and scrammed.

She poured a generous amount into a tumbler and held it to his lips. He drank, and after a bit he did indeed start to look better. His eyes opened a little, and she placed the tumbler into his hand, closed his fingers around it. She moved back to behind the table and her hands drifted over the books.

The whisper came again as she touched the pages.

Your books, your tower, your magic.

"Peter, tell me what's going on. Do you know what's happening?"

She went to the shelves that ran down the entire length of the room. Running her hands over the bindings of the books she noticed how her ring lit up like Rudolph's nose.

A History of the Durlailian Years. The Wizard Wars: Volume One. Hugor's Song. She could read them all. They were history books. *Hagnar's Song* was in a different language from the other two. Was it all history? *Yawn.*

She drew the book out. As she read the words from *Hagnar's Song*, the black ring blazed.

Where dale and daffodil lie on sandy river's bosom in Mar/there the body of Hagnar lay for seven hundred years/a skeleton in armor/his glorious deeds unsung

She looked back at the gorgeous elf-man. He was sitting up, leaning forward, his face in his hands, cup on the table. They were well-shaped hands, matching well-shaped legs. She was particularly taken with the little bulge of his thigh muscle just where it met the dent above his knee.

She picked out another book, *Wizard's Cats Throughout the Ages*.

"Look, Peter, it's all right. Let's get to the bottom of this," she said, tired of waiting.

Peter looked at her, then back at the elf.

"Master, you're under a grave enchantment," he said to the elf.

A cold itch of horror started to spread through her lower gut.

"Sorry?" she said, looking at them. She shook her head. The gorgeous elf-man's head was leaning way back against the chair, the maid—Dorcas—waving her apron to fan him. He looked unconscious again. He'd gone back to the dirty marble color.

"Peter?" she said. "I'm sorry. You were saying something?"

He began to talk, but somehow it put her into a heavy doze.

She perked up again. "I'm so sorry, I must have drifted off. What did you say? Oh. Oh! Poor man!" The elf was vomiting onto a rug.

"Peter. Peter, get a basin."

Once all was calm, Peter opened his mouth, but she held up her hand to stop him.

Your ring, your power, your tower, your books, the voice inside the ring said, lilting and with a little feminine echo. She looked down at the blue ring. It glimmered across the surface of the stone, like light behind cracked ice.

"I'm a sorceress," she said, lifting her head up and speaking to the ceiling since she was a little too nervous to speak to the men. "Well, a new one." She grimaced, not feeling like she sounded at all credible. *Say it like you mean it.*

"The sorceress Zephyr!" *There. Sounded much better.*

"I knew a beautiful sorceress once. Beautiful and treacherous." The elf-man spoke. He slowly sat up again, his eyes still closed.

"Did you know Hulgetta? She's not what I would call beautiful exactly."

"He killed your mistress," Peter said, pointing to the man. "He did it. He killed Hulgetta."

"Really?" She studied him again. So Hulgetta really was dead? He didn't look like a killer. He looked like the exact opposite. She couldn't take it in. "How? She's immortal."

"He cut off her head."

"I don't remember that," the elf-man said. Zephyr took a step away from him. Her mind tossed around the words like a hot potato.

The blue ring blazed.

You are the mighty Sorceress Zephyr.

What's happening?

Your books. Your tower. Your magic.

"Did the other sorceress die as well? The beautiful one, I mean," she asked the elf-man.

"Gabrina? No."

"Tell me, what is your name?" she said.

"I don't understand. What's going on?" He looked up at her, then Peter.

Not what I asked, Mr. Elfy-pants.

"Master." Peter stepped forward. "Master, she's to blame for all this."

Zephyr put a hand to her forehead. If only this sick dizzy feeling would go away. The room stank. Really stank of burning hair. *Ugh.*

"What were we saying?" She turned and looked at the elf-man in the chair. He looked ghastly pale. She could see the veins under his skin. "Oh, yes. I told you my name is Zephyr. What's yours?"

He rose and swayed before her. Even as she watched the white color started to drain.

"Watch out!" she said. He fell like a tree. She caught his head and prevented it from bouncing off the stones just in time. Kneeling beside him, her robes pooling around her legs, the square front sagged open. She quickly gave his slick, sweaty, cold face a few little slaps.

"Elf-man! Gorgeous elf-man," she said, but he was out cold. She whirled around.

"What did you do?" she said, accusing Peter. *Something in his eyes.* He knew what was going on. "You're playing with us. I demand you stop it at once."

He gave her a furious stare. "Me stop? You're to blame for all this—"

"For what?" she demanded.

"It's working upon you—upon both of you."

She came to in the chair. Had she passed out? She felt vile. Swallowing down the knot of nausea at the back of her mouth, she looked at Peter, furious. Somehow this was all his fault. God, would that smell of burnt hair just go away? He looked back at her, grave and unhappy.

Make him fear you.

"I am the mistress of this tower, Peter. Is that understood?"

"Yes."

"Whatever you just did—don't do it again."

He ducked his head. She accepted it as a sign of agreement.

"Where did the elf-man go?"

Peter nodded with his chin at something behind the table. She saw boots. *Oh no.*

Your tower, your books, your elf.

She ignored the greedy voice, and went behind the table, sinking onto her knees, trembling with concern. The elf-man was lying there, pale as parchment, but his eyes were open and blinking. *Poor man. Poor, poor man.*

"Here," she said, pulling on his sleeves and hauling him up so his head could lie upon her bosom instead of the cold ground. He'd been through the wringer. He was dripping with sweat and trembling slightly. "You can't just lie about on the carpet all day," she said, trying for a little bit of humor.

His face was chalky white, but he turned and looked at her with big eyes of confusion. *Oh my god.* She forced herself not to bury his heavy head into her breasts, howsoever much she wanted to. His face was the glowing white one gets from fainting.

When she got him up and back into a chair again, she said "Where do you hail from, stranger? And why are you here?"

"Hail?"

"Who are your people?" His face fell. *Whoops. Bad question.* Suddenly he was watchful, struggling with some emotion at the same time.

"I have no people." He stood, so she stood as well, her hands out in case he grew wobbly again.

"A man of mystery, eh? Come on. You can tell me. What's your name?"

"Eldred Fire Eater."

She pulled away and studied his face. He wouldn't meet her eye. He was a terrible liar.

"Hmmm. I don't think so. Try again."

"This tower was once Eldred Fire Eater's. I was his apprentice."

"And where is Eldred?"

"Dead."

She was starting to get the feeling that being a magic worker resulted in a shorter life span.

"I assume from all these books that he was a sorcerer."

"No. He was a wizard."

"Well, possession is nine-tenths the law. This tower and these books are mine now."

Your tower, your books, your magic. The gentle voice of the blue ring took on an edge in her head, while the stone glimmered and flashed. *Cool.* She looked back at the elf.

His hands were gripping his hair.

"Master," Peter said.

"That's enough out of you, Peter," she told him. "Why are you even here? Isn't there something useful you can do elsewhere?"

Peter gaped at her.

Your desire. Your books, your tower, your magic.

"I just want you to tell me what your name is," she said to the elf. He looked at her with fogged eyes.

"Theodorus. Theo." He stared at her, his voice thick, his mouth open, his eyes staring at her own lips.

"Thank you. Was that so hard? What happened to you, Theo?"

"Master!"

"You," she snarled at Peter. "You can stand here and shut up, or take yourself off. Your choice. But if you stay, just shut your pie hole. Got it?"

He stood there, silently.

"Very well," she said, and turned back to the elf.

CHAPTER TWENTY-ONE

His head was splitting and he was dismayed to see such a gentle lady, her tone throbbing with compassion, a vision of simple prettiness, suddenly turn snarling upon the servant Peter.

How odd that she wore an oversized black robe much like he wore when doing magic in the study. Yet this robe was too large for her more petite form. It sagged across her shoulders and the square-cut front slid low, revealing taut, milky breasts. The robe pooled over her thighs, outlining them clearly in black. Her naked body underneath the shifting cloth was tempting, even as the room still spun around him. That little suggestion of a dent in her stubborn chin drove him mad. He felt the restless fury and passion of his inner fae stirring. His eyes throbbed and the room filled with colors that should not have been there.

He blinked. He took a deep breath and regained some measure of his equilibrium. *Right.* "Since my master's death, I've been…here," he said. No, that couldn't be right. He'd been too wretched after the debacle three months before to do much more than make a pretense of studying. Every day he wanted to leave, to avoid these objects that reminded him constantly of his master and his death. But go where?

He must have decided and eventually left. How long ago had that been? He had no idea.

"Where did you get these?" she said, pointing to Hulgetta's books.

"I—I don't remember…"

"Peter says you killed the sorceress who owned them."

He looked at the books and blinked. They looked vaguely familiar. Vaguely, but that was all.

"Such is the way of magic workers. I remember none of it."

"No?" Her manner was decisive for such a young and fair maid. Who was she? Where had she come from?

"And your master? How did he meet his end?"

Woe smote him afresh. He looked at her and his eyes filled with the beginning of tears.

"I killed him. I killed him, too." Remorse flooded him as if it had happened yesterday. He touched his heart, which ached with guilt and loathing.

"There was a sorceress," he told the fair maid. "Named Gabrina."

"And she was beautiful?" She had leaned against the table and clutched her hands around her knee, lacing them together.

"Very beautiful, yes. She seduced Eldred, my master, and so confounded his senses that he would do anything she desired. She called upon him to fight a dragon."

"A dragon!" She was breathless, her eyes aglow. "Did he actually fight a dragon?"

"We tried."

"Both of you! But why did you decide to kill a dragon?"

"Gabrina wanted the dragon's blood. She'd been wounded, she said, by her enemies and needed it to live. So she said."

The maid seemed to read his thoughts, her eyes scanning his face.

"But you were dubious."

"I saw no wound, nor sign of it. Dragon's blood, when used carefully, can make a mortal age backwards."

"She wanted the blood to stay young. A woman of a certain age, then."

"So I thought. But I could not convince my master she lied. We fought the dragon, which bit him, and the poisoned venom drove him beyond reason. At one point he rushed at me, thinking I was his sworn enemy and fighting me with his sword in his delusion." He looked at Peter. Then back to her. "It was her fault. She cursed him, and it drove him mad."

"Then what happened?"

"We fought and—I killed him."

"Murderer!" hissed Peter, aghast.

"I meant to confess my crime against him, but…"

"Horrible," she interrupted. "Horrible for you, I mean. So Gabrina was an enchantress?"

"No. No. A sorceress."

"Sorceress! Are you sure? Did you ever see her do any sorcery?"

"No."

"She sounds like an enchantress to me. I suppose they sneak up on you. At any rate, that's what I've heard."

He didn't respond. Gabrina, an enchantress. It seemed rather obvious, and a fresh welling of shame and loathing poured over him.

"You murdered our master!" Peter pointed at him with an accusing, trembling finger. "We trusted an elf and you betrayed us. They'll hang you when they find out," he promised.

"They won't hang him if they don't know," the maid bit out, and her voice held a warning in it.

"You lied." Peter said, nothing but contempt in his tone. He did not even see how he was stirring the pretty maid to wrath. "We saw your meek demeanor, we saw your burns, and we told ourselves you'd been injured helping him. The whole time you deceived us all. Laughing up your sleeve."

"Now, does he look like the type to laugh up his sleeve?" the maid demanded.

"Never trust an elf."

"Nonsense. You see how it was," the maid said. "He had no choice." She seemed singularly free of the prejudice that was so common he'd begun to take it for granted and lower himself in the estimation of all others accordingly. It was not their estimation of him that caused him to willfully murder the man he was closest to, he reminded himself.

"I don't know how to live with myself." His voice broke, and his throat was thick with emotion. It was all flooding back. Touching his chest, his heart, it felt somehow more sensitive and tender than before. He felt worse, if possible. The pain welled up fresh all over again, as if it had happened just the day before.

"Deceiver. Murdering dog." Peter's voice was shaking as his face turned dark pink.

The maid rounded upon him. "If you say anything of this, Peter, you will suffer for it." The maid—Zephyr—stood toe to toe with the tall servant, staring him down, even though she had to tilt her head back to do it. Peter's mouth tightened in a downturn but she did not back down, though he was older than she and had lived in the tower and the lands surrounding it his whole life.

"Put yourself in his shoes," she told the servant. "Imagine Eldred decided you should go with him to fight the dragon and left Theo here. Imagine it was you he had turned against in a maddened state."

She waited, watching the servant's face, until a glimmering of understanding crept into Peter's face. "You were the one who staggered back to the tower. And they all assumed that the dragon had killed your master. What would you have done, tormented, with remorse gnawing at your heart? You look a clever fellow. Would you have confessed all? That you killed your master even though you didn't mean to?"

Yes, she had a will of iron. She stood there confident she was in the right, and Peter's confidence wavering, he dropped his eyes before her.

"No," he said, frowning. "No, miss. I mean, mistress. I would have hid the truth."

"Why should Theo be blamed? Clearly the whole thing was this Gabrina person's scheme—if anyone is to blame it is her. Could none of you see she was an enchantress?"

He looked up at the ceiling. Being called a gullible dupe somehow did not soothe the canker in his heart. No more than being called a guilty murdering dog. His inner fae, watching her form, that long hair and her deep blue eyes, gave a strong thump. He breathed in and felt the throb quicken behind his eyes and down below.

"And then?" She turned, addressing Theo. "Where is this Gabrina now?"

"While I fought my master, Gabrina cursed him and ran away."

"Did she come back here?"

He looked at Peter who shook his head.

"The last time I saw that mistress of evil, she was on a mountainside mocking me with laughter while my master lay at my feet, the life leaking out of him."

He stifled a sob. "His senses were restored before he died. He forgave me everything, Peter." He ground his palms into his eyes, remembering how he had knelt over Eldred's limp blood-covered body and wept.

When he looked up again, Zephyr was watching Peter with a cunning expression on her face. "Peter, what compensation do you receive for your service?"

"Eight dreckles a quarter, miss. Mistress."

"What if it were twelve?"

"Twelve!"

"On the understanding that you keep your mouth shut. Not that Theo wasn't justified. But because you're right—he should have told everyone when he came back. Why didn't you explain?" She turned to him again abruptly. "Not right away—I can understand that. But eventually. Why didn't you say?"

"I hadn't attempted to conceal anything. They all assumed my master fought the dragon and lost. No one asked what happened."

"He shut himself up in the tower," Peter said, "and let his wicked deed fester. We assumed he was mourning."

"I was too ashamed." He turned to the sorceress. "I still am." He rubbed the area over his heart. It ached acutely.

Zephyr looked at Peter. "Now he's confessed. It's time to think of yourself. What are we going to do with you, Peter? Can we trust you with this secret?"

"Of course, mistress. I've loyally served the tower since I was a lad this high." He put his hand at the height of the table covered with books.

"Well, you've proven your loyalty today. In addition to the extra dreckles, why don't we find some new responsibilities for you."

Theo watched Peter who was listening with all his might. The sorceress was very shrewd to have observed Peter and gotten the measure of the man so quickly. He lived to serve, but preferred to serve in larger measures, rather than smaller deeds. Before his very eyes, Peter came out of his stoop, his eyes filled with wary calculation, but a helpful eagerness too.

"There are the crop reports," Peter said, only hesitating a little. "Master Theo was to look them over days ago. The farmers urgently wish an assessment." He looked at Theo. Yes, Theo hated assembling the reports. A tedious task, and frankly, he'd rather do just about anything other than read about or discuss farming.

"There you go," the sorceress said, gliding about in her black oversized robe. "I myself know nothing about crop reports, but perhaps you can look them over and explain them all to me. You can write, yes?"

"I can. I mean, yes, mistress."

"Good," the sorceress said. "Well, go write out a report then. A report on the reports."

"And record the—the dreckles, mistress? In the accounting book?"

"Of course."

Peter pulled his forelock and began marching out of the room with his shoulders squared. Then he remembered and turning, ducked a quick bow to Theo. The sorceress turned and aimed her full attention on him and Theo felt a new flood of self-awareness, even a hint of alarm.

"So. Your master is dead. What will you do now?"

He wandered over to the window, crushing a leaf of fragrant geranium and smelling the scent of the leaf. "I don't know. Leave. Wander."

She didn't seem to like that answer at all. She strode restlessly up and down the carpet, kicking her feet out from the long hem of the robe. "But where will you go? Where is your home? What is to be your purpose in life?"

"My home is here. At least it *was*," he said, defensively. He knew not how she came to displace him. His memory was in a fog, out of reach. Her every question plucked at awful feelings he'd tried to bury deep, exhausting him. He felt the need for penance with every wretched memory she called forth.

"Did you grow up here? Your master, was he your—"

"No. Not at all. I grew up in the East. I'm half, you know."

"Pardon?"

"Half elf. And no, he wasn't my father," he said in answer to the question in her eyes.

His head hurt and his memory of the last few days remained enshrouded in fog.

"Where did you grow up?"

"I grew up with my father in the north. He's an elf, but then war came to our land. He did not trust his people to care for me while he was away fighting, so he sent me east, to my mother's people."

"Oh. Did your father come back for you when his battle ended, or—"

"He did not. I waited for him. Then I grew tired of waiting. Eventually, I left the humans to find him. By that time I had reached the age when the fae side begins to emerge, and it became more troublesome as I journeyed."

"That doesn't sound good."

"When I went home… Things happened that I could not take back. My father would not allow me to stay." He swallowed down a lump of shame. Why did he not go to the river and drown his worthless flesh? With all his faults in clear array about him, it seemed the only way for him to avoid bringing down disaster and shame upon other innocent people. And then he killed his master. Clearly his father was right to shun him.

Bleak emotions like sharp rocks on a stormy sea shore began to wash over him. A wild frenzy of fresh grief threatened to engulf him once more. He looked up to find she'd crept closer to him. She grasped at his sleeve with her gentle hand and held his wrist and hand in her own smaller ones.

"How does a father abandon his son?" Again her sympathetic sorrow was an arrow right into his heart. "How could he abandon you to strangers and not come back?" Her tone was so very sad on his behalf. The sympathy utterly undid him. A feeling of sweet solace began to steal through his veins. The memory of her long fingers holding onto his head comforted him. He wanted to lie with this maid—in the worst way. Worse still, he was already half in love with her.

His heart strained towards her. *It is you who are the enchantress.*

No one had sympathized with him over his past in such a way before. He looked at her and felt his eyes begin to throb with emotion. With her fair hair curling all down to her waist, she—the thrumming of his eyes grew stronger. *No. No, that can't happen.*

She blinked at him and he realized she'd caught the change. He took a pull upon himself, stuffing his fae side down. He turned away, gently withdrawing his hand from hers. He needed to be stronger than this. He rose and pulled away from that hand on the sleeve of his arm. He turned away.

"You should stay here," she offered to his back. "Would you like to learn sorcery?"

"No. My old master scorned sorcery and those who practiced it. A lesser art, he always said, until he met the cursed Gabrina and was confounded."

"What!" She sounded so outraged, like a wet hen, that he had to smile. "Sorcery is the finest magic there is."

"Not if Gabrina is any example."

"Gabrina was an enchantress. Clearly."

"I suppose we'll never know."

He did not like women who worked magic. Already her impulsivity terrified him a little. But where would he go? He remembered the lonely road back to the tower, the smell of his master's blood in his nostrils, his master's blood staining his wet clothes, the icy rain pelting him all the way back.

"I want," she hesitated, and looked down at the smaller ring on her right hand. "I want you to stay here. To become my apprentice." She twisted the blue ring on her finger. He turned away again, resolving not to look at her another time. But some bewitching force of personality spoke to him, took him by the neck with a sinuous shake of authority. He must stay here. He must see what she knew of magic, and make sure she didn't hurt herself or anyone else with her impulsive whims. He couldn't see the landscape outside the window. All of him wanted to accept her offer.

"I've been an apprentice." Resisting her was surprisingly hard.

"But I want you to stay." Her words were forlorn, and yet a blast of her will hit him full on, like a giant cold wave washing over his head and through his heart. He mentally staggered beneath it and found her terrible, not kind at all. No, no, he would not. But before he could even think, the next wave washed over him, and the next.

Stop. "Stop. I'll stay," he heard himself say. This was magic. He knew it, and gave into it, at the same time marking it for examination later.

"You don't have to," she said in a rush. He found himself staring down at her again, puzzled. Now she seemed guilty, twisting and twisting the ring about her finger, pinching at the blue stone. That ring. She'd used it on him, and now she felt bad. It was some kind of wishing ring.

He couldn't stay. He did not want someone using him against his will. Yet all the same, a wanting poured through him and tore him in two. He was weary of loneliness and full of longing. He wanted her company, and the desire to pull her close into his own body and whisper nothings to her was a compelling need. If he left, sharp teeth of wanting would gnaw into him, not leaving him alone.

"I will not learn spells."

CHAPTER TWENTY-TWO

She sputtered as if to say, *What person in their right mind wouldn't want to learn spells?*

"So you won't stay, then?"

He was grave. "I'll stay."

"But not because you want to study spells."

"Because I have nowhere else to go."

Her eyes went big and wide when he said that. The dark cornflower blue watered up with tears and sympathy. He observed it, but made no move towards her, a little afraid of her now. The fresh feeling of bitterness and doom from his confession about his master's death mired him down as if a heavy, wet net had been cast over him. And now this—he was a pawn to a sorceress.

Dorcas put her head in again. She looked flustered as she curtseyed. "Have you seen Peter, master? We're low on firewood."

"Dorcas?" Zephyr said.

"Yes, miss?" Dorcas looked confused.

"Is firewood really that important at this very moment?" Zephyr asked.

"Tis, miss," Dorcas said. "Dinner must be cooked, bread baked, ale brewed." The heart of an abode ran on an endless diet of firewood.

"Then Theo shall assist you—Dorcas, is it? And ask Peter to draw up the apprentice articles."

Dorcas seemed struck into stone. For a full five minutes she stared at them both unmoving.

"Who for?" she asked at last, wiping her hands on her apron.

"For him," Zephyr gestured in his direction.

"Where's Peter?" she asked him, her voice hoarse, eyes wide.

"He's upstairs," Zephyr answered, "assembling the crop reports, I imagine. Is there a reason that Theo will not do?" The sorceress gestured to him.

Dorcas stared at him, consternation writ upon her tired face. "Theo?"

"Yes."

Dorcas looked at her and then at him, then back at her again. "Crop reports?" she said distractedly, and began twisting her apron between her hands.

"Yes, and for that, I've given him a raise. From eight dreckles to… I think we agreed on twelve."

"Twelve dreckles? Twelve!" Dorcas cried. She put her hands up to her head.

"Is there something wrong?"

"Nothing. A man can marry and raise a family on twelve dreckles a year," she said. "Oh, mistress!"

"Is that so? Well." She eyed the maid carefully for a long moment. "Provided he chooses a good wife, Peter should be quite happy, then."

Dorcas's face went blazing beet red. "I'll have Peter write up the prentice articles and come find you," she said, and ran out of the room.

Zephyr turned to him. "I guess we don't need to be so formal, do we? I never actually signed any articles with Hulgetta. Just took a vow."

"Without the articles your mistress could have killed you. She could have compelled you to do countless horrible things."

"Then that's probably why she never had me sign any," she said with a wry smile. "If that's the case, though, how could you—harm—your master?"

"I was no longer his apprentice. I had just finished a journeyman contract, but hadn't signed another."

"Why not?"

"I wasn't sure of what I was going to do next." He frowned.

"I don't understand you." She shook her head. "Whatever. Bring on the articles. I mean you no harm and will happily sign them."

He left the study. Dorcas was skipping up the steps of the tower, her skirts bunched up in her arms, calling "Peter!"

He turned to go down into the kitchen, where he removed his jacket, hanging it up on a peg and then rolling up his shirtsleeves.

The other maids looked at him like he was going to bite.

"Dorcas said she needs firewood," he murmured.

"It's been fifteen years since you chopped wood for the kitchen, sir," one of the maids said with a bob of a curtsey.

He shrugged. Yet he welcomed the distraction. Outside he enjoyed the bite of the sharp axe and the sound it made as it planted into the wood. He inhaled the scent of fresh wood shavings. All the while a part of his mind thought and thought.

He had no idea how long a span of time had passed from his master's death to this moment. It was difficult, his thoughts sliding about like mercury. It made his head ache. For some reason one particular memory would intrude. He was in the study, examining a heavy book he'd placed on a special book stand. Some movement at the other end of the room attracted his attention. The tapestry seemed to move. He looked up, and he saw the tapestry on the wall bulging in an odd way. Then a tiny hand came around the corner and began to pull it aside.

That was it. His memory ended abruptly there. The memory seemed significant. His head ached, trying to remember beyond that point. The next thing he knew he was being sick in the study, she was there, and Peter was looking like someone who'd been run through with a sword.

Yet how much time had occurred between those two moments? A day? At least. It had been late in the day with the sun streaming through the study as the tapestry began to bulge. Now it was early morning. At least a day, but it could have been years.

He stared at the large pile of wood he'd created. A sorceress occupied the tower. How at home she seemed in the study. How unhesitating she was at commanding the servants.

Then she came stalking out with Peter behind her, still wearing the black robe. He looked around, the elf inside him not wanting the eyes of other men upon her in such a state of undress. They swiftly went through the apprentice articles ceremony. Peter held the apprentice scroll that she'd already signed above and below, and she said the words for the apprentice contract. Theo said the words then signed the indentures above and below. With his signature a line shimmered and snaked across the contract, leaving behind a thin burned trail that undulated like waves in the sea. Sparks flew from the burnt line and a buzzing passed through him, tickling his torso and stomach like he was a lute string that had just been plucked. The contract was struck. Peter ripped the contract along the burned line, showed how the unique halves fit together perfectly, and then gave one half of the contract to Zephyr and presented the other half of the contract to him.

"Done," she said, "And that, by the way, was sorcery."

"I did not say sorcery was unnecessary," he explained. "I merely consider it a low form of magic."

Her eyes lit up with fire.

"I didn't mean to twit you about sorcery." However, he enjoyed the way she became so indignant and huffy. Taunting her was such a pleasure, it was almost physical. Again a stream of pure lust shot through his loins. Still, he spoke the truth.

"Sorcery is a lower form of magic, erratic and unpredictable."

"That is completely untrue," she said.

"The whole point of creating magical items instead of working a spell is that the item will work reliably and for a much longer time period than some mere spell."

The storage closet was stuffed full of dangerous items made by sorcerers that worked fitfully if at all. That he did not say, however.

Looking down at her, he realized that not only did he feel compelled to stay, but also to be close to her, to be in her confidence. Given the chance she'd grab the wrong end of the stick and everyone would suffer for it. He would try to prevent that from happening.

"Forgive me, Mistress Zephyr, I must finish stacking the wood." She backed off, and looked like she was going to say something. Then, whirling around rapidly, she strode away in her oversized robe, leaving as quickly as she had come.

He stacked the wood neatly, brought Dorcas the three armfuls she needed, then turned and went to the horse trough to wash. He stripped off his dripping shirt and splashed about. He came up from the water to find his new mistress watching him from the balcony. She held out a towel and he went to stand below her, so she could drop it down to him. He toweled himself thoughtfully and slowly, watching her, until her cheeks turned scarlet and she disappeared back into the tower.

He sat on the edge of the trough, waiting. The blood throbbed in his skull and behind his eyes like he was going fae. He sat, aware of how it throbbed in his groin, and waited it out. He already felt a powerful hunger for her, a need to bury himself inside her and taste her in a way he'd never felt for any woman before. The feeling took a very long time to fade. He worried it might not fade the next time.

She'd used her ring upon him, but she didn't need it—he wanted her already. He wanted to take her robe off and then take her rings off, leaving her bare, naked and human, vulnerable to his touch and—he had to stop such thoughts. His skull was throbbing with the beat of elf drums, a music that led folk into the woods where they were lost forevermore. He buried his axe in the stump of the tree and went to ask Dorcas for more chores, eager to keep his body moving, his wicked mind still.

CHAPTER TWENTY-THREE

The morning was a-wasting. Dorcas pulled hard on the corset strings and her breasts were pushed up higher and plumper.

"Almost done," Dorcas mumbled. She'd brought reinforcements into Zephyr's bedchamber early that morning. Zephyr woke up and sat up bolt upright as Dorcas entered the chamber with a basin, followed by a string of maids with a bucket of heated water. They carried clothing stretched across their arms, and other toiletry items. Zephyr had never cared for dresses and other girly stuff, and eyed the apparel with suspicion.

To the study! All those glorious books, all hers, and she was going to plunge in as soon as she could untangle herself from the glam squad.

They scrubbed her with a basin of warm water and lavender soap, then put her into a shift, and attacked with the long, fierce corset.

Now, it's not like she wasn't used to corsets. But the one she'd been used to wearing at Hulgetta's was more of a bodice, and only came down to the bottom of her ribs. It laced up the front and only had four stays. It was cut with large arm holes and tied loose enough that she could move about and breathe with ease. The corset Dorcas shoved her into was a whole other beast, with long stiff boning that came to a point right above her pubic bone. They squished and squeezed, pulling at the laces until her body created the proper carrot shape.

"But I'm going to be in the study today," she protested. "I wouldn't want to spoil this pretty dress," she said, petting the strawberry-colored gown they'd brought her. It was very sweet, really.

"Oh, no, mistress. You cannot wear that man's robe again," Dorcas said. "It's scandalous."

She pouted. At Hulgetta's castle she'd worn the same style wizard's robe while concocting potions. Admittedly, she usually wore it over her other clothes, but it was much colder at Hulgetta's than it was here.

"You must look proper before you see the men."

"Men? Who?"

"The men waiting below."

Peter entered the open door. She saw his eyes involuntarily drop to the plump edge of her bodice.

"Yes, Peter?" He jerked his eyes up to her face suddenly. Then, a flush mantling his cheeks, he moved over to the window seat and looked out the window instead of at her. Sort of ridiculous, for she was covered from boobs to toes. She pushed away the white lead paint rouge presented to her.

"Thank you, no," she said politely. Another maid came forward with a complicated set of threads stretched between her hands.

"And what are you going to do with those?"

"Pluck Mistress' hairline. Tis the fashion for it to start much further from the face."

"I'd rather not. Not right now, thank you."

Dorcas approached her with what strangely looked like the kind of neck pillow people used on airplanes.

"And what is that?" she asked.

"A bum roll." Dorcas tilted her head in a way that Zephyr was beginning to realize meant Dorcas was prepared for a fight, so she embraced the bum roll while they continued jerking and sewing her into the rest of her clothes. She kept her arms out, her eyes wandering over to Peter.

He was wearing a light grey jerkin and wine colored robes over it. He was a whole different man, his shoulders twice as wide as before, his height more noticeable. On his head was a matching wine colored pancake hat. Put a fat chain of gold around his neck and he could be any successful mayor of London, circa 1600 whatever.

"Mistress Zephyr," he said, interrupting her thoughts, "I have here a petition."

"From whom?"

"The local knights. Seven of them downstairs are here to wait upon you. They have armored themselves and acquired suitable horses. They are begging to join King Linus's army before the war is decided."

"It is still undecided?"

"Not really. Tis mostly over by this point, I expect," Peter confided.

"What do they normally do with their time?"

"They hunt and lose their dogs in the woods," Theo said, coming up the stairs and entering the room. "They drink too much, and pester the people of the countryside. They dress themselves in fine robes and strut about." This last remark seemed aimed at Peter.

Just then she disappeared into the dress. She re-emerged to find Theo looking at her, his eyes hot and bright, before he turned to look out the window exactly as Peter had.

He too was dressed up today. Everyone seemed to know they had company but her.

All in black, from head to toe, he was in elegant contrast to Peter. He wore a black velvet surcoat with wide split shoulder sleeves that set off his narrow hips. Below the surcoat, black tights highlighted and outlined every muscle of his ass and legs. The only part of his lower body not revealed in full was hidden under a modest codpiece. She wanted to eat him up with a spoon.

As Dorcas pushed her down onto a stool and began to divide and comb out sections of her hair, she eyed the magnificence of that backside, but the sight of him brought back memories of the day before. She bit the side of her lip and frowned, feeling uncomfortable about compelling him with the ring. It was wrong. Very wrong. On the other hand, she couldn't bear the thought of all his gorgeous, wounded elfy-ness wandering off to who knows where, confused and awash with guilt and grief. No, he needed to be here. Yet today he looked far more collected. A thick flood of uncomfortable feelings shot through her. *I'm never using that ring on him again. Ever.*

Dorcas pulled out a little metal container about the size of a compact. She opened the lid and a rolling smell assaulted Zephyr's nostrils. It was as if someone had taken road kill and drenched it in perfume.

"Ew. What is that?" she said, sniffing at a box of pomade.

"Civet musk."

"No, thank you."

"But—"

"Just—no."

Dorcas brought out the comb. Wetting it in the basin, she grabbed the ends of Zephyr's hair in her fist began exacting revenge for the spurned civet musk, attacking the ends first.

"Do these knights defend the tower lands?" she said, trying to sit with some dignity, despite tugs on her scalp jerking her head continuously. Dorcas was pulling her hair back in a severe central part, then twisting each side down flat.

"The tower lands do not need defense," Theo said. "There's nothing here but the tower and farmland. No significant rivers or cities. No vast woods or shorelines full of merchant ships. The land is too small and the people too poor to invade." Peter, with many a look and glance, seemed to indicate he agreed, pretty much. It was funny how the new clothes were bringing out his expressive features. He said so much with a few broad looks and glances. She watched as Dorcas looked him over once and turned away blushing with satisfaction.

"If they are drunken louts, shouldn't we send them off to war, then? Get them out of the way?"

"The other reason no one attacks the tower lands is because no one remembers we're here," Theo said, legs apart, hands behind his back. "To send out these men who will immediately be slaughtered is the same as waving a big flag that says 'Over here! We're poorly defended, fatuous idiots.'"

She smiled. A trickle of cool water made its way down her scalp. The morning was already warm and heating up this chamber, which was in full sun and at the top of the tower.

"True. Very true. However, they are very persistent," Peter remarked, turning to her, his eyes big with caution and concern. "I fear if you deny them, they will continue to petition and pester you."

Dorcas was now pulling out some very long hair pins with pointy needle-sharp tips. This was going to hurt.

"Before you meet with the knights," Peter said to her, "there's another matter about which I must beg a moment of your time."

"Certainly, what is it? Ouch! Dorcas!"

"Patience, mistress. One moment." The maid pinned a double braid across the crown of her head and now was wrapping up the rest of her hair into a loose bun at the base of her neck and placing it into a kind of snood or caul. That wasn't the problem; the problem was the long pins she used to skewer the dratted caul to the braids on the crown of her head. Was this a hair style or acupuncture? *Sheesh.*

"Theo—No, no, I already said I'm not letting you put civet musk in my hair. Where do you people get these things?—Theo, why don't you wait for me down below. Is there an inventory for the study and all the magic books?"

"But the knights?"

She tried to peer at him from where her head was shoved forward, her chin almost touching her breasts. More pins scraped along her scalp. *Ow.*

"Right. Okay, first Peter, then the knights, then you and me. In the study." She stifled a sigh, looking outside across the green and yellow green crosshatched fields. People! She didn't want to deal with people. All that hocus-pocus lying about below just waiting for her. She itched to dive in. *Your tower, your books, your spells.*

Well, if the ring was urging her to do it, then she was definitely going to think twice before following that impulse.

"With great power comes great responsibility," she mumbled. "I'll be down in a moment, Peter," she said, giving Dorcas a poke in the ribs. "If only this one would hurry a little."

"Mistress," Dorcas groaned.

∞

When Theo came up the stairs looking for her almost an hour later, he found her on the fourth floor.

"Theo," she said listlessly. "The news is not good." She patted at her hair. The crosshatched gold ribbon and seed pearls seemed rock solid. Theo took her in from head to toe, but she was too filled with woe to care at the moment. He sat next to her on the bench and took her hand.

"What would mistress have me do?"

About a thousand indecent things. With me. Upstairs.

"I don't know. Peter says we're headed into a famine."

"There are grain bins with surplus grain, not only here at the tower, but also about the land."

"I know, I know. But Peter says it won't be enough. We agreed he'd go and do the measurements again. You know, all by himself this time, just to make sure. But the farmers are saying they're mostly empty because last year was a poor harvest too."

She looked out the window again, seeing the yellow-green landscape with new eyes. No longer did she glory in the giant checkerboard of happy fields below. Now she saw a patchwork of green and sickly yellow-green plants already parched from a lack of water.

"Something needs to be done," she said, rubbing her forehead, which ached from tension. "And sooner rather than later. He says that the rainy season is late, but if the crops don't get enough rain in the next three weeks…" She shook her head. Peter said the little ones were often the first to go in a famine.

"I'm gut-sick just thinking about it."

She bit at her upper lip and put her elbows on her knees and her chin on her fists, but it felt like the corset was trying to stab her, so she sat up straight again.

"And the knights?"

"Oh my god, the knights." She struggled to stand. "I completely forgot."

It was as if he walked around in a magic cloud of gold sparklies. Something about him—perhaps the elf magic—made all the internal parts of her leap up to attention when he helped her up from the bench. She found herself lost for a moment in a rapt contemplation of his lips. In his suit of black, his hair was copper, his lips rose-pink, and she felt a little weak in the knees as he offered her his arm, though maybe that was just lack of air from trying to bend her upper body in the corset. She put a hand to her now flat abdomen. No wonder women fainted all the time back in ye olde days.

She clung to his arm on the stairs. Soon enough she'd get the hang of trailing skirts, but when she'd left Peter's funny little office on the fifth floor the first thing she did was trip on the first stair and almost plunge down to her death. She'd sat on the bench, shaken.

The muniments room, Peter called it. It served as a kind of office, full of old records of the tower and dust. She'd sneezed a lot and wondered at Peter, very much in his element. She would go mad in such a cramped, boring space. He didn't seem to mind it, though. He had one little birdcage-sized window near his desk and puttered about happily while spelling out the doom that faced everyone below.

"I asked Peter about buying grain from neighboring lands. He looked at me like I had suggested he try to fly. I guess it's just not done."

"It is, but not often. It's a clear sign of weakness."

"And no one wants to look weak. Because they could face attack. But it is a possibility?"

"Where's the coin to come from to pay for such a scheme?" Theo countered.

"Heaven knows. Isn't there a treasury or something?"

"No."

"Then what usually happens when something like this occurs?"

"People die."

"No—I mean, what did you do the last time you were facing famine?"

"I advised Eldred to build the grain bins."

He was so frustrating! "I mean, what does a wizard usually do?"

"Nothing."

"Someone must be in charge."

"I don't think you quite understand how things work."

"Obviously."

"Once, all was common land. The people farmed all together and shared the harvest. There are still some common lands the poor use near the tower. But there is no king, no leader, and there never has been."

"So why are the knights coming to see me?"

"It is traditional for people to consult the wizard. Usually he has wisdom to share. The grain bins, for instance, were the result of my suggestion. Without Eldred's influence, they never would have been built, but he did not command anyone to build them."

"The wizard's influence."

"Influence. That's all."

"Who's the nearest neighbor from whom we could buy corn or barley?"

"Magor."

"So the tower fills up its bins with corn from Magor."

"If they have corn to spare."

"It's always something." She stood up. "If they don't have corn, then we'll find some elsewhere. And when the people run out, we can share. I don't want to deal with this. I just want to go be by myself and learn more magic." She heaved a sigh.

They had made their way slowly to the landing of the third floor.

"Where are they?"

"The dining hall."

∞

While the study was filled with bookshelves and sunlight pooling on the dark tables, the grand dining hall was full of gloomy formality. The hall sat on the third floor of the tower, The windows overlooked the towering pines of the black forest that stretched out across the entire northern horizon. The trees threw their shady forest gloom into the room. The formal, extravagantly carved dark benches were twins to the one at the foot of her bed. Here they lined the walls as if they'd been squatting in the tower for longer than they'd been trees.

Half the dark-stained, oak paneled room contained an open space with wide plank flooring, just now filled with jostling and bumptious knights. At least, that was her first impression. Thirty people crowded together into such a panoply of chaos, noise, and color as to set her heart racing. She rapidly backed up, stumbling into Theo as she did so.

It was already near midday, and a sharp wedge of sunlight poured over the company of men, along with their multitude of servants. Little pageboys darted like tiny fish in and out of the winking sunlight beams.

Tall-backed dogs with arched tails well tucked into their bodies were scattered throughout the company and joined to the noisy hallooing with their barks.

Last night she'd sat all alone in the other half of the room, at the massive slab of a table formed from a single plank of an outrageously enormous tree. In one of the high-backed, spindly dark chairs she'd felt very small picking at her sorrel salad and roast goose. Looking down on her were row upon row of wizard portraits that hung from the paneled walls. Deep-set eyes gleamed as if seeing into the depths of time. They looked upon her with pity for mixing with the rabble, instead of escaping to the calm of the quiet study below. She agreed, frowning, wishing she were there too. Was she ever going to get to the study today?

Meanwhile, the sudden onslaught of masculinity made her stop. When was the last time she'd faced such a riot of male laughter and jeering. Her eyes widened upon spying many an exaggerated upthrust codpiece. One in particular was topped with a leering demon's head. *Decidedly vulgar.*

Peter slid into the room behind them. "I took the liberty of telling Dorcas to bring up food and drink, mistress," he said.

"Of course. Of course," she said, thinking just the opposite. *Go away. Leave me in peace.*

Theo tried to lead her forward. The men saw her, and at that point everyone, young and old, turned and stopped talking. Instantly. She stopped too, but Theo almost dragged her along with him and she heard the soft scuff of her slippers as she stepped into the middle of the open space. The room was so silent she could hear the hiss of her dress against her petticoats.

Slowly the crowd surrounded them. She noticed hands on sword hilts. Faces looked daggers at her. No, not her—but at Theo. *Elf.* The word caught her ears. *Bespelled*, someone else muttered.

Not good. The smallest, scraggliest little pageboy was frowning at Theo, his thin mouth in a hard grumpy line as if he were wishing the elf dead over and over.

She turned in a slow circle and saw Peter on the edge of the crowd, a head taller than everyone else. *What's going on?*

CHAPTER TWENTY-FOUR

Peter in response to her silent call strode forward at once.

He said, “It’s not what you think. She’s not bespelled by that elf.”

“So say you,” a giant man with an enormous belly in a dull green leather jerkin said. “Yet since the death of Eldred what have you been, Peter, but that elf’s boot licker?”

She heard the scrape of a withdrawn sword before she saw it. Then she could see nothing because Theo swept her behind him.

“Sir Wiley!” Peter called. “You much mistake the matter.”

She was trying to see around Theo, but he had grabbed her farthingale and held onto the ribbed boning, effectively keeping her in place. All she could see was an expanse of his black velvet back. She almost punctured a lung trying to bend sideways in that wretched corset just to see.

The giant knight had gotten his sword caught up in his scabbard. This was not tragedy—it was a farce. Peter kept trying to explain while other knights began offering up helpful suggestions to their friend.

“He signed the papers—articles of apprenticeship.”

“It’s the tip, man. You’ve got it—there—no, use your fingers.”

She decided to put an end to it all. She gripped Theo's shoulder hard and wrenched herself away, stepping out in front.

"Amahan hehov isles arolha!"

Everyone hushed, just as the giant man freed his sword. He turned in triumph towards them, his tongue between his teeth. She quickly rolled out the final words, feeling a simultaneous inner push towards him until her nerves felt spent and empty. The giant man paused with sword raised, then crashed at their feet like a falling tree.

So fun. Better than hop toads. It never gets old, does it?

Theo looked aghast at what she'd done. Hands on her hips, she turned and eyed everyone else as they gaped at their fallen comrade, then back at her.

"Anyone who dares to threaten my apprentice will face far worse than that man," she said, pointing to the fallen body. "Understand?"

Then she spoke the waking spell. Within a minute or two the men were helping the giant man up into a chair. Sir Wiley was shaking, a bloody foam spooling forth from his mouth like a rabid mastiff, which alarmed her, but Peter explained he'd bitten off the very tip of his tongue.

Theo handed over his very own handkerchief, and she told Sir Wiley to hold it to his tongue until the bleeding stopped. And maybe even after that. The crowd nervously chuckled at her joke.

Peter started up again.

"Her apprentice," he panted, almost stammering. "I saw the contract signed myself yesterday, do y'hear?"

Theo, impatient as she swept her forward and presented her to them all. "Gentlemen, make your leg to the Sorceress Zephyr," he said.

The seven knights turned to her and made her a "leg." She nodded her head gravely in return, but, felt a strong qualm. They were one and all looking her up and down in a way that felt quite icky.

"She's occupied the tower. Understand?" Peter said.

"Enough Peter."

She looked stern, and tried to look taller than she was as well. *I am a stern sorceress with powerful secret knowledge. Fear me.*

"You've heard Peter. This man is my apprentice and therefore under my protection. Attempt to harm him and you will face my wrath."

"We meant no offense, milady," one fine fellow in white with red hair said. He was like a young Henry the Eighth.

"I'm sure you had the best intentions." Her voice dripped with irony. She didn't want these men here. She wanted time with her books. And Theo. Alone time. *Please let me have him. Please please please.*

Behind her, she heard the servants enter. Dorcas and the maids trooped in with laden platters. Dorcas looked harassed and hot, her cheeks pink. They laid out goblets and wine decanters along with large polished pewter trays upon which rested dabs of cheese, brown bread, and lady pears. All of these went upon the large table, along with a tall pie of meat and black pudding that shared pride of place next to a braised rabbit stuffed with parsley.

"Gentlemen, I hope you will relieve your thirst," she said, gesturing, the hospitable words stiff in her mouth. Several little boys, whom she assumed where the knight's pages leapt to serve their masters. She took the opportunity to notice Dorcas had raised an eyebrow of disdain towards the knights. One of them held out his foot, barring her way around the table. One look from Zephyr and he turned away. She snagged Dorcas's and whispered in her ear, "What think you of these fine folk?"

"They rove the tower lands like locusts, eating lords and peasants alike out of house and home."

Turning back to the men she said, "You have taken the time to honor me with a visit and have broken your thirst. Now, state your business."

The one in white with bright red hair like Henry the Eighth stepped forward. "Sir Bertram," he said, and made a leg, by way of introduction. Then turning, he addressed himself exclusively to Theo.

"King Linus has prevailed in war, elf-wizard. The Valdeans who fought for Rupert the Rogue have fled his lands."

"What has this to do with the tower and its lands?" Theo asked.

"They head south, seeking their home by land. They will pass right by us," Sir Bertram continued to Theo as if she was not even there. "We can attack them in the valley of Eglacia."

Was she invisible?

"Where's Eglacia?" she asked Theo. If Sir Bertram was ignoring her, she would do the same.

"Western Magor," Theo answered. "About one hundred leagues from us."

"We want to form a cavalry," Sir Bertram said to Theo.

The knight with a crude laughing codpiece joined Sir Bertram, stepping forward from the others.

"And who are you?" she said, eyeing the codpiece. She didn't like it, and she didn't like him either. He had a youthful smooth cap of dark brown hair that went oddly with the harsh bracket lines about his mouth.

"Sir Ingham, milady," he said with an easy smile that did not reach his eyes. He turned to Theo. "Dread Wizard. The ravine of Eglacia forms an easy bottleneck. With even our few numbers we can capture their forward scouts, men and horses. We mean to show those Valdeans what for."

Ginger Beard said to Theo, "We could be there and back with the heads of the Valdeans tied to our pommels in a fortnight."

A crude image. Peter came up to her side. "I was told the Valdeans will pass through Tempolian Valley, not Eglacia," he said to her.

"And who told you that?" Sir Bertram demanded.

"A traveling merchant."

"Well?" she said, turning to the knights. "Is this true?"

The knights turned to her as one. They all made a leg in her direction.

"A good point. Yes, milady," Bertram said soothingly, "you do well to be advised by Peter." Yet he did not look like he was at all happy with Peter, and she noticed his baby blue eyes were cold.

"Sorceress," she corrected.

The men turned back to talk to Theo.

"Tempolian Valley is a wide flat valley," Theo said to them all. He looked down at her. "Quite different from the narrow pass of Eglacia," She liked this feeling of her and Theo together. He was letting them know whose side he was on, and his support warmed her through and through.

"As near as makes no difference," Sir Bertram said, waving away the problem.

"But it does make a difference. If you don't meet them in a bottleneck when you hit the wide open plains you'll be outnumbered and swiftly slaughtered."

Really, why did she care? Let them go out and fight if they wanted to. She looked back at the door. Which led to the stairs. Which led to the study.

"Not, perhaps the best of plan," she said lightly.

They turned to her, looked at her with great curiosity, like one would look at a cat that suddenly reared on its hind feet and began talking.

The one with the offensive codpiece, Sir Ingham, stepped forward and said to Theo, "We've made arrangements to acquire a complement of war-horses, as you suggested, elf-wizard, and each of us has a full suit of armor being fitted to wear. Even outnumbered, we would take the day."

"Why?" she demanded. "Weren't you listening to what Theo just said?"

"We have superior weaponry and valor, milady," he explained, with a small bow in her direction.

"Sorceress. I am the Sorceress Zephyr." She put some gravitas in her voice. A dog whined. At least it understood she was getting peeved.

Sir Ingham made a leg, a hand on his chest, the very picture of courtesy. "So sorry if I have offended, mi—Sorceress Zephyr."

"You are not a brave force of knights," she said. "You are wealthy country provincials." Now she had their attention. "Your fathers are farmers. You know sheep and oats not arms and tactics. Have you ever actually drawn your sword, Sir Bertram?"

Sir Bertram's face turned brick red.

"I thought not," she said.

The other men jumped in.

"We may not be battle seasoned, we are still worthy of earning honor," one with curly blonde hair said. The others gave loud noises of assent. Theo said nothing. She just wanted to go downstairs and get her freak on with all the magic.

"Apprentice Theo," she said, and paused. "Apprentice *Theo*." A large wave of murmurings swept around the group when she mentioned his title again.

"Do you know much of these matters?"

"My father is a warrior. I held a sword as soon as I could walk and trained all through my youth."

She blinked at that. *Right.* It was just that he didn't look like he knew how to fight. He looked like he knew how to compose a love poem, or play a lute with a bevy of sighing maidens at his feet.

"Yet, I too, am not battle tested," he admitted.

"You were trained in combat as a youth?"

"I was."

"That's more than any of these men. Peter said they want to go off and fight, and won't stop bothering me until they get permission. What am I supposed to do?"

"Send them home."

Of course.

"Even if no longer ill-equipped, these men are still untrained. It will take three weeks to get to Western Magor. Once there, they will be slaughtered in less than three days, and that will be the end of them. Unless they bolt for home and the Valdeans follow them all the way here."

"Honest, decisive words, Apprentice Theo. I thank you for them." But they weren't the words she needed to hear.

She turned back to the knights. "I am sympathetic to your desires." Go out and get yourselves killed, just leave me in peace, please. But no, she couldn't say that. "You wish to earn glory. However, I see the wisdom in what Apprentice Theo says. I cannot endorse your desire to go into combat."

"Milady, no! I mean, sorceress—" the room erupted as one and they all protested.

"All we ask is to carry the tower's banner into conflict," a tall knight exclaimed.

"Without the banner we would be seen as bandits," Sir Bertram said. "And treated as such if captured."

Sir Ingham added, "Under the tower banner we can be ransomed. So you see," he added with a rather nasty smile, "we will not be slaughtered after all." *No, only your servants and animals will die. And why should you care about that?*

"Milady, you must say 'yes' to our quest. Otherwise our parents won't let us go," the young knight with fuzzy blond hair and very red lips said. She forced herself not to smile.

"Perhaps your parents don't want you to go, because they don't want to pay a ransom," she suggested

"Oh no, milady. They wouldn't pay the ransom. You would. It's traditional," he explained.

She wondered about the parents of these men. Did they relish their offspring as little as she did? Perhaps. They did not seem to mind at all that their sons planned to go off to be slaughtered—perhaps there were may more sons at home to replace them.

"I've made up my mind. No banner. No ransom, no permission."

"The sorceress has decided," Theo crossed his arms, unrelenting.

"You must train first," Zephyr said. "Training takes time. A weekly tourney will help. We'll donate the grounds," she said, with a look at Peter, who was shaking his head no. She ignored him. "But you'll have to build it. An open space devoted to training and maneuvers."

"This will not answer our purpose," Sir Ingham said to Theo.

"Ignore me one more time," she said to Ingham, her chin coming up, and her voice going low. The man eyed her with cold dislike. "Forget to call me Sorceress Zephyr again and see how long you stand on your feet." The men all backed off a pace. The dogs whined.

Ingham looked furious. And dangerous. She would not show any fear to that man, and did not feel any, though the back of her brain was prickling with the need for caution.

"They have taken you in," Theo said in an undertone, coming up to her with his arms still crossed.

"Not at all," she murmured in a low voice. "We need some kind of protective force if push comes to shove. This is at least a beginning. And jousting will keep them occupied. You will help them set up the tourneys."

"Me?"

"Well, you *are* the authority on fighting. They clearly look up to you, and you might as well teach them something if you can."

"I don't like the way they look at you in that dress," he said, and she saw his eyes flash black. A bright arrow of lust pierced her down low, right where the corset stuck into her when she tried to sit in it.

CHAPTER TWENTY-FIVE

Dorcas had come with more food, but Zephyr was too restless to eat. She wanted them all gone. However, she'd learned more about Theo because of their dog and pony show. "Was it battle that made you leave the tower? The war with Rupert?" She still could not fathom why anyone would ever abandon the tower, but clearly it was not all fun and games.

He shook his head. "I remember not." Just standing near him was like standing near a shelf of magic books. That faint joyous feeling filled her whenever he was near. Her veins sang around him.

They were interrupted by the tall knight in dark grey. He reminded her somewhat of Peter, only with more hair, and more charming finesse. Sir…?

"Fair Sorceress Zephyr," he said, bending over her hand, "You are as pleasing a sight to one's eye as the summer's sweetest honeysuckle o'er covered with dew." *Did he just say something suggestive to me?* She slowly pulled her hand back, unsure.

"I thank you," she said, after a slight hesitation. "Just who are you?"

"Sir Reginald, milady," he said with a twinkle in his eye and made his leg. It was a long leg, and there was no missing the long codpiece as he displayed it to her. Theo gave her a look that as plain as day said: do not check out Sir Reginald.

Jealous much? He need not worry. She looked at Sir Reginald and the knight twinkled back. Theo fumed at her side.

"'Twould be a thrill to fight for the favor of a lady in the stands and test one's skills against another." At least he seemed to approve of her plan.

"It will be delightful," she agreed.

The rest of the men ate and the room filled with exclamations of *zounds!* and *lackaday!* Everyone was full of a restless good cheer. She had to quell an impulse to burst through them and flee down to the study. She was not so good in crowds, preferring face-to-face time with a spell book instead.

The hounds went over to the long table and stretched themselves out beneath it, panting with contentment in the warmth of the day. There was only one woman amongst all these men, and this whole time she had remained seated on a bench near the window, but now she smiled invitingly every time Theo looked her way.

"Who's she?" Zephyr asked with a nod of her chin.

"La, milady! I am Rachel Trumbull," the woman said, rising and crossing the room, her eyes bright and bold. She gave a sweeping curtsey. Feathered pancake hat, striped farthingale, outrageous flirt, and a pungent, penetrating odor hung about her in a cloud that made Zephyr's eyes water. Civet musk, no doubt.

"Sir Bothswell's mistress," Peter whispered in her ear. "She was determined to come see—that is—"

Zephyr turned just in time to see a deep dimple appeared near the small beauty mark next to Trumbull's mouth as she made eyes at Theo

"Tell Miss Trumbull," she said in Peter's ear, "that if she keeps looking at my apprentice that way I'm going to bitch slap her."

"I don't understand what—yes, mistress."

"Thank you."

People were still discussing the fate of the Valdeans.

"Five thousand mercenaries are said to have escaped Linus's blade," Sir Betram said.

"Five thousand!" Zephyr said.

"When they reach the Bald Mountains they'll skirt east at first. When they reach the large central valley of Magor, tis all open fields and farmland. They will roost there, out of reach of Linus's forces, letting their horses rest, repairing armor."

"Magor. Magor with the corn?" she asked.

"Yes, mistress," he said.

"Then no corn for us," she said.

"If they take the Eglacia pass," Sir Betram continued, "they wind up here," he tapped on the map, "in Western Magor at Tempolian Fields."

"How far is that from us?" she said. On the map, their land was a grape. King Linus's kingdom the big grapefruit along the coast. She did not like where Sir Bertrams finger tapped. It was a plum quite close to their little grape.

"Not one hundred leagues away, milady," a particularly ugly man said. His bald forehead wrinkled up above a squashed-potato nose.

"Sorceress. And you are?"

"Sir Pettish, an' it pleases your ladyship."

"Sorceress." She turned to her apprentice. "Well, Theo?"

"Let us strike hard and slaughter them all," Sir Bertram urged, "before they take the winter to fatten up again. We'll strike and bring their heads back on the tips of our poinards." Like he was doing her a favor if she acted right now.

"Unless they don't take the pass," Theo mocked. "Then you'll be facing five thousand of the enemy in open land on broken-down horses."

This riled up the men.

"Rape, plunder, robbery—'tis all Valdeans know."

Sir Reginald turned to him. "They have been separated from the rest of their army. They are hungry, desperate, and far from home."

"You are in sympathy with them, then?" she asked.

"I think they will harm anyone weaker than they are." He pulled on his earlobe, thinking. "No one is safe while they roam about the land."

"If they are such strong, ruthless fighters, and well-armed," she asked, "then why would we ever want to tangle with them?"

"For glory!"

"For honor!"

She'd set them off again. If sheer force of will could kill, then these men would be fearsome indeed. But now that she could look at them a little more calmly and try to judge their age beneath the big beards and stiff clothing, they seemed young. They intimidated her the way a bar full of male college students hooting at a basketball game on TV are intimidating. Why, oh, why was this suddenly her problem?

"Is anyone else harrying the Valdeans?" she asked. "What is King Linus doing?"

"Dying." King Linus was on his deathbed, apparently.

"He fought and was wounded."

"Hardly a scratch, but its turned bad, they say," Sir Pettish told her. The man's high tenor voice was lilting and in complete contrast to his ugly face.

"They had to take his leg."

They all shared a moment of silent reflection on the imminent demise of King Linus.

"I curse the Valdeans!" Sir Bertram said. "They will overrun Magor next and after that take Proxia. Then they will be upon us like fleas on my dog."

"Theo, tell us more of your training," she said, trying to quell her anxiety at these words. "You say you have never fought."

His expression clouded over at once. "I said I have not been tried in battle. I have, however, fought—and to the death." His expression instantly flooded with remorse and sorrow. She felt sympathetic tears rise in her own eyes.

"Is that—you had said there was a time when you could not control your elfin side."

"I fought any who insulted me. Many were grievously injured."

Good job, Zephyr. Poke your finger right into where he hurts the most. The knights looked like they'd edge away from him if they could.

"Can Magor defend itself?" she asked Sir Reginald.

"Doubtful," He replied. "They're like us, farmers, with little in the way of defense. No army. No castles. Peaceful people."

"How have you avoided attacks in the past?" she asked him.

"We had a powerful wizard to protect us," Theo said. *Zing! Ouch.* Okay, this *was* her problem. Well, they might not have a powerful wizard anymore, but if she got to work, they might somehow escape a famine.

"Gentlemen," she said. "You have work to do. So do I. I shall leave you now." But it would not do. She must stay and drink with them, they cried. She hesitated near the door. Dorcas came up to her, a pitcher at her side.

"It's traditional, Mistress," she said. "Elderberry wine. 'Twould not make my grandmother tipsy."

Theo came up to them, took the pitcher from Dorcas with a look, and, holding out a hand, said, "My mistress." He led her to the top of the table and poured wine all around.

"To the Sorceress Zephyr!" His voice rang out in the hall.

The men cheered and knocked the hilts of their knives on the tabletop. When the rapping noises stopped they drank and cheered and drank again. She put a hand upon his arm.

"Thank you."

The toasts went on, but Theo said into her ear, "They have hoodwinked you."

His voice was neutral, but in his eyes she read some of that heat that she saw when his eyes changed, and her entire body below her waist responded.

Dressed head to toe in black, he might have been made expressly to crush Sir Bertram's ego. He was the model of a man. She watched him go back to the table where the talk about fighting in armor with the other men. As they dove deeper into the discussion, his face underwent a transformation. The black wavered back and forth with the green, waxing and waning. His features grew animated, and even joyous until finally he joined in.

"What's a poignard?" she asked him, enjoying that suddenly it was the two of them together as allies.

"It's a small knife for thrusting."

"Ahh."

CHAPTER TWENTY-SIX

It was not until dusk and little black bats were flitting about the white tower that the knights were got rid of. Still calling out for more drink, they staggered to their horses. The last three were red-lipped Bothswell, ugly Pettish, and Sir Reginald. They were engaged in an enthusiastic discussion of sword stances.

"Come on, elf," Sir Reginald was saying. "Come on. Show us what you're nattering on about. I'm ready." He staggered out into the dirt yard, and turned about, while servants and horses scattered back, creating a circle of golden dots from their lamps. The three tried to engage Theo under the warm summer moon, wanting him to demonstrate combat tactics he'd described around the dining table earlier in the evening.

She watched them from the balcony. All the toasting through the afternoon had made her tipsy and heavy-headed and she had the hiccups.

"A master of sword under our noses all this time," Reginald was saying, "Theo, you dog."

Theo was a different man. She couldn't get enough of it. He was showing Pettish when to relax the wrist for more finesse when striking an opponent and when to stiffen the wrist and raise the elbow so the whole force of the arm landed behind the blow. He moved with vigor, all elastic action, suddenly demonstrating a quick lunge at Pettish, finger and arm extended, tapping the knight on his flank. Pettish responded, but couldn't land a touch on the elf even in jest. Theo showed the young man how to turn his head and keep his torso perpendicular to his sword arm so he only presented his side as a target.

"Distance is all in all," Theo said. "A man cannot kill you if you are out of his reach. Control the distance and you control your enemy." A light smile floated across his features while attempting to impart knowledge to the other men, yet overall, she was most struck by his sincerity.

Her stomach hurt, watching him. Yesterday she had wanted to soothe his wounded sensitive soul. She was far worse today. The most god-awful, painful crush began to envelop her. She was rapidly becoming lovesick. She felt something between them. Surely he felt it, too. All day she swung back and forth, one minute convinced he did, the next convinced he didn't. Right now for instance, he seemed too happily occupied to give it much thought.

Just as she thought this, he sent a sideways glance up to the balcony. There—.

She could not turn away even if she tried. Every sign, ever gesture or accidental touch set her alight. The effect swiftly faded, leaving her hungry for more of his attention, more proof that he liked her. She quirked her mouth. Her gut said he was the key to protecting this land as danger came closer. Yet she just didn't know if she could handle him becoming even more heroic. She might spontaneously combust.

He cared not a whit for her magic studies, her enthusiasms for spells and potions, and he abhorred her ambition. Even her determination to help the people was suspect.

She'd become attuned to the special feeling of magic near him. It was a manic feeling like all her fairy dust was alive and agitating to be by his side. She chewed her lower lip.

At last, young Sir Bothswell, much the worse for drink, staggered about the yard chasing Sir Reginald with a stick. Then he was violently ill in the dust and his servants poured him into the saddle for the ride home, his wolfhounds following at a trot. Pettish and Sir Reginald mounted up, hallooing their good will into the night. Servants lit their way with lanterns mounted on poles, and the giant moon painted the road white like illuminated chalk.

"They should not be invited back here."

She was agreeably surprised at his possessive tone. She hadn't liked the way they looked at her either.

"You are too pretty, too young," he observed. Her heart leapt.

He took her wrist in his earnestness. "Forbid them from coming here every day. They will take it as an encouragement to fight for your favor."

"I won't."

"I wouldn't trust any of them alone with you."

"I'll take precious care never to be alone with them. Or even in a situation where their people outnumber my own," she promised.

"Good."

Her heart leapt, even though he spoke as if stating facts. He was no flatterer. She suspected it mattered little to him whether she was pretty or not.

Peter came out into the yard. She called out to him from the balcony.

"Peter, I wish you would take particular care never to leave Dorcas alone around Sir Ingham. I don't like the look of him, and from his behavior this afternoon, I think he fancies her."

Peter gave a double take.

"Dorcas?"

"After all, it's not like she's married."

"I doubt marriage would make much of a difference to Sir Ingham," Theo said, calling up to her, his brow lowering as he tilted his head up to look at her.

"You're right. Sir Ingham is particularly loathsome. Therefore we don't want him tormenting Dorcas, do we, Peter?"

Theo turned to go into the tower, not looking at her. "We don't want him tormenting anyone," he said.

Every part of her body thrilled, convinced he was bothered by how Ingham treated her. She fled down the stairs and met him at the bottom.

"Mistress?" He looked tired, or sad. What to say, what to do? She wanted to be alone with him. She wanted some way of teasing out his feelings and seeing if he returned hers at all. Deep down she knew he didn't. Or he didn't mean to. Maybe only a smidgen. But she kept blindly hoping anyway.

"The moon is so bright tonight," she said. Theo was silent. She tried again with another tactic, a little more pointed.

"When it's warm like this, and the moon is so lovely, I can't stay inside. Where do people go on a beautiful night?" She despised herself a little for being so obvious.

"Nowhere."

"Surely the young people—?"

"There is a waterfall."

"Nearby?"

"A short way into the woods."

"Would you show it to me?" He looked up, alarmed. The see-saw teetered back down with a thump on the *he doesn't like me* side.

Your apprentice.

"I want you to show me the woods."

His head went back like he'd just taken a blow to the chin. *No. Absolutely not.* "I didn't mean that." She didn't want him that way. She pushed down the will of the ring till its whispering voice died down.

She smiled, even though it was hard to make her expression playful, her tone light. "Theo, would you show me the way?"

Like someone sleepwalking, he turned and began walking. She followed. He guided her through the cluster of outbuildings just beyond the tower. He took her past the stables where the servants were housed above the horses. In the dark he showed her a little winding path that twisted into the dark fir trees. She tickled her fingers on their needle tips, and in a bold move, put out her hand for guidance while holding up her gown as they encountered roots and rocks in the path. He took her hand and patiently waited for her and did not let go. Into the gloaming they went on the soft pine needles, down to the sound of rushing water. She was so nervous she bumped into him when he stopped at the waterfall. It was twenty feet high and narrow, with a frothy white foam that glowed in the evening gloom. He let go of her hand.

A few mosquitos attacked. The water's spray and thick smell of balsam threw a cloak of cool pungent air about them. He stood with a foot on a rock, watching the waterfall, and taking a deep breath, and said, "I'm your apprentice, am I not?"

"Yes," she said, and held her breath. "What is it, Theo?" She couldn't stand the tension. "Are you worried I'm going to flirt with one of the knights?"

"It is not the knights that worry me, mistress."

"What then?"

"The Magic books. Promise me you won't use them."

She felt herself turning pink. So this was his agenda.

"I can't do that." She was piqued. At the same time the smell of burning hair floated through her memory. Something had happened. Theo suspected it was her fault. Maybe it was.

She lifted her chin. "If Magor is occupied and we can't buy corn, then we're going to have to resort to other means of feeding everyone."

"You mean the books. I should have known you'd find an excuse to plunder them."

With great power came great responsibility. Could she somehow use her powers to avoid the famine? Were there spells that could help? It was a bold thought.

"Why do you disdain sorcery?" she asked him. "All your elfin abilities—"

"Which I do not want—"

"Which are amazing—If only you would realize it."

"You are ever optimistic about magic. Too much so. I've seen how evil magic can be. Even when you never intended—to hurt—" He had to stop speaking. As she watched, one perfect tear dropped down his face in the bright moonlight.

She changed tactics, and pressing his arm with her hand, she said, "I saw you discussing war craft, battle, soldiering, fighting. You forgot your sorrow; you were passionate, alive—even happy. That's how I felt around those books when compounding a spell. It's what I was meant for. Don't you ever feel that way?"

He glanced at her and then looked off over her head.

"No."

"Come on. Teaching the others stances, lunges, and distance—I saw you. You loved it."

"It makes me remember my youth. That is all."

"It's more than that."

"I was well taught. There's a feeling of satisfaction in mastering the drills. I'm no warrior. Don't let your fancy run riot and imagine I am."

"Say what you like, but I saw you."

"If I seem to know anything about fighting it is only because the other men know nothing at all."

"Fine—but magic? When I'm in the presence of magic… When I'm near you, for instance," she said, taking a step closer, her face upturned. "I can feel it in my breast. It stirs me more than anything else that I've experienced in my entire life. Don't you feel something like that, Theo?"

He looked uneasy, but he did not move away. His breathing grew harsh.

"Don't you?"

"I studied the practice of wizardry and mastered it, but I've never felt the way you describe."

She tilted her head, lightly playful. "No?" She let her voice lilt, teasing, playful.

"I made one magical item. It doesn't even work right."

She bit her lip.

"When you're around," she said, not able to look him in the eye, "I feel strange. Different from how I normally feel. Do you know what I mean?" She waited but he didn't answer. She turned and played with her fingers. "At any rate, I've never been near an elf, so I thought perhaps it was that." He looked at her with a distant expression, as if to say, "So?" *He wasn't going to make this easy, was he?*

"And I think it is, partly. When I was with my mistress, I felt an agitation of the air, spirits—molecules—whatever you call it—around magic. But nowhere near as much as I feel around you."

He didn't respond.

"I mean, even the books are different in the study when you're around. Did you know that?"

"Different how?" His face was unreadable, but the muscles leaping in his throat gave him away.

"When you're gone they're more… inert. Do you think that spells can feel whatever it is too?"

He was standing very near her, and looking at her nose, no, her mouth. She fluttered all inside. She stilled, waiting breathlessly to see what he would do next.

He still wasn't saying anything. But there was the cutest little wrinkle between his brows. She let her hand float up to his arm. Then, as he stared at it either fascinated or horrified, she slid her hand down his arm and took his hand into hers and opened it, despite some initial resistance from him.

"When I hold a spell that hasn't fully formed yet, I can feel it. Right in my palm." She took his fingers, stretching them out, and he stared at his palm.

"It's a feeling—well, it's hard to describe. Sort of nubby. Like the feeling of tiny animal feet tickling your palm. Warm. Any moment it could spring away, and the trick is to hold onto it in your mind, let it form and feed it with a kind of elemental energy. Or it's lost." She gestured with her hand the motion of a spell springing into the air and let go his hand. His eyes darted to hers and away. Then back again. The cold smell of him was rapturous like burying her nose in a bouquet of rosemary and mums.

"Do you understand what I'm talking about?"

"You want me to stay and be your apprentice so I can improve your magic."

"Because you *are* magic."

He frowned. Her guts felt shredded. She wished he would reject her, just hand over the pain and get it over with. The suspense was killing her.

His eyes half-closed, she let her hands creep up to his shoulders, and then when he did not protest, let her hands drift up higher to his neck. She drew his neck down so his head hung just above hers, and she could almost reach his lips. Then he suddenly snapped upright. He pulled both of her hands down, holding them in his.

"You know we can't."

"What do you mean?" The feel of his large hands, dry and strong, surrounding hers made her whole pelvic girdle do a happy dance inside.

"Are you blind?" Theo said, his voice grating. "Did you not see the men—how they responded when they thought you were mine? They could have slaughtered us both."

"I'm not so sure. Anyway, they thought you had enchanted me. But you haven't."

Not yet.

"We can't."

"Why not?"

"Because of the articles. The apprentice articles expressly forbid this."

She stood very still as this particular sword blade of rejection split her body in half.

Fuck me.

"Seriously?"

"Didn't you read the articles?"

Ugh. "Not the whole thing," she confessed.

She felt the springy pine needles under her slippered feet and the mist falling as it clung to her skin and hair. She forced her brain to start working again. She contemplated telling him to hell with the articles.

"It's for our mutual protection. Otherwise, I never would have signed it. Or stayed."

She said a long string of other very bad words in her head. The blue-green enormous pine trees cast their shade over her despair.

Stupid apprentice contract—and it was her idea. She made a little gesture of shooting herself in the head, and sat cross-legged on a large stone, putting her hands behind her because the corset practically stabbed her in the belly otherwise.

He stood before her, putting his foot up on the rock, frowning deeply.

"There's another reason we can't. I didn't tell you the whole truth about my master's death. Gabrina maddened Eldred further after he'd been bitten and burned. She told him we had lain together."

"Did you?"

"Yes."

CHAPTER TWENTY-SEVEN

"But not the way she said. She said I'd put the black eye upon her and she had no choice."

"That's a very serious thing, Theo."

"I know."

"But you didn't? Put the black eye upon her?"

"I—Yes." He twisted his hands in his hair. "Yes. No. I did, but I didn't mean to. She came to me in the middle of the night, stealing under my covers when I was half-asleep. She touched me, and did things. I had never lain with a woman before. Sometimes you remind me of her, you know," he said, giving her a darkling look. "I told her what was happening to me. I told her to go, but she wouldn't. I warned her to leave me be, and yet at the same time as she kept touching me, I… I changed and we—I—"

"Did you hurt her?"

"No, no, no. She was on top of me. I did nothing to—I didn't *want* any of it. Or…rather, I didn't want to want any of it. She did all she desired with me underneath her."

She really didn't like the date rape territory they'd wandered into. Not one little bit. Instinctively she assumed that if this Gabrina claimed she'd been forced then she probably had been. She frowned at him and moved away.

"Of course. I would never—with my master's—no."

"This is what the men were afraid of—you would do this same thing to me and I would enjoy it, but the next day—?"

"The difference is—with you I want—no, that's *not* what I mean. I did not force her—not in the way of men. If the sounds were anything to judge by, she did enjoy it. She enjoyed herself mightily and from the very beginning, even before I changed." His lip curled. "All the while, across the camp, my master lay in a fever, delirious from the dragon's poison. I kept telling her to be quiet. I was sure he could hear us."

"Theo, the problem is that the way you're describing this, it sounds like she took advantage of *you*. She initiated sex with you. You didn't want to, but she coaxed you along and then your change took over." She thought about it. "She made sure to humiliate you by being overly loud and then the next morning she made sure your master knew that you'd betrayed him and she claimed she had no choice."

"If, as you say, she was an enchantress, then yes, she did. She manipulated me. Used me. But don't you see? It doesn't matter. I've enchanted a woman, and I can never let that happen again. If such a thing happened back where my mother's people lived, they would have killed me. If it happens here, these knights and all the folk from the village would slaughter us."

"But here, where no one can see us—" *And I'm willing.*

"Not even here. We cannot do this. Ever."

She stood there stunned. So sad for him. If it was important to believe someone when she—he in this case—said they'd been manipulated and harmed by having sex, then it was her duty to believe him or her. The whole thing was a terrible snarl. She didn't know this Gabrina—she didn't *know* she was an enchantress. It was horrible to doubt a woman who made such a claim. But he was making the *same* claim. Sort of. Whom to believe?

Wait a minute. If he loved her, such an enchantment wouldn't matter, because what happened between the two of them would be mutually consenting. But he didn't. He didn't like her. She would happily have foregone the physical for a time to be with him romantically, but he didn't want that either. He might desire her because of whatever physical chemistry they had between them—in the way he desired Gabrina physically, but ultimately she was not important to his heart. She felt sick. Her pride was in tatters.

She didn't want to look at him. It hurt too much. She turned and looked at the waterfall. Narrow and spilling milky foam, it underwhelmed her. She turned to stare into the black forest, which was growing ever darker, and pursed her lips together.

Fuck.

"Back to work, then."

"Where are you going?" he asked.

"I have work to do. A famine to stop. I'm going back to the study to look through all those books until I find something that will help."

She strode along, tripping over roots and her skirts from time to time, shaking off his hand on her elbow whenever he steadied her. She was going to give up her foolish obsession for the stupid elf. She was going to bury herself in the most glorious work she knew. It was what she'd always wanted anyway.

She was still deeply peeved. Not at him exactly. He was at least honest. He didn't have to tell her about

Gabrina at all. They entered the tower and she turned into the study, rolling back her sleeves.

"I want—I mean, please put all these books away. Everything except those books that would seem to have some sort of spell for multiplying grain, making crops prosper—you know what I mean. Anything like that."

He began pulling out books and stacking them on the table, putting others away.

She looked around on the table that was covered with Hulgetta's books.

"Hey. I see all Hulgetta's books here, but there was a lot more than just books in the castle."

Theo's eyes crawled all over her face, but he remained silent.

"Peter!"

Peter came into the study with a lantern, several fluttering moths trailing behind him. His robes were gone, his jerkin gone, his shirt unlaced. And hidden in the fold of his collar—was that a red mark upon his neck? A hickie?

She turned away, unable to bear the sign of another couple's happiness. "Peter, what happened to all the magical devices brought from Hulgetta's castle?"

He took so long answering that she turned back. He was studying Theo carefully. Then, moving his lantern, he peered at her for an even longer time. She stiffened up under his gaze, her breath huffing in and out despite herself, not meeting his eye. Her tattered pride hurt so much she was in agony.

"Peter!"

"They were left in the storage closet. Will mistress want to examine them?"

She held her eyes on Theo's. *The storage closet. What storage closet*? Theo stared back. It was a contest of wills between them.

"Yes, Peter, thank you. I would. Show it to me." Peter went over to a part of the wall with an ornate gothic arch molding, pressed something, and a door swung out.

"Will that be all?"

She swallowed with difficulty. "Yes, thank you," she said, her voice hoarse. Her foot tapped hard on the floor for several moments. She pulled back the secret door once more and stuck her head in. Bright moonlight and dust motes moved through the long narrow rows of shelves. She went back into the study and grabbed the big lamp to carry into the room. Three tall free-standing shelves made the space cramped, but they more than made up for it with the contents of their wooden trenches. Each deep shelf held various items nested within, some with tags dangling, some without.

Ba. Nanas. Her eyes flicked around the room, ogling various mysterious, interesting items. On the shelf before her was a peach-colored hand and forearm made of stone. It was sticking out of the shelf like it was waiting for a high five. On the shelf above that was what looked like a stuffed dead crow on its side.

Yours. Your books. Your tower. All yours. The ring rippled.

She drifted about, marveling, letting her fingers trail over a golden pair of manacles. The fairy dust inside her was prancing in response to the magic inside each item. Sometimes less and sometimes more. Such a joyous place! She almost swooned. She looked up suddenly to find Theo in the doorway. His face was inscrutable, but she sensed he was displeased, distressed even.

"You were going to tell me about the closet when?"

"If you are the rightful mistress of this tower, why didn't you know about it?" *Touché.*

"If you're my loyal apprentice then why didn't you *remind* me?" Before he could answer, she spotted a basilisk on the shelf.

"Baz!" she cried out and reached up to touch it. But it wasn't Baz. For one thing it was dead and stiff. For another, it was much larger. She tried reading the tag around its neck. Pulling on the tag caused it to suddenly tumble down to the floor. It hit the stone, its jaw dropped open, and a plume of flame shot forth from its mouth.

"That's why," he said, as the tip of a blue velvet cloth hanging down from a higher shelf caught fire. She pulled it out from under the fossilized arm and ran with it to the narrow window. Opening the window, she hastily dropped the flaming cloth into the yard.

"This is not a game, Mistress Zephyr."

"I know it's not a game," she said testily. "I'm going to find a solution. With or without your help."

He folded his arms. "Mistress, I presume you know the story of Silver Tom."

"Never heard of him. Who's Silver Tom? You can stop looking at me like that. I'm not from around here, not even from this world, so how would I know?"

"A wizard passed through a small village street," he intoned, "without noticing a silver coin had dropped from the pocket of his robe. A boy named Tom found the coin and picked it up. He instantly turned to silver. The villagers gathered around and could hear him crying, but he could not move or speak, or even be lifted. There he stayed in the street of his village night and day. Sometimes people came at night, when no one was looking, and shaved off slivers of the boy to sell for money. Over the years he was slowly whittled away until there was nothing left of Silver Tom."

She waited. "That's it? That's the end?"

The muscles in Theo's jaw pulsed. God, he was so hot. She wanted to bite his lower lip, imagined the feel of his tongue against hers while kissing him. She could imagine it so very clearly, in all its warm perfection, even down to the very taste of him.

"Okay, I get it, I get it, when it comes to magic, don't touch unless you know what you're doing. Look, Theo, I don't know how many ways I can say this. There's magic here!" She threw out her arms hitting the cramped shelves. *Ow*. "If we can use it to stop people from starving then I say what we are doing is a worthy endeavor. Now you're either a part of the problem or a part of the solution. Which is it?"

"There's nothing in here that can help you." He walked out of the closet. She followed him, watching as he resumed pulling books out onto the table and putting others back on the shelf. She lit two candelabra and placed them in the center of the table. Giving him dirty looks, she sat with all deliberation in the uncomfortable tall chair and pulled the first book towards her, opening it up. Soon she was absorbed in the table of contents, her resentment entirely forgotten.

Towards the middle of the night she found something. "This! Theo, look at this." She tapped her finger on the page of the book. The hunk of coal on her finger had been blazing on and off all night long. The book she was reading was in High Anslod.

"Cloud Bird," he read over her shoulder.

"It brings to life 'a bird who has fragrant wings that caress the airy breeze and leaving behind the scent of spice. The bird's presence encourages gentle rains, and such a rain sounds like bird's feet pattering on the roof.' Which is what we need, right? Gentle rains? And it's a simple spell. I'm sure I can do it. This is the one," she said tapping the page.

"I wouldn't attempt it."

"Why not?" she said. "You haven't even looked at it."

"It's Anslod."

"So?"

"It's incredibly imprecise."

"Granted. Maybe." She didn't know, actually. "But I'm very familiar with Anslod. I'm going to do it."

She stood. "I'm going to get changed out of this gown. I need this list of ingredients, and I'll be back."

When she came back downstairs in her robe, he had a whole new stack of books piled up before her stool.

"I've assembled all the history books I could find related to weather and birds in general."

"Great. What for?"

"Study."

She examined the stack closely.

"But—this is far more than I could read in half a year. I don't have time to read these."

He looked uncertain. "You have time to glance through them, surely. It's not like you're making the spell today."

"In fact, I am."

∞

"How are you coming with the Parthian measurements?" She took out a piece of parchment and began mending a quill. She started scratching out the basic ritual from memory, ignoring Theo, who sat there looking rather forbidding. He might not have been in a position to openly forbid her to do the spell, but he made his displeasure clear.

"Theo," she said at last. "Stay or leave. But if you stay, you can't glower at me the whole time. Get me these supplies." She slid the parchment across the table towards him.

"That hawkweed has to be fresh," she said. "And I need a mushroom."

"What's it called?"

"Bleeding tooth. It's small, like this," she said, holding out the tip of her thumb to show him. "White. On the top of the cap it weeps bloody tears. Make sure it's whole."

He nodded and left.

She bit her lip and scratched away at her page, ignoring the slight trembling in her gut. Intense. That was the word for how he looked. She liked intensity. She liked it a lot, though it was making her self-conscious.

He came back with the mushroom.

"What about the hawkweed?"

"We have some over here." He started getting ingredients from the long apothecary box along the wall.

She sniffed at it. "How fresh is it?"

"I don't know."

Was that considered fresh? She had no idea.

"And you think this is acceptable?"

"Yes." He sniffed it. "Of course."

Once everything was gathered on the table she rolled up the sleeves of her black robe.

"Don't do this," he said, standing on the other side of the table.

"Do what?"

"The cloud bird spell. It's dangerous."

"Not true."

"Uncertain. Inconsistent."

"Consistency comes through practice. But you forget what happens if we can't make rain. Do you have a better idea?"

"Only magical devices can be used safely."

"Have you ever made such a device?"

"I have."

"A rain stick? A box that's full of grain every time you open it?"

"No."

"Well, then, this is our only alternative." She was measuring the hawkweed but stopped to peek at him.

"So what'd you make?"

"A spyglass."

"Yeah? Cool. Is there any way this device can help us in our current situation?"

"No."

"Right. If you don't want to do sorcery yourself, fine. I can't make you. But if you're going to have a bad attitude, then get out of my way."

He gave her such a dark, burning stare that she got up and went into the storage closet, shutting the heavy door so she could hyperventilate in peace. She clung to a shelf and put her forehead against it. He looked as if he wanted to leap upon her and—and—it flustered her. More shamefully still, it set a flutter of nerves down low between her legs.

Resolving to be the bigger person was much easier when his bad elf vibe wasn't present. When he was there, and looking at her like that, she wanted to provoke him, tease him, and when he was good and angry, she wanted to suffer the consequences. What he was like in bad elf form? She leaned against the door, trying to control her breathing.

Your apprentice.

Stupid ring.

Your tower, your books, your rings.

Shut up.

She shook her head. That way lay madness. She emerged from the closet and went back to her preparations.

"Eight tries before we run out of hawkweed. Hulgetta often took twelve or more tries," she told Theo. "Also, this seven-toed left front paw of a mole looks a little mushy," she said, weighing it in her hand. "I hope it still has some juice left in it. I'd say probably only four more tries. And it's the only one we have."

She took a big breath, gathering up her nerves into excitement because really, was there anything better than magic?

"Ready?"

By then everything was neatly laid out on a table near the windows where the white moonlight spilled down. She moved the ingredients out of the range of the burning beeswax drips from the tapers above.

She folded back her sleeves, read the spell four times and looked up at him. "You know, this'll go much faster if you help me."

He removed his surcoat and rolled up the fine linen sleeves of his shirt. She started in with the tincture of eagle's feather. The smell of burning feathers made her head hurt and she went to stand near the windows, opening them wide and trying to breathe some fresh air.

They continued, and as he handed her items, she could tell he'd been an apprentice before—a much better one than her. If nothing else, he'd been at it longer. She tried to imagine doing a demonstration of a spell for him and couldn't. He was probably already much more accomplished than her when it came to performing magic.

By three in the morning, she was ready to give up in despair.

"It's not working."

CHAPTER TWENTY-EIGHT

"I can't even get the base to catalyze. Here, you try." She pushed the mortar and pestle over to him.

"Me?"

"Yes. Maybe I'm doing something wrong." She picked up the bundle of hawkweed and inhaled. She watched him and was impressed. Everything he did was with precision. He was much better than her at every point when it came to assembling the base in the right order, through the right procedures. It was a lowering thought.

"It doesn't work," he said.

She came and stood over the spot and looked at the sticky straw lump. She poked at it, and it gave off a few crackles of energy.

"We're close, Theo." *Not close enough.*

"Wait a minute," he said, "is this spell translated from the Parthian?"

She looked at the spell. The ring on her finger blazed brightly as she looked at it. There—she suddenly recognized the grammatical construction he picked up on—how the adjectives were always placed at the end.

She frowned. "So?"

"Anslod does not have the same measurement scale as Parthian. The measurements are off."

It's always something. She lifted up her hands to look at her rings. *Some help, guys.* The rings stayed dark. *Okay, think.* She leaned over the book.

"This part here, where it says a small cup—"

He didn't seem to be listening. He seemed to be sniffing her hair. She paused, that fizz between them bubbling up once again.

"Show me the cup you used," she said. "It seemed large to me."

He pointed to the cup measure. She stared at the array of implements, and examined the metallic cup. "These are different from what Hulgetta used. Hers were fancy little wood things. Much smaller. They were shaped differently as well." She tapped her teeth with a finger. "Do we have the measuring spoons and cups from Hulgetta's lair?"

"I have no idea."

She went into the storage room and poked around. *Cups, cups, who's got the cups?*

There was a beautiful copper hand mirror with some writing on it. She picked it up. Around the edge, in Parthian no less: *Your True Love's Reflection.* She turned the mirror around, only to give a jump and a squeak as his hand came around behind her and gripped the mirror, twisting and pulling it away from her.

"Don't lose your focus," he said into her temple. She turned to glare up at his face, well, his chin at least, crowded together as they were.

His arm stole around her waist, his eyes flashing black for a moment. She felt the throb of him, and her bosom was suddenly heaving.

"Remember the famine."

Right.

Still.

He tucked the mirror up on a shelf out of her reach. She counted to ten again, this time in all the languages she could think of.

Okay. Okay. He's right. Don't lose focus. Just don't look at him, okay? They stood for a moment toe to toe. She quavered, her insides melting.

"Ah! Here," he said, plucking something from the shelf just over her head.

The cups! Familiar and a little greasy to the touch, they were not perfectly cylindrical like Theo's cups, but rather hand carved into four quarters—like a four-leaf clover. Her fingers felt for the notches inside.

"Huzzah! Bring them into the light." She left behind the darkened study and darted into the dirty golden glow of the candelabra. He carried the cups to the table and held up the lantern.

"It's smaller, see? There's also this notch inside. That's the line we used for a cup." She pointed out the grooved line.

"For a 'generous' cup Hulgetta always filled the liquid to the brim instead, so the cup was almost overflowing. You see? This is her handwriting. She translated the original and in doing so created a kind of code. It's obvious to her—the exact difference between a small cup and a generous cup—but would pass unnoticed by anyone else who tried the spell."

You were a paranoid wench, Hulgetta. But I've got the measure of you. The problem, of course, was in deciphering the rest of the spell. And she needed sleep, desperately. Her eyes were crossing, she was so tired.

"It's been a long day, Theo. Aren't you weary?"

"Not at all, mistress." Of course not.

"Okay. Then here's the plan. I'm going to retire for a short nap. You're a clever fellow. When I come back I want you to have this code cracked."

"I wouldn't know how to begin."

Was he being deliberately obtuse?

"You'll figure it out. She could have used a code word to stand in for a specific measurement. Small cup. Generous cup."

"What else?"

"We also need some understanding of Parthian measurements. See if something on the shelves will help us?" She gestured at the books.

She turned to go and then turned back. "There's something I want to say. Tell me that you'll help me on this project. I know you don't lie." *Don't make me say it, Theo. Don't make me use the ring.*

"I would never hurt my mistress."

"I know." *Don't make me say it.*

He came forward towards her and she found herself backing up to the door of the study. He looked offended, but he kept getting closer, and closer.

"I will help you," he said softly. There! His eyes turned black. She caught it, but it was only a flash. His mouth hovered over hers.

"About us," she said in a whisper. "No one would have to know. If that's what you want."

"It wouldn't be honorable," he said.

She backed out of the room and shut the door. *Grrrrr.* He was so forthright and sincere at times, so enigmatic and maddening at others.

By the time she got to her bedchamber, and with the help of a maid got her corset off she was in agony. The more she thought about the things she had said and done around him, the more superficial and power grabbing she felt she had been. Flinging off the rest of her clothes, she climbed up into the big bed. Burying her face in her pillow she screamed and screamed all her frustrations out until she was exhausted.

She fell asleep, heartsick to the core.

∞

She looked tired. She sat in the study wearing that black square-necked robe that was too big for her. He looked at the hem. It was actually his old robe. Her eyes were puffy, and she'd pinned a sloppy braid into a crown across her head. She sat on the stool, looking ahead at the table covered with the ingredients for the spell, her back hunched.

"Have you broken your fast, mistress?"

"Thank you, I'm not hungry. I'm more excited to see what you've got to show me." She leaned forward, peering at the cups, but wouldn't look at him.

"I checked the measurements from Hulgetta's cups against the Ligean measurements.

It turns out that the small cup measurement is the same as the Ligean vulta-cup. I compared the rest of the Ligean measurements with the other cups and items I found. They're the same."

"What about the Parthian measurements?"

He shrugged. "One civilization follows another, or is corrupted or influenced by a previous culture. The Parthians invaded Ligea. Maybe they adopted their mathematics when that happened."

"Well done. Clever apprentice."

"And once we looked for it, the code Hulgetta used was easy to crack."

"Good."

"I still feel that—"

But she wasn't listening. "This is your conversion list?" she asked, leaning over it.

He gave up. It felt odd seeing his master's favorite table covered with metal bowls and little bundles of dried plants, instead of books.

He had been careful in the months since his master's death to preserve everything just the way his master had left it. Now all was deranged, and it felt sacrilegious to him. She rolled up her wide sleeves with twists so they were tight and bunched around her forearms in a practical way. Like she was about to knead dough. She got to work measuring out the different herbs and elements from a row of silver boxes, and, like Eldred, seemed to see or hear nothing around her while she was absorbed in her work.

"You can measure these out for me, ahead of time, when we do another spell," she said. Then she began ripping up hawkweed as if it were available under every bush. The only reason they had any was because it grew on the mountain where Eldred died, two hundred leagues from here. It was the only mountain so far where he'd ever found any, and he'd gathered it to burn on Eldred's funeral pyre. Watching her rip it up, he suddenly hated her. Hated her with a passion. He felt his elf side throb with it, and tried to think of something else.

Handing him the little rubbery mole paw with seven toes, she said, "Boil this for me over the chaffing dish." He went to the table near the windows, a table with a small chaffing bowl the size of a large goblet set up in its place. He placed the small bricks of charcoal in the bowl, got them burning and placed the metal cup of water on top. She went back to her grinding.

Just for an instant, her manner brought Eldred back to him again, and he felt the sting of his master's loss afresh. As he stirred the mole's foot in boiling water, he felt less burdened by the tremendous weight of responsibility for his master's death. He looked at her still grinding away at the hawkweed. She thought him imbued with magic. He'd never thought about it that way. He was used to hearing himself derided as not entirely elf, or eyed with suspicion for not being wholly human.

Certainly magic affected him, unsettled him deeply. Not nearly as much as she unsettled him. In that first moment of his suffering, she'd been so kind. Her intentions were good. It was her overweening lust for magic that raised his ire. One who would do anything for magical power was evil. It was up to him to find a way to thwart her. He would have to pick his battles, and when the time was right find a way to pluck her power from her.

He added in the water that had been boiled with the mole's foot to the hawkweed she had powdered. The ground up mixture of herbs turned bright purple when she used it to cover a dried eagle's claw.

"It calls for a pigeon's claw," she said, "but I think this is fine, as long as it's coming from a bird. It's the only one properly dried. We don't really have time to dry another."

Her expression had become intent and almost wild as she arranged the gloppy paste over the claw. Then with the claw she drew a set of designs with the paste.

"If you're copying those from the book you're doing a slipshod job of it."

She looked and corrected her design, but the whole was rather imprecise, which offended him.

"This next part requires patience," she said.

He almost snorted. He'd seen nothing of patience from her, ever. Yet as she kneaded the eagle's foot, adding more and more of the hawkweed concoction, the oblong claw shape eventually became a ball about the size of his fist and as the ball grew around the claw, becoming more and more stiff while her hands kneaded the shape along the pattern of the design on the table. He watched, mesmerized by the dance of her hands, until at one point she ripped the ball apart.

"Where's the claw?" he asked. The center of the ball exuded a sort of spray like an orange when the skin was torn.

"It transmuted. That's why it's called magic, Theo," she said in response to his expression. "If you are amazed by that, then watch this next part."

It happened so slowly that he did not quite know when the ball became transparent. She'd been at it for hours. And now she flicked her fingers and shook her wrists to relieve their fatigue.

He could feel the faint tickle of magic coming from the ball, and saw the near-empty weight she scooped into her hands.

"Good, good," she whispered. "See the suspended mist in the air? Feel it. Put your hand through it."

He passed his hand through it, and enjoyed a brief sensation of clammy moisture, but something else as well. He pulled his hand back quickly. She gave him a smile radiant with conspiratorial glee. It lit her from within and for an instant she was so beautiful he found looking at her painful. Yet only a few minutes later, he caught the hesitation and desperation that flashed across her face.

"What is it, mistress?"

"I think I need some kind of stabilizing element. Something it can feed upon to give it substance. The spell calls for all this clagipher skin stuff. Do we have any?"

"No, mistress."

"I didn't think so. So here's the thing—we never had any either. And Hulgetta said it wasn't important, but it helps the spell build structure."

"What do you need?"

"Well, to build structure hair has keratin in it. That has a kind of cellulose structure. Also, it's pliant, but stable." She combed the fingers of her free hand through her hair, and taking hold of a single hair, slowly, gradually, let the hair touch the ball, just the tip.

Slowly, over time, the single long hair shrank away. Then it was gone. She combed through her hair again. More hairs came away, tangled about her fingers. Again they were consumed.

"What do you think?" she said, eyeing the ball in her hand.

"Looks the same."

"I know." She made a moue with her mouth, then quirked it.

"Maybe it just needs more. Here, you feed it," she said handing the ball over to him.

"Me? I couldn't possibly—"

"Stop being a baby. Come on."

She swiftly left and then returned with a comb. She began to thoroughly go through her hair, until there was a flat little nest of it on the table.

The feeding went on all day. He got four hours of sleep in the evening while she took over, but when he came into the study at the blue light just before dawn, she was lying with her head on her arm, asleep. He woke her.

"It didn't take," she said. She looked at the puddle lying on the center of the table, and he saw the dried tear tracks on her cheeks. She covered her eyes with her hands, shook her head, and then buried it in her arms again.

"Leave me alone," she said.

CHAPTER TWENTY-NINE

"We've got to try one more time," she said. "This time it will work," she assured him, giving his hand a squeeze. Her smile was a travesty.

"What happened to make the others fail?"

She paced back and forth along the strip of carpet, arms behind her back. "It wasn't the amount of hair, it was…" her thoughts went inward and she fell silent.

She was staring at him, her head tilted. What a peculiar expression on her face. He felt a tangle of dread twist around his guts.

"Theo."

Evil. The drive to accomplish this feat of magic was all in all to her. A mania.

"Theo." He didn't want to respond.

"Give me your hand." She took his hand and then a very sharp knife. He braced himself, but all she did was carefully trim his fingernails with a knife. Then they started the whole process over from the beginning. She ground up the hawkweed and looked at him over the mortar and pestle. Their last chance. Despite himself he felt her excitement infect him.

When she fed the ball his fingernails the results were immediate. The misty ball grew and a vague form of a curled-up bird took shape within the mist.

"Yes, yes! I knew it!" she said, and began dancing around the room, throwing her arms up with joy. She came prancing to him, her eyes ablaze.

"We needed keratin, but it had to be magic keratin," she said, taking the ball from him and weighing it in her hand. She carefully transferred it back to his palm. "And it's taking on resilience and weight. Look!" She showed him the moist slick of water on her palm.

"Ha ha! We found the batteries!" He couldn't follow her thoughts. She gesticulated and talked about storing magic up, how she'd used all her store, but because he was magic, his store was ever available.

If it was true, it was still not enough. They fed the shape, and he was the first to notice.

"It's stopped growing."

Her face was stark white, and her eyes bloodshot. Her skin was shiny from lack of sleep and exhaustion. She disappeared into the storage closet.

"What are you doing?"

"Stay there," she called. "I need to find something." He didn't think it wise to let her rummage around in the closet on her own, but she came back out almost immediately with a small tin. Opening the tin she dropped the contents out across the table. The claws scattered all about with a rattle. Greenish black and quite long, he noticed they continued rattling after they should have stopped.

"No. What are they? No, you can't use them."

They rolled about like weevils, until one almost rattled off the table. She scooped it up in time.

"We need some magical oomph."

"I don't recognize them."

"Does it matter?"

"Yes, yes it does."

"I'm trying it."

The ball of birdfluff liked the claws. It consumed them greedily and continued to grow. It also began spinning much faster and making little sharp popping noises.

"What's that?" he asked.

"I think it's shifting the air pressure around it." A louder pop.

"Gah!" She pulled on her ear and shook her hair. "It's making my ears pop."

He moved closer to her as she held the ball in both hands, because despite himself, it was interesting. The head and wings were forming.

Her hands were wet like they'd been dipped in water. The cloud form grew, and as he crept closer the beak began to form upon an impossibly scrawny neck. It was peering around and holding its wings out from its body.

"Is it hurting?"

"Oooh, you're just beautiful!" She cooed at the bird and leaned down to kiss the misty air about it. "Though I wonder if that really was an eagle's claw. You're a little more vulture-like to me."

"What's it supposed to look like when it's done?" he asked.

"It's—ow! Stop it. It bit me." She had a faint pink gash across her thumb. The cloud bird formed a longer neck. It opened its beak, waggling its bent finger-like tongue up and down. She fed it the penultimate nasty claw.

"Eagle or vulture, you're still my little miracle. Aren't you? Aren't you?"

She picked it up and bent her head down closer to it.

"Ow!" The tip of her nose was turning bright pink, and she rubbed it with her free hand. The thing climbed up onto her forearm and gripped her there, the size of a small sharp spur hawk. Again the beatific smile lit her from within.

"You want this?" The bird eagerly opened its maw. She fed it the last claw and the creature continued to grow.

"Is it heavy?" He could see that it weighed more; her arm had dropped a few inches. The bird was now almost two feet high.

"Sorta. Like a heavy waterlogged towel."

The form grew feathers, and the wings began to stretch out again, the bird first holding out one then another. It started biting her arm.

"Zephyr! Mistress, I mean."

"Ow. Ow. It's alright. Just a sting. Feels like the snap of a wet towel He's not breaking the skin." More pops followed.

He was impatient, alarmed. "Why's it biting you like that? The book said 'gentle and mild.'"

"I don't know."

Now the bird was moving as it grew, stretching out its claws, shuffling from side to side on her arm and ducking its head, bobbing it down and then back up. The wings stretched out and flapped a few times. She threaded her fingers gently through the creature's legs and held it to her forearm, as it began flapping its wings in earnest wanting to leave its human perch.

"I'm trying to hold it, but it's really strong," she said, her arm braced and her other hand holding on.

"I'll find a basket or cage."

"Good! Or a chain or net. Quickly!"

He stretched out a hand towards it. The thing's head reached out in his direction, mouth open. There was a big pop. She was right; it felt like the snap of a wet rag. He shouldn't have been surprised that it hurt and stung, but he pulled his hand back, shaking it. The red splotch was like a wasp's sting.

He could have sworn the creature turned and looked right back at him. It hunched its vulture shoulders and bobbed its head up and down a few times, as if to insult him with body gestures. He didn't want to leave it alone with her. It was eerie. As if reading his thoughts, the bird opened its misty jaws and screamed at him.

The noise was intensely loud, ending in the hissing crackle, a sound reminiscent of the noise that comes just before a lightning strike. With the scream, the bird fell *through* her arm and plopped onto the table, rolling around in its surprise while Zephyr stared at it with her mouth open. Theo almost wanted to laugh. It quickly righted itself, but when Zephyr began trying to pick it up again, it scooted away from her hand. She chased it down the table and it turned its head diving at her hand, biting left and right. The whole spell was going out of control. In addition to everything else, a smell of burning hair and ozone filled the room. He involuntarily stepped away, his body feeling fizzy with danger and magic, the elfish side of him thrashing to get out.

"Let it dissipate, let it dissolve," he said from the doorway.

"I can't," she called back while she chased after the bird. "We're too close. Look, it'll be alright, just find a net. Hurry!"

By the time he got back with a small hay net from the stables, the beast had grown three times as large. Now it was perched on the back of a chair. Nearly three and a half feet tall, it stretched out its mighty wings, almost tipping the chair over in the process. Zephyr was at the far end of the study looking dazed and blinking rapidly. At first he thought she was trying to escape the bird by going out the window. Then he realized she was hurriedly trying to close the windows.

"Close the door. Quietly," she called.

But the bird was ignoring him at the moment, so instead he quickly crept closer, the net outstretched, ready to be thrown over its body. The bird gave a casual hop over to the table, and proceeded to rip a long strip from the page of a book and begin chewing. It looked back at him suddenly, stopped chewing, and swallowed. It turned back and ripped another strip from the page.

He threw the net over it.

The bird stopped chewing and spat out the pulpy scrap of page. From under the net it turned to look at him and gave an *urk* of warning.

"What should I do now?" he said, keeping an eye on the bald black head. The plumage was almost purplish where it was darkest around the shoulders and mottled dark grey down the belly like angry thunderclouds. Across the breast and neck, a rainbow sheen caught the light across the feathers, that turned lighter grey and downy on its legs. The bird looked at him with eyes of yellow-green.

"Grab it!"

He lunged forward, hands out, and the bird shrieked. It panicked, diving all over the table, crumpling the open book pages, while he tried to hold onto the net and gather the bird to him. Wings flapping, the bird grasped the net with its clawed foot. It chewed upon the net with its vicious beak then launched itself towards him. He stood his ground, but the bird got tangled into the net and fell off the table.

Zephyr was there suddenly. Her hands grabbing the net and suspending the bird before it hit the stone floor. With one echoing scream the bird melted through the net, bounced off the floor and then ran across the stones before lurching into flight.

"Why is the door still open? Theo!"

The cloud bird took to the air, scraping past his head, and flew out the open door, leaving the study to fly off into the stairwell.

"Now look what you've done," Zephyr said and with an angry, frustrated look bound out of the room towards the stairs.

"Hurry! Close the other windows," she panted.

He followed with the net, though realizing it was of no use, he cast it down behind him. As he watched, the cloud bird glided about the vertical open space, clumsily, bumping and bashing into the various ornamental projections of the vaulted stairs. He could hear Zephyr panting up to the top floor. The bird stopped to grip a respond and looked around, hanging off the stone ornamentation like a bat hanging off a stalactite. It opened its beak when it saw him and the strange white-and-black tongue protruded almost like a panting dog's. A gargling screech emerged and echoed about the tower walls. The bird was mocking him.

She was now on the sixth floor. He could hear her slam the bedroom chamber closed. He saw the bird lazily fly up to the balustrade on the fourth floor and hurriedly he followed. It launched itself into the air and began circling around and around.

Zephyr's form flitted by him on the stairs and slammed the dining room doors closed. Theo followed her down.

"Second floor," she panted. "Balcony."

But before he could make it down to that landing, the bird came zooming straight at him and perched on the railing of the stairs between the third and second floor. Zephyr looked up at him from the second floor, her expression half awed and half alarmed.

"Not sure exactly what to do now. We need to leash it and get it—whoa!"

The cloud bird flapped its wings, ducking its head down at her while screeching. She threw up her arms, waving them, and it sheered away from the second floor balcony. Outside, the sky was rapidly becoming covered in a thin scrim of cloud and glare.

"Nice bird. Come back down here," she said, tapping the railing, her voice melodic and calm, authoritative but pleasing. The bird gave her a look then dive bombed her. She stood her ground, but it was dense enough to knock her over, and he rushed down towards her.

"I'm fine! I'm fine—just get the bird."

From outside they heard the sudden spatter of rain and a peel of lightning.

The bird cried out in response and wheeled about back up to the fourth floor. So he followed. Rain dropped from its wings, soaking the flagstones below. It circled around again, gliding more steadily, to perch on the railing again. He had picked up the net and had an arm through it.

He kept eye contact, yet crept forward. *Distance. Know your distance*. The bird eyed him and ducked, but almost seemed like it was waiting to be caught. Less than three feet away. Then two. He leapt, hearing Zephyr's scream echo across to him.

"THEO!" The net wrapped over the bird, his arms wrapped around it, and they were falling.

The bird broke through the net, but his arms were still about it as it briefly carried him into the stair well. They were rapidly dropping before the bird screamed and misted through him. Something wild, something almost evil touched off his inner elf as he felt himself fall. From thirty feet up he heaved himself towards the second floor railing, bounced off it and crashed onto the flagstones below, knocking his head.

The world pulsed all around him. *Stupid bird.* The world went black.

∞

He came to, his face wet and long strands of Zephyr's hair tickling his cheeks. Colors appeared all around him, not just from the door of the study, but also from her rings as she held his hand to her breast. And behind her colors burst out from the stupid bird. It held onto a vault beam over the stairs and peered down at him. He felt himself pulsing hard and involuntarily because of her nearness.

His head turned into her lap. He buried his face in her gown, smelling her through it for just a second. A clutch of servants huddled over near the stairs down to the kitchen, apparently too afraid of the bird to come help.

Meanwhile, she was patting him all over.

"Are you alright? Anything broken?" her voice cut off on a sob. "What were you doing?" she said, thumping his chest. "You almost got yourself killed."

"I'm fine, fair mistress."

She got up and stared down at him. "Your eyes are black."

"I know," he gritted out, fighting the furious need to crush her in his arms, to bruise her lips against his, to carry her up to the top of the stairs away from everyone else. "I'm fine. Go get the bird," he said, rubbing the back of his head.

"How?" A tremendous crackle of lightning came from outside the tower. She looked up at the bird, who looked at her and then launched itself into the air.

“It’s playing a game,” she said. “Are any other windows still open?”

“The balcony,” he said, pointing. She was up and running for it. He followed, slipping on the wet step. She fell too, and then he was past her, his head splitting with pain.

They arrived together. But it was too late. Completely horrified, he watched as the bird aimed for the balcony door, and Zephyr stood right in front of it. She crouched down low, so he thought she meant to duck the bird, but instead she tried to imitate him. She launched herself up, caught it, and tried to hold it to her breast, while the bird clawed at her and dragged her over the railing.

CHAPTER THIRTY

He caught her gown, her knee under the gown, and around her hips, before she went entirely over. The bird turned its neck and screamed in her face. As it did so, the bird misted through her arms. Her weight sank over the railing suddenly, but he hauled her back, pulling as hard as he could so they both fell onto the balcony floor together.

They sat up, watching as the bird did a circle. With a powerful flap of wings it launched itself up to the tall black pines. It screamed out at them a few times as a hard, drenching rain began to fall. Then, with an enormous flapping of wings, it flew up and off towards the western horizon, its body sinking under its large size. Despite these difficulties, it soon caught a draft of air, and swept up away towards the sunset.

"Blast, blast, BLAST YOU, STUPID BIRD!" she shouted after it, leaning over the railing and shaking her fist in the bird's direction. He pulled her back from the railing and back into the tower, out of the rain. They panted together, wet and out of breath. His hands remembered the feel of her naked leg, the back of her knee. She looked up at him, and the piercing tang of his desire made him turn away. He could hear her stomping up the stairs to go change.

"Don't talk to me," she said, when he tried to follow. Furious, she stalked up to the third floor. Leaning over the railing, she called down below. "All of you there. Open all these windows again. It might come back."

∞

For the rest of the week he watched his mistress limp about like an old woman and rub at her hip when she thought no one else was looking. Servants said they heard the bird in the woods at dawn. She limped off to the woods as they called out all the men, little boys, and clever girls who trapped forest creatures for food for their families. No one saw the bird. For days Zephyr practically lived in the woods, but it was useless, there were no more sightings of it anywhere. Plainly it was gone.

He'd offered her the spyglass he'd made under Eldred's tutelage, so she could see if the bird was lurking somewhere nearby. Certainly there were more clouds dotting the sky off to the west. He thought that if she had something to do, she might quit poring over all the books he'd laid out on weather and birds, and pushing away the food that Dorcas brought. He wanted her to study, but not in such an obsessed fashion, refusing to do anything but read, falling asleep in her chair. He wanted to shake her out of this melancholy spirit. He was not used to seeing her silent and quelled. It alarmed him greatly.

"How does it work?" she asked listlessly.

He showed her how it telescoped outwards and stood with a hand on her shoulder.

It was like when they were alone in the forest. She kept her head averted, but a mutual feeling, an understanding, coursed back and forth between them. He needed to comfort her. This was the only remedy he could find.

"How is it magical?"

"Do not worry about that, mistress. I never got it to work the way I wanted."

"I understand. We were so close, Theo."

"I know."

He came back not half an hour later and she whirled around, her hands behind her back, looking guilty as sin.

"What did you do?"

"Nothing. I was looking for the bird."

"What did you *do*?"

She brought out the glass from behind her back. "I moved this little lever."

"Why would you do that? Show me."

"See, I fiddled with the little knob sticking out here, and suddenly it clicked over to the far end of the semicircle. But then it hung loose afterwards."

"Must you destroy everything you touch?"

She was as red as if he'd slapped her.

"I'm so sorry."

"Why did I show it to you? Why did I even let you touch it? I should never have trusted you."

"Theo, I'm scared. Look," she passed him the glass and pointed east. He looked out over the valley below, focusing on the far road that wound up and down towards the border.

"I see nothing."

"Hold the knob. There, like that." She pushed the lever over and held it with one finger. He did so and raised the glass again.

On the East Road he spied an army. Inside a giant peach cloud of dust, they came riding from far away. Men on heavy destriers. Their armor glinted in the strong sunlight, almost blinding his view through the glass. He tried to count them, but they moved along in a seething mass. Behind the riders marched men with pikes, and behind that, a long thin line of carts. He put down the glass. Her face looked up at him with a pinched expression.

"We don't have a standing unit of soldiers in this region. Some kind of militia?"

"You know we have not."

"Because no one would attack a powerful wizard in a defensible tower. Only there is no wizard now. Can you fix it?" She put a finger on the glass.

"I don't know," he said. Turning over the spyglass, he started taking it apart.

"I'm really so sorry, Theo. Believe me."

"I don't believe you. I don't trust you. Right now I don't even like you." It hurt. It hurt down deep. He stormed off, not trusting himself to stay. He wanted her stripped of anything to do with magic. She was a force of destruction and must be stopped.

∞

Her face was grey-white, her eyes fluttering closed as she slumped before a pile of books. He was there reluctantly at Peter's insistent request.

"She's not eating. Dorcas has been in the kitchen cooking every dish she knows, trying to tempt the mistress," the servant whispered.

He walked into the study and stood before her. He slapped a book down on the table and she jumped.

"Trying to find another spell?" he asked. "One that might help the crops?"

She gave a sigh and shrugged. Books lay open everywhere.

He was still feeling the wicked urges from his encounter with the bird, his elf side harder than ever to control. The throb had started to come up when he was around her, when he thought of her, when he remembered how she smelled in her robe. So he stayed away, down at the building site for the tourney ring. Color leaked from items all around them in the study, making the ordinary world look dull and grey by comparison. Pink, purple, and blue spilled from her hands, the books around her, and even from his own fingernails when he looked down at them. A vague pulse occurred now and then, stirring his cock, his old ability to quell it gone. He was beginning to crack. As a result, he avoided her whenever possible.

She looked up from where she leaned over the table in her unwashed robe, head resting on her hand.

"Is there anything else, apprentice?"

"Do something," Peter hissed from the doorway, and gave him a little push motion.

"Have you eaten today?" he asked.

She shook her head. He noticed she was quirking that rosebud mouth in the way she had. It made him want to throttle her, but it also signaled she was hiding something. He came closer.

What was she up to now?

"Why didn't the spell work?"

"It did work. You saw the bird. It worked."

"That was no bird of gentle rain and mist. What were those claws you fed it?"

"Just claws. They were in the cupboard."

"You knew what they were, didn't you?"

She wouldn't answer. The ripe *O* of her lips began quirking again like mad as she shuffled her books about, stacking some on top of others. Almost as if she were hiding them from him. He tried another tactic.

"Mistress? As your apprentice, I have earned your confidence, haven't I?"

"Yes."

"Then why will you not confide in me? What were they?"

Her eyes went wide. "What does it matter? You want to shame me, tell me I messed up the spell."

"That's not an answer. What are you hiding?" He paced another step closer.

"Nothing," she said, her voice quieter, shrinking back into her chair. He went to the table, pulled her out her chair, and hauled her up by her wrists.

"Hey!" she protested. At least she was waking up.

Nose to nose with her, he said, "Do not ever lie to me."

"I used demon claws."

He threw her away from him—utterly disgusted.

She rubbed her wrists. "It made the spell work."

Between fighting his inner elf and not giving her a box on the ear, he was beside himself. "Demon claws. It's astounding that you're still alive."

She gave a huff of breath like she'd been holding it. "I didn't know you cared."

He didn't. He didn't want to, certainly. Unfortunately, she was rapidly becoming an obsession with him. An obsession as mad as her own fixation with magic and spells. He wanted to claw into her, to knock that indifference out of her. Her flaws twisted into him like burrs digging under his skin, making him throb with frustration.

"Look to your character. What have you done but lie and hide the truth? Look at the result. Deceivers never wield magic well."

"I am not a deceiver."

"Something odd has happened in this tower. What is unclear, but I'd lay down my life you're the cause of it."

She looked like she was holding back tears.

"I'm in as much of a fog as you."

"You are ruining the reputation of this ancient tower, which has been a pillar of good and righteousness for the last six hundred years."

She wrung her hands. "I confess, yes, I knew they were demon claws."

"An air of deception hangs about you." She flinched like he'd struck her. "I should never have become your apprentice."

A tear spilled down her face, but with a look he knew well, she said, "You're telling me you've never committed any sins of omission? I don't believe you. It is difficult to be candid with someone whom you suspect is always concealing his thoughts and feelings."

Shrewd mistress. I hide the desire to throw you down in the dark woods and...

He tightened his lips and managed to scrape out the words, "I see."

She said nothing. *Very well.*

He turned to leave. Catching sight of one of her books, he said, "What's that?"

"Nothing," she said lightly.

"Liar!" he said, and his eyes throbbing, changing, churning, the room filled with a pinkish red hue with various blues and purples—which poured from the book. He grabbed it in one hand, her wrist in the other.

"Ow," she said. The book tumbled to the table. He let her go and reached for it.

"Immortality!" He cursed her.

"I just found it on the shelf. You said you're immortal. Why shouldn't I be?" she said.

"Because you're not ready. Never attempt such a thing with inferior spells. Promise me."

"I promise," she said listlessly. He took a deep breath to stop the anger that was pushing him to the brink.

Tossing the book down, he hustled her out of her chair to the stairs. He was going to have to do something about this whole situation.

"You have not eaten in days," he said. "Dorcas has laid out a meal for you upstairs."

"I'm not hungry."

"I don't care. I thought you respected Dorcas. She's been straining to cook something that would tempt you all day."

"Fine. But don't touch that book while I'm gone."

"Mistress, I would never destroy any book in the library," he vowed. He escorted her upstairs and left her seated at the massive dining room table all alone. She looked like a starving orphan, her eyes big. He excused himself.

"I thought you might join me," she said wretchedly. He excused himself. Then he went right back downstairs, determined to hide the book where she'd never find it. He'd hide several other items while he was at it. He wouldn't reveal where everything was hidden. Not even if she punished him for it.

The idea of her punishing him for his wicked deeds set his brain on fire. Many other incendiary mental images followed that one, until he went out and doused himself in the horse trough.

"Theo, we need more firewood," Dorcas said from the kitchen door. He gave her one look and she instantly vanished back into the kitchen. That and the throbbing of his brain told him his eyes had changed yet again.

He doused his head repeatedly, and when that didn't work he exercised his feelings with the axe upon a hapless pile of firewood. While he chopped wood, he began to devise a plan that would strip her power from her. She had to be stopped.

∞

Theo wouldn't stay, but Peter came up to join her in the dining hall while she ate. She felt as bad as she had that first night, and as unworthy of being waited upon by all the servants in the enormous tower. All the wizards above looked down upon her in judgment and she squirmed in her seat. She noticed Peter once again wore the short, poofy striped breeches that stopped well above his knees, plus the robe over his usual jerkin.

"Been out and about, Peter?"

"Merely checking on the tourney ring, mistress."

"How goes it?"

"Theo has it well in hand. Well in hand."

"Can't we do something about this famine, Peter? Dig ditches. Use irrigation from the river?" She'd spent considerable time explaining these concepts to him.

"Excellent schemes one and all. There isn't time, unfortunately, mistress."

"What about a conjuror?"

"Well, yes, the question of a conjuror is certainly an interesting one. We could certainly use one, if not two or three. I've heard conjurors know how to make rain. Yes."

"Why not get one, then?"

"I'm afraid they are all up north. I've never seen or heard of one so far south."

"You mean they mostly stay where it rains all the time." Her tone was dry.

"Why, yes. Perhaps that's true."

She liked Peter, and saw something now of what Dorcas saw in him. He didn't seem plain at all to her now, but rather warm, meticulous, intelligent, with large bedroom eyes. They weren't brown; they were pale grey, with dark, spikey lashes. He was very patient with her. He reminded her of those incredibly charming British fellows who displayed the best sort of breeding via their manners and character.

Unlike her. She was of a low character, according to Theo. She went over to pick up the spyglass and looked out the window as a matter of habit.

"Sorry, I'm afraid I didn't catch that," Peter said.

"Nothing. Mumbling to myself."

"Still a week left, mistress, before the crops are done for. And plenty of clouds off on the horizon. We may get rain yet." She stood and looked out the window. There were clouds, but nothing else. Just the fields, and a large cloud of dust from the future tourney ring site to the south.

"Have you used your glass recently?"

"Theo's glass," she said listlessly. "It's not good, Peter."

She swiveled the glass out towards the western horizon, but saw nothing very different than before. Empty sky. However, when she looked over towards the main road that led from the east into their land, she spied several giant trees that weren't actually there now. Putting the glass down, she peered out with her own eyes. So odd. Nothing but bare hills, devoid of people. She looked through the glass again, and once more the giant trees emerged. She tried holding the glass in one spot on the road, and then swung the little knob, holding it in place at the far end.

They were still there. Along with a small army riding forth in fierce determination down the road and straight towards the tower. Squinting, she tried to peer through the dust obscuring them. In the center one individual stood out from the rest—a man with long hair—or was it a woman? Whoever it was, the others who surrounded this long haired figure rode their destriers, heraldic banners fluttering in the breeze. She couldn't make out the tattered heraldic devices through the low dust. Seasoned men, no doubt, mercenaries with enormous grizzled beards. She felt such a surge of fear watching them. Valdeans. They were coming. But when?

She moved back to the dining room table. She wanted to talk to Theo about it. She hung her head, wondering what Peter and Dorcas had said to him to get him to show up at the tower.

"Pigeon pie?"

She returned to her seat and the towering pie was set before her on the table, a slice cut and set on a plate in front of her. Haunted by what she saw, she picked at the dish. It was full of fowl, burdock root, leeks and peas. The last of the vegetables from the winter, as well as a few from the spring. The whole sat in a savory gravy with rosemary bits swimming in butter. Taking up her knife and using her spoon in place of the fork these people had never heard of, she nibbled at the pie. "Mmm," she said, making an effort. Peter's chest puffed up with pleasure.

Actually, she was a little hungry. The back of her jaw and her throat almost cramped at the taste of food. She took another bite. Not bad. The meat was rather delicious. It was so strange; she couldn't quite identify it. Tender, like a puff of cloud. Like cotton candy chicken. However, chickens were rare on the menu at the tower. The castle had ten of them, and they were worshipped for their eggs. They only wound up on the chopping block when they could no longer lay, and by that point they were often tough and stringy. So this was not chicken. Definitely not rabbit. Did he say it was pigeon pie?

She tasted it again. But she'd had enough pigeon to know that it tasted more like dark meat than like the most melting, tender chicken breast. Suddenly she spit out the bite, dropping her knife and spoon with a clatter.

She knew what it was.

CHAPTER THIRTY-ONE

"Peter, where did these birds come from? What is this?" He shook his head. She asked the maid waiting with a pitcher near the door.

"Tis pigeon pie, mistress," the maid said with a curtsey.

She held up a bite on the tip of her fork. White meat. Grey meat, really, but definitely not dark. "I hate to disagree, but this isn't pigeon."

She wiped it free of sauce with her napkin. The meat was so fine grained it was translucent. Wispy.

Her voice shook with emotion, "Dorcas!" She flew down the stairs, dizzy from lack of food, but nevertheless leaping down the steps two and sometimes three at a time. "*Dorcas!*"

She arrived in the kitchen panting, putting her hand to her ribs.

"The pie. Something in the pie," she said, trying to get the words out and breathe at the same time. "What's in it? Who caught it?"

"The pigeon pie? Old Felig brought the birds by."

"Felig! The one with the," pant, "field out west?" *The one with all the clouds hanging all around it?*

"Yes, mistress. He said he couldn't wait longer to sow his seed and yet he could not get his harrowing done till Thursday on account of his ox was lame. So he took a sling to the birds so they would not steal his seed." Harrowing signaled the start of pigeon hunting, because farmers didn't want the birds eating all the seed they'd just planted. *Right.*

"He brought them down with his sling?"

"Tis what he said."

"Them? Them? Not just one?"

"Aye?"

"Find this Felig. Find him. Peter!" she cried, as the servant hit the bottom of the stairs. She clutched his robes with both fists. "Tell Felig if he kills another one of these birds, I will murder him in turn. Understand?"

Peter gave a series of nods. She started out the door.

"Mistress, where are you off to now?" Dorcas said, following her.

"To Old Felig's field. It's that way, yes?" She pointed off west.

It would not do, of course. Ever since the cloud-bird debacle, she'd been roaming the tower in her spell robe, refusing to see anyone, refusing to get dressed. Now Dorcas herded her like she was some beloved cantankerous chicken, right back up the stairs. By the time she'd argued that she'd only be stomping around in a field and would never subject the gorgeous persimmon-colored gown Dorcas brought out to all that dust, Peter had gone to get Theo, who entered the bed chamber.

"Theo, I'll need your spyglass."

"I've got it. You're not going alone."

"Surely—Oh, fine, fine." Dorcas held out a black gown with black and white stripes in a long herringbone pattern down the front.

"Very well, only hurry." Theo turned his back while she scrambled into the farthingale and skirt. Dorcas tied on the sleeves as Zephyr sat to have her hair done, only begging Dorcas to stick it all up in a snood and be done with it.

"And we should get some nets. Well, maybe a cage. But how did he catch them? Dorcas, what are you doing?"

"Pattens, mistress," Dorcas said, sliding one metallic wedge up over her slipper. "In case it rains."

She grabbed Dorcas and pulled her up to kiss her forehead. "I love you, Dorcas."

"Miss!"

"You have—you have such faith in me." Her voice thickened and her eyes watered.

She wiped her eyes, and turned to let Theo assist her up from the bench. She tried to sweep out of the room like Dorcas said the grand ladies did in their gowns. Instead she almost fell on her face, for the damn pattens were flatfooted. She clutched at his surcoat, while his eyes glimmered and flickered, but he righted her and they went down the rest of the stairs very carefully, if loudly. By the time they emerged into the open air and turned onto the road that led to the village, the sun was covered with turgid clouds, the sky streaked with pink.

They stopped only long enough to tell a few lingering souls outside the tavern what the cloud bird looked like, what it was, and that no one was to eat it on pain of the sorceress's very grave displeasure. The men listened, tankards in hand, toothless mouths agape. Did they understand? Theo demanded. They nodded to Theo, peeked at her, and promised to spread the word.

"Now they'll exaggerate everything fearfully and spread panic around the land." Theo stalked along the raised field furrows.

"More like everyone will now try to hunt cloud bird on the sly. But I think we're justified—I mean, a bird's made from demon claws. I'm not sure we actually want people eating it, do we?"

"Not sure we can stop them."

∞

They crossed three more fields before they saw old man Felig, broadcasting his seeds into the furrow trenches.

"Hi, you there!" Theo called. "Are you the man that caught the cloud-bird?"

"Don't know no cloud-bird," The grizzled man said. Theo described it.

"Oh, them."

"Them!" Zephyr said. "How did you ever catch one?"

"Sneaky devils. Crept up upon them eating my barley corn."

"Right." She looked up at Theo. "We've noticed the cloud bird is rather, um, evasive."

"Warnt no evasive with me. It went to squawk, but I had my hand round its throat, like this I did," he showed them, "and it could make no noise then. Wrung its head off."

"Look, don't do that again," She said.

"They're eating my barley corn."

"Well that's just too bad, but these birds are necessary."

"Then ye can pay me not to hunt them."

"Where did you find it?" Theo asked. They followed him to a patch of tall trees and scrubby green that clustered near one edge of his fields.

"They et a third of my barley corn. Had to wring it before—"

"Never kill one of these birds again! Understand?" she said, standing tall and imperious.

"They're—"

"*Never*. Theo here will make arrangements if you are so mercenary. Now please go away," she begged.

Theo took out the spyglass and started peering into the trees.

"There!" he said, passing over the glass.

"Where? Where?" She could hear the cry of at least a handful of different birds in the trees, but couldn't actually see any. The clouds were gathering thickly, making it almost dark.

He pointed them out and she looked through the glass. High up in the treetops they hovered in a dozen nests like patches of fog. They were more substantial than the original cloud bird, and smaller. They were two feet long instead of three or four, their heads were a beautiful purple mauve color.

"You've found them," Theo said. "What now?"

"We catch one," she said. "At least one. Preferably six, and then we can have breeding pairs. But it doesn't matter, as long as they make it rain."

Theo had taken the old man's sack of seed. He tossed some onto the field. "We're still far away, you know."

"They're breeding awfully fast, aren't they?"

She tried counting the birds as they walked up to the trees. Say one hatchling per nest plus parents, that's three times a dozen. Thirty-six birds in fourteen days. It was much more complicated to work back and figure out the breed rates. A few of the birds nested with pigeons, but most seemed to be mating with their own kind.

"Now what?" she said to Theo.

He shook his head.

"Birds!" she declaimed at the top of her lungs. "What are you waiting for?" She threw a clod of dirt up into the trees, hitting a trunk. The birds exploded all about with a huge cacophony of noise. They rose up into the air and circled, making a tremendous racket.

"There, throw the seed. Oh, Theo, there he is!" she cried, and clapped and held her head. The largest bird began to wheel around high above their heads. He was easy to spot with his black head and enormous wing span. A few of the birds would drop down to dive bomb the sorceress, pulling up at the last minute.

They hunkered down in the field as birds began to take an interest in the seed broadcast all about.

"What's our plan?" she said, squatting on her haunches, trying to keep her skirts bunched up out of the dirt.

"We wait for them to become absorbed in eating, then we catch them."

"Just like that?" she asked.

"Just like that."

Many birds were soon eating seed as if they were starving. However, the big cloud bird seemed suspicious and riled up. He screamed out his displeasure. Rain began to splatter across the field. She stood up.

"Rain, Theo. Rain." She felt all at once weary and contented. "We did it."

"You made it rain." It was a big concession. Her entire lower face was one big grin, and she couldn't stop. The clouds grew and grew until the rain was covering not just the field, but as far as she could see. She laughed and hugged Theo. She spun around with her arms out and didn't even care when suddenly a wall of rain fell upon them.

Rain ran down her face as she looked up into those dark eyes, burning orbs that lanced into her. A shock ran straight down to her pubic bone, where it set up a fierce ache. The slide of a treacle-thick yearning poured through her. She was suddenly in his embrace, his mouth over hers, his tongue tasting her, tasting of rain. He kissed her thoroughly, as if that was what he had to say to her and he had needed to say it for a very long time. She absorbed the kiss, tasting rain on their lips and skin. His hands pushed at the shoulders of her gown impatiently, gripping her naked shoulders, and tasting her skin as it became drenched in the storm. He bit and kissed and tasted the rain on her flesh.

His lips heated her skin to scorching, even as the rain cooled it. His mouth kissed the rain off her face, her cheeks, her neck, and then her mouth again. Her body locked into his; they rubbed together, and the jolting harsh pleasure of his tall frame against hers caused a numbing buzz that started in her pelvic girdle and spread out across her entire body. She kissed him back, her mouth open, tasting the charge of his desire, an addictive tang mingled with the wet, making her squirm to get closer, more intimate. His tongue was ardent against hers, one hand scooping into her bodice and stroking her there, as she groaned softly in the back of her throat all tight with craving.

Just as she felt the first big wave that would rock her towards an orgasm, a whistle crack of lightning poured through her eyes. She felt like she'd just suddenly bit down hard on a copper plate—an electrical discharge and the smell of ozone hung over them as they sprang apart from the shock. Her teeth hurt from the snap of electricity that has passed between them, and her fingers were numb.

"Pah! What was that?" She spat, trying to get the taste of metal out of her mouth. Her nipples hurt; everywhere hurt except her fingertips, which she still couldn't feel.

"It felt like lightning? Are you all right?" she said, leaning towards him, reaching for him with a hand.

He backed away out of her reach. "It was the apprentice contract."

She stood there, her woolen dress growing sodden and heavy, rain running down her hair and into her lips.

She swallowed, looking at him. "Do you love me?"

He considered, a brief pause, then said, "No."

The honest deep tone of his voice was gentle, but it was a blow.

"You are without honor," he continued. "I could never love a woman like you."

Honor stood for a code of behavior. Which was all nice and pure, but frankly, she got shit done. The rain on her face was a reminder of that. Yeah, she was willing to step over a few rules and moral qualms if it meant staving off death for the people around them.

His face looked absurdly youthful. "Always with you it's a mad scramble from one thing to the next. No caution, no concern for others. Your reckless, heedless behavior could get us all killed."

"I just saved us all." She blinked from the rain in her eyes.

"In this instance, yes."

"Would you rather I sit in the tower sewing, all polite and composed and honorable, while the crops died and everyone starved? Even wizards must eat."

She should be mad. She wasn't, though. She looked off over the fields and then back at him. She was too disappointed to stay mad, and her feelings deflated as fast as they had risen not a few minutes before. She hurt, so very much. Gutted.

"We should be getting back." She picked up the wicker cage.

The rain did not seem to matter to the birds who gobbled the corn. Several of them had begun pecking on the edge of the field only five feet away.

∞

The rain clouds made all the world grey. Her ridiculous pattens squished into the deep mud that had once been dust, until she was making one slow, gloppy step after the other through the field and he had to pull her along while she held the cage out in her other hand.

They got four birds in a cage, Theo simply grabbing them up from the field before they could fly away. She couldn't believe that it worked, but the birds were too desperate for food after the long winter, greedily swallowing up corn before the other birds could get it. While Theo held a caught bird's beak closed with his hands she tore off strips of her petticoat and tied up their beaks before stuffing them into the cage.

She lost three of the birds before she got the hang of it, and her fingertips were bloody. But they managed. The hybrids couldn't dissipate as easily. They needed to get a full throttle cry going first. A few of them flew right through Theo. At that point his temper took a turn.

Now as they slogged along the rain continued to fall, but it was gentle.

"What are you going to do with them?" he said with a nod to the cage.

"Release them at the tower and see if they stay." She peered up at the others crying and shrieking their displeasure. "That's the plan, anyway."

When he'd ripped her petticoat he had such a wicked look in his eye. And when he took her fingers in his own to bind them up she shuddered with a want so strong she wouldn't have been surprised if she set off the contract spell again.

They talked not at all after that, and eventually came upon the village. Cloud birds up in the sky continued to heckle them from above. The village, already drenched from the rain, endured a torrential downpour.

This did not stop the young women and men in the village from running out into the fields in the scantiest of undergarments. They romped about in the rain, until the girls were flapping in their muddy shifts as they skipped, and the youths, tired of tackling each other and rolling about in the mud, began to eye the girls and gleefully chase them about. Zephyr noticed among the older teens that not a few of the girls relished getting caught. She turned her eyes away from their shocking behavior in the mud with the lads and caught Theo's eye. Then she didn't know where to look.

Not everyone went frenzied with the rain, of course. While the pagan rituals went on in the mud, the more respectable villagers gathered under the eaves and in doorways to stare at the sorceress and her apprentice, soggy with wet, as they picked their way along the road.

Her emotions sank as deeply as her feet into the thick stew of mud. She stopped mincing along, having lost a patten. While she balanced on one foot, a hand on Theo's shoulder, he knelt and dug his hand around in the mud to find it. She cursed Dorcas and all ridiculous women's apparel, her cheeks heating from the humiliation of needing his help. Then she noticed the villagers shooting dagger looks at Theo.

What's he done?

Wet, bedraggled, and dirty, it seemed to take forever to pass through the small semi-flooded street. She lost another patten in the mud, at which point Theo did the sensible thing and, after retrieving it, hoisted her up into his arms. They could not leave the village fast enough for her comfort. Just as they had passed the last building she heard a whistle and a thump and saw Theo wince.

"What was that?"

"A stone," he said, lips tight.

Stones. She craned her head around. Women throwing stones at the apprentice. Another rock whiffled past. Then another one hit his head. He staggered and blood began to run down his cheek.

"Stop!" she insisted. Theo marched onward. "Stop!" More rocks flew. "They'll hurt the birds."

He let her down and she did an about-face to march back into town.

"What gives?" she said. They looked at Theo with sullen hatred. Silently cursing, she held up the birdcage. "Do you know what will happen if these birds die? We'll have no more rain. Is that what you want?"

"No use," said a woman who reminded her quite a lot of Lanky Sue. "Raiders are coming."

She thought of the spyglass and the vision she'd seen.

"Who says raiders are coming? What proof have you?"

"Merchant Davies came through yester morn. Said raiders asked him for the East Road. He sent them about to the road would carry them back to Magor."

She listened aghast.

Another man spoke. "Matter o' time, is all. They'll find us soon enough."

They still kept looking at Theo with murder in their hearts. She turned and stomped away, as much as one could in the squelching mud. She was scared.

"Naught but bad luck since the elf came," a man cried out.

"They're coming," another woman added, "and we'll all be slaughtered."

"Go," she whispered to Theo, "Go ahead of me." He looked around, and at that moment she saw him like they did. Dressed head to toe in black, covered in mud, his brow angry, his face stark white, lips tightened down until all the color left them. He looked as if he wished ill upon the entire world. Wicked.

But he would not go ahead of her, and insisted upon carrying her over all the puddles.

"Fine," she muttered, looking at the trickle of blood coming from his hairline, her teeth chattering with fear and cold.

CHAPTER THIRTY-TWO

"They know," Theo said, putting her down as they reached the gravel path up to the tower.

"Know what?" she asked, holding the birdcage away from her. "Pesky buggers."

"What is it?"

"Oh, sharp claws. What do they know—that we kissed?"

"About Eldred. That I killed him."

"How?"

"It doesn't matter. But they know."

At last they reached the tower. He followed her dripping form up the stairs. She put the cage on the balcony railing, and without so much as a by-your-leave, dug into his pocket for the rest of the corn, bestrewing it across the railing. Then, taking out one bird at a time, she held each bird to her breast and undid the bindings about their beaks.

"Ugly little critters, but I love them." She stroked the bird's chest for a moment. "The feathers are so soft." The bird held up its beak to her as it was stroked.

He was no longer sure cloud birds hated being handled. She slipped the cloth off the beak, and the bird immediately demanded the corn along the ledge, scrambling to get to it. She placed it there and the bird was soon joined by another single-mindedly focused on the corn.

Perhaps he was jealous. He never took to magic in the same way she did. Never felt as connected to his master, or to his spyglass, in the same way she felt towards the magical birds. In fact, he never felt connected to anyone. Except her.

She was gentle with the birds. He would be gentle when taking her power away from her. Very gentle. He stared at her hand, the one with the blue ring. It served to compel others. Get that ring and all the rest would be easy. Yes, suddenly his plan was clear.

"Did they break the skin?" Theo asked, taking her bandaged fingers to examine them. "Here," he said, giving one fingertip a kiss. "Let me." He started to draw the ring off.

"It's fine," she said, withdrawing her fingers into fists. "Let it be." He drew her small fist into his hands and kissed it open.

"I don't understand you," she complained, but she couldn't pull her hand away, and she closed her eyes as he kissed her palm.

Just then a lightning flash drove them back from the balcony into the tower. He tried to recapture the moment, but his heart was pounding and the free birds wheeled around the sky making an unholy noise. Zephyr closed the balcony doors just as it started to pour. She had smelled like wet wool in his arms.

Her dress sagged upon her form, fifteen pounds heavier with all the water it had absorbed. They listened outside.

"What hoarse, ugly cries they make," he said.

Her hand in a fist pressed to her chin, she turned towards the stairs. "I feel as if my soul was crying out the same way," she said, and mounted the stairs.

∞

He stood next to Zephyr in the dining hall four days later, watching the birds below. She was thoughtful, elusive. He wasn't sure what she was thinking. He watched at her side as the cloud birds chased the wild pigeons past the balcony.

"I can't tell if they hunt them, or mate with them," she said.

One pigeon dodged adroitly back and forth before alighting in yard.

"Mistake!" she called out. It sank in the thick, sticky mud, and fluttering, got mud all over one wing, making things worse.

A cloud bird attacked it, dropping straight down from above. The pigeon, caught in the claws of the cloud bird, panicked, chest heaving, waiting for the end.

"That answers your question."

"Poor thing," Zephyr said.

The cloud bird could barely hoist its prize into the air, but finally did so, taking it off into the tall pines where they were roosting. He could hear the bird's racket at dawn down in the basement. At Zephyr's insistence, he was sleeping on a cot in the laundry. She didn't think the servant dorm safe. All night long as he listened, lightning poured down over the tower until it was like an electric birdcage. Outside, birds called back and forth, excited by all the ruckus. He wondered how she slept all alone in that big bed. When he saw her tired eyes the next morning he was sure she didn't.

She turned away from the balcony.

"You're like that pigeon. We have to figure out some way to keep you safe."

He was going to fix it. He was going to get the blue ring from her, gently convince her to abandon magic.

Your ring can keep them from harming me, if necessary.

Her hand fisted up, the other clutched around the ring.

"Where are you going?" she said.

"To the tourney field." The tourney ring was almost complete, though it still lacked a viewing stand.

"You shouldn't go alone."

Dorcas tapped on the door, wiping her hands on her apron. "You wanted me, mistress?"

"Villagers seem to know about Theo and Eldred's unfortunate end." She waited. Dorcas said nothing. "I asked Peter and he said he only told you, so if other people know…" She paused. The silence stretched out for an uncomfortably long time.

"Dorcas said nothing," he observed, "because Dorcas never says anything."

"Then how—"

"Peter told you," he said to the maid.

"Yes."

"Where?"

"At the waterfall."

"Where lovers go to meet." He turned back to Zephyr.

"Someone was listening."

"Dorcas, I feel like an ass for even *thinking* of blaming you when you've been nothing but loyal."

She was looking at Dorcas's belly.

"We need to build you and Peter a house so you can have some privacy," she said.

"Tis forgotten, mistress."

"They're just waiting to get him alone. I can feel it." Zephyr crossed her arms across her chest and hugged herself.

Dorcas turned her soft brown eyes upon him.

"It's not him, exactly, mistress. People did like the old wizard, and then people is worried 'bout the raiders, see?"

"I don't see."

Theo stepped in. "She's saying that while the raiders are near, and the crops are failing, the mob looks for a scapegoat."

He knew as well as Dorcas how humans withstood pressures until they built up and erupted into violence. Better he was the target then they tried for the tower. Or the books. Or her.

Zephyr looked over at him. "All I could dream about last night was Theo lying chained up with a bloody head, but I couldn't find him."

"People are excited about the tourney ring being built. If Master—if Theo fought well, people might be inclined to forgive a little faster. People don't give much thought to a person's misdeeds if they've done something grand."

Zephyr turned over several ideas in her mind.

"Yes. On the other hand, Theo smiting down the local gentry with his sword might remind them of Eldred all over again." She looked at Theo. "You can't trust the knights."

"I don't. But the knights won't hurt me."

"Some of them wouldn't, mistress."

"Small comfort. Well, the first thing we can do to reassure people is to watch our borders. Men—even older boys. Clever but not weasely. You know what I mean. God, if it's not one thing, it's another."

Peter burst into the room. He was wet. Throwing off cloak and cap, he tossed a sickly yellowish spotted plant out upon the table. A pea plant.

"Are they all like that?" he asked Peter.

Peter shook his head. "Perhaps a fourth. Maybe less. Maybe more. When you look across the fields, many plants are densely packed and vibrant green." Peter put his hands apart. "It's the borders that look most affected."

Theo held up the plant stalk and then let it fall. "So far."

"The farmers don't know what it is," Peter continued. "It's not blight. Or insects. Nor rodents."

"It's everything," Zephyr said suddenly, and, standing, began to pace. "The plants are stressed."

"Stressed?"

"Distressed. And when they are distressed, they put out a—well, a scent. Bugs come running as a result. It's nature's way. The strong crush the weak."

"Suddenly you farm?" the elf said.

"Look, five of my uncles are farmers. You can't help but have some of this stuff rub off on you over the years."

"There are always insects," Theo said.

"Sure. And if the plants were healthy they could repel these attacks. But they've been weakened for too long, so they can't. What are we going to do?"

"What can we do?" Peter said. "Wish for dragon's blood?" He sat. "The heavens are clearly against us," he moaned. "We're all going to starve."

"Not all of us," Theo said.

"The children will," Peter said. Dorcas suddenly fled the room, hands clutched to her stomach. Zephyr just looked at her servant aghast. Peter followed Dorcas from the room.

"We just have to think of something." She sat down suddenly at the dining room table. "God, it's always something, isn't it?" She put her head on the table. "I feel so responsible."

He put a reassuring hand on her shoulder and whispered in her ear. "This responsibility is too much. Let it go."

"What do you mean?"

"You can't solve every problem, even if you wanted to. It's not what you're here for. You wanted privacy and solitude."

"To study magic."

"To study, yes," he said. "But it's not working, is it? You neither solve the problems nor study in peace. What do you really need? A horse, a cloak—some coin—you can leave. Be free of these woes that are dragging you down."

She rubbed her face. "But what about—everyone?"

"They'll get through the difficult times," he said. "They always have, and always will. It's what they know—"

She gave a big shudder. "Leave it all behind. You. The people."

"Leave behind annoying villagers, the books, the rings—"

She looked down at the blue ring as if she was listening, but then her head came up again.

"You're right. I'm giving up too easily."

"That's not quite what I—"

"Oh, I know what you're saying. Why am I being so egotistical to think that I alone must take care of everyone? We're all in this together, not just me. If they wind up better off that will have to be our reward, but frankly, how could they do worse?"

She rose from the table and hugged his hand to her cheek. "I was giving up. Thank you, thank you. I'm over it now. Thank you for pointing me in the right direction."

She let go of him and looked up into his face, her eyes dreamy.

"You thought I should leave…" her head swiveled towards the door as if hypnotized. That same dreamy, abstracted look overcame her face. A look that made him want to kiss her, those lips, but he knew her better now. That look on her face meant gears were turning behind her eyes. He was learning to fear that look. Her face turned towards him again.

"What Peter said. Tell me more about dragon's blood. What's it supposed to do, exactly?"

"No, no, no—I'm not going back there," he said.

Did she *know* he was determined to stop her? *She can't. She can't!*

"We're just talking." She put a hand on his arm to reassure him. The hand with the black ring. Suddenly he wanted to overpower her, simply take the rings by force. Could he do it quickly enough and get it off before she could make him stop? Peter stepped into the room. Would Peter interfere? She looked as if she was listening to something they couldn't hear. She knew. Somehow she knew. He could turn on her, let her struggle with his elf side. She'd lose. No, he wouldn't descend to that level just yet.

He took her by the shoulders. "If you send me back to finish off the dragon, you'll get me killed."

∞

As Theo talked, she watched the blood drain from his face. The grinding gears of her emotions made her shudder—she loved him to the point of acute pain. At the same time, the solution was crystal clear.

"You have to go. I'm not asking." He would save them all, and he would be safe. At least when he fought the dragon, he knew who his enemy was and where it was.

"You've wounded it, therefore it won't be as fierce—if it's even still alive. Eldred was out of practice, you said, but you've been drilling the knights in battle at the tourney ring. All your skills are sharp, fresh. I know you can kill it and bring its blood back to us. We need that dragon's blood."

"I know why you're doing this."

She sank down on the bench, pulling him along to sit beside her. "You've seen how they've all been acting around you," she said. "With this quest you'll redeem yourself in everyone's eyes. You'll be a hero." *You'll be safe*.

He stood up as if he couldn't bear sitting next to her for even a moment.

"What happened in the field. That's why you're sending me away."

Yes, that too. He'd gotten to her, like a poisoned arrow that doesn't kill its victim, but leaves it to slowly languish in misery.

"You're hiding *my* things. *My* books."

She sounded like the ring.

Where are your books? Who thieves here? The elf. She knew what was going on.

The galling thing was that even though he was misbehaving in this way, his apprentice contract never activated and zapped him hard.

Yet without Theo, she didn't know if she could get the spell to work. He was like one of those fire wands you used to spark a gas stove burner. He was her catalyst that got magic going, and she swore to herself up and down that while he was gone she would only resort to nice magic, if she needed to. *Mild and sweet things. Nothing demonic or nasty. Promise. Just this one little immortality spell, that's all.* She'd found another immortality spell in a book. It was a good one, too. She'd hidden it away where he wouldn't see it, but they couldn't go on like this.

"If I ever meant anything to you, you would not send me away like this," he pleaded. "The way my father did."

Ouch.

"I'd forgotten. Oh, but Theo, you must return to us. To me. This isn't a banishment." It was a rebirth.

"Your pride is stung or you would not send me away." His voice cracked with contained emotion.

Any time he went down to the tourney ring she held her breath. In every home across the land, there were hand sickles, scythes hung near the door. No end of sharp, pointy objects. No end of clubs and heavy sticks. One good solid lop across the back of his neck was probably all it would take.

Meanwhile, with the sickly crops, she knew people were even more cranked than ever. Who would be the first to go from hunger? Dorcas had given her the key, she saw them now with fresh eyes. How they worried, how wound up they were.

Someone like Sir Ingham could set them off. Set them to torment an outsider, and afterwards they might feel ashamed, but it would be too late. A mob could do hideous things to one elf. Even if he was immortal.

She looked down and played with the chain at her waist.

"You'll come back to me, and when you do, you'll no longer be my apprentice."

His eyes were scanning her face and she raised her chin, determined.

"Please."

"I'll play the hero you want me to be," he said, crushing one of her palms to his lips, then the other.

"You don't even love me."

"No, it's more of a madness."

She felt his lips on her skin, the delicious tickle of his kiss going all the way down to her toes. Did she feel his lips smile against her palm?

"Perhaps this quest will kill the mad feelings I have for you. If not, I don't know how I can go on like this." He laid his cheek against her palm.

She reached out and tugged the rope pull, a fine trembling throughout her body

∞

The next day he set off reluctantly on horseback, a long spear and shield strapped to a white palfrey, with enough money jingling in his purse to buy an equipage once he had the blood and needed to carry it back. *Your rings, your books, your tower.*

He spoke of honor, but he'd lost his when he killed his master, hadn't he?

A handful of reasonably smart and agile peasants accompanied him. They were to stay back and watch near the border, remaining hidden, but sending word swiftly if raiders came near. She watched him leave on horseback. There was something about him that she just couldn't trust without his acknowledged love.

Out on the first floor of the tower Peter was assembling a moss maid statue. She'd decided that this would be her magic battery. She went out into the stairwell where it stood in the shadows and petted its mossy sides. The thing was human sized, taller than her, and unfortunately, its hulking form reminded her all too well of Hulgetta.

She took a patch of moss and brought it back into the study. The first step to immortality was an elphidora broth. It bubbled and boiled without heat, without stopping, and with delight she realized she'd finally gotten through the first part of the immortality spell. Each level was harder than the last, but with the moss maid on her side, she wouldn't worry now. She had her catalyst.

The immortality spell was described in a history book. *Ha!* She wished she could show it to Theo just to see his face.

CHAPTER THIRTY-THREE

A few days later she looked up from her cauldron in the laundry room. There was more room here, and a fireplace. "Peter, how goes the new house?"

"Well, mistress, very well. You wanted me?"

"I wanted to see if the system was up and working."

"Tis." The system they'd arranged was for a long string of signal fires so that she would know the instant Theo was on his way back. The system worked fairly well at night, but much better during the day, when the dark smoke was more likely to draw notice. The cloud birds had ceased causing much rain at all, but she noticed through the spyglass that they were molting, so perhaps it was a down time for their rain-making.

"I'm afraid that the moss maid is going to have to be restructured and made larger."

Peter's shoulders dropped. "Might I ask why?"

"No reason, really. It just seems like it needs to be bigger. Massive," she said, holding out her arms. She could feel the moss maid inside the effigy, battering about like a moth in a lamp. She wanted more room. But Zephyr wasn't going to tell Peter that.

∞

Four weeks later, at midnight, she became immortal. It was like flying into the air up high and then dropping. There was no way to stop the fall. She felt that she was dying at the same time she felt she could endure the rush forever, burning with fever. It was not what she expected. The feeling connected her with the earth, and she could feel all the turf, the roots, the gravel and down, down further into the cold ground. In the same way she'd flown, the moss maid magic brought her lower and lower and lower still.

There was no end to the deep. She emerged from her trance at dawn, and could not shake off the sense that the moss maid magic was there for her to touch. Like setting down a fork in front of you, where it is ready if you need it. It stayed in her awareness.

She did not sleep well night after night. In her dreams Theo was locked up in chains and it was her fault. He was dragged along unconscious, stolen by evil trolls that went through Hulgetta's castle. She was scared. Diving into the moss maid magic was as easy as diving into a pond, except it had no edges. The power was so big that it even seemed like it could yank her along with it. She was not used to that.

At the same time, she yearned to tell someone all about it. She wanted Theo back, wanted him home. The knights came to the tower to show her their fine new fat and shiny plow horses dressed up like war horses, and their new armor hammered out from old suits left in corners to rust. She greeted them with smiles on the balcony, but let them stay down below in the yard, as the maids circulated with platters of drink. They didn't seem to mind that she kept herself aloof, and she felt she was doing at least one thing of which Theo would approve.

The rest of her days she spent with her eye to the spyglass hour after hour after hour. Sometimes she would grow tired of the empty landscape and flick the lever that Theo had attempted to mend. There would pop into view the magnificent giant trees. She should plant them now. Theo knew not how far into the future this vision lay, but she marked the varieties of trees—oaks, mostly—and their location. It gave her something to do, along with making a knot garden and herbarium out of the yard below. Many plants would help absorb all the puddles. Now and again she would train her eye on that army. Doing so alarmed her. *We're so vulnerable*. She was stronger in magic, but more afraid to use it. She thought of the Valdeans and pined for Theo with all her heart.

∞

The dragon snapped his long spear to bits. He took out his sword, keeping his shield higher than normal. He'd been taught to fight men hand to hand in single combat, or alone surrounded by a pack of warriors. He had not been trained to fight a five-hundred-year-old lizard, twenty-five feet high, with a giant muscled neck and a very mean temper. *Wounded? Sickly? Weak? Ha!*

It slithered out of sight back amongst the massive boulders, the wily bastard, hiding and whipping through the twisty turns of the hills with far too much agility for a cold-blooded, oversized snake that was supposed to be injured and hovering on the brink of death.

His own temper had grown nasty during this time as he was forced to eat rodents and dandelion grass. He thought of Zephyr and went elfish, wanting her with a wicked lust to the point where he temporarily lost his ability to go back. At last, he resolved to walk right in the dragon's cave, knowing it was suicide, but he was hungry and would rather die quickly than starve slowly. First he climbed up on top of the cave to gain a better view of the world below. While he was there, an idea so obvious, so easy, came to him. He turned his head just as the dragon slithered out from the cave. It saw him first and bit him by the shoulder, lifting him from the ground, exactly as it had done with Eldred. But there it made its fatal mistake. He had learned from that experience and mentally practiced for it. Once the dragon had locked onto his shoulder, the distance was closed. With great precision he grabbed around the dragon's muzzle with his bad arm and held on. With his sword arm he angled his aim and stabbed the dragon in its squinty eye. He could feel it squeeze his shoulder, feel the venom enter his bloodstream. But being elf, his body was better able than a human to resist the poison flooding through his system.

The dragon sent out a flaming snort, torching the air in one breath and singing his hair.

Fight me, you beast. I'll destroy you and write a poem rejoicing in the deed.

He continued jabbing the dragon behind him with his sword, poking into its eye over his shoulder, rapidly growing weak as his blood spilled around all the dragon's teeth on the ground.

∞

"Mistress! Mistress!" Another gorgeous summer's day, and she was sitting on a bench on the fourth floor, snoozing over her spell book, while Dorcas and the maids sewed on their stools. It had become a habit in the long summer afternoons to gather like this. Sometimes she sewed too, and sometimes they sang. Far below a voice was calling her name.

"Sorceress!" She sat up on her knees and turned to the window.

"It's Peter," she said. Dorcas popped her head out the window next to hers.

"Fires—" He pointed. "The elf is come!" he shouted.

Then he was off, running. A myriad of field hands who had been digging a large hole for another tree dropped their spades and ran off towards the East Road as well. The maids all looked at her. "What are you waiting for?" she said. They hurried down the stairs in a flock, her persimmon dress in the lead, belling out as she flew down the stairs gracefully in her little horn heeled slippers.

They tumbled out the door just in time to see the tiniest speck of a cart on the road headed towards the tower.

Passing the new baby knot garden, and the beginnings of the herbarium, she ran up to Peter, panting for breath and holding her side.

They were at a high point of ground, and in a good spot to observe Theo's progress.

"Our early warning system could stand some improvement," she commented to Peter.

"Certainly."

"I'd rather have half a day's notice of Theo's coming than half an hour's notice. What if it had been a raiding band of Valdeans?"

"Yes, indeed. Yes, I take your point."

He was coming. He was coming. Soon, they could make out the odd creature pulling the cart. A giant ram with curled horns and big leathery wings. *How extraordinary! How magnificent!*

She clapped her hands with delight.

He came back up the next hill and into view once again. "Is he—Peter, something doesn't look right. Oh, get my spyglass. Somebody."

The spyglass was brought to her and she used it the way Theo had taught her in order to measure the distance.

He was still half a league away. One and a half miles.

She kept the spyglass upon him, and once he was past the next two hills she exclaimed, "He's bleeding!"

She gathered up her skirts and went running back into the tower. Frantically searching through the books, she found one on dragon wounds and burns. Down in the laundry she plucked out a salve made of elderflower, sage, and tansy. It would serve as a base for the rest. She ran back to the study and pulled upon the moss maid statue that rose section by section, as if through the floors of the tower, to the third floor.

The magic potion, activated with a tiny bit of moss, ignited with just a small squeeze of the dead basilisk. She stirred it up into a paste of elderflower and beeswax, laid out some fresh, clean clothes to use for binding his wound, and darted outside again just as his cart was pulling up the crest of the hill to the tower. He drove it past the knot garden and into the yard of crushed gravel.

He's not dying, she told herself, even though the blood looked fresh on his shirt and was leaking down into a great puddle onto the seat near him. *He's not.*

He was a bit of a mess, however. His surcoat was ripped, one shoulder exposed with both puncture marks and burned streaks of skin, and his face was a blank mask of streaked dirt.

He's immortal. Not going to die.

"I've read elves are perilously hard to poison," she said to Peter.

"Perhaps it's because they've spent thousands of years poisoning each other," Peter jested. She was not amused.

"Mistress," Theo said. The ram stopped and dropped in its traces, dead.

She skirted the ram and went up to him.

"You're back. I'm so glad," she gushed. Then he swayed and all at once everyone launched themselves towards him. Several men caught at him, but she was there first, and he would only lean upon her, only let her get a shoulder under his and support him as they moved in the direction of the castle.

He gestured to the ram as they passed. "My gift to you, unfortunately, has died. Please accept my apologies."

"Don't be ridiculous. Did you get the blood?" she said.

He craned his head around, wincing, and behind his seat the men were drawing forth two large ceramic vats topped with wooden lids, sealed with scarlet wax, and corded for good measure.

"Oh, well done," she exclaimed. "Peter will take care of all that," she said, turning back towards the tower. For the last few weeks they'd worked together on gathering the dimensions of each field, the acreage, and how little dragon's blood would be needed to pull the crops back from the brink. The trick, her book had said, was not using too much. Too much of the dragon's blood and the plants would regress back into being seeds. Peter was ready to tick off which fields got what dose and administer the cure.

She watched his black eyes devour her, as she in her turn assessed him. He was filthy, unshaven and exhausted, with dark circles under his sunken eyes, his lips pale, like he hadn't eaten in a month. His face was flushed with fever, but his gaze held a black flame when he looked at her.

Just now he was puzzled, his eyes narrowing as he scanned her face minutely.

"You seem… different." She was different. Like the snake that consumes its own tail, she'd consumed her passion for Theo, partaking of a gnawing need for him morning, noon, and night. She was a wreck.

Best to get it out in the open now.

"Ageless, perhaps?"

"You didn't."

He's the one who's different. She pulled him towards the vestibule. Then they were inside. When she put her hand on his cheeks and forehead, trying to gauge his fever, he dodged her touch, turning away. Those black eyes examined the three-story moss maid with affront.

"You're wounded," she protested.

He turned back to her, hard to read. "Not badly. It looks worse than it is."

"I prepared a salve."

"What I really need at this moment is food. My money was stolen."

"Of course, of course," she said. She scrambled down to the kitchen and soon half the maids were heating up kettles for his bath, while she and the rest toiled up three flights of stairs with an enormous tray holding a hero's feast.

CHAPTER THIRTY-FOUR

He ate slowly, taking small bites of food. The hollow of his cheeks was new and her heart hurt to look at him.

"I brought you this," he said, and took her hand as if to kiss it. Instead, he placed some rubbery pink little squidges into it. She looked closely at them. They were seven-clawed mole's feet, tied all in a line to a red string.

"Oh, you remembered!"

She admired them.

"Are these all left front feet?"

"They are." *Reading her mind, was he?* To her ear his voice seemed dismissive. He was looking over her head.

"Where did you find them?" she asked, curious and full of dread at the same time, her hands fisting up the persimmon dress under the table.

"I bought them on the road from a starving apothecary and his family, in Magor," he said, his voice expressionless. "They were displaced by the war."

"It's war, then?"

"Yes, and spreading. They're going to lose. The Valdeans are very strong. They don't coordinate their raiding parties, and so their movements are chaotic, unpredictable. And there are so many of them."

"The knights have been training rigorously ever day with the drills you gave them," she said. He ate, his eyes on his food, and didn't respond.

"I assume you kept a low profile and never said where you were from?"

"No need. The tower lands are all anyone talks about in Magor—aside from the Valdeans."

Dread pooled in her stomach.

"What—what are they saying?"

"A beautiful sorceress lives in the tower now, though some say she's an enchantress."

"Oh no."

"Oh yes. She tests warriors in battle, and she takes those who triumph into her bed."

"God."

"Raiding parties of Valdeans are already casting around the borders of Magor, trying to find you."

"Is there some enchantment preventing them?"

"Not at all. They lack maps. And the populace flees before them."

"Theo, what are we going to do? Act like sitting ducks until some roving band of Valdeans stumbles upon us?"

"Then myself, Pettish, Reginald, Bertram and whomever else can sit a horse will go out to meet them and we'll see who takes the day. At least they won't be expecting us. There's only the one road in. The other ways are blocked by the forest and the river. Your system should allow us some warning."

He looked at her. Underneath his calm air she could feel his desire, like a knife stabbing into her and twisting.

"I've prepared a salve down in the laundry with a bath," she said. "Also some sage tea."

"To drink or bathe in?"

"To drink." Several moths were fluttering around the candles on the banquet table. "The honey water is to bathe in."

Giving him a side glance, she saw he was looking back with those eyes. Some elemental force pulled upon them both.

"Well done," she said again, more faintly, staring down at the claws, touching each one with the tip of her finger, treasuring them.

He stood. "Pardon me, mistress. If it pleases you, I will go bathe now."

"I'll get the salve."

"I can put it on."

"I'd rather do it myself."

"As you wish."

She looked down at her feet, her heart full of uncertain tenderness towards him, missing his formerly sensitive self, but equally, if not more, attracted to this other side of him. His eyes had been black the whole time. Had he lost his human nature for good? Would he ever forgive her for sending him away?

She lingered a little after he left, touching the moss maid body for courage, petting the moss, running her hands along the curling witch hazel branches that served for hair.

Then she went below with her salve. The maids had all deserted the tower for the night. There was one last large kettle of hot water on the banked stove. Picking up the kettle with a thick kitchen cloth, she brought it over into the laundry and paused. Sheets on the drying racks screened him from her view. She peeked her head around.

He stood in the bath, naked, and though he was wet, he appeared to be waiting for her. She added more hot water to the bath, and then, picking up a cloth and some lavender soap, she washed him all over, taking care to first go over his shoulder, dapping the washcloth gently to remove the blood, and putting the salve on his cleaned wound.

"I'm surprised you didn't pop a little dragon's blood onto this," she said, a finger smoothing on the salve.

"Are you mad?" Oh, how she adored his frowny perturbed look.

"Dragon's blood doesn't work upon dragon's wounds," he said. "It makes them worse."

"Oh, of course. How silly of me."

His eyes followed her hands as they wrapped the bandage under his arm, around his shoulder, around his biceps, making a neat triangle that conformed to his lithe, taut muscles. Her fingers seemed to have an extra sensitivity during this task. He remained silent, his damp skin steaming a little in the cool cellar. She felt his eyes just the same, a prickling awareness as they roamed over her face and then dropped to her body. She finished binding up his wound and turned to the rest of him.

She devoted herself to sponging his body, the flat abdominals, feeling a peculiar drag to her fingers whenever they lifted from his body to soak the cloth again in the honey water. He remained so still, looking down at her hands. Why did touching him have such a huge effect on her? Her heart raced, her pelvis urged her forward towards him.

She might be his mistress in theory, but from now on the chains were around her heart. *Be wary*, said the voice in her head.

Though would it be so bad if we were equals?

∞

He got out of the bath and took her into his arms, crushing the dark orange dress. She avoided his burned shoulder, but her mouth sucked the honey water nectar from the hollow of his collarbone, until his breath was short and harsh. He stood there, willing himself not to move. Her hands found his chest, and her fingertips brushed over his nipples, feeling them harden, and then lower down over his ribs, tracing them along his lean figure.

When she reached his straining shaft and gripped him, he let his eyes close and a sigh of contentment escaped his lips. There was a pounding at his temples. He would kill for her, if needed, would rip apart the world to get to her. Yet here she was, trembling as much as him. He looked at her, his cold black eyes seeing her through and through.

"You're no longer my mistress."

"No. Your apprentice articles have expired. We can be together now." He could feel the way she responded, her body going slack with acceptance of the need for him, the anticipation for his touch.

"You want a night with me in your bed," he said. "It's not enough."

"I want more than—what do you mean?"

∞

"Elf marriage?" She turned and sat on a stool. "What's that?"

"There are two forms of vows that elves take," he said. He was wearing his breeches, and nothing else. The rest of his clothes were torn and bloodied. They would have to be burned.

"One type of marriage is a formal affair between families, clans. These are public vows, formally taken when one or both bring a large amount of property or valuables into the marriage. Gifts of land are usually exchanged. After fighting, they signal peace.

"They are binding vows, but they aren't love marriages. The other kind of elf marriage is a love pact. The vows are private—secret, even. A couple vows to remain loyal and true to each other, no matter what, and are bonded thereafter for eternity."

She looked like she was having trouble breathing. She put a hand to her chest, yet she walked away from him, to the other end of the chamber and then came back. She clutched at the blue ring on her finger.

As she hesitated, he let his expression become wounded, and then hurt.

"Sometimes, Theo, I feel you have—a will to power. To power over me, I mean."

He set his jaw. He had to mean it. "If you do not want this, then I must leave here."

She came right up to him. "No, I accept."

He stroked her cheek with care. She was weak around him like this. His caress tumbled the locks within her. "Alone at dawn, we will speak a few simple words and be bound to each other."

"You mean, I don't sign over the tower to you, or shower you with all my magic books?" She laughed.

"You will give me one love token," he said. "Something you hold dear."

"A token?"

"Your ring."

The tower was silent. No voices outside in the yard. The room was cold. She opened her mouth several times but did not speak. The cloud birds out in the trees were quiet for once. It was the stillness that came before great violence or an earthquake.

"You don't sound very loving, Theo." She folded her arms. "You sound a little irritated with me. I can just see you when you were younger. I doubt you tolerated fools lightly. Are you sure you're not trying to deceive me?"

He stared.

"When have I ever lied to you?"

"When I first met you, you lied about your name."

"All magic workers are not so frank and open as you. I was taken by surprise. When have I ever lied since?" He came near her and held her by the arms. This had its usual effects, but she would not look him in the face.

His black eyes burned and throbbed. Something was very different about her. Streams of purple and blue radiated from her form.

She babbled nervously. He was stony silent, his fury building, his glance bent upon her.

"You're leaving me no choice," she said, fretting. "I couldn't bear it if you went away."

He had her against the wall by then, and pulled her dress up enough to stroke her. While he did so, he held her face and looked her in the eye until she was sighing and seemed spell bound. She was already excited, and he'd never kissed her like he did now, his mouth taking hers, his hand fisting into her hair, pulling her head back as he explored her tender throat. The small, hard bites on her neck made her cry out in pleasure and delight. His hand down there stroked against just the right spot. She'd do anything with him, and was telling him so with every bit of her traitorous body.

He pulled off her dress and then his breeches. Other layers of her clothing fell like petals around them until she was down to her shift and he could see her pink form through the linen. He wanted her to crave the feel of their flesh touching, rubbing together. By then she was kneeling, sucking him, and then it was his turn. He laid her down on top of her dress, and pulling up her shift, kissed the sweet, tender flesh between her thighs.

He shifted her around onto her knees, tipping over the lamp, which went out, and penetrated her from behind. Hard then harder. And she gasped and he could feel the rolling clenches that let him know she was reaching the pinnacle of delight. Her back arched and sent him into roiling, intense release. She was crying out his name while he thrust for much longer before burying his face in her hair and hissing her name through his teeth.

When it was over he stripped off her shift and let their bodies greet flesh to naked flesh. Eyes closed, she purred with satisfaction as he tasted the exceedingly soft silk of her upper arm. He was bending over her, working her with his fingers while his torso met her flank. Her back bowed, her pelvis came into his hand. Her most secret self felt like a sea shell, slippery, soft and wet, and his fingers followed the curve into her until again he was overpowered with wanting and slipped inside her himself.

Afterwards he undid her long hair, and stroked its silken length. He drew her closer to him, then pulled aside the blonde curtain to pepper her shoulder blades with kisses and small nips.

"I feel like I've been rent in two," she complained happily.

"Tired, love? Should I let you sleep?" He knew he would lie awake all night, the elf side of him so in control by now that he would make love to her repeatedly, to the point of madness, if she let him.

"I want sleep, but I want you as well." She pushed her neck back to him, and he caressed her everywhere, awaiting the dawn. He nibbled along her jaw line, along the curve of her breast. Their skin now knew the feel of each other, and she pressed herself to him, her foot coming back to his shin, her glorious plump thighs twitching back against his own hairy length. Her arm came up to bury her hand in his hair, pulling his head back down to worship her skin again. He did not think he could want her with such deep, profound pain, if she did not love him back the same way… It made what he had to do much harder.

CHAPTER THIRTY-FIVE

A horn called into the distance. His love gave a start.

"The signal. Someone's lit a signal fire."

He whispered to her to get dressed, kissing her cheek and willing lips. She was sitting up, her eyes swollen and sleepy, her breasts pert and lovely. He pried the linen sheets from her hands, but still she was slow to move off their improvised bed on the pea gravel in the laundry room.

It was not yet dawn by the time he had dressed. Finally, he pulled her up off the floor, ruthlessly pulling the shift down over her, cinching up her corset. She was pliant in his hands, her skin icy cold, her lips almost blue.

"How much time?" he asked.

"If they signaled properly, we've four hours."

"It's enough." He listened, aware of her hands on his arm. They were like ice. She was afraid, he realized, chaffing her hands together between his. All outside was quiet. They snuck out of the tower and went down into the dark woods. They had just hit the tree line when voices began to call out. First for her and then for him.

"They want us. Should we go back?" she said, turning, looking behind her towards the voices. "Can't this wait?"

"It's a secret. No one must see us."

"I hate it—this elf marriage."

"Don't say that." He pulled her into his arms and kissed her until she was breathless. He would have his elf marriage. His love for her was a painful hole inside his chest.

"I worried for so long that you didn't really love me."

"I can think of no one else but you." It was not love, but it was true.

They went down by the river to the willows.

"I have no token prepared," she protested, following him, fumbling over the rocks and holding his hand as the moon gave only a sickly quarter light. His shirt stuck to the patch of his burn and pulled, the salve sticking to the cloth.

"I told you. Give me your ring."

"Not the black ring, it's my favorite," she protested, absurdly covering it with her other hand.

"I'm your favorite," he replied with a grin. "Confess it, you adore me far more than any ring."

"True. And this one," she said, looking at the blue one crackling with fierce light. "It says such horrible things. I hate it. I don't want you to have it either. What if it told you bad things about me?"

He kissed each of her hands. "Either one, my love. I know you treasure them above all others, for they never leave you. Sacrifice what you love to make me happy."

"What are you giving me?"

"Perhaps the same ring back again."

The voices hallooed out with panic.

"No," she said, looking trapped and wary suddenly. "This isn't a good idea."

He had to push her against a rock and kiss her, caress the gorgeous mounds of her breasts, and finally take her harsh and panting against the rock to put her into that softer, more malleable mood again.

"My affections for you have reached the point where either we must bond or I will die from being lovesick if I stay here with you. If you cannot sacrifice for me—"

"The blue one, then," she said, holding out her arm like she was allowing him to cut off her finger.

He slipped the ring from her finger and onto his smallest finger.

Your ring, your woman, your power.

He couldn't tell if the earth was rumbling or horses were stampeding towards the tower. The horn sounded again. Much closer. They were at the edge of the forest now.

"I want your black ring too," he said.

CHAPTER THIRTY-SIX

"Take it," she replied, and held out that hand as well, her face full of triumph that she could please him.

How flushed she was. She clung to him as the smell of burnt hair filled his nostrils.

"I'm stopping you, you see," he said, rubbing the top of her head with his chin, not letting her escape his clutches when she began to struggle. "You'll no longer rule the castle, and our land will be safe once again. I know you'll hate me for it, but I must sacrifice my feelings to trim your wings, now, before you do more harm."

Yet as they sank to the forest floor and the world began tilting, she was shaking her head. She looked at him as a stranger. He felt her being torn from his memory. He resisted with all his might, as another rumble sounded, this one from the earth, as if the deep stones below were grumbling, turning against him.

He watched her, so sick he'd wish for death soon. She lay there on her back, clutching the ground, a fair maid, her face streaked with tears of betrayal. *But who—who could have treated such a beautiful girl so horribly as to cause her this pain? What did they do to her?*

∞

Through the trees a crowd of men burst forth, led by Peter and followed by Sir Bertram, anxious that Theo lead them against the raiders swiftly approaching. They found the two lovers dirty and tumbled, bewildered and ill, memories washed away. Peter cursed the heavens, and Sir Bertram moved forward to haul up the elf.

"Memory or no, he understands how to fight," Sir Bertram said, "And just now we need every body we can muster."

∞

Thirty two years later…

Peter heard the bell jangling in his office and craned his stiff neck up to the ceiling. He looked out the birdcage-sized window and threw down his quill. *Botheration.* Muttering, he crawled off his accounting stool, and like a stiff, long legged heron, he limbed it up the stairs. *Too old for the night watch. Too old.* But a smooth beginning made everything else so easy.

The bell jangled wildly again and again.

"Coming! Coming." He wished she would stop or the birds would wake and they'd have miserable weather for the tourney tomorrow.

Grimacing as he grasped the chamber door, he scratched and then gave them a second. You never knew what brazen display you'd encounter with those two. Twenty-some odd years of it but they still went at it like it was the very first time.

The Sorceress Zephyr was standing behind a tall-backed chair, clutching the master's old black velvet robe, which was on inside out, up to her neck, her hair tumbled.

She was looking pathetically young, her face full of shock and surprise.

Peter spied the rings were on her fingers. *Again. Clever woman.* By this point they spent four-fifths of their time with her as mistress. *And the master?*

Master Theo groaned on the floor, starkers. What must needs be done must. Inwardly rolling his eyes, Peter snapped his fingers.

"Why, I know him! He's a wizard. Why, he was a wizard here in the tower once."

He let that information sink in. She sat quietly in the chair still clutching the robe, her face pale and preoccupied, but she was listening.

He pretended to suddenly remember. "But he was here back in the master's day. The wizard before you, that is. 'Twas long ago, but yes, he was the old master's apprentice. What happened to him, you think?"

She looked all around the room as if seeking an answer.

"You know, some other wizard could have magicked him something awful."

"How horrible." She looked at the man and then looked away again, anywhere but at Peter or Theo.

"What d'ye think we should do with him, then?" Like leading a plow horse through its paces. Her brow furrowed up. Every year she was a little less chatty than before. He gave her a nudge.

"Give him succor or toss him out on his ear?"

"We must help him, of course. Give him, er, succor."

"Excellent idea, mistress. Excellent idea. I'll get him sorted out then, shall I?"

Theo was easily seized in Peter's grasp.

"Up, man, up!" He got him sitting up and then hoisted Master Theo under the arms until he got up onto his feet.

Leaning his master up against the door frame, he turned back to his mistress.

"Does mistress happen to recall me?"

She shook her head. *Of course not.* It never varied.

"Not to worry. Yet my face seems familiar, perhaps."

She peered at him for a minute. "Yes, yes. Your name, it's on the tip of my tongue."

"Peter, mistress. I'll take this one away, no harm in him, really. But I'd advise you to read that," he said, pointing to the carved limestone lintel above the door. "'Twould help you out, I'm thinking."

Retrieving the bundle of Theo's clothes, he started to leave.

"Not to worry, not to worry," he said, rushing from the room.

She stood up. "Poor old Peter, you should not stay up so late at your age." She walked with him to the door. She gave him a kiss on the cheek. That's how sweet she could be if she wanted.

"Should I whip up a little something for you tomorrow?" she suggested. "An age restorative, perhaps?"

"No!" he said, alarmed. Then at her expression he collected himself. "Very kind of you to offer, of course, but I've had more than my fair bit of good living and all the excitement I can handle. And tomorrow there's the tourney, you know."

"Very well, but if you change your mind—"

"Good night, mistress. You can rely upon me to take care of this one. Come along, Master Theo," he said, and they began down the stairs.

"Good night, Peter," she said, distracted and sad. He closed the door and limped his way down with the young master following along behind. Going up the stairs was not so bad. Going down at his age was another matter altogether.

"A minute." While Peter waited on the third floor, Theo pulled on his breeches and shirt, and looked around.

"This place has changed much from my day," he said. "Especially that." He gestured to the giant moss maid. Each segment was aligned to give the illusion that she rose through the floor, bursting through the next and then the next until her head met the vaulted ceiling at the top, just under the attic.

The moss maid's body was living patches of green and made the air in the tower feel clean and cold. Little plants dotted with tiny wildflowers ran across her hips and in between her breasts. Moths traced out her legs in the dark and then up higher around her belly. Her eyes were crude circles of cut-up beech branch segments, white and staring. On the shoulder of the giant maid sat the skeleton of a ram with wings, arranged tilted slightly back on its hindquarters, as if about to leap up in flight, the skeletal wings splayed out like white fingers.

"Who is that woman upstairs?" Theo croaked.

"A sorceress now occupies the tower. Ye've come back after a long journey, having battled another wizard after you were forced to kill your master."

"I have?"

"An evil wizard," Peter continued by rote, "and ye won the battle, but as he lay dying, from spite he took your memory." Such a lot of tarradiddle, but it served. "Now ye've come back to the tower, 'cause the people have invited ye to a tourney, and you must get a good night's rest, so that ye can dedicate your victory tomorrow to the memory of your former master."

Finally, Peter heard the door to the chamber above open and close.

"Good, good, she's found it," he said, half to himself.

"Come along," he said, and led Master Theo down to the cot in the laundry room. The poor man fell asleep quickly. The heavens willing, he would be fit in time for the tourney, and continue on as always.

∞

The line above the door was carved with letters in English that read: Check Out the Attic Upstairs Before You Do ANYTHING Else! Yes, YOU, Zephyr! She looked around the chamber she was in, but there was no door to anywhere except the stairwell, and no kind of attic trap door to pull down. She looked over and over again. *Nope. Nothing.* She took the lamp hanging on a hook and opened the chamber door cautiously. Peter and that man were gone. She closed the door and immediately noticed an arrow carved into the stone that pointed to where the transverse rib ran down to a respond. A little gargoyle sat there. After some time, she pressed the center of the gargoyle head and a door above her opened up. A narrow thing, but she had to dodge quickly as an unfolding ladder clattered down. She grabbed the lamp, climbed up the ladder, and found herself up against the roof of the tower.

CHAPTER THIRTY-SEVEN

There were planks laid across the unfinished floor, creating pathways to an island over in the center. She picked her way there slowly and carefully. The tower was too high to repair the roof from the outside, of course. The workers must have to use this space to repair the roof from the inside.

Resting in the center of the floor was a large square of wood that said LOOK UP. There was a scroll bound in ribbon dangling down from above, and she untied it and flattened it out on the floor to read it.

10 important things:

1. Yes, you can trust Peter in everything. ***** Dorcas too. (Who's Dorcas? I don't know.)

2. You might want to take a day or two before making the elf your apprentice. If you DO make him your apprentice, FYI you can't boink him for a year. Think it through, is all I'm saying. *************

3. Best place to pick up gossip: The tourney. But don't think the ladies will give it up. They seem to be in awe of you. The knights are the ones who lurv gossip.

4. A lady doesn't touch her face in public. It's a thing. Also the maids will groom you like a prize cow, but you have to go along with it. Seems everyone

frowns upon traipsing around the tower in spell robes with no corset on, and you've got this image to uphold. Without it you get all these people dropping in on you and you'll never get anything done.

5. The cloud birds are going to annoy you. I mean REALLY annoy you. But if you get rid of them there's going to be a drought and then you'll just have to create them all over again. ***

6. Okay, something funky is going on. I don't know what it is, but if there's something you need to write down, do it now. No, you're not going to lose your memory at the end of the day, or anything like that. It seems to be more of an occasional thing. (Something to do with being immortal???? Spell gone wrong???) I dunno, no one tells me anything. *********************

7. Listen, lady, you're going to have to really do something about those Valdeans bastards at some point, because reports are coming in and they are sick, sick, sick people. We want none of their kind here. *****

The last three were ripped off – which was maddening. What did she say? Why were they removed? Did she remove them or did someone else?

Along the side was written:

—important it's got an asterisk next to it.

Giving a hasty sigh, she turned away from the board. From the center of this bull's eye more planks stretched out like the points of a compass. She walked down one and found slips of paper held down by a rock, bottles of ink in different colors, as well as a pile of paper, neatly titled. It said:

Castle Stuff: Peter & management

She walked down the other paths and found three more.

Magic Stuff: Apprentice, cloud birds, & storage closet

Knights: tourney rules, Valdeans movements, etiquette

Village: crops, irrigation, & compost/sewage initiatives

It was an artificial memory, and she felt her cheeks quiver a little, and her nose sting like she was gonna cry.

What was worse was, if the thickness of the village pile vs. the magic pile was anything to judge by, she was more farmer than sorceress. *Ouch.*

She didn't want to think about that. Gritting her teeth, she turned to Magic Stuff and, picking up the sheets, started reading.

CHAPTER THIRTY-EIGHT

By morning she was reading in the casement window and gave a mighty yawn when the maids bustled into her room. She had just finished the castle pile when they entered, no knock, no nothing.

"Mistress, what cheer?" Four fresh-faced young women with armloads of clothes and basins of water, shoes and hats presented themselves with curtseys. They were dressed simply, but seemed more than servants. *Maids-in-waiting perhaps?*

"And you are?" she said, turning to them.

"Anne, mistress."

"Jane, mistress."

"Mary, if it pleases you, mistress."

"Pomfret, mistress."

"Pomfret!" Zephyr exclaimed. "How did you ever get such a ridiculous name?" Once she said it she could feel herself turning scarlet and wished she could have bitten out her tongue. Pomfret, however, seemed to take no offense.

"'Twas mistress herself named me," she said, and went back to stripping the bed.

She managed to get them to go away for half an hour, stole the papers back into the attic, and washed herself and scrambled into a clean shift before they came back.

"It's tourney day!" Anne said.

"Must I?"

Apparently she must. They poked and prodded her until she was ready to choose a dress and hat. She chose the purple dress, and they thought it rather plain for the occasion.

They offered her a red velvet pancake hat, striped with pearls along the sides and topped with some limp grey feathers that would look more at home in a feather duster.

"Oh, I think not."

"But they are cloud bird feathers," Mary pointed out.

She shook her head. Mary looked rather miserable that she'd rejected their choice of a hat.

"Don't you have anything more… saucy?" They looked at each other, then looked back at her. Finally, they popped forth a hat that was like a mini-cowboy hat, only it was in cloth of silver, with a poofy top and the lighter cloud bird feathers—the ones that were more silver and purple colored—the feathers curling all around the brim of the hat and over it.

"Yes." She tried it on, enchanted. Clearly the maids still preferred their choice, but c'est la vie.

It turned out that they were all to walk to the tourney grounds together, and they left the tower in plenty of time, strolling through the vast knot garden, before crossing into the herbarium that stretched for one fourth of an acre, before walking through several orchards full of ripe pears. The maids chattered about the men they would flirt with. Pomfret apparently fancied a pair of twins, and her sisters twitted her over which one she preferred.

With a huge blush she said, "Both together." Pomfret was a handful, apparently.

Everything seemed familiar. "Where is Dorcas, by the way?"

"Dorcas has much to do in the castle today," Jane said, her tone brisk. They would not look at her, though.

"And how—how is her baby?"

"Do you mean my mother, mistress?" Pomfret said.

"I do."

"She died a few years back."

"Pomfret!" The others said, and elbowed her hard in the waist. She held her stays, but defended herself, saying, "Yet here are all her babies well and grown—Tis true, Mary, and she should know it. And our mother's namesake is now a mother many times over herself."

The girls smiled sadly at her. She began to cry, though she had no idea who Dorcas even was. But she walked onward, kept her mouth open, unobtrusively wiped her eyes, and made herself think of other things.

Keep it together, Zephyr. You've got an image to uphold.

The tourney grounds were paneled with upright planks along the sides and open on the ends. On each end, many horses gathered, tourney clothes draped across their rumps. The knights were calling out, and despite the fact that it was not safe amongst the snorting horses and the plank walls were very high, many little boys and not a few little girls scampered through them. Not a few had monkeyed their way up the gaps of warped wood between the planks to hook their arms along the top, their little rumps all in a line.

She headed towards the stairs to the raised stand that ran the length of the tourney ring, but was gently led in the other direction by the maids. There was a much smaller raised stand on the opposite side of the oval, layered in tapestry cloth and mostly empty.

She was abashed to be brought in to the larger of the two compartments of the fancy stand, and worse still, brought to a special seat that had a little gold-fringed fabric top to it. Even more frightening was when the maids attempted to desert her there.

"You're not leaving, are you?" she asked them, ashamed to hear a note of panic in her voice.

"Of course we'll stay," The three said, and promptly sat down.

Pomfret, however, came and bent down towards her ear.

"It's much easier to flirt, you know, over on the other side. 'Tis much closer to the horses."

"Go, go," she said, encouraging them. The noise of the jousting field was all around her, though it was still and empty in her fancy booth. Smells of sweating horses, the buzz of people in the stands across from her, and the smell of hay, horse shit, and dirt all assaulted her nostrils. What would happen next? An air of expectation hung about the place, and the clatter of armor as the men began mounting their steeds set off a burst of birds from the trees that shaded the open stands opposite. They settled again below the people along the ground, pecking up the bread crumbs below, where clumsy toddlers chased them.

After the maids-in-waiting left it felt like a thousand eyes stared at her from the other side of the stands. The people ate, drank, and watched her. The worst was when they stared, then leaned over and whispered to their neighbor. She twiddled her fingers, craned her neck to see the knights and their horses, and smiled when Jane reappeared. Jane was far too sensible to flirt with the boys.

Apparently not. Jane handed her a filmy purple cloth with a beautiful silver sheen to it.

"Tis your favor, mistress. You must grant it to the knight you wish to win the tourney today. Or elf," she said with a wink, and left.

Zephyr gave a low groan. Apparently everyone in the tower knew about her anonymous hook-up with the hot elf-stranger last night.

A blowsy looking woman wearing a hat just like the one she had earlier rejected appeared.

"Sorceress Zephyr, good morrow," she said with a duck of the head. The woman was highly rouged and had a large mole or beauty mark next to a dimple at the corner of her mouth.

Exactly the same hat—pearl striped scarlet, right down to the ugly grey feather. *What's up with that?*

"Nice hat," she said, because somehow she didn't think she liked this woman. Why did she have to deal with all of this anyway? She just wanted to do magic.

Just then a string of horses and their riders came prancing out to stand in front of her.

The favor, right. One sat taller and straighter than the rest. There was something about him that drew the eye. Perhaps because his black horse's cloth was purple, like her dress. She was in a purple mood today.

While the others stayed back, the guy in purple came forward, putting up his helm.

Oh god. Oh no. Not him, please no.

"I'm expected to be champion today," he said. "You're supposed to give me your favor."

There was no help for it. There went the scarf.

Then the woman in the awful hat appeared to gird her loins. Leaning close, she said confidentially, "Dearest sorceress, you may not recall, but I once did you a great favor. You said at the time you would reward me. In fact, you said you would give me one of your finest rings."

"Tis unlikely the sorceress ever said such a thing," a fat old red-headed man said, as he entered. He made her a leg. "Sorceress, may myself and my companions join you for this joust?"

Somehow in the hustle and bustle of the men coming, the woman was edged out until she was at the entrance and there was not a stool or chair for her to sit in.

An ugly, old bald man saw the woman with the hat lurking. He made a *go away* gesture and the woman gave a huff, turned about and disappeared.

"Thank you for shooing her away," she said to the ugly old man on her right side.

These men were all knights with a strong predilection for the tourney. While the jousting went forward they kept up a running commentary, informing her about the names of the knights taking part and crucial elements of competition.

Servants brought food and drink, and after a while she realized she was enjoying herself far more than she had anticipated, though she still cringed and winced at the rattle and clatter of the armor when the men swiftly crunched together over the jousting barrier. It was like hearing a car crash where the cars were made of tin.

There were two complaints, however, that perked up her ears. One was about someone called Knight Trumbull. Not Sir Trumbull. He was out in the field today on a white horse with light blue cloth. He was the son of the woman who'd accosted her before and a dead man named Sir Ingham. The knights would not say just what he had done, but she got the feeling that he was raping young women, or terrifying them, or both. The other issue was the recent rumbles of war from the Valdhors, their neighbors to the south.

"Valdhors."

"So they call themselves now."

She frowned and shook her head. The name sounded wrong to her ear.

She focused on what they were saying. Linus the Third, however—and at the name Linus the Third she felt her body go numb all over—and the Blue Sorcerer were rallying forces against these horrible marauders. She knew those names. Why were they so familiar?

"Anyone in allegiance with the Valdhors will *not* be considered an enemy to the Valdhors," Sir Bothswell said. The man had grey fuzzy hair like a dandelion, and red, red lips.

"Which, of course, no one believes. Valdeans have always invaded, decrees or no."

"I thought you said they were the Valdhors?" she said.

"Who are ruled by their warrior class—who were all born of Valdean parents."

"Ah."

It was hard to keep track, and on top of that he was out there jousting and he was just mowing down the other knights—whom to her eye looked pretty damn good themselves.

"I thought the knight with the scarlet banner pretty good, don't you?" she said between alternating mouthfuls of gooseberry tart and the best cheese she'd ever had in her life.

When she mentioned this, Sir Bertram began puffing out his chest like a pigeon.

"That's my son you've honored me by mentioning, sorceress," Sir Bertram said. "His twin is over there," and he pointed. "He goes next."

Ah! The twins. She spotted Pomfret tucking a large white handkerchief into the twin's fist. Sir Bertram's other son was unseated and sat in the dirt before he fell over to one side and was carried from the field.

With that, the jousting portion of the day was over.

"If the enemy is really knocking at the door this time, then what—"

No one was listening. There was a huge stir amongst the stands.

"What's going on?"

"Theo has agreed to join in the melee."

"By George, it'll be something to watch if he does."

"Who's Theo?"

She watched as the men entered on foot. Then the crowd went from a huge roar to a scream and *God*, it was him.

She suffered a thousand agonies, a scarlet face. Everyone watched her. They all seemed to know something was up.

Turning to the knights, she tried to act disinterested.

"I see the determination at this table," she said, "and I, too, am alarmed that an enemy is this close. Clearly something must be done."

She was drowned out by a flood of shouts as the men began to fight in teams.

"Theo's team is taking on three teams at once," the ugly man said, leaning towards her from her right. "And winning."

Three teams at once. Craze-balls. Wow.

"What?" she said, not catching Sir Bertram's words as the melee came to a climax.

"When the knights join Linus's force, we must have Theo to lead us."

"Okay."

Sir Bertram shook his head.

"He says he won't."

There was a break, and Sir Pettish said she was expected to invite the champion to sit next to her while the younger men tilted at small iron circles dangling from a string and the like. He showed up, looking sweaty and reluctant, but he sat next to her while she offered him food and drink. She tried to talk to him about the threat of the Valdhors.

"Sir Bertram says that they are fighting within three hundred leagues of us."

He stood. "A youth has asked me to give him some pointers before he goes out today. If you will excuse me, fair sorceress."

She turned back to the knights.

CHAPTER THIRTY-NINE

"Why won't he lead our force?"

"We don't know," Pettish said, looking around at the other men and then back at her. "We thought you might."

She shook her head.

"Whatever his reason, it must be overcome," Sir Bothswell said. "You could convince him."

"You can wrap him round your little finger when you've a will to," Bertram said.

"So you all would go with him, support him, and form an army."

"We're too old, sorceress. War is a young man's game."

"Nonsense," she said, looking around. "You're only—what? Fifty? You're in your prime." Pettish looked flattered at her words, though he looked the most decrepit of the lot.

"We went off to fight years ago. You don't recall, but the men on foot got the worst of it," Pettish told her. "We were all on horseback, and were protected by our armor."

"We were almost routed," Bothswell confessed. "I, a mere lad, rode through the fray on a first pass, when my horse was struck. It fell upon me, and I was pinned. I feigned death, but heard men slaughtered all around."

"Only one fighter prevailed. He pulled the enemy off their horses and ran them through like they were made of butter. He never ceased in his attack and they shied away from him. He chased them and slaughtered their leaders until at last all turned and fled."

"Then he harried them to the borders."

"We joined the chase, but we learned caution that day."

"Who was this genius of war craft?" *Why don't they make* him *leader?* "Which of you was it? Oh, let me guess." She rolled her eyes.

A second melee was underway. This time the elf and three knights fought fifty men. She counted them again, making sure of the number. She couldn't tear her eyes away. He fought half the pack, while the three knights covered his back.

He would bring down his foe and shout out to the third knight until the man changed what he was doing.

"Look at him," she said. "Right now, see how they protect his back? He can't do it all on his own. Young men need wiser heads to urge caution."

The men had a particular look on their faces, one with which she was very familiar. It was the look her father had gotten on his face when she talked about going to South America. He didn't like it but was struggling to remain open minded and embrace the idea.

She got a total thrill out of it. She had the warm fuzzies for this place and these men. And it was a gorgeous, glorious day.

"I'll convince him to lead if you agree to follow. Do we have a deal, gentlemen?"

They struck hands on it. The melee was over. Groaning men out on the field climbed up onto their feet with the help of their wooden swords and retched or limped off.

"Why won't he fight?" she asked.

"No idea," Pettish said.

"Look at him." He was helping the men up and was shining with sweat, but looking around as if to say, *That was fun. Who wants some more?*

"I mean, look at him."

Still. Walking home with the girls as the long shadows stretched across the orchards, she didn't want to get too far on her high horse. Today had been like joining a card game mid-hand. Is this poker or hearts? She didn't know, but she was expected to play the next card. So far she was rolling with it, wincing all the while.

A man drew up on his horse. She recognized the horse, a giant dappled white beast, and she paused politely.

"Good morrow. Did you fight today, sir?" she asked.

"Good morrow, fair sorceress. Perhaps you don't remember me?" She looked him over. He was twenty-three or twenty-five. One of the men who had jousted.

"Forgive me, sir, and my wretched memory."

"Tis Sir Reginald. You spoke with the friends of my youth today. They told you of our exploits so long ago."

"Friends of your youth—Sir Reginald," she said, shaking her head in wonder, "you are wonderfully preserved."

"Tis the dragon blood you gave me," he said, walking alongside the maids. Jane was riveted by his every twitch. *Jane, you wench!* Still, she quite liked Sir Reginald.

"And how did I do that?" she asked.

"I was brought home from battle mortally wounded. You had the tiniest bit of dragon's blood dotted upon my tongue." He gave a laugh. "Thus here I am!"

"You have not aged a day!"

"Not quite, dear sorceress. I aged backwards some thirty odd years. Was left an infant and have grown up all over again."

Lack-a-fuck-me-day.

Her mouth dropped open and the maids and Sir Reginald laughed at her expression.

"My greatest apologies, dear sir. I regret my mistake."

"Oh, I would much rather grow up twice than be dead once," he assured her, and remounting his horse went off into a cloud of dust.

∞

The next day she went into the village for Pomfret, who needed aglets. Aglets were metal dangly things that went on the end of corset stays and other fancy cords people used for tie-on sleeves. She heard her name called and turned to find Trumbull in the street accosting her.

"What is Mistress Zephyr doing then?" Trumbull asked with a degree of familiarity that made her inwardly cringe.

"I've been visiting the tower chatelaine, who just had a child." She patted the now empty basket that only held a few aglets wrapped in a twist of cloth.

"Giving succor to her as married one of the Magor scum."

Had she? Zephyr did not know. She didn't answer, since it didn't seem to be a question. "I am told bringing baskets to those unable to leave their bed is what any upright woman of noble birth does. But you, sir," she said, switching to the aristocratic tongue as her black ring blazed red, "you wouldn't understand that, would you?"

She did not know it, she only guessed, but she hit the bull's eye. Trumbull turned deep, dark red in the face. He was not actually a knight, she'd found out, and not legitimate either. He was the son of that horrid woman from the tourney, and he fought with a horse and armor he'd inherited from the father who never recognized him. She didn't think any of that was his fault, but didn't like his stinking looks just the same.

"Ho-hooooo! Other knights may like a saucy tongue," he said.

"Are you a knight? I had not realized," she said. "Certainly you are lacking in courtesy."

He was deliberately blocking the way in the street, and a faint feeling of alarm made her wary.

"I charge you, lady, for you are a harlot. I accuse you of meddling, of demonic arts and foul, unnatural intercourse with elves. I name you enchantress!" He pointed at her, and it seemed like a big deal. Suddenly, the entire village came circling around them.

She stood there rooted to the spot. She wanted to go back to the tower, go into the study, lock the door and never come out. Sweat popped out along her body while she swore to herself.

"By rights," Trumbull bellowed, more out to the crowd now than to her, "you should be placed on the cross, flogged through town, dunked in the river and stoned to death."

So this was not good.

She considered a good swift kick to his balls, but she had on flimsy flat shoes instead of a stiff, pointy slipper. She was wondering if he'd even be able to feel it beneath the ridiculously enormous codpiece he was wearing.

So she lost her temper.

"Do not play with me, scurvy knave! An enchantress can do naught but seduce by her manipulative powers. There is little magic about her, and even that is weak and poor."

She changed to a sincere tone, as if telling him for his own good, but she wanted the entire town to hear her.

"Yes, I am a most powerful sorceress. Good citizens have no cause to fear me. While bullies like yourself should fear my vengeance."

A little ground trembling. *Whoops, didn't mean that. Shit.* She could feel it pull at her, a kind of chaotic, destructive impulse. The pull had a wild feel to it, making her gaze turn inward. *No, don't. Don't go there. Ah-ah-ah.* It felt good.

Stop that right now.

Many villagers who had at first pushed forth now looked a little uncertain and began backing away.

"Aye, we do not fear you," Trumbull said, though he had now gone very red in the face. She couldn't let herself be intimidated. She had to control these people through confidence. "We have your measure. I have only to say that the rings on your fingers are a cursed enchantment that you've—"

What? She was blinking.

Jeering laughter surrounded her on all sides. That dreadful man was calling out to her again.

What?

∞

Peter found him at the tourney ring giving lessons to Sir Reginald, who was impressive for one so young.

"Trumbull is plaguing her in the town," Peter said, limping up to him. Reginald turned and began running. He turned too, and followed, sword in hand. He looked behind to see Peter puffing behind him.

∞

"Let me stop a minute, please," she said, and holding her stomach, trembling, she was sick on the side of the road. Reginald held her arm and Peter her basket, but Theo gave Reginald such a look that he dropped her arm, and Theo took it instead.

"This Knight Trumbull," he said. "He fights at the tourneys."

"Yes? What of it. Oh, I have no idea what just happened. Whatever it was, I didn't like it. Oh God." She clapped a hand over her mouth.

"Deep breaths," Peter said. She gave Peter a look of sad thanks, but it was Theo's arm she clung to.

"Let's not talk about him. Will you walk me around the fields? Thanks. I have another matter I need to discuss with you," she said.

They walked through the orchards that spread out below the tower.

"What about Linus the Third and this blue sorcerer?" She said, plucking a leaf from a pear tree as they walked. "Will there be war?"

"Certainly."

"What about the men here—if they join Linus's force, how well do you think they'll fare?"

"They need drilling in weaponry, close quarters combat. Someone to sweat the fat off them."

"Someone like you."

"Not me."

"Who else? If they ask you, would you say yes?"

"Sir Bertram or Pettish may lead them. Not me." She took her time and gathered flowers for a posy. Asters and goldenrod with horse mint.

"I'm giving these to Pomfret. She's going to freak when she finds out what happened in the village." They continued walking. By now he started to feel she had some sort of ulterior motive.

"Wouldn't your father be proud to see you at the head of all these men?"

"To see me leading an army of warriors, yes. These are not warriors."

The heady smell of ripe pears was in the air. A servant approached.

"Dominic, is it?" she said.

"My father is not well. He said I should follow you and assist you in whatever way you need."

"Another guard dog. Thank your father for me. All in all, though, I prefer the elf."

She gave a little titled head nod for him to go. He exchanged a glance with the young man who gave him a look and a shrug as if to say *Better you than me*, and left.

"Why won't you lead the army?"

He wouldn't say.

"Today, you saved my life, you know that. Did you do it for me—or would you have done it for any woman?"

"I hope for any woman."

"And if she was an enchantress?"

"Any woman I believed to be innocent."

She grinned. "You believe me innocent?"

He blushed to his ear tips. "I believe you capable of great mischief. But not evil."

"You would protect any innocent woman, then," she said, quickening her stride towards the castle. "Against any bully like Trumbull, even if he were a fearsome foe?"

"I would."

"Then why not the innocent of this land? Against their great foe?"

He kissed her hand, trying to avoid a response, but she gave him a look as if to say she was not fooled by his gallantry.

"You are a clever lady and have built a neat trap."

He left her in sight of the tower, watching as she walked back with her posy, sniffing at it, foiled no doubt in her purpose. Yet that last dreamy look she gave him made him very uneasy.

∞

A week later he was up before dawn to birdsong and left the dormitory, restless. He washed himself in the trough. It was still quite early; the sun had not yet peeked out from around the tower, and blue indigo shadows shaded his cold limbs. He had slept little, uneasy, and unable to calm himself. A flicker from above caught his eye. It was the sorceress, watching him from her room at the top of the tower.

Her long hair hung out the casement window, the ends curling around the ivy leaves that reached up towards the window. She watched him wash. It made him feverish, both hot and cold as she pinned him with her eyes.

At last he stood looking up at her. For a long time he did not move, letting her look, and letting himself be seen. Dragging on his shirt, he was just about to leave when she called out.

"Theo," she cried, and he turned back to her, reluctant but courteous, as he made her a proper leg. "There's something I'd like you to see," she said, and disappeared inside.

He met her on the third floor. In the dining hall stood a man, his back turned. Rather, not a man, but a suit of armor. Black and richly detailed, it gleamed like a beetle's shell, like a raven's wing.

He approached it and put his hand out.

"Take this suit of armor. I had it made for you. You shall be my black knight, dressed in this armor, and carry my banner as your coat of arms."

"And as the black knight lead the others? I can't."

"The enemy is now closer than ever before."

He shook his head. Fighting brought out his inner elf, making it so much worse to control and tamp down.

She bit her lips. "The armor is still yours, of course, but I'm disappointed."

"I can't." He couldn't tell if it was the constant bouts or her, but something was going to give soon. His inner elf was raging, and it became harder every day to crank it down and keep it within.

∞

"What do you wait for, sir?" Trumbull said on his knees. "Let it be done."

Trumbull wasn't an idiot. Theo finished him off and left the tourney ring, his elf raging with the glory of triumph and vengeance.

∞

He came up and knelt at her feet, his head resting against her ribs. Her hands went to his hair and he felt her shudder. She showed him her fingers. They had touched his armor and came away with blood.

The worst agony was her touch. Her other hand was moving lightly through his hair when he wanted her to dig her hand into it and—it was an agony to be in her presence.

"You had to do it, I suppose," she said at last.

Theo closed his eyes as they throbbed with co-mingled want and satisfaction. "He humiliated you, a powerful sorceress. And he delights in other people's pain. What he tried with you—Reginald says there are other women he tormented and hurt. Yes, it had to be done."

Her fingers flexed in the air before she snatched them back and stuck them up her sleeves as if she was forcing herself not to touch him again. He dared not look in her direction as he left.

∞

At the next tourney no one would fight him. No man would go near him for fear of insulting him and being challenged to a duel.

The sorceress invited him to sit near her but he would not. The restless feeling burned within him in her presence. Fighting was not making his elf side worse. Fighting relieved his feelings for her, feelings that were swamping him.

∞

It was the middle of the night, and she was in her shift, a robe hastily thrown over it, as she descended the stairs quickly behind Peter to the third floor.

Peter put the lantern on the hook, gave them both a look and then turned and left the room.

"Theo, what is it?" She said, alarmed. His face was pale, his eyes black and wild with agony.

He sank to his knees before her.

"Are you ill?"

"I'm sick from desire," he said.

CHAPTER FORTY

Pressing his fevered face into her ribs, he said "I'm blinded by love for you."

She was riveted with shock. *Love?*

She could see the whites under the bottom rim of his black irises and her heart began to give queer leaps.

"If I say no?" she asked.

"If you have no mercy, I will go to the river and drown myself rather than live one more day in such misery."

She made the mistake of looking him in the eye. Like a dart striking her, a sensation of desire embedded itself in her flesh. Her breath became short, and yet a divine feeling of giving in to him pervaded her, removing all resistance.

She kissed him. He was up in a flash, yanking her into his arms and savagely kissing her back. Before long she was on the table, her skirts up, his tongue working at her down there, melting with his heat any hesitation she might have, undulating his mouth until she opened her legs wider as he deepened his kiss. As she looked into his eyes, her whole pelvis responded in a strange but unmistakable cramp. It was such a new melting sensation, communicating loud and clear her body's insistent desire. She felt it all the way up from her loins to the back of her jaw.

His hands measured her ribs, tore away her robed gown, tore away her shift. He pulled her with those hands, so competent at wielding swords, up to his mouth and sucked her breasts until they were slippery and hard, the thrills of sensation snaking down to her pubic bone and stabbing there, while her womb throbbed for him.

He penetrated her with his fingers, filled her as he thrust into her, before sinking with her back down to the table, covering her, his bulging arms and shoulders level with her head, as he thrust harder and harder in response to the way she clutched his hair and wrapped her legs around him. The sensation in her pelvic girdle, this ache, this cramp nagged at her. It almost tickled and hurt it was so insistent and strong. It grew and grew, alarming her not a little. She whispered filthy things in his ears and tongued him from the lobes to the tips, taking time along the way to penetrate his ears in a very naughty way as he unleashed himself upon her with more urgency than before.

Quickly spent, he was quick to rise again, and this time he was loving, caressing, and teasing. She meanwhile was in a torment, and somewhat fearfully tried to hide it from him, afraid of how he might tease her if he knew what power he had over her body.

"Will you fight for me?" she said, panting.

"If that's what it takes to bind you to me. The images in my head—things I've imagined doing to you up in your bed—night after night," he gasped. "I cannot sleep for pining."

"Show me," she said. "Hurry!"

He stripped away their clothing until she lay before him naked. He pinned her arms above her head and held her down with his weight, staring into her face.

A thick sort of bliss stole through her brain and grew down her torso to meet that sublime ache. Pleasure-benumbed, she didn't know what to do with herself, she was going to go mad. She made a pretense of struggling as he turned her over and took her that way, then took her bottom as well. The violence of her orgasm plunged through her over and over again, until like a boat spinning over the falls, she felt herself riding the tumbling waves of blissful sensation from her pelvis releasing. Rode them down to a deep place within her soul, surrendering something of herself up to him before surfacing again. She succumbed to a deep, hard lassitude in which it felt like she would be content to lie there forever. Her body felt no desire to move, speak, or even think ever again.

Later, in her bed, he slept deeply, head upon her breast, his arm and leg across her possessively, while she lay awake, still in the thick dregs of the lazy bone numb feeling, her head propped up upon the pillows, eyes staring out at the harsh moonlight that spilled in through the diamond-paned windows, illuminating all the naked glory of his ass and legs.

Hot, molten sparks flew through her mind recalling the way he took her. Possessiveness burned into her like a brand.

Why was she full of gloom at the same time? The lightning outside cracked in chorus to the croak and screech of nesting birds in the vines below her window. Green lightning poured from clouds above and showered down through spatters of rain, so that damp worked its way through every little crack and crevasse, making her soul want to shrivel. Meanwhile he was fever hot, and where his flesh touched hers, she was warm, while the rest of her shivered.

She remembered his eyes. Sick with desire, he said. Thick with the molten power to create such bodily effects within her. She felt an awe at his being able to create sensations. She felt afraid, too.

"Awake, my love?"

"Fretting. This is going to end badly."

"How so?"

"I don't know. I just feel it somehow."

Another shriek from the birds, who sang out in agreement. He sat up and pulled her down to him, making love to her once more, with such vigor and frank lust that she was left exhausted, and yet wanting more. *I can't take this*. Her mind at last sinking into a restless sleep while she lay in his arms.

In her dreams he twisted her about his finger, and she woke with a start.

Still half asleep, she peered through slitted eyes at the bright moonlight on his face as he lay upon his back. In her dream there was no softness to him, no love. Oh, but she loved him, loved him madly. She was forced to be hard on him, commanding him to go lead the army. It was like reaching inside him to the insane, relentless lover she had here in her bed. *This man. This is the man I want all the world to see*. She twisted to one side, repositioning one tender buttock, and he put his arm across her, onto her hip, while she stroked the heavy weight of his head on her breast.

Lying here now, tumbled, the stink of sex all about her—this was who she really was. She was not some idealized image to look at from afar. Yet he seemed to love her—kinky sex, screaming, cursed birds, and all. That thought was what made her heart hurt the most.

Outside the tower, two or three bolts of green lighting burst forth in the clouds. Suddenly the hard rain began to fall, and the birds shut up. Still unable to sleep, she continued staring out into the night, the feel of his head a heavy weight upon her.

∞

In her dream she was the formidable Theodorus's apprentice. Life was difficult, and often tiresome, but she was happier than ever before. There were sleepless watches, midnight events in rainstorms. Often she worked in total blackness, in graveyards, at crossroads. There were things she bumped against in the night, things that crawled out of tarns and put a scaly claw around her ankle. There were words in books she didn't understand, didn't feel she'd ever understand, and didn't know that she even would want to understand.

She awoke with another start. For a moment that world had seemed more vivid and real than this one. In her dreams she'd been happy. He kissed her shoulder.

"I shouldn't have done that," he said.

"What?"

"Made love to you. Used my elf enchantments. It's hard not to, it's—I can't always control it now."

The sweet agony she felt—that was his elf side?

She snuggled down into the sheet. "You have no idea how good it felt. None. And I'm here with you willingly, aren't I? Don't worry about it."

"I never thought I could be this contented," he murmured. He kissed her shoulder again, and rested his head on her once more with a deep sigh.

As if his lips were magic, she fell deeply asleep again.

∞

The men trained in armor. The black knight was now never seen without it. Belly cut, wrist cut, flank cut, head blow. From the stands she and the maids watched, riveted.

He showed them how to jump on a horse, how to run, how to swing an axe, how to swing a hammer. He climbed up a ladder from the inside of the ladder only using his arms till he was at the top of the viewing stand. He did all this with alacrity and his suit made the noise of fifty angry people slamming metal boxes shut at more or less the same time.

Dash and squat to the side, dash and squat opposite direction. They practiced the direct blow, where they reached for the middle of their own sword, pushing aside the enemy's sword at the same time, and aimed for the enemy's eye slit. *Gah!*

"Another place to land the tip of your sword is in the gap here, under the lance rest, on the opposite side of the pauldron. He'll have chainmail, yet you can still inflict some internal damage if you go in, and then angle your sword back.

"It's a wrist action here. One fast jab can inflict all kinds of damage."

Sir Reginald was his favorite practice partner.

"Use of overwhelming force. I cross swords, sweep left hand inside his sword—see, now it's immobilized under your arm, push back with your sword on his arm, while with this hand, you push, and if you can sweep your heel to catch his—down he goes." Down Sir Reginald went. But he was back up again, with almost a bounce and the noise of someone dropping a hundred cans down the stairs.

"Again, what if it doesn't work? What if he doesn't fall?"

"Take back your distance or break the distance," Pettish said.

"Very good. In this instance, if he staggers but he doesn't go down, you need to stay close. If you take back the distance what happens? His sword'll be right there. Once you've freed it from under your arm, press hard. Then reach down beneath his tasset, grab his chainmail at the back, pull up and yank."

Sir Reginald went down hard. He had the wind knocked out of him.

"Rise, Reggie. We'll do it again." Sir Reginald was busy crawling away and either didn't hear or didn't want to. With a sigh, Sir Pettish took his place.

"Elbow and forearm are parallel. I'm pushing on his gorget. His balance is off. I keep my arm pushing there, but at the same time go down and reach. Your head stays up, your body is pushing back, while the arm reaches. All part of one action. Stay low, right leg forward—" Theo gave a leaping spring forward and Pettish was perfectly horizontal in the air for a moment. His face was patient, resigned to the ignominious pain that was to follow.

"You'll notice something—how am I pulling on the fellow and holding my sword? I'm not. The sword falls free of my hand just as I reach. Once he's down—look, it hasn't moved far, I grab it, and we're on again."

Whenever the twins did particularly well she joined the other girls in staring at Pomfret, who always obliged them all by going beet red.

He demonstrated. "Dagger to the eyes."

He looked up for a moment at her, his shy glance saying—*this is so much fun*. The men were breathing hard as they tried to stay on their feet. They hustled about with purpose and energy, and she felt very proud of them all.

He did flips, he demonstrated how to get up swiftly from being on one's face, how to get up if they were knocked upon their back. The armor made a huge racket. She wanted to climb his armor and take him down to the ground.

She called down. "Sir Reginald! What do you think of Theo's new armor?"

"Beautiful," he grinned. "Only, he won't be able to sneak upon on someone, unsuspecting like."

When it came to the men getting off their faces or their backs, it was like watching the same film in slow motion, which sent her and the maids into giggles.

"On your feet," he snarled, banging his sword against his shield, making a dreadful din. She could only imagine what it would sound like inside the suit of armor. The men slowly got to their feet.

"Do you think the battle stops because you're tired? On your knees!"

The men sank down to their knees.

"Up!"

They got up. Groaning. Almost before they got up, he was calling out.

"On your knees!"

They sank.

"Feeling tired? Well! What are you waiting for? On your feet!"

She watched the men weep as they rose to their feet. The men rising and falling in their armor filled their ears, a giant mechanical gate opening and closing shut with a tremendous clang.

He'll be in danger every day. And this was all my bright idea.

"He seems to have them well in hand," she said to the maids. They agreed and as one rose to go back up to the tower.

CHAPTER FORTY-ONE

He loved her, but his capricious elf side said she was not nearly distraught enough over the fact that he was leaving for war. He still burned for her, but his elf side saw her as a cold-hearted temptress and wanted her to beg him to stay. There were soft chinks in the armor of her heart. He would exploit them, pry into them. He was learning her weaknesses for physical pleasure and decided to destroy her with his caresses.

He told Reggie his plans to capture her heart for good. Reggie nodded and yet looked doubtingly at him. When he asked why Reggie looked so, Reggie said something about women always finding a way to get the upper hand.

"Now is a dangerous moment in the history of our people," she said to the crowd, "Enemy soldiers are not more than five days' march away. Linus the Third welcomes you and will provide you with support from his supply lines."

A rather ragged cheer for Linus the Third went up from the men.

"Only one man can best you all. Only one man will strike fear into the heart of the enemy. The man who will lead you into battle and glorious victory is the black knight."

He rode forward. He raised his helm. His eyes were as black as his armor, winking in the sun. He knew this from their familiar throb.

"I do this to protect you, sorceress," he said, looking straight at her.

"Do it to protect us all, your people and your land," she called out and the crowd went wild. She gave him the look that said *crush me in your arms*. She had no idea how uncomfortable he felt in this situation. Who was he to be leading a small army of human men?

The maids bedecked him with garlands. Before a large crowd, he spoke:

"My mistress, I would have a token to remember you by." The crowd cheered so loudly he knew she could hardly hear him. She took the ring from her finger—the one with the blue stone upon it—and pushed it into his bare hand. He put it on his own smallest finger for all to see. It whispered to him.

The other ring. Your ring. Take it.

As he was asking her, no—*telling* her he wanted the second ring, he saw the hit of magic in her eyes. Her jaw went up, her teeth clenched and she was stretching her arm out towards him, her fingers, reaching. At the same time the crowd bodily picked him up and carried him out of reach, onto his horse. With more cheers the crowd, swept away by their adoration of their new hero, drew his horse down the road and pulled the army south. Girls threw down flowers before their horse's hooves. Girls who were bold and agile grabbed onto a horse's mane and saddle stirrup cup before climbing up to steal a kiss from a startled knight and hop off again just as quickly.

He became the vortex for a writhing, seething mass of people, all shouting, all touching him. Had he not been protected with armor and his men not come in to circle him with their own horses, he would have been mauled to death. He was swiftly carried off and out of her reach, not even able to look back so their eyes could lock upon each other until the dust from all the people and horses obliterated her from his sight.

∞

She looked through the spyglass, her frustration growing worse. Closing her eyes for a moment, she gave in and changed it to the other setting. By now she recognized the shining figure in a black breastplate in the center, as well as the other bearded, older men.

She was looking at her own men, riding home in fierce exultation at their victories. Battered and dirty, wounded and glorious, they were nothing like what they had been when they left last autumn. The long line of carts following them was full of war booty and prizes. She fretted with impatience. Why weren't they here yet?

"What are you doing?

She turned back to the table.

"Reading the dispatches." She stood beside the massive table, shuffling through the many pages of reports. Finally, she threw them down and began to pace.

"Really, as a de facto ruler of this land, I have no idea what I'm doing," she said.

"Nor does anyone else," Peter replied. "It makes you very hard to predict." He chuckled.

"You think it's funny?"

"This land has not seen war in five generations. We know nothing of war. You're doing well enough, my dear. I'm not sure any of us could do better." He was very decrepit these days. She had him carried up and down the stairs in a chair.

"Peter, you should be at home."

"You need me too much here."

"Well, certainly."

Peter was like a father to her. She confided all things to him and him alone.

"At home they want to put me in a big bed and watch me die. It's rather tedious. I'd much rather be here with you," he said, patting her hand.

They sat together most afternoons in the banquet hall, where there was room to spread out papers and maps related to the war all around the table.

"I do not see you in your study anymore, mistress."

She was afraid to do magic now. The catalyst was not under her control, and she was leery of using it. She turned back to her dispatches. It was the only news they received of the black knight.

"What do the dispatches say?" Peter asked.

"Another woman tries to woo the black knight. The king's sister, Princess Allame. Remember when he scorned that duchess and then the plague broke out?"

Idiot mages had suggested burning the elf to stop the plague, since clearly the two were related. *Pah.* However, King Linus the Third had forbade it, saying Theo was the most astounding warrior he'd ever laid eyes on.

"Our black knight is the heroic idol of the century," she said.

"His reputation as a warrior is rather good," Peter said with a smile. "But had he not been ensnared by a certain sorceress, I'm not so sure people would have taken much notice."

She smiled back, wrinkling her nose at the same time, letting him know she thought him a smart ass. She wrote Theo letters. Tender love letters scrawled with hot passion towards the end, but he never replied. When one of her letters went astray and became widely shared around the war camps and at Linus's court, she understood why. Her last letter was turned into a popular raunchy ballad about the black knight.

She read on. "He's kicking ass, Peter, but it hurts, because there are all these songs and poems about women trying to seduce him. Now the enemy is calling him Virgin Killer. Says human women are literally dying for the love of the black knight." She tossed down the dispatch again. "It's adding a sinister edge to his reputation, don't you think? I don't care for it." She picked up another.

"See—now this dispatch claims the enemy side has been betrayed in several key battles because women bring him information as their love tokens."

Peter nodded, and grinned, clearly quite pleased with this treachery.

"Look at you. So bloodthirsty. I for one would rather that beautiful women not throw themselves at his feet. They're wooing him by foul means and fair. One woman, spurned by him, tried poisoning the king's banquet. Linus's food taster is dead as a result."

"You're worried he's not true to you?"

"I'm a little worried that he is. They say he's so wicked and cruel to these women. He wasn't very happy with me when he left. What's he going to be like when he comes back?"

Peter carried on with his task of making a fair copy of the latest harvest accounts.

"And your other project, over there in the corner. You don't mind if I have a peek?"

"Not at all. We're rebuilding grain reserves and depleted soil. And I'm grinding out a chronicle about these times. Notes on how to protect the land from famine and war."

"See, you do know what you're doing. Though, I must say, I always thought you were someone who would be making history, not recording it," he said.

"I will make history," she mumbled. But there was much to do.

"You do not remember when you first came here. I did not expect that this land and the people at the tower would thrive under your care. I was wrong. You have been a boon to us all, mistress. Many blessings upon you."

Her eyes filled. "Your blessing means so much to me, Peter. Thank you." She clasped his gnarled hand.

The horns sounded. She couldn't believe her ears. She went to the windows. "You hear that? Peter! They're coming back." Four days. She had four days to prepare a celebration. "Peter?" She went over to her old friend.

Holy creepers. "Peter, you're not well. I can help you, I can—"

"No!" he said. "Call my children."

CHAPTER FORTY-TWO

They were walking back from Peter's funeral when the cloud of dust warned them of approaching warriors. The signals had not been lit. Their own men were returning.

Today they would feast with the victorious men. She was still saddened by losing Peter.

"Set aside your sore heart," Anne said, putting an arm around her waist.

"Our father was a very practical man," Jane reminded her. "He would want us to use the funerary meats at the victory banquet. He's with mother now, and in the end, that's all he really wanted."

They went and changed. She wore a midnight blue dress with long cap sleeves, a high lace collar around her neck, and an open work skirt that was silver underneath. Her dress was full of mystery and elegance, and in the glass she seemed distant and imposing like the sorceress of a tower should.

Then she decided the hell with it, took off the collar and put a crown of flowers on her head. Apothecary roses, Lenten daisies, and tiny pink and yellow toad flax. If joyous was feeling like you were going to climb out of your skin and shoot off into the sky, then she was joyous. Without the collar the square cut neck line was quite low, but she left it that way.

She stared through the glass from the balcony, examining the tattered banners they had captured. Few were familiar to her. Their own banners were torn and bloody—but carried with pride by the foot soldiers of merit.

These were the men she had spied over and over in the glass all those months, battered by war. Sir Bertram's beard was mostly grey and he came home missing one eye. Even the horses bore scars upon their flanks. She'd never have recognized them for the lily-white pampered folk who'd played at being warriors on the tourney field not long ago.

Anticipation ran through her body. Trembling with excitement, she spotted him as he came into view.

"There he is," she said to the maids and Dominic. Clean shaven, his armor polished, the sun glinting upon it. She had to squint. They were in half-armor. Chainmail, helm, and greaves. Breastplate and boots.

She looked through the glass again. The black knight was the bright hero amongst them, hands fisting the reins of his charger, but he was talking earnestly with someone. Someone with long hair and blue robes. A stranger. Perhaps another woman, another magic worker.

"All those dispatches," she muttered to herself. "All this time, I've wondered—Tell me, Dominic, the person riding by his side—is that a man or a woman?" She let him look through the glass.

"Can't tell." He passed the glass to the women, who also couldn't say.

"It's a man," Pomfret said at last, and Zephyr could have kissed her.

Yes! How that long flowing hair had gnawed at her through many a sleepless night. Looking at the ceiling, she had cursed men, she had cursed elves, but most of all she had cursed herself for being a fool. At last the proud eagle nose of a long-haired man came into focus. His cliff of a brow and a strong jaw. Androgyny never looked so beautiful.

"Oh, it's definitely a man," she said, beaming. "A sorcerer, too, I'd guess."

They all bristled with anticipation, while below in the kitchen twenty different roasts were on the spit, and upstairs on the third floor a grand banquet was being set upon the table.

∞

As they rode across the land, Rhine had to be constantly urged onward. He wanted to get to the tower as soon as possible and again sped up their pace, despite footsore, injured, hungry men.

"I had not heard the land of the great tower was so beautiful," Rhine said.

"Tis beautiful, but not my land, and not my home. War has only made me long for my true home."

"Ah, north of the Zahra Freeth border?"

"Yes. The elf land where I spent my childhood. Where my father still lives. At least I hope he does."

"I've never seen such magnificent trees," Rhine exclaimed after another hour. "Magic?" he asked, suddenly suspicious.

"Dragon's blood," Theo agreed.

"I've only ever met one elf before, but I understand you can see auras and colors that we never see. Can you see the aura around each tree that tells you it's been treated with dragon's blood?"

"I can. And round Sir Reginald too," he joked. Though it was true: Sir Reginald shot out streaks of yellow and green. Theo could spot him across an entire battlefield, even at night.

"So you can see an aura around anything with magical properties—and even identify what magical property it is."

"If I'm already familiar with it."

Rhine nodded. "Being familiar with dragon's blood, you recognize it. I see. Can you tell good magic from bad?"

"In principle, I can."

"How so?"

"Good magic tends to shoot sparks. Bad magic seems to quiver in my vision, as if surrounded by some sort of miasma."

"Fascinating. And you know the Sorceress Zephyr personally? Do you discuss magic with her?"

"Is that why you insisted upon accompanying me? Do you seek to woo her yourself?"

"Stop!" Rhine said. Theo looked down to see his blade in his own hand, already halfway drawn.

"Have no fear, elf. I know her not, I seek her not," Rhine said. He forced himself to relax. "So you *do* know her well," Rhine continued with a grin, as they began to ride forward again.

Theo tried to smile.

"My own mother was an enchantress," Rhine said. "Rather embarrassing for my father's side of the family when they found out. My curiosity is so wide reaching, might I just ask—can you tell if a person or an object is enchanted?"

He pondered the question.

"That is to say," Rhine continued, "you observe the dragon's blood, but it does not affect you. Yet say someone, well, hands you an apple—"

"An apple," Sir Reginald said on the other side of Rhine. "I'd die for an apple. I am famished. My belly is touching my spine."

"A growing boy needs his mush," Theo said with a grin. Sir Reginald made a crude gesture back, but with good cheer.

Rhine continued. "If the apple was enchanted would you be able to tell? By its aura, say?"

He looked at everything with elf eyes now, and thought in elf terms. He'd lost the ability to only be half himself and could not bring himself to regret it. *Home, home, home*. The longing for elfin lands beat like a drum in his heart. Yet the nearer they drew to the tower, the more this drumbeat was superseded by his heart calling for *her, her, her*.

"I do not really know, sorcerer. I was not aware of any enchantments when I felt only my human side. Can humans spot enchantments?"

"Oh, certainly. Enchantments are funny things. There are many signs to look for, if you observe closely," Rhine said.

They continued discussing enchantments as they climbed up the very last road and he saw the tower appear at once close up and massive. For so long it had been a white pillar in the distance. He'd been so happy and miserable together in that tower that he knew not how to feel. *Her, her, her*. He became deaf to all else, even the rainbow land they passed as they crossed a new channel running like a dark, slow-moving snake through the fields. Much magic had been used here, and all was now a pastoral paradise.

Up on the roof of the tower, cloud birds roosted all in a row. To him they were the color of the darkest pink he'd ever seen with his eyes. They seemed impervious to heat, holding out one wing and then another to soak in the sun.

∞

The warriors pulled up on the pea gravel in the tower yard. Above, on the balcony, she welcomed them. First, she gave thanks to the heavens for his return and the return of all the men, speaking out in a carrying voice as best she could against the waves of cheers from all the people who clustered round the tower like a many headed cape of movement. Eyeing a small card in her hand lest she forget anything Peter had jotted down, she continued. During her speech, people kept joining the crowd, jogging in from the fields. She couldn't keep her mind on her rehearsed words. She kept nervously glancing at him and finally let silence take her. With a large breath she gestured to him in the crowd and begged for him to speak to their people.

He got up on the back of his horse and then climbed up the stonework onto the balcony, landing effortlessly by her side.

The people cheered, and she noted that his destrier was led away to the stables by three young grooms. The horse snorted and continued prancing its giant feet. She winced and hoped the young boys were careful of its hooves, but they seemed overjoyed with pride at handling the black knight's horse. She looked back up at him.

"I have showed you who I am with deeds, not words!" he said out to the crowd. They strained forward to hear him.

"Some of you have lost husbands. Some have lost fathers, brothers. Some of you are from other lands and lost your homes. I charge these knights to divide up our booty according to each his merit in war. The rest will be dispensed by this honest sorcerer here," he continued, gesturing to Rhine. "A handful of coin to each citizen down to the smallest child. Tonight with your family drink to these men—their valor was such that any army twice its size met defeat. Drink to the knowledge that our enemy is no more. That our deeds will go down in the songs our grandchildren will hear!" He motioned for the war booty to be brought forth. The knights below picked up handfuls of gold and threw it out to the crowd, who roared their approval.

The entire time she could not take her eyes from him and could say nothing. It was as if a strong current of electrical ions went through her when he took her hand and kissed the ring.

As he came towards her, his eyes were black. Reports had it they were black all the time now. She swallowed.

"Sorceress Zephyr, it has been a long time."

Her face felt hot at the emotion that thickened his voice. Cheers rose and fell like waves around them.

Her arm was taken by a black-armored greave that pressed into her linen sleeve with merciless power, and she was pulled from the balcony, to the steps and down into the study.

He was already kissing her as he pushed her up against a table. Those eyes were as shiny as his black-armored breastplate. Stripping off his greaves, he pushed her up onto the table.

"Zephyr," he said. A part of her noticed he hadn't even closed the door.

"I'll never forgive myself for sending you away," she said. She clung to his armor as he pulled up his chainmail. Soon her skirts were up to her thighs, the filmy shift torn away in haste, and she fell back against the stack of open books, struck by his blazing glory, as afternoon light from the high windows ignited his hair.

The chain mail was rough and made little cuts in her skin, but she couldn't be bothered to care. Grabbing her legs, he held them up in the crook of each elbow, making his thrusts harder and deeper until her eyes practically rolled up in her head. *Yes, that.* She missed it and wanted more. "More!" she cried out, and then lost herself in his thrusts and the caress of his hard palm squeezing her breast.

He crawled up onto the table and turned her over, shoving invaluable books to the floor in his haste.

Finally, he was thrusting with a strain that let her know he could feel her quicken. She felt the honeyed lick of dazzling release and he drove into her in time to her involuntarily clasping muscles. Even after it was done, he continued for the pleasurable feel of it and she rubbed her back against him like a lonely kitty. When it was over, she shifted around and he was content to let his head lie upon her naked breast. She breathed in the smell of him. He stank like sweat, he smelled like his horse, and the faint nitrous smell of war. His face came up again and caressed hers, his nose stroking her nose, her cheeks, as he inhaled.

"You smell like lilies," he breathed. "And sex." He kissed her for a long time, slowly, as if wondering in her. She was as transfixed as he was, shuddering.

"Mary and Pomfret say I must now grant you a boon," she told him. "What should it be? Land? A rich wife?" A wicked dimple peeked out in her cheek and then she composed her face again in all seriousness. "Name what you want. All I have is yours," she said. "Including my heart. But that you already have in your keeping."

"I would have your black ring," he told her.

She began to draw it off her finger, frowning. *That's all?* It didn't seem enough, not nearly enough.

The ring had once glowed with red fire, but these days it barely gave off a spark.

"Don't," a voice said.

∞

"I wished to break the enchantment for good," Theo said, rising and sorting his clothes. She swooped down her skirt and didn't know which way to look. The long-haired man was not six feet away and must have seen everything. Everything. She wanted to sink through the floor.

"Do not give him the ring."

She slid the ring back on her finger and hid herself behind Theo, pulling at her clothes, frantically trying to restore her dress to order.

"You don't want this ring on," Theodorus said to her, taking her hand, drawing her forth, and trying to unkink her finger knuckle gently, so he could pull it off. "And you said you'd grant me anything," he reminded her with a charming smile. Which was true. He began forcing the ring upward over her knuckle even as she involuntarily clenched her fist. His expression became determined.

"No!" the blue-robed sorcerer said. "Not just yet."

"This is not your business. We don't need your help," Theodorus said. "Nor did we ask for it. These rings are enchanted. You pointed it out to me as clearly as you could."

"As clearly as the enchantment would let me."

She decided she liked this Rhine. Up close his eyes were a deep velvety dark blue and very large. His voice was melodic yet assertive, commanding.

There was nothing about a curse or enchantment in her artificial memory, and she looked at the ring again.

"Should I remove it or not?" she asked.

"Do you know where the rings come from?" Rhine began.

∞

Theo had gone into the storage closet and found the petrified hand. It lay on the table—right where they'd been going at it, and *oh, God, how long had the sorcerer watched?*

She looked over at Theo. *Say something*, she indicated with a nod of her head to him, but the awkward pause grew excruciating.

"Now," Theo said. They both took off their rings, and placed them on the fingers of the petrified hand.

Rhine moved over to sit on the window bench. She drifted to a stool and sat across from him, knees together, back ramrod straight, feeling like a sluttish schoolgirl. Theodorus stood impatiently behind her.

"There is nothing more dangerous than to use magic that you don't understand. I happen to be very familiar with both of these rings. Shall I tell you about them?"

She stared and gave an uncertain nod.

"Perhaps I could look at them first," he suggested.

Theo seemed peeved, but made an impatient gesture for the sorcerer to do so.

The blue sorcerer Rhine turned to speak to her. "He's right to be very cautious," he said, his deep-set eyes woeful. "There are many out there who would harm you in order to take what you have. I, however, am not one of them. I am not a thief. Moreover, you and I have fought on the same side, Theodorus. I was with Linus the Unlucky, as well as Linus the Second. Linus the Third would give me anything I wished for, as long as it was not his kingdom. You know he's trying to foist his sister off on me now."

"I remember you now!" she exclaimed. She turned to Theo. "This sorcerer is my mistress Hulgetta's former master. But they were not friends." Memories began seeping up into her consciousness. She turned to Rhine. "You know he killed Hulgetta," she said.

"I did not kill her! She was already dead. I didn't even take off her head, it just popped off suddenly."

"I never trusted Hulgetta. At this point I much prefer the pacts and true friendships of simple men than others interested in magic and spells." He stroked the rings, which flashed and went dark.

"These rings are exceptionally dangerous. At this point you both remember your past and present. But you don't remember the moment you met. The moment you first met, I should say. And every time you switched the rings, you forgot each other all over again."

"If someone mentioned it or tried to tell you—all would remain a blank. Much like if you came out of a slight dizzy spell."

They looked at each other.

"Yes, it will begin coming back to you now that the rings are off." He sat back. "I have never told another this story. It brings great feelings of shame. You see, I did not learn of these rings from another, the way you have. I had to figure it out all by myself."

CHAPTER FORTY-THREE

"My father was a powerful sorcerer, my mother a woman of determined will. She had learned a bit of conjuring from an uncle—a great uncle of mine, I believe—who once had some small magical skill and saw sensitivity in her. But she hungered to learn even more. Most of her reason for marrying my father, I think, was her belief he would teach her all he knew. Indeed, she often said he'd promised to reveal all his knowledge to her after they married. Her family was not happy, you see. They'd planned an alliance for her that was to their advantage and she had run off to marry my father instead.

"My father was entranced by my mother when they were first together, but he was a little less than trusting. He'd seen the thirst for power in her and knew corruption and misery often follow when that desire leads. While he lusted after my mother, he feared who she would become if she gained more knowledge of his powers.

"However, once I was born, he became even more concerned. Times were very unsettled. Should anything untoward happen to him, he would not be there to teach me all he knew. So he decided to make this ring," the sorcerer said, tapping the surface of the black ring. "Once it was completed it would soak up all his knowledge. Upon his death, it would be given to me. When I wore it, I would instantly understand all that he knew and his magical knowledge—so carefully earned through much secret hard work—would never be lost.

"It took much time and energy to make such a ring. Through it all, he kept the project hidden from my mother. She assumed he had taken another lover and became spiteful towards him, and even towards me, for by then I was an infant. He encouraged her to go visit her family and show them the new baby—myself. While she was gone, he worked as hard as he could to finish and perfect the ring." Looking at Theodorus he said, "As a wizard you would understand how hard that is. How unusual for a sorcerer, too, but he wanted to make sure the ring lasted and that its magic was consistent." Theo gave a short, frowning nod.

"He was a patient man. Slowly and surely he put his knowledge of fire and air into the crystal, and it began to come to life.

"When my mother returned, he hid the ring. He did not know that her jealous nature had caused her to have him spied upon while she was absent. As a result, she knew all about the ring, and guessed some of its purpose.

"She thought about how to make him give it to her. For by this time she knew quite a bit of magic herself, having picked it up from my father in some small ways. The women in her family had protected and passed down an old book of love spells and charms for at least one hundred and seventy years. With the knowledge from this book and the small bits of knowledge she'd gleaned from her husband, she decided to make a ring of desire. With such a ring she could bend him to her will. He'd want to please her so much that he'd show her everything he knew.

"She and her sister together conjured the blue stone that they placed in the ring of desire." He tapped the blue chalice ring. He tossed it in his hand and weighed it.

"Working with a desire spell as a base, the sisters made the original spell into a powerful enchantment once it was seated in the ring's stone. Its magic is sorely drained now, but at the time, whoever wore the ring could compel another to do almost anything. Yet it is a twisted sort of desire. The wearer at once attracts and repels others. When my mother returned from the hinterlands with the ring on her finger, she was confident that she would soon have the black ring as well.

"What she did not know was that one of her servants had broken down after she left and confessed everything to my father. Her desire for the ring, her book of magic spells, everything.

"My father had little time before she arrived. He tried to make some final adjustments of the ring to protect it."

"I'm sorry—you said these people were your parents?" Zephyr said. Rhine's mother sounded like a real piece of work. Her tone of sadness seemed to provoke Theo. He deliberately took her hand—strangely naked now without the ring—and held it in his own.

"He thought it would confound her—without actually harming her.

"Alas, the magic my father devised did not work exactly as he hoped. My mother came to the castle with her ring of desire. She demanded the black ring of my father and he gave it to her.

"She slipped it on her finger and they both promptly forgot each other.

"Because of this unintended effect, they both forgot about me as well. Since they did not know each other, they did not know they'd created a child together. I was a very young boy at the time and was simply thrown out of the castle by an unscrupulous nurse and her accomplice who decided to use my parents' weakness for their own gain.

"It took my mother's family years to find me. It took me until I was well into my twenties to understand what had happened. By that time the black ring and the blue ring had passed back and forth between the two of them several times. You can imagine the havoc it was wreaking upon the entire countryside. Wars in the land went on for close to two decades.

"I studied magic all that time. Once my aunt finally told me about the spell book, the whole history finally became clear." He shook his head.

"I came to discover a safe way to store the rings when I discovered the stone hand of St. Marna, which renders all magic null and void.

"This ring," he said, holding up the black ring, "now possesses all your knowledge, Zephyr. Should I put it on, we'd forget each other, but I would know the spells and incantations that you know yourself. However, if I put this ring upon the petrified hand of St. Marna, the ring is rendered null. Your magic and memory are both safe, and no one can affect either, though you wore the ring last."

"How came you to lose these rings?" Theo demanded.

"My apprentice, Hulgetta, stole them. I had not realized this was the case until I received a letter that told me the two rings were missing. At first I dismissed it as rumor, or unsubstantiated gossip. I knew the two rings were in my chambers and were safe. In fact, my chambers are rather cluttered and the hand could have been anywhere, but in my own confident arrogance I did not actually look for them. For that, I am entirely responsible.

Then I saw the famous black knight ride onto the battlefield."

He waved his arm towards Theo. "By then, people talked of a sorceress and her enchanted elfin lover. I thought the tale exaggerated, yet here was the elf lover, transformed into the black knight. Everyone talked of his adoration for the Sorceress Zephyr, and the great black ring with which she ruled him. I also heard he had been a wizard once, until she stole this same ring and usurped his power. As you can imagine, that made me look at you twice," he said to Theo.

∞

"I rejoice that you finally figured out how to break the enchantment," Rhine said, standing.

"Because of you."

"Not at all. You had to see the enchantment for what it was yourself. An enchantment can almost never be broken from the outside."

They stared at the rings. She felt sad that Rhine's one legacy from his father was ruined. The father's knowledge the ring once held was long erased by now.

"May I ask how you got these rings from Hulgetta?" Rhine asked Theo.

"When we went back to the castle via a magical door, she had expired from injuries."

"She was magicked," Zephyr said. "On the field fighting Rupert the Red."

"Interesting."

"Zephyr, not understanding the complexities of Rhymaeic magic, thought she could burn a certain spell book, but the flames were gradually consuming the entire castle. We dived in before that happened and saved what we could."

"The maids?"

"There were no maids in sight," Theo said. "There was a lizard. We tried to grab it, but it ran into a crack in the wall, and then off down a corridor. We grabbed what we could and fled. I expect the whole castle went up in flames."

"It didn't," Zephyr said. She turned to Rhine. "I went at one point, shortly after getting both rings." She knew this because she had read it in the artificial memory. Even as she spoke the words a dim memory began to return. "I went looking for Wart. There was no sign of her, or of anyone. The entire castle was blackened, but most of it was still standing."

"You threw a Rhymaeic book in the fire?" Rhine demanded.

Zephyr looked at Theo. "Yes."

"Where is it now?" Rhine's voice took on an urgent edge.

"I–I don't know. It was a while back."

"How long ago?"

"Oh," Zephyr blew out her lips and tried to tally up the time in her head. "Thirty years?"

Rhine rose and said, "All Rhymaeic books must be obliterated. By throwing it in the fire, you've made it much stronger. We must find this book. Immediately."

"You're going to the castle. To see if the book is still there?"

"Yes."

"Would you like to use our green door?" Zephyr said, but he held out his hand.

"No need." Blue smoke had already started wheeling around him.

"Wait!"

He looked impatient, jaw muscles clenching. His manner had changed so swiftly that she felt shy of him suddenly. Here was the man who commanded King Linus's army.

"How can we contact you?" she asked.

"I will visit you this winter," he promised. Suddenly an enormous cloud of blue smoke wiffled up from the ground. He walked into it and disappeared.

They followed the last snaking bit of blue smoke outside. It slid into the herb garden and disappeared.

Now Theo was looking at her with grim death in his eye.

"You're starting to remember," she said.

"I am."

Her face went hot. Not only was her memory was affected. The languages, the things she thought she knew—everything was evaporating fast from her mind, like dew lifting from a field as the sun heats up. Pouring in memories from the last three decades left no room for the rest.

"At least I'm still immortal," she said. "Lots of time to relearn everything else," she joked.

"Zephyr, you're not immortal anymore."

Zephyr felt like she'd been kicked by a mule. "Am too."

He shook his head. "Listen. The cloud birds are gone. That magic is no more. It follows that other spells you cast have ceased as well."

It was true. She listened. For once the tower was deafeningly silent. As if by undoing the enchantment they'd undone in one stroke all the magic she'd worked through the power of the black ring.

"At least I still have the books," she said, looking around biting her lip.

"Books? You mean *my* books?" Theo looked down at her. She looked around as his rage started to gather. Rhine was gone. "He took the rings."

"*My* rings," Theo said.

"Who cares? Did you really want them around?"

"Thirty years. You deceived me, betrayed me," he said, as if he was trying to overcome his disbelief. "We lost thirty years." She shut her eyes. *Here we go*. She focused on him, prepared for whatever might come. Zaps emerged through space from the elf warrior and struck her like electric shocks. This time they flowed into her and through her. She became a conduit to the ground. The electric current ran from her fingers down through her core and out through her sex, making her rise up on her feet from the sensation. Into the ground those zaps flowed, pulsing, going deep and wide. A part of her became very, very scared when that happened. Her fingers were smoking and she couldn't feel her fingertips at all. The rest of her body felt as if she'd been suspended from a large hook. Tingles cascaded through her body in shudders.

CHAPTER FORTY-FOUR

"I regret nothing," she said, hating the way her voice choked up feeling trembly, unsteady. The aftershocks from all the zaps left her unsteady. "It was the only way I could stay here. With you."

She crossed her arms over her bodice. The sky was clouding up in response to her feelings. Of late her moods were connected to the weather. She knew she should try to stop it, but the bad feelings welled up hard and strong. The sky was turning black as she turned to him again.

"I was wrong," she said, her voice twisting with emotion. "But you're the only one I've ever loved, and I did not—I didn't want to leave you."

"Your only thought was grasping more magical power."

"No! No, you know it's not true." Nothing but one giant *I'm sorry!* filled her mind. She was shaking with the need to convince him.

"Don't bother with your base feminine tricks. You brought me to your mistress to be slaughtered, and then almost killed me yourself."

"I didn't *know*." Her cry of ignorance fell on deaf ears.

"Thirty years or more. You heard what he said—we could have gone round and round this way for another century."

"I did it to stay with you." Her voice went deep, as large sobs welled up, filling her lungs and making it hurt to breathe.

"You did this to stay with me, and what next? What will you destroy now to get your way?"

"You are a better man than when I found you—and you know it," she said, wiping her nose with her sleeve.

"I am no longer blinded. Yet all along I knew it! I could *never* have married you—I could never love one lacking in honor and possessing such a cold, wicked heart."

"I have feelings!"

"For yourself."

She crossed her arms. The wind stirred her long sleeves, and compared to his armor, she felt as insubstantial as a leaf that could flutter away. She trembled, feeling the rush of nerves a warrior experiences on the battlefield. The sky began to grow greenish black, like a bruise colored by her displeasure.

"You will not stay here," he said. "Begone."

"What?"

"I banish you."

She couldn't believe her ears. "You—banish—me?"

"Yes, banished from this land. I will have my men escort you to the border on horseback."

"Your men. Your land!"

"You can take Hulgetta's books and your clothes."

She had never been so angry in her life.

He turned to go inside. The ground rumbled.

"Your land. This is not your land—not anymore. Come back out here and face me, elf." She had never called him that before. Not to his face. "These people acknowledge me," she said. "King Linus acknowledges me."

"King Linus would back me over you without a second thought. How can you stand there completely shameless after what you've done?"

"Who has looked after these people and worried about their survival for three decades? Not you. You could not be bothered in your guilt and remorse for killing your own master."

She thought she was going to have a fit, and the raging fury felt as if it occupied not just her body but also a ridged column seated in the ground like the bony spine of a dinosaur beneath the earth. Her rage went down, spread out and went wide. At the edge of it, far down below, something stirred. She was distracted and could not hold back as her fury poured into the earth. She felt the power tremble there deep below, could feel it ever so slightly, but it was already too far gone to call it back again.

"How is it you're proposing to remove me from this land?" She turned and pointed at the orchards, her hands shaking with anger or elf zaps. "I dare your men to come near me. I dare them." The knights and everyone else had by this time already shied off from her and Theo. Theo looked around. She saw him realize that his men were so far away he'd need to shout for them to hear him.

"I will remove you myself," he said, turning back to her.

She stared at him, her nostrils flaring. "Try," she said.

For a split second, he hesitated. Then he took a step near her, his hands out. The ground trembled hard and birds suddenly shot from the tower and nearby trees, their cacophony adding to the sudden peculiar swirling winds as clouds began to form overhead and green lightning flashed within.

She stood there, a small figure with a pale face, golden hair falling down the back of her head. Lovely, blazing eyes, her mouth set with an expression deadly serious, as if just by thinking it she could send ten sword blades through his body.

He could feel his own forced knowledge of sorcery lifting from his mind like a dream only half-remembered. He knew her vast learning—stolen from his mind with the help of the black ring—was fading fast. She was already opening and closing her hands as if they were ached. Soon she would be little more than the tiny maid from the castle who he had tried to woo for his own purpose. A feeble sorceress's new apprentice, who knew one little sleep spell and had a rare genius for getting into trouble.

He made a grave mistake and took another step towards her. First there was the sound of each floor of the tower being punched through by an enormous force. A giant cloud of dust came rushing out of the open entrance, and servants, including Mary and Anne, poured out of the kitchen entrance. Dominic and Jane were the last to come rushing out.

"What have you done to my tower?"

She didn't answer.

The weather began to lash the fields and crops as lightning burst like a green electric birdcage over the entire tower. The jagged display faded two-thirds of the way down, as the streaks snaked out towards the maid and were absorbed. At her feet they burst into small fairy-sized sparkles that hit the ground and vanished.

He turned and looked at her in shock.

"That was you. You're doing this." He turned and advanced upon her, reaching for a sword from the wagon that stood to one side.

"It's not. At least, I don't mean to."

He was going to go to battle against her, fae and warrior alike. He was coming for her. She was terrified. Stumbling, her heart was numb with hurt, torn with heartbreak. She shouted at him over the wind.

"If you slay me, you'll never control the rage within. You'll feel twice the guilt and the misery you felt when you killed your master."

His eyes were inky darkness. A heavy frown marred his perfect brow. She watched his vision bend inward. Never before had she witnessed such furious swift calculations from him. Never before had he faced her as a complete enemy. Then she felt his self-control crack. She began to back up, her hands out to her sides, for the first time feeling threatened.

The rain began lashing them. She put her arm up and sobbed even harder. Never had she been so unhappy. In her own anger and upset she imagined ending this unbearable misery by simply throwing herself on his sword. She backed up automatically, though she felt five times heavier, not just with the rain soaking her dress, but with the weight of her shattered heart.

"Slaughter me, then," she cried. "But I know your heart. You won't do it."

He lifted his sword. Looking up she saw it high overhead. The tower roof shook, while his face was stark white against the stones. A big wind blew up, accompanied by a ripping, tearing sound from the ground. She twisted around and her heart stopped.

∞

The sweet sound of her voice almost tamed him. *No, no, no!* He flung off the influence, letting hot passion course through him. If she loved him, the voice inside him said, she wouldn't torture him like this. He was in an agony of disgrace that she had snapped her fingers under his nose and played such tricks. He couldn't hurt her. He'd vowed he wouldn't, long ago. Yet it was as if something within him felt such agony he was compelled to stamp out the one thing he loved and revel in the destruction.

A part of him rejoiced and trembled, ready to destroy her. He aimed his sword.

He would create a bier bedecked with flowers for her corpse.

He would burn himself up with her corpse in the fire.

The smell of burning hair filled his nostrils. He heard the rumbling, felt the ground move. There was a breath of silence, and then the tower stones began to fall.

The moss maid had come to life. She wrenched herself away from the tower. The ground shook, stones toppled, and a quarter of the tower came tumbling down as she ripped herself free.

CHAPTER FORTY-FIVE

The moss maid twisted her upper body, but her feet were caught. Theo's head craned upwards to take in the entire monolith, from the witch hazel hair to the dried bracken feet.

The monolith saw Zephyr and straightened up again before bracing her hands on the edge of the torn tower and freeing her feet one at a time. Then she turned to look about the land. Spotting Theo below, she rotated towards him with a menacing rush of her upper body. The skeleton of a winged ram came with her and flew about her form in the air. Violets and green moss showered down from the enormous creature, while a train of dark blue butterflies fluttered about the massive rounded breasts or followed after the flying ram skeleton.

He ran to Zephyr, raising an arm over them as more stones tumbled from above, striking his arm, almost bringing him down on top of her. Other stones begin to fall from the tower, and items toppled out. He tried to encircle her waist and lift her off the ground, set her in a westward direction, so she might run away and be safe. But she pounded upon his already bruised arm, and he dropped her. The moss maid, slowly turning, made the ground shake. She crushed the cart flat with one foot. The horses bolting off into the woods, dragging their harness after them.

He felt all toppled inside, his anger sinking into caution and instinct.

"Let me die for you," he said, and meant it, pushing her behind him. "Run!"

He swept her back. She clung to him as he tried to give her protection, wishing she'd flee, knowing they'd both soon die anyway. The moss maid was coming right for him. They both knew it aimed to destroy him.

"I won't leave him!" Zephyr screamed up at the moss maid, and ducking underneath his arm got in front again. With an arm flung back about his neck, she held her other arm up protectively in front of them both. The maid's enormous arm came at them like a massive tree trunk, her fist about to drive through the elf in his armor, through them both. Zephyr turned her head and braced herself against him.

"No!" Zephyr cried, the sound stretching out, prolonged. *Neeeeeeeeeooooohhhh!* A scream of sheer will, it echoed out over the air.

He picked up Zephyr but could not move fast enough as the mountain of angry magic swooped her massive fist down right at him—towards them both. At the sound of Zephyr's voice, however, the arm swerved, swooping past them at the last second. An enormous whoosh of air followed in its path as Zephyr's scream continued to echo off the tower stones. Before the cry had died away, the moss maid, as if in obedience to the shout of protest, burst apart.

An explosion of green plant bits and brown dirt suddenly enveloped them in a small tornado cloud. Clods struck them with force from all sides, specks of moss clung to them. They shut their eyes tightly, holding together, as the storm ended as abruptly as it began with a shower of dirt and plants raining down upon them from above.

She was still trying to shield him with her body, on tip-toe, one arm about his head. He let his sword arm drop and instead covered her head with his arm, protecting her, turning her around, and pulling her away from the tower as stones tumbled all about them, along with enormous clods of heavy dirt.

∞

She was still clinging to him minutes later as he sat on the edge of the water trough and tried to bathe her face clean of dirt. He pulled her down to sit on his knee, and using the long sleeve of her tattered dress, bathed her face. A part of him was buzzing and alive. Coming close to death always made his soul sing. The sensation was like a heady wine and made him understand like never before that the flesh mattered little. One's immortal deeds sang for eternity, whether one was alive or dead. There was much food in this day for the poets.

"It's over," he said, putting his arm around her.

She burst into tears.

"My god, she almost killed you," Zephyr said, covering her eyes from him in her shame. "I almost killed you." Then she twisted her face away from him and sobbed bitterly into her arm. She didn't pull away as he held her. Loyal and true. Self-sacrificing after all. He felt his spirit reach out to her as if he had never seen her inner beauty before. His blood was singing, and there was a strange turbulent shift inside him, as if pieces were finally fitting together, and the ground at last solid beneath his feet.

This new sensation made him touch her fingers with his own, and revel in the current of feeling flowing back and forth.

CHAPTER FORTY-SIX

"The elf marriage is only a naming of the words already in both of us," he said, pulling her up to stand with him. People were slowly creeping closer to the tower, stopping to look and listen a hundred yards away before coming forward another foot and then stopping again. He ignored them and bent towards her.

"It's not a trick like before. But we must do it now."

He stood them up.

"There is no answer in my heart but you," he continued in Elvish, "no name in my heart but your name. That is the elf marriage. Do you acknowledge this?" He translated back into Berbainwick.

"I do."

He took her hands. "Do you feel the same?"

"I do. There is no answer in my heart but you. No name but your name." He helped her say it in the old words.

"Will you stand with me through time, without shame, no matter who or what tries to part us, with the exception of death?"

"Yes," she said, her eyes big.

"Then we are well and truly married and none can part us except the heavens, may they show mercy on our love." They said it all again in Elvish and it was done.

She looked around them at the dirt and tumbled stones. She turned back to him in her wet and bedraggled dress.

"I have no token to give you."

"Give me that leaf in your hair, your faith and trust, and in return I vow to teach you all the magic you desire."

"I give you this leaf, along with my faith and trust. Take this clump of moss," she smiled in a wry way that twisted at his heart, "and give me your forgiveness."

"You have it. I know your heart. You never intend to harm anyone."

"I will learn to be more cautious."

He gave a skeptical laugh.

"I like to hear you laugh. You never even smiled when we first met."

"Your love controls my fae side."

"What does that mean?"

"It means I think you're heroic. But never make me jealous." He waved the people to come forward. They rushed to the tower.

∞

The pounding of nails rose up to the sky as birds flew away in a quiet stir of wings. He climbed down the ladder and went over to her where she sat on the edge of the water trough. The sun began to gleam with scarlet as it slowly sank.

"I've destroyed your beautiful tower." Her shoulders hunched and she put both hands over her face and sobbed like a small child. These bursts of strong emotion had been overwhelming her off and on for most of the afternoon. He watched over her cold, wet, and dirty form. She had faced what seemed certain death that day, not just at the hands of a warrior, but at the hands of brutal magic gone awry. Were she one of his soldiers he'd say she was holding up well overall.

The sun was going down, but the summer sky was alive with the call of birds and a pale primrose light that highlighted the last clouds remaining. Without the cloud birds it was very peaceful.

"It can be rebuilt," he said tenderly, bending over her. His own heart hurt over the destruction, but his first concern was her—as always.

"Can it?" she said, not believing him.

"The men have propped up the lower two floors. They will have to build a scaffold to prop up the rest. It will take a few years." *More like decades.* "Don't cry! Please don't."

"We'll be living in a willow hut by the river."

"No, we'll travel to my home instead. I am going to rejoin my father. I am one of them now, a warrior, and not as I was before. They will be wary, but I can control my fae side now, thanks to you. I will demand my place at my father's side."

"You're leaving?"

"I'm not leaving you. You will come with me, be at my side." A troubled look appeared on her face, and her lip was quivering.

"So many tears." He stroked the side of her face. "It's been a long day."

She plucked at his sleeve.

"What is it, sweetheart?"

"I—just—the stories you've told me about the elves."

"You are the only woman I would ever conceive of taking to the elves." She looked dubious. "You don't know the meaning of fear." He was shocked to see her actually appear timid.

"As a powerful sorceress, you are someone they will respect," he reminded her. "I will teach you wizardry and the language aristocrats use along the way. I'm inviting you on an adventure."

She embraced him.

Holding her he said, "To visit my family as I am now, and to present them to you—I cannot express my complete happiness. I've never felt so content in all my life."

"I want to see your people, and understand them. But it will make me so sad to leave the tower lands."

"We will return soon enough."

She looked over at the men propping up the open sides of the tower with long nailed boards. Her forehead wrinkled again and her lips began to quiver.

He pulled her face back to look up at him instead. "I have been snared by you, fought with you, and loved you. After this, how could I shy away from a few scheming fae relatives? Come—the choice is up to you. Will you travel at my side to see the elves, to witness things no human eyes have ever seen? Would you enjoy such a journey?"

He felt sublime awe and not a little dread around his own kind, so what would she feel? She would be at odds with them for being human, for not knowing their language.

Yet he could feel a pull inside her, what she called her fairy dust. It was sparkling like diamonds at the thought of going to the land of the elves.

She let him cradle her in his arms as they watched the sky turn purple, the boards propping up the tower walls dark with raindrops.

"I will go with you," she said. She pulled his wet head down to her own and kissed him over and over.

In the end, she tentatively offered him a solution to the problem of the tower. He agreed and held onto her as she took the twisted, broken remains of the vines that had covered the tower and held them in her mind while she held up one end of the vine in her hand.

Closing her eyes, she said, "I'm not tapping into the moss maid, I'm tapping into you." She began to speak the animating spell she had first used so very long ago.

The vine snaked and writhed as it animated. It grew up and over the solid part of the tower, winding itself round and round the stones, across the open gaping wound, up and under and around the boards that propped up the floors. It wove up and down and right and left, until it reached the bottom.

Like a bottle covered in woven mesh, the tower was now safely protected from the elements.

"That'll keep things safe till we return."

"*If* we return," Theo said.

"*When* we return."

THE END

Madeline Iva

Madeline Iva writes paranormal, fantasy, and contemporary erotic romance.

In 2013, she started Love Fest, a day of romance panels at Virginia Festival of the Book. That year she also co-founded LadySmut.com, a blog devoted to hot men, hotter romances, and all things sexy.

Her work "Sexsomnia" is included in THE LADY SMUT BOOK OF DARK DESIRES published by Harper Impulse.

Find her at:
http://www.ladysmut.com
http://www.madelineiva.com
or email her at madelineiva@gmail.com.

74227373R00259

Made in the USA
Columbia, SC
27 July 2017